Storm clouds over Ireland

STORM CLOUDS OVER IRELAND

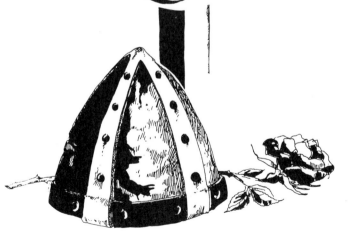

DONALD WILLIS

Published in 1992 by
The Self Publishing Association Ltd
Units 7/10 Hanley Workshops
Hanley Swan, Worcs.

A MEMBER OF

in conjunction with
DONALD WILLIS

British Library Cataloguing in Publication Data

A catalogue record for this book is
available from the British Library

ISBN 1 85421 143 9

Designed and produced by Images Design & Print Ltd., Hanley Swan
Printed and bound in Great Britain by Hartnolls Ltd., Bodmin.

$\mathcal{A}$CKNOWLEDGEMENTS

$\mathcal{I}$ would like to thank many people - most of whom must remain unfortunately unnamed - for their help and support in the writing and publishing of this book. My thanks go especially to my wife for encouragement on countless occasions - without her I could never have completed it -, to Dr Oxley for assistance with research, to David Haynes for help with the preperation and finally to Dana Harvey, a most skilful editor, and my publisher, Tony Harold.

To Judith

who has always shared

my love of history

PART ONE

1166 – 1173

And now the Irish are ashamed

To see themselves in one year tamed:

So much one man can do

That does both act and know.

CHAPTER 1

The dense oak wood was almost completely obscured by an early, low-lying mist, tinged pale yellow by the light of the hidden sun. A group of horsemen waited impatiently for the mist to disperse; the sound of their voices was muffled and silver droplets clung to the long hair of their horses' manes.

Lord Henry FitzAlan yawned and drew his cloak closely around him. The horses snorted restlessly and the younger men chatted idly as they waited for the sport to begin. Gradually the almost uniform whiteness of the area was subtly imbued with colour until the rich hues of the men's clothing and the deep green of oak leaves filled the glade. Henry watched the transformation without being aware of it, his eyes still heavy with sleep, his face taut with boredom.

The sound of jeering laughter roused him and he looked over at a group of men who stood round a shamefaced-looking boy. He had been trying to fly a hawk to a lure, had failed to judge the swing correctly and had hit the bird with it. The bird stared at him from its perch on the falconer's arm, its arrogant stance parodying the men's contempt.

Henry snorted derisively and turned to his son Robert. "Come on, lad, show us what you can do."

It was clear to Robert from Henry's expression that he wasn't expected to do any better. He took a deep breath and squared his shoulders, filled with determination to prove his father wrong. Handing the reins of his horse to one of the grooms, he strode out to the centre of the field and took the lure from the falconer who winked encouragingly at him.

Tall and with a proud bearing, Robert immediately commanded the attention of the surrounding men and Henry found himself regarding his youngest son more keenly, realising with some surprise that this was no weakling child straight from his mother's school-room. Intrigued, he watched as the boy swung the lure until it caught the eye of the hawk.

Robert's voice was soft as he called, "Merlin, come Merlin," his tone conveying that he had all the time in the world. The hawk stirred restlessly, unwilling to be drawn from its perch. Robert ignored it and continued patiently swinging the lure until he was sure he held the bird's interest. Then, to the surprise of the onlookers, he stepped slowly backwards, coaxing and teasing the bird to come to him.

"He'll not do it now," one of the men muttered. Henry turned and glared at him and the man fell silent.

"Merlin, Merlin." Suddenly the hawk took off, swooping for the piece of meat. Robert swung the lure down, judged it perfectly, and the bird missed it by inches.

The falconer allowed himself a covert glance to where his lord sat. Henry was watching Robert avidly, an expression of satisfied pride on his rugged face. This was good: failure was apt to be blamed on Henry's servants and in any case the falconer was fond of the boy who had worked diligently to improve his skills, showing little sign of his elder brothers' arrogance.

The hawk had returned to its perch and Robert swung the lure again, this time allowing the hawk to catch the piece of meat and settle contentedly on his gloved arm. A shout of approval went up from the surrounding men and a small flock of birds, disturbed by the sudden noise, flew screeching from the trees. Robert took the meat from the hawk and rewarded it with food from his pocket; then handed the bird back to the falconer.

Henry was a large man in whose face time had sculptured lines of pain and arrogance. A man's man, he was bluff and hearty with his comrades, feared and respected by his family and Robert approached him with some trepidation.

"Well done, well done, lad," Henry said, and his voice rang out loud and clear in the cold morning air. Robert stood a little taller and tried to suppress the smile of pleasure which his father's words aroused. He couldn't hide his flushing cheeks, but Henry was already talking to his steward and didn't notice. "What other skills do you suppose my son has kept from me?" he was saying, his voice jovial.

The steward smiled and shrugged. "What else indeed, sire?"

"I thought he'd been wasting his time studying Latin," Henry reached out and squeezed Robert's bicep, "but by God, he never grew these fine muscles doing that. He'll be wasted in the church, this fine son of mine." Robert bit his lip to keep down an angry retort.

Henry turned his horse swiftly, showering the men around him with dust. "Come," he called to Robert, "let's see what you can do with the lance and sword." His son fell in behind him, riding next to the steward. "What are you doing, riding in my shadow, boy?" Henry exclaimed. Robert caught up with his father and their knees brushed as they cantered side by side along the narrow path through the trees.

After a while, Henry turned and winked. "You're a quiet lad, aren't you? Not like Hugo and Gerald. For someone who has no desire to fight and be a man, you show an unexpected aptitude."

"I have every wish to do so, father."

Robert's words clearly startled Henry. "You've never said anything to me about it."

"You showed no interest. You already have me relegated to the life of a churchman."

"No need to be bitter, lad. Gerald's my heir, Hugo's a warrior through and through and making his own way. Third sons go into the church – it's not what I'd want but – ," Henry stopped and shrugged his shoulders expressively, lifting his eyebrows and his hands. The effect was almost comical. He wasn't skilled at looking helpless and his mime was grossly over-exaggerated.

"It's not obligatory. Such decisions could be overridden – if circumstances so warranted." Robert suggested.

"I fight with Gerald, I hunt with Hugo – what need have I for any further filial associations? No – the wisest move is to give you to the church – in good faith." It occurred to Henry that his choice of words had a double meaning and he laughed, delighted with his own wit. The group of sycophantic retainers who surrounded them joined in and Robert was hard put to control the despair which threatened to spill out in anger.

"You're not amused, boy," observed his father, "tell me why."

"I have no wish to be a sacrifice." They were riding through the lush Welsh countryside towards the castle where they would practice at the tilts; where Robert would have to excel yet again if he was to impress his father. The castle, high on its motte, filled him with a mixture of pride and regret. It was an impressive sight with its square stone walls, built four storeys high and silhouetted against a brilliant blue sky. Its powerful image filled him with courage. "Father, I don't believe you really want a son in the church."

"Maybe not. We'll talk about it later." Henry's tone was amiable and Robert felt a little of his tension subside.

15

Arriving at the castle for breakfast, Robert followed his father up the stone steps to the dining hall on the second storey. The long wooden table was laid ready for them and Robert took his usual place some way from where his father presided at the head of the table helping himself to a selection of the cooked meats, bread and beer. Henry pinched the serving wench and laughed at her surprised shriek.

Noticing his son again, he roared, "What are you doing, boy?" Robert lifted his head in surprise. "Come and sit here, by me." Henry sounded impatient at having to ask, yet again, for his son's company.

Robert picked up his plate, hiding his elation. In seventeen years Henry had paid him scant attention, now it seemed he needed his younger son constantly at his side. Robert felt honoured, for the place his father indicated had always been his brother Gerald's, reserved for him even in his absence. He had impressed his father that morning, more than he had realised.

Henry picked up the conversation where they had left it earlier. "Well now, boy, what could you do with your life which would give me greater pleasure than sending you into the church?"

Give *him* great pleasure? Robert paused. "I could travel to Ireland with the great Strongbow, win myself lands and titles and give ever increasing weight to our family name," he said.

Henry raised his eyebrows and said nothing. Robert, too, fell silent, unsure of how to proceed.

"A valiant, but idle dream, I think," Henry said after a pause. He sounded disappointed, as though he'd expected more.

"Father, this is no boyish dream." Robert's look was compelling, and his blue eyes turned steely grey as he held his father's stare.

"Then what is it?"

"Reginald d'Evreux will take me. Silas Strongarm has trained me and will train me further."

"Silas is retired, how did you convince that surly devil to help you?"

"By offering to take him with me." It was an insolent thing to have done and Robert held his breath waiting for his father's reaction. The men around them did the same.

"By God, did you?" Henry thumped the table with his fist. He looked at his men. "Do you hear this? He offered to take Silas to Ireland with him." His hearty laugh filled the hall. When his laughter subsided he looked seriously at his son. "I'm seeing you in a new light, Robert. Has d'Evreux really agreed to take you?"

"With two conditions. One of which I've fulfilled, the other I hope to secure today."

"The conditions?" Henry asked.

"To become well versed in the skills of a warrior."

"And have you learned all there is to know?"

"Not yet. But I have some months before Strongbow leaves. The rest I'll not know until I've fought my first battle."

"And then some," Henry nodded in satisfaction. "The other condition, what was that?"

"I beg your pardon?" said Robert, thrown off balance.

"You told me you had a condition which you hoped to fulfil today." This time Henry saw the sudden rush of colour to Robert's cheeks.

"I have to secure your permission and your blessing."

"Today?" Henry's expression had become inscrutable. He dropped the bluff manner from his shoulders as he would a sodden cloak. Father and son faced each other across the table, their eyes made contact and neither wavered. They resembled two men about to launch into combat.

"You're my father. I know how quickly you can assess a situation. You have seen me fight and hunt. You've heard my proposal and I would expect from this that you will already have made your decision."

The silence in the great hall created its own sound, filling Robert's ears. It dragged on whilst he forced himself to eat and drink – as if he cared about the taste of his food. Henry leaned back on his chair and looked up to the ceiling, his hands clasped across his belly. When he moved it was startling. His chair thumped onto the ground.

"Have you stopped to consider your mother's feelings? She missed you when you were with d'Evreux at Llandrinoch." Henry could have said nothing to surprise his son more, he had never shown a moment's concern for his wife's wishes.

Robert was caught off guard, but answered carefully. "I have always tried to please her by attending to my studies. But I am not my mother's plaything."

"No indeed," Henry answered slowly. He stretched out his hand and Robert looked at it stupidly.

"Shake on it then, boy. You have both my permission and my blessing."

Behind the smile, Henry felt a flash of irritation with his Lady Katherine who had deceived him into thinking Robert was interested only in music and Latin. She wasn't going to like this, but then it wasn't for her to like. The decision had been made: when Richard de Clare Earl of Pembroke, departed for Ireland in a few months' time, Robert would go with him.

Sleep eluded Robert that night and the elation he felt at having been acknowledged by his father was tinged a little in anticipation of his mother's reaction. Despite his attempts to warn her, she had deliberately misconstrued his unwillingness to enter the church as a desire to remain at her side; but he had grown impatient with her blandishments, felt entrapped by her pitiful need of him. There was a gentle side to his nature which had allowed his father to think him unmanly, but he was no mother's boy: the need to fight and prove his worth was in his blood. He thought back to that moment, nine months ago, when Reginald d'Evreux had first expressed confidence in him and encouraged him to train as a soldier. "But how can I go about it?" he had asked, hampered before he had even begun by his father's expectations of him.

"You have an old veteran working at Taffowey," said d'Evreux, "Silas Strongarm. He was wounded and nearly killed during a campaign and now champs at the bit, longing to fight again."

"Yes," said Robert, remembering him. "So what would you have me do?"

"Approach him. Offer him a deal. He coaches you in the art of war – you take him with you when you go off to fight. Both of you will benefit from the bargain and his friendship could prove valuable to you."

Robert remembered the day when, as a rangy and overly sensitive youth returning to the castle, he had first sought out Silas. He had wandered into the courtyard where the men were practising at the tilts and addressed a page who was patiently holding his knight's war horse. "I'm looking for Silas Strongarm," he said.

"Over there," was the dismissive response, accompanied by a laconic wave in the general direction of the stables.

Robert had found Silas eating his morning repast, and approached him, swallowing his nervousness. "I'm Robert FitzAlan and you are Silas Strongarm, I think."

The man didn't look at him, but continued spearing a piece of meat and putting it in his mouth, chewing it slowly. "Aye. You are, and I am," he said, uncommunicatively.

"I've recently returned from Reginald d'Evreux. He tells me you are the man I should talk to – about making me a warrior."

"You?" Silas said, looking at him in subdued surprise.

"I need your help," Robert ploughed on, ignoring the implied contempt.

"And why would I wish to help you?" Silas asked.

"Because you are bored with your duties here and wish to return to campaigning."

Silas chewed on, silently. After a long, thoughtful pause he nodded, indicating that Robert should continue.

"I have been trained in horsemanship and in the use of arms, but have little experience in the art of fighting. You are well versed in the art of fighting, but without the resources to use them."

Silas nodded again.

"Teach me your skills, teach me everything you know, and when I am ready, I shall take you with me to Ireland."

"And if you have no aptitude for it?"

"That you will never know until we try," said Robert, his heart thumping. "We will work in secret. If I fail, no slur will fall upon you, if I succeed, you will have earned your chance of joining Strongbow's men."

In the months that followed Robert's conversation with his father he continued to train hard with Silas, his enthusiasm inspired and his excitement mounting with the prospect of proving himself in battle. He rose early each morning and went riding in full mail for two hours, becoming accustomed to its weight and restriction of movement. After a light breakfast, he trained rigorously at the tilts and with the sword. Sometimes Silas made him chop logs of wood with a heavy axe for an hour or more, and Robert's body grew firm and ever more powerful, his long limbs stretching and filling, transforming the rangy youth into man and soldier.

Silas sometimes allowed his pleasure in this unexpected new lease of life to show, and occasionally even praised the boy, although more often he was critical, forcing Robert's exhausted body to ever greater feats of physical endurance. Silas trained alongside Robert, showing little sign of the neck and shoulder injury which had kept him away from battle for many a year.

"How did it happen?" Robert asked once, looking at the long, jagged scar.

"I looked away. It's a valuable lesson to learn, and better learned second-hand. Never turn away from your adversary." But beyond that, Silas wouldn't say. He was a taciturn man to whom words were so much wasted air and he wasted as little as possible.

Robert was painfully aware that his knowledge of military skills was confined to his reading of the works of Caesar and Tacitus. He questioned his father and brothers continually about issues of leadership and tactics, but it soon became clear that only experience would truly satisfy his growing thirst for knowledge.

More delighted than he cared to show, Henry seemed pleased to help his son in every way he could, and insisted that Robert take with him to Ireland, not only Silas, but six other men, all armed and equipped for war. His brother Hugh contributed generously to his expenses and Robert cared not that his motives were only to get a troublesome younger brother out of the way.

The night before his departure for Ireland, Robert spent a sorrowful evening in the company of his mother. Finally letting down her stoic guard, she allowed the tears of bitter loss to fall. "I shall miss you, Robert."

Her careworn face, already old and disillusioned, filled him with sudden pity. "And I you, mother. But we shall see each other again and I will have become a son you will be proud of."

"I have always been proud of you." Her voice was tremulous as she spoke, for she had no daughters to keep her company in the long days when her husband and sons were away at war; her efforts to hold onto her gentle Robert had come to naught, and had incurred only the angry, sullen, disapproval of her lord. Some of her feelings were expressed in her final words to him: "It is not easy to be a woman, wife and mother, Robert."

For the first time in his life, Robert considered his mother's point of view: how it must feel for her to watch those she loved, her protectors, go off in the cold light of dawn, not knowing if and when they would return, and with nothing but household matters to divert her. Quickly he brushed his musings aside, knowing how his father would rail at them. "But women are different from men," he told her.

She closed her eyes, hiding the distress she felt. "Yes, very different, Robert," she replied.

The morning dawned, a grey drizzle obscuring the hills and woods which on a clear day could be seen stretching away from the castle as far as the eye could see. His mother stood at the top of the stone steps, a small lonely figure in the rain, and Robert forced a smile. Whatever anguish she might be feeling, she kept it hidden from him, for she had said all she had to say on the matter, and he dismissed her resolutely from his mind. It was easy to do. His eyes sparkled in his tanned face; his light hair, darkened by the rain, clung to his well-shaped head. His excitement allowed him no time for doubt, fear or sorrow and the world spread before him, its possibilities endless. If he returned, he vowed, it would be as a conquering hero and he would see his mother smile again, pride in her eyes. Robert lifted his arm and dropped it again, and his men followed him, away from the castle, towards Llandrinoch, and from there to Ireland, where his life would truly begin.

CHAPTER 2

$\mathcal{S}$tanding on the hilltop, which from as far back as he could remember had been the traditional assembly site of the sept, Rory MacGillingrouth gazed down at the village of wooden houses over which his chieftainship held sway. His own dun stood out clearly, surrounded by a protective barrier of hedges and bushes. Smoke drifted up from the many cooking fires of the dome-shaped hutments. At the far end of the village stood the tall pencil-shaped building that had once housed the beginning of a monastery, but was now only partly used as a place of worship, the rest of it having been allowed to fall into ruin. A badly constructed drainage ditch ran the length of the homestead.

Rory felt a strong sense of responsibility towards the men, women and children who moved about the village. He could just make out the figure of Aifel, like an ant crawling about beneath him, probably busy preparing his forthcoming meal. Until very recently she had been his woman, his wife, the mother of his children; then he had discarded her in favour of the younger, and far more beautiful Dvorvild, daughter of his own chief, Patrick O'Flerty. Rory had been right hand man to O'Flerty for a long time; just recently, however, he had felt his position being threatened. His own brother, Cashal, had gained increased popularity for his wisdom in the war council and his exploits on the battlefield, so marriage to Dvorvild had been expedient. For the time being, he felt he had done as much as he could.

Rory sighed. In many ways he regretted taking Dvorvild. Although he was pleased by her beauty she showed little aptitude for homemaking and seemed more than happy to leave everything to Aifel and their daughter, Aileen. He spared no thought for the feelings of Aifel: the workings and ways of women were not for him to question, any more than he would have expected women to question the ways of men. If Aifel desired his protection he would grant it in recognition of her years of devotion, and she was lucky that he was still there to protect her, for after all, she was aging now, losing her looks, and there would be no one else of his standing who would want to keep her.

The MacGillingrouth sept, tied in so many ways – through family relationship and tradition – to the large O'Flerty tribe, had lived in the village of Seandale for ten years or more. For decades the sept had been at loggerheads with the MacTillings, one time owners of the territory around Seandale, until they had been driven away during the recent inter-tribal wars that had plagued Leinster for almost fifty years.

The MacTillings had suffered severely in the struggles between Dermot of Leinster and Tiernan O'Rourke, Lord of Brefne. When O'Rourke, in alliance with the High King, had succeeded in expelling Dermot McMurrough from his possessions in Leinster, Donal MacTilling had been driven out of the country of Loswellery, into the fastness of the Wicklow hills. This had delighted Rory MacGillingrouth, who had promptly led his sept into Seandale, the most westerly village in Loswellery. These reflections further coloured his feeling of self satisfaction, as he gazed down upon the sleepy village.

Rory was aware that his position could be threatened. Word was about, fed by wandering priests and travelling bards, that Dermot McMurrough was away enlisting further help from foreign mercenaries. Rory had already suffered at the hands of Dermot's earlier allies, the soldiers of Robert FitzStephen, and he could not suppress a feeling of unease. The controlled ferocity of the Norman Knights and the skill of the Welsh bowmen had been experienced to his cost and their reputation had spread abroad, like wine spilled from a drinking vessel. Rory shrugged, he could not afford to be frightened by rumour and much could yet happen to prevent the Leinster chief from renewing his struggle for power.

Rory made his descent into the village and strode along the main street which ran the length of Seandale. Children playing in the dust, pigs rooting in the rubble and chickens scratching in the dried mud of the street, scattered before him, setting up a cacophony of sound. Ignoring them he went to his dun.

"Look, father, we've been fishing," Rory's son Donel called proudly.

"And Donel fell into the water and nearly got drowned," added his twin brother Corvild, his voice shrill in his excitement.

22

"So you've caught me my dinner from the Loge stream, have you now?" Rory said, ruffling their hair and smiling at them. The Loge bordered the village, flowing by to join the Liffey, and the twins, still young enough to spare time to play, often fished its sparkling waters. Losing interest in their lively chatter, Rory pushed past Aifel who stood in the doorway, ignoring both her and the angry look which his daughter Aileen threw his way.

"Excuse me," Aileen said, her voice dripping sarcasm.

Rory scowled at her. Though still young she had a formidable presence and he often felt unable to cope with her defiance.

"Where's Dvorvild?" he demanded of Aifel.

Aileen looked up from her work again and stared him in the eye. "She's out picking berries," she said, her voice insolent. She might as well have added, "whilst we remain at home and work," but she had no need to, her taut body spoke for her.

"How about some food then?" Rory said to nobody in particular. Aileen turned her face from him, pretending not to have heard. Suddenly her attitude maddened him: with so much on his mind he had no wish to contend with a recalcitrant daughter. "Did you hear me, Aileen?" he shouted, and the children outside the dun scattered like leaves before the wind.

"It would be difficult not to hear you, father," she said, her eyes flashing coldly at him.

"Then do it."

He took a step towards her and she felt the muscles in her body tense, ready for flight, but she stood her ground. "You have a wife to cook and fetch for you. Ask her."

"She's not here," he said, drawn easily into an argument.

"That's your problem. You wanted to marry the chief's daughter – you did. Now that you've turned mother into an old woman, you prefer Dvorvild's beauty – enjoy it. If your wife isn't here to look after you, look after yourself."

"You'll obey me, or I'll have you whipped."

She turned her back on him, feeling the hairs on the back of her neck rise. At that moment, perhaps just in time to save her from a beating, Rory's brother Cashal appeared, bending his head to enter through the low doorway. He was a giant of a man; his bewhiskered face was smiling now, but Aileen had seen how he could turn the blood of men to water with just one ferocious stare.

"Good day, Rory," he said. His rich voice filled the dun as he greeted his brother, but his eyes were on Aileen.

"Cashal," acknowledged Rory, inclining his head angrily.

23

Cashal brushed against Aileen and she let her body lean into his as he paused to receive her welcoming kiss. His lips were warm and filled with promise but the greatest pleasure was in enticing them to linger for just a moment longer than they should have done, as her father stood by helplessly.

A brotherly kiss – no more, Rory told himself, but he saw the way Aileen's eyes lingered in Cashal's and the kiss itself wasn't quite right, leaving him feeling uncomfortable.

Cashal sat down at the table with Rory opposite him.

"Leave us," Rory ordered and instantly suffered a moment of agonising fear that Aileen would defy him again. He relaxed as she obeyed, but in doing so she again brushed past Cashal, pouting her lips seductively, and Rory knew that his daughter was mocking him.

She stood in the doorway, concealed from her father, and watched as they talked. Cashal could see her from where he sat and turned his head periodically to smile in her direction. "Patrick O'Flerty is angry with McMurrough," he said to Rory, his face growing serious.

"And hardly surprising, for what's to prevent him from recruiting more help? MacTilling will join any forces he may amass and try to win Loswellery back."

"I think we should prepare ourselves for a bitter struggle," Cashal said, nodding sagely. His right hand grabbed the hilt of the dagger he always wore.

Rory was gratified that Cashal saw things his way, but his more immediate concern lay with his own standing in O'Flerty's war councils. Further conversation did little to curb his growing bitterness over the way Cashal was steadily usurping his place in tribal affairs. It was clear that Cashal was very much in favour with the old chief, and this had the effect of trivialising his own political marriage.

He noticed his brother look over to the door and realised that Aileen was still there. At fourteen the girl already had the mature body of a woman, and Rory was uneasy. He had seen that look in Cashal's eye before: he was a man with a roving eye and a passionate nature, Rory had no argument with that, but would he be prepared to indulge himself with his own blood relative? Rory would put nothing past Cashal, yet it appeared to be Aileen, and not Cashal, who was the instigator. Was she truly aware of the effect her swaying hips and half closed eyes were having on his brother, or was she still an innocent child, accidentally parodying the behaviour of the village girls? Much as he wished to believe the latter, the former, he was sure, was true.

Whilst Cashal and Rory talked, Aifel took Aileen to one side. Her anxiety was clear from her expression. "You provoke your father too much,

Aileen. I warn you, be careful."

Aileen smiled nonchalantly. The idea had been forming gradually and had now crystalised: if she was going to succeed in making her life comfortable, she had to take charge of it now. She didn't want to be another Aifel in ten years' time.

Aifel read her mind with the almost uncanny ability which had led Aileen to hold her in awe as a young child. "You are determined not to let a man hold sway over your life, aren't you? You're afraid of ending up like me."

"That's part of it," Aileen said carefully. She loved her mother and was afraid of hurting her.

"It had to come some day, my love, your father is ambitious for power. Dvorvild is merely an end to bring him that power."

"Is that all she is?" replied Aileen, her voice bitter, thinking that Dvorvild's incredible beauty must have something to do with it, but as soon as she had spoken she wished she could withdraw the words.

Aifel ignored the implication. "I still have Rory's protection and can live here with my children. I'm fortunate." There was a hint of warning in her voice, she had no wish for her upstart daughter to upset the fine balance of her life.

"Fortunate! Why don't you fight Rory, mother? Why continue to act as his servant?"

"You already know the answer," Aifel said calmly.

"Nothing can be worse than demeaning yourself." Aileen's cheeks were flushed in indignation.

"Yes it can. Try starving, Aileen, try surviving alone without any protection. Don't belittle me without giving some consideration to the facts of my life. You've never known any hardship – since before your birth Rory has been chief of this sept and you've enjoyed the privileges which that has brought you." Her eyes took on a dreamy, faraway look. "I haven't always been as you see me now, Aileen. Before I married your father, and when we were newly wed, I too knew the thrill of power." She looked at her daughter, but it seemed to Aileen that her mother saw not her, but another scene. "Things will change before long, I can feel it. And change us with them." Aifel focused back onto Aileen's face and she shrugged, her eyes crinkling as she smiled. "Things change continually, be prepared to go with them." Her voice was suddenly practical.

Aileen felt her anger drain away and hugged her mother warmly. Aifel was thin and vulnerable beneath her shift and Aileen experienced a surge of powerful love. They leaned against one another for some time, until Aifel pulled away and went about her business and Aileen, catching Cashal's roving eye, forgot their conversation.

Rory's thoughts remained with his wayward daughter long after Cashal left the dun, and when Dvorvild returned he looked upon her with relief, as a diversion. He forgot his earlier misgivings as they sat down to eat, idly comparing the manners of the women to those of his twin sons, who ate busily and noisily. He forgot, too, who had prepared the meal they ate, as he looked at his new wife, comparing her with the older and more familiar woman.

"Has your day been a happy one?" he asked Dvorvild.

She looked at him with her great blue eyes and tossed her fair hair, bound by a cowhide strip, back over her shoulder. "I've been out in the woods collecting berries for Aifel."

Aifel looked up briefly but made no comment.

"Good, good," he replied vaguely. He looked at his daughter who seemed absorbed in her food.

Aileen ate as she lived her life, with great enjoyment, and appeared to have no interest in the fate of her mother or Dvorvild's tenuous hold over her father, but, in fact, they played a large part in her thoughts. Aileen realised that her looks and the fact that she was a chieftain's daughter would not keep her position forever; more was needed – as her mother's fate demonstrated. She rarely resented Dvorvild for long, they had the affinity of youth, and Aileen could clearly see that one day Dvorvild would share the same fate as her mother. She took stock of her own position. She had as good or better physical attributes than Dvorvild and she intended to use her brain as well as her looks to avoid the fate that seemed inevitable for women. She had tried playing on the village boys with great success. Her body and eyes made promises which she taught them she could break if she chose and she'd found out that, whilst in the grip of passion, a boy would give anything, do anything, to possess her.

The idea had been forming gradually and had now crystalised: if she, Aileen, was going to succeed in bettering her life, she had to take charge of it. And Cashal, the most desirable man in the village, a warrior and a true man, was responding to her wiles in a most encouraging fashion.

He took her breath away with his good looks and the sheer power of him. She had lost interest in the boys; now she had eyes only for her uncle. The sense of fear and importance she experienced when he looked at her was beyond anything she could ever have imagined. She knew that once she had him under her control it would no longer matter if her father threatened to whip her. She would only have to tell Cashal of his cruelty and he would put an end to it. She was sure that Cashal's power was waxing, to the detriment of Rory's. And powerful men could still be malleable if a woman was sensible and clever.

They had just finished their meal when Corderg, Aileen's elder brother, came in. Aileen noted how Aifel's face lit up at his arrival, whilst Rory made only the most sullen of welcomes. Aileen liked Corderg and felt no jealousy at her mother's obvious love for him. It was hardly surprising, for he was always gentle and considerate. Destined for the priesthood, he was a quiet, scholarly boy, which was why his war-like father could spare him no time. Aileen too thought him rather weak, misconstruing his gentle nature and not realising how much inner strength it must take to stand up, in his own quiet way, against the wishes of his father. For herself, she preferred the Cashals of this world. Such men could make a woman feel like a woman, and such men provided a challenge which Aileen was determined to conquer.

Sitting down at the table and pouring himself a drink, Corderg told them of the new English prioress at Whitley. "Father Seamus is most unhappy about the new Roman ideas she is trying to introduce," he said. Rory drained his cup, slammed it on the table and got up to go. "But I'm more concerned about her relationship with the Welshman, FitzStephen, knowing his support for Dermot McMurrough."

Rory, just on his way out of the dun, hesitated and grunted his agreement. For once, he thought, Corderg is talking sense.

"I've heard it said," Corderg continued, "that Patrick O'Flerty's not taking kindly to any increase in English influence. He sees it as part of McMurrough's plan to regain his lost lands."

Aileen was excluded from the conversation, with no hope of encouraging them to include her. When fighting started she would be expected to keep out of the way, yet as a young and beautiful woman she would be fair game if her tribe were the losers; but still she must show no interest in the talk of men. Even Corderg had more status than she. She unrolled her pallet and laid it in a dark corner of the room, curling up on it with her cheek on her hands, listening half-heartedly to Corderg and her father and thinking of Cashal until she fell asleep.

The following day was hot and sultry. Aileen watched the swine as they wandered amidst the undergrowth at the edge of the copse. She was uncomfortable in the unaccustomed heat, despite the simple linen smock she wore. Sweat ran down her face and body and her head ached. She thought longingly of the cool water of the stream which formed a pool nearby as it twisted round the copse – known as Donel's Folly – on its way past the village. She'd been told by Rory to bring the swine to the woods and knew he would be annoyed if she disobeyed him. She shrugged and went further afield to cool herself near the water. His anger was of little consequence anyway, it had become a part of her daily routine now. Either she did as Rory wanted and was unhappy, or she did as she chose and dealt with the brunt of his anger. Preferring the latter, she drove the pigs to the water's edge.

She lay down beside the pool but still the heat was intense. Even the pigs were loath to move out of the shade and many of them were asleep on their sides with their rounded flanks gently heaving.

A constant hum filled the silence as bees and flies went drowsily about their business. Across the open field that separated the wood from the stream, the heat haze shimmered and Aileen felt alone in the world. The afternoon's silence enveloped her, isolating her from her village. In the nearby fields men and women had laid aside spade and hoe in order to seek the shelter afforded by the trees and hedges, and the village itself seemed almost deserted; other than the hens who picked their way in the dirt, nothing moved. Time itself stood still.

Lifting herself up onto one elbow, Aileen looked into the tempting depths of the pool. Rising suddenly to her feet, she stripped off her smock and dived in. The pigs will have to fend for themselves, she thought. They had barely moved all afternoon, in any case.

The coldness of the clear mountain spring water took her breath away and she could feel the blood pumping around her body as she splashed and played in the rejuvenating waters. The sun glanced down, making silver crystal from the drops which sprayed around her dark head, each filled with the multi-coloured hues of the rainbow. The trees sheltered her and she laughed in sheer pleasure as she played.

Cashal MacGillingrouth, weary after a day spent in negotiation at the dun of the O'Flerty, slowly made his way homewards. He had chosen to go through the tangled undergrowth of Donel's Folly, rather than use the longer, well-worn track to the north of the copse: not only was it quicker but the trees offered protection from the scorching rays of the sun.

Nearing the edge of the wood he heard the splash of water, and, curiosity getting the better of him, he crept with the caution of a born hunter toward the source of the sound. His hand on the hilt of his dagger, he peered through the veil of leafy branches and saw a girl swimming in the pond, droplets of water following the curve of her tanned arms. He let out his breath in a long sigh and relaxed.

With strong, powerful strokes Aileen swam to the edge of the pool and stood up, her long black hair clinging to her body like a cape. His tiredness forgotten, Cashal stared at her from the trees which Aileen had thought would hide her from prying eyes. Not that she appeared to care much about that, he thought, as he recognised his brother's daughter. He smiled, the girl was a wanton, asking for the attentions of a real man. He had heard the boys talking in the village, she had them all panting after her.

Perhaps he should do her a favour, and show her what her body was really made for.

Aileen stood momentarily with water dripping from her body, and Cashal realised with a thrill that the girl he stood admiring was no girl after all, but a woman, far more beautiful than he had imagined. Her breasts were large and her smoothly-tanned flat belly, led excitingly to the black triangle of hair between her long, athletic legs. Her wet skin glistened in the rays of the sun and Cashal was fascinated, unable to take his eyes away from her.

Breathing more quickly as his excitement mounted, Cashal continued to watch as she lay at the edge of the woods where a patch of white sunlight could warm her now icy body. For a few brief seconds he felt concern: he was, after all, looking at the body of his niece. But Cashal was a man of action, and if he allowed himself to ponder for any length on the morals of his actions he would be lost. His needs would always take priority over the consequences of his behaviour and the needs he had now were not something he was prepared to over-ride.

He stepped out of the woods, the undergrowth crackling beneath his feet. Aileen looked up, startled, and threw her arms protectively about her body, but as soon as she saw Cashal her expression of fear faded, turning to one of excitement. She let her arms drop, stood up and looked into his eyes, her own gaze unblinking. Then, unexpectedly, she moved over to him and cupped his face in her hands.

"It's you, Cashal MacGillingrouth," she whispered.

"Aye," he said, smiling at her. "So the moment has come at last, pretty one, that you have been promising."

"I've made no promises, Cashal," she said, trying to lead him as she did the village boys. She assumed a coy expression but he wasn't interested in playing games. He kissed her fiercely, urgently, his beard scratching her face and when her knees buckled she let herself fall to the ground beneath him.

CHAPTER 3

It was a warm, bright August morning in the year 1170 and Strongbow had completed his preparations for his Irish enterprise. The business of embarking was well in advance of schedule, for he had spared no expense, and his men and equipment were comprised of the best that England and Wales had to offer. Strongbow meant to recoup his fortunes during this campaign and an air of confidence and efficiency pervaded.

The sun beamed down from a cloudless sky onto the flat countryside which stretched from the distant hills to the small harbour town of Milford Haven. The land between the hills and the harbour was mostly flat, with only occasional farmhouses giving any sign of human habitation. Small copses and some larger areas of wood added variety to the peaceful landscape. Gorse and heather flourished on the common land where oxen, cart-horses and sheep grazed.

The town itself consisted mainly of small wooden houses crowding in on the central market square and creeping up the three roads which entered the town from the east, north and west. Here, ale-houses and stalls selling food and vegetables vied for the custom of the farmers and merchants who came to sell produce and livestock. More ale-houses were perched along the edge of the quay to service the needs of the fishermen and harbour hands and the crew of the occasional merchant ships which berthed there. The larger port of Bristol took the bulk of the traffic for the west of England, and Milford Haven had remained a quiet backwater.

Today the town's quay teemed with Strongbow's soldiers, shouting, swearing, sweating under the weight of their equipment. Rank upon rank of massive horses were roped together waiting to be loaded, and the ground was slimy with dung and heavy with the smell and sound of bluebottles and horseflies. There were carpenters, blacksmiths and other craftsmen filing on board ship – their task when safely ashore in Ireland would be to build such engines of war as might be needed once the battle commenced. Seamen and those engaged in loading stores rushed unconcernedly amongst the packages and coiled ropes which lined the sides of the quay, forming human chains to convey the stacked cargo into the holds of the waiting ships. Protesting horses were led up narrow wooden gangways, snorting and lifting their feet high, frightened by the hollow sound of the thin wood which separated them from the water underneath. Seagulls wheeled and cried above; some perched on the rigging and the furled sails, staring with glittering eyes upon the unfamiliar hub-bub below them.

A gentle south-westerly breeze played around the dock area and Silas wiped his face with his shirt sleeves, letting the wind gently fan his sweating brow. The scene looked chaotic but he could remember the earlier, smaller expeditions led by FitzStephen and Maurice FitzGerald, and to his experienced eye, it was clear that this was an organised army of conquest.

Among those busily supervising the loading of men and stores, Robert FitzAlan took his place, revelling in the atmosphere and vitality of the scene. A great deal had happened to influence and change him since he'd left his home. At Llandrinoch he had been welcomed by his old master Reginald d'Evreux, and shortly afterwards he had been assigned a company of men-at-arms which he was to command.

Since arriving in Milford Haven neither Robert nor Silas had had much sleep – the business of seeing d'Evreux's troops embarked had seemed unending – and both men were impatient for the fleet to sail.

"Is all well with you?" asked Silas, noticing an odd expression in Robert's eyes.

Robert smiled. "Yes, I was only thinking how lucky I've been to have got this far. It's more than I've ever dared hope for."

"Aye," said Silas, clapping him on the arm, "You've done well, Master Robert. Perhaps you'll win yourself some lands – be a lord in your own right."

"And perhaps I shall be killed in battle," Robert retorted, only half in jest.

Silas put his hand up to his scarred neck. "Just remember not to turn your back," he said and winked.

They watched the proceedings in silence, leaning against the ship's rail as the last of d'Evreux's men filed past them up the gangway of the *Fortune*. Most of them carried arms and armour, as well as their personal effects, and all of them looked cheerful, pleased to be on their way at last. Many had the added difficulty of leading their nervous horses, but without exception they filled both Robert and the taciturn veteran Silas with a sense of pride.

"I hope I'll not let them down," Robert said, suddenly aware of his tremendous responsibility.

"It's a grave task," agreed Silas. It was good that his master should not be overly confident, for it was in that way that trusting men could be led into unnecessary disaster.

Threading their way below decks to the comparative peace of the cabin which had been allotted them, Robert breathed a large sigh of relief. "It's good to be finally on our way, is it not?"

"I'm pleased to be away from Taffowey with a sword in my hand once more," Silas replied, peering through the porthole toward the horizon.

Robert looked at him, wondering what it had been like to return home half-dead, believing he would never fight again. Silas's left arm was still stiff and clumsy from the damage caused by a blow intended to remove his head, but it seemed not to impair his fighting abilities. His recovery had been slow but sure, yet even without the full use of his left arm Silas was a worthy companion to the inexperienced Robert, and the latter was well aware of it.

"Tell me," Robert said, "are the Irish as easy to defeat as reports suggest?"

"No man is easy to beat, whether he be Irish, Welsh or English."

"Yet Maurice de Prendergast has told me that FitzStephen captured Wexford last year with only five hundred men. We have far more in our army."

"He had five hundred men – of his own. Did you not know he was aided by Dermot McMurrough's Irish?"

"No, he said nothing of that to me. What about that story he tells – how he fought his way out of an ambush simply by clever use of his bowmen?"

"He lost more men in that one battle than in the whole of the rest of the campaign," Silas concluded.

"Is it true then, that the Irish wear very little body armour and can fight only with axes and slings?" Silas nodded. "Our chain mail must give us great advantage – why did FitzStephen lose so many men?"

"The Irish leaders use cunning, their men will not give up. They win through good planning and strategy."

"And how does Dermot McMurrough fit into this description of good leadership?"

Silas grimaced. Clearly he didn't approve of Dermot, yet Robert had found him charming when he'd met him at Llandrinoch. Indeed his good humour and the courtesy he extended to all those with whom he made contact, had endeared him to most of the men.

"Dermot McMurrough is a man with two faces," Silas said, his expression wary and closed. "I've been told that Dermot had the heads of two hundred of his enemies brought before him and he gnawed on each one of them."

Robert laughed at the grisly picture this conjured up. "What you're saying is that I shouldn't believe everything I hear?"

Silas shrugged, his face still unreadable. He would say no more and Robert was left wondering if he actually believed the ridiculous story. A pensive silence fell on them both and remained unbroken until Silas jumped up suddenly, almost knocking a pile of armour to the ground.

"I need food," he shouted. "Is there no food to be had on this God-forsaken ship!"

"Go and find some if you wish," said Robert, laughing.

Except in combat Silas rarely moved quickly, but his stomach was a hard taskmaster; he seemed to have to fill it continually simply to maintain his hard muscular frame. He returned shortly with bread, meat and beer, which they ate quickly then made their way on deck.

After checking that all was well with their men, many of whom were sitting or lying wherever they could find space on the crowded decks, they stood at the side of the ship watching the activity on the quay. With much creaking of rigging and shouting from the seamen, the *Fortune* moved slowly out into the bay, giving place to another vessel, upon which further troops began to embark. The sails cracked as the breeze filled them and the ship heeled slightly. Robert gazed at the receding shore-line. The houses of the town stood out sharply against the cliffs to the west and the rich purple of the distant hills. He wondered what lay before him. There was nothing left for him now but to succeed. Everything was under control and tomorrow he would be in Ireland.

CHAPTER 4

Strongbow's invading army arrived off Waterford on August 23rd, 1170. His nephew, Raymond le Gros, had gone on ahead to choose a landing site which afforded the ships a safe berth from which to disembark and defend their troops. The area was deserted, with a wide view over the surrounding countryside and Raymond had already had a huge mound built and look-out guards posted. The men were in the best of spirits as they went about the business, and, in a simple ceremony on the beach, Strongbow gave thanks for their safe arrival on this most propitious St. Bartholemew's Eve.

The following day the Norman force was joined by the last of Raymond's contingent, flushed by an easy victory over an Ostmen army from Waterford, and the two leaders met at Raymond's camp in Baginbun to decide how best to move against the walled city.

Robert and Silas, along with the rest of d'Evreux's men had been glad to step ashore, and, after a comfortable night on dry land, were impatient for the approaching battle. Fired up with Raymond's accounts they felt assured they would soon be masters of Waterford.

As they marched toward Waterford, Robert and Silas discussed the le Gros fight.

"Did you learn anything more about the Ostmen battle?" Robert asked.

"It seems that Raymond's men stampeded five hundred cattle to upset the Ostmen," Silas told him. "Many of the men took fright and were driven over the cliffs into the sea. The rest were taken prisoner."

"And what became of them?"

"Harvey de Montmorency had their legs broken and cast them into the sea," replied Silas, shrugging. The fate of prisoners was of no interest to him. Robert grew quiet and Silas wondered what ailed him. "I hear Raymond argued with de Montmorency," he added, guessing what was on his young master's mind.

"To what end?"

"He wished the men to be saved."

Robert looked at Silas in astonishment. "Saved? Then what would we do with them?" He had not thought Raymond soft. How could they spare men to guard prisoners of war who would otherwise have nothing to prevent them returning to fight again? And yet, he remembered, they were men and such cruelty was a bitter way to end a man's life.

Silas didn't answer. Could his master not see the fields about him, the same fields which he hoped soon to dominate? How did Robert think they would be worked if all the Irish were slaughtered? Silas watched him struggle with the dilemma, knowing that Robert would come to understand in his own time: he was a thinker, a born leader of men, the problems of leadership and morality would plague him for the rest of his life. He realised how much he had come to respect the young man, a rough affection born initially out of respect for his mother, who had made it her business to ensure Silas's injuries had been properly treated. He would have died but for her.

The English army were now within sight of Waterford. Robert gripped his horse's reins tightly, trying to control the panic which he could feel building from the pit of his stomach. He stole a furtive look at the men who surrounded him: they were grim-faced and pale, their lips set, their backs straight. He felt a surge of pride as he realised that he was part of this group of daunting warriors moving forward towards the town.

Soon Robert could clearly make out the citizens lining the walls. They were shaking their fists and hurling abuse at the soldiers and he felt a similar hatred suffuse him: the Irish had ceased to be men, they were an obstacle to be overcome. The Enemy. He adjusted his armour, as he had done a thousand times in practise, to ensure the freedom of his sword. A shiver of excitement tinged with fear washed over him.

"I pray that we're to be led by Raymond and not that cold fish de Montmorency," he remarked, grateful that his voice sounded terse but unafraid. Silas nodded his agreement. There was little more time for talking, for the front line had reached the town's walls and the attack of Waterford had begun.

From their vantage points on the walls high above Strongbow's army, the defenders repelled the Norman attacks with apparent ease. To continue to follow this course of action would be suicidal and soldiers drew their excited horses to a halt as they reached the bank of corpses of men who had gone before them.

Robert saw what was happening. The blood which had been racing through his veins felt as if it had turned to thick mud as he realised it was more likely to be a siege he was engaged in than a real battle. His shoulders slumped with disappointment: a siege would tie them up for several days, or weeks, depending upon the amount of food and livestock available to the town; the soldiers would become bored and fractious, forced to raid the outlying areas to forage for their own food. It was one thing to attack the enemy in battle; another to starve out a whole town – men, women, children – until it was forced to surrender. Robert saw himself and his companions as soldiers, not the inhumane jailors a siege would force them to become. Worse still, whilst they kicked their heels waiting for surrender it would be possible for the Irish to rally more forces and creep up on them unawares. The Welsh and Normans' strength was in their speed and the surprise of their attack, not in sheer weight of numbers.

Strongbow, too, wished to avoid a siege at all costs: speed, he knew, was essential. Raymond, ever a skilled strategist, devised a plan which was readily adopted. He had noticed that there were a number of wooden houses built into the wall which projected outwards and were supported by beams from the ground outside. These beams, if ignited, would – or so Raymond hoped – collapse the dwellings and so make a breach in the wall through which his men could move.

Robert and his men watched with interest as a small group of volunteers, crouching behind their long shields, took lighted torches and made their way towards the wooden beams. Strongbow's own Welsh bowmen gave them cover with a hail of arrows which shielded the firemen from attack.

At first Robert couldn't understand what was happening, but as the fire took hold and the smoke cleared he saw the houses begin to fall in, leaving substantial gaps in the wall through which he could see the town. Robert's own shout of triumph was drowned by exultant cries from the men around him, and the army seethed once more with excited anticipation.

As the fires died down the Norman forces poured into the breach. Raymond led the attack and Robert was close behind with his men as they drove into a melee of Irishmen who screamed their fury with ear-splitting venom. He was surprised, almost caught off balance, by their ferocity. They whirled their axes in the air and several crowded around Robert's horse, driven by the pressure of those behind. The horse, terrified by the noise and the smell of blood, plunged and flailed, nearly unseating him. He felt his diaphragm tighten in panic as he imagined himself falling to the ground and to the mercy of the Irishmen.

The Waterford men were not soldiers but civilians. Though they wore no armour and most fought on foot, they were fighting for their lives and the lives and freedom of their families, and as such had the strength of madmen. The initial fight they put up unsettled Robert who was used to order and strategy, but his training soon began to tell and he felt an icy calm take over as the Irish fell back under the superior skills of his men.

Holding his sword out before him at arm's length he faced a man who, axe in hand, was bearing down upon him. The man was very close – Robert could see drops of sweat on his forehead, darkening his uncovered red hair to brown – and he hesitated for the briefest of moments, loath to attack someone who was so obviously an unskilled civilian. The man saw his opportunity and lunged with his axe. Robert reacted instinctively, shielding the blow with an outstretched arm. Though he was aware that the blade pierced his chain mail and the skin beneath, the blow lacked speed or power and he felt no pain. The shock was enough to alert him to the danger of hesitation and in one swift movement he pierced his assailant in the gut. He felt a cold detachment as the blade entered the man's body and he pushed and twisted before withdrawing it, his eyes riveted upon the face of his adversary. The man doubled over, clutching at the hole in his body as blood poured between his fingers from his half-exposed stomach. He fell slowly to his knees, his head touching the ground before he finally collapsed, lifeless, at Robert's feet.

Robert had killed his first man but he had no time to react, for almost immediately several more were in his place, axes raised, threatening. The huge faces loomed toward him, mouths wide open, for the Irish screamed as they leapt in the most blood-curdling fashion. With his sword, Robert cut through the mass of faces, watching the shock of death mask each one. In his euphoria he heard nothing but he saw everything. The men fell before him like dry firewood.

Looking about him during a brief lull, he saw Raymond le Gros stumble whilst scrambling over some fallen masonry. Helpless in his heavy armour le Gros tried to regain his feet as a huge Irishman came at him. Robert got there first and had speared him before he even knew he was there. The Irishman fell, a look of astonishment in his eyes before they glazed over to stare sightlessly at the empty sky.

Catching his breath, Robert reached over and hauled Raymond to his feet. Their eyes met over the dead man's body. The older man inclined his head in silent acknowledgement; within moments they were in the thick of the fighting once more.

The battle was quickly over, the citizens of Waterford overwhelmed by the skill of their opposition. Casualties among them were high. Robert realised it would have been impossible to control the initial blood-lust of the Norman soldiers, who had almost been cheated of their fight. But he was sickened by the shambles before him: Dermot McMurrough's followers had indulged in wholesale slaughter, slicing through the vulnerable and unarmed bodies of women and children, Many of the lesser-injured still ran, panic-stricken, through the town.

Robert, observing the carnage in the silent aftermath of the battle, felt a rush of pity for the people of Waterford who lay dead and dying around him, many with severed limbs writhing in agony in their own blood. From one tangle of bodies an arm twitched. It was a small limb and, walking over, Robert realised it belonged to a child, a little girl, no more than eight years old. Her injuries were obviously fatal and he closed his eyes briefly, unwilling to face this bitter reality of war. Opening them again he saw her looking up at him, her face white and her eyes wild with fright. He bent over her, stroking her forehead, desperately wanting to give her comfort.

"Don't die," he whispered as he gathered her in his arms. But his words went unheard: the girl was already dead. He laid her down tenderly and felt tears sting the back of his eyes as he remembered with shame the wild, almost sexual enjoyment he had experienced as his sword had cut through the wall of men in the height of the battle.

Shortly after the capture of the town a fanfare of trumpets announced the arrival of additional men in the shape of contingents belonging to Robert FitzStephen and his half brother, FitzGerald. Strongbow was delighted to receive reinforcements; moreover, FitzStephen was able to assist Strongbow in his efforts to save the life of a leading Waterford citizen. He had been arguing with Dermot McMurrough who wished to have the man put to death as an example – as if the city were not overwhelmed by such examples already. Dermot had become ugly and recalcitrant following Strongbow's repeated requests for lenience, but FitzStephen, demanding some recognition for his intended support, provided Strongbow with the necessary lever to prevent the killing. Dermot yielded graciously once he could see he had no real option, and the man was set free.

Dermot hid his anger, cloaking it with warm charm. Barbaric by nature, he had no wish to upset Strongbow and his allies at this stage and he agreed with Strongbow's advice that the town be properly garrisoned and its defences rebuilt. The Normans had obviously come to stay and he saw himself not only King of Leinster once more, but as King of all Ireland. With Strongbow beside him his enemies would be defeated, for together they were invincible and he felt sure the dark days of defeat and exile were now over. He had only to bind the Welsh Earl to his cause.

"I think the time has come," he said to Strongbow, "for me to honour my pledge to you. I promised to give you my daughter in marriage. Eva is bored and I'll wager you are willing?"

Strongbow, ever ambitious and desperate to gain more power, curbed his excitement. In earlier negotiations, Dermot had offered to make Strongbow his heir, a highly controversial and illegal move, and a marriage would be one way of achieving this. It would also be safer to secure lands now, rather than waiting for Dermot's death.

"Marriage with Eva will be welcome. Your daughter has both beauty and charm."

Dermot smiled, his daughter meant a great deal to him and he liked to hear her praised.

Strongbow continued carefully. "We've fought well together, Dermot, and I think you need my help as much as I do yours."

Dermot nodded, knowing what Strongbow was about to propose.

"It would give me added security if I were to own some of the lands I help to conquer and I fight better when I feel secure." He looked directly into Dermot's deceptively gentle eyes.

"Of course it has always been my wish that you should keep and hold whatever lands you conquer." Dermot smiled benignly.

Such promises were easy to make and the two men, who held so much of Ireland's fate in their hands, shook upon the deal. Strongbow's only remaining problem was in trying to gauge the reaction of Henry of England. Royal approval was essential: what lasting value would the crown of Ireland have, if it meant the active opposition of the Plantagenet?

And so it was that the celebrations following the siege of Waterford included the wedding feast of Eva McMurrough to Richard de Clare, Earl of Pembroke. Strongbow officially marked the occasion – and demonstrated his pleasure at being acknowledged as McMurrough's heir – by announcing his decision to knight a number of young men who had excelled in the assault on the town. Robert was to be one of those knighted, singled out by Reginald d'Evreux as having played "a conspicuous part in the fighting" , a fact confirmed by no less a personage than le Gros himself.

So he didn't forget, thought Robert, recalling the promise in Raymond's eyes.

The festivities over, a decision was made to march on Dublin, the capture of which was essential to the conquest of Leinster. During the knighting ceremony Strongbow had spoken briefly, outlining his plans and promising that if they all continued as they had been doing, they would be well rewarded with land, becoming his own tenants.

Robert sat by his camp-fire that night looking into the hot flames. His body ached and the wound in his arm throbbed painfully, but he was content. He had been taken into Strongbow's confidence and won praise from le Gros; he was determined now to prove himself worthy of the great men's trust. It was the beginning of a dream coming true. He would build upon this modest start because soon, he was certain, he would have a chance to win the lands which Strongbow had promised. Not so long ago his grandfather had achieved a similar ambition, following William the Bastard from Normandy to Saxon England and in so doing making a fortune for his family.

Silas, coming upon him, smiled – a rare sight indeed. "You have done well – Sire," he said.

CHAPTER 5

$\mathcal{A}$ileen smiled in satisfaction as she walked through the village. Two weeks had passed since the beginning of her affair with Cashal and the repercussions had been felt not only in Seandale village, but throughout the O'Flerty sept. The liaison was now common knowledge and the basis of much gossip. The other young girls of the village viewed her with a new respect and envy, for Cashal was quite a catch. To be his lover was an achievement recognised even by those who criticized a liaison between uncle and niece.

Rory was furious that so few supported him in his opposition to the relationship. He had at least expected Father Seamus to be with him, yet curiously only Aifel and Corderg supported him. To rub salt into the wound, Aileen was flaunting her new power at every opportunity, reminding him, at the same time, of Cashal's ever-growing influence and his own steadily waning popularity.

When she entered the dun her radiance was not lost on Rory and he could contain himself no longer. "You will put an end to this immediately," he flung at her as she entered the dun, angered by her glowing eyes and flushed skin.

"I shall do nothing of the kind," she retorted, her chin tilted upward so that she could meet his eye. As a further act of defiance she tossed her hair back over her shoulder; it was loose and tousled and he turned his head away in disgust.

"Then you will be the loser in the end. You know the reputation Cashal has amongst the women of the village. He is fickle."

"He is besotted, father. Even the mighty Cashal cannot withstand me."

He lifted his hand to strike her, but she stood firm and unflinching, her eyes flashing green fire. "Cashal would not care for you to strike me, father," she said, and she actually laughed at him.

"Cashal is my brother and your uncle. Your behaviour is an abomination. Corderg says such a relationship would be damned."

"Corderg says, does he, father?" she jeered. "And do you now listen to the words of wisdom Corderg speaks, over those of your brother? Over those even of Patrick O'Flerty?"

"Patrick has no interest in the matter," Rory flared, his handsome face marred by a purple stain.

"No interest perhaps, but it would seem he sees no harm in it."

Rory, incensed beyond reason, lunged at her, but he was made clumsy by his rage and she was cool and haughty in her pride. She ducked his swinging arm easily, and walked from the dun, her head still held high.

Greeted by a group of girls gossiping in the street, Aileen smiled and winked at them.

"Good day, Aileen."

"Are you keeping well, Aileen?"

"Very well, thank-you," she replied, basking in Cashal's reflected glory.

Her twin brothers ran over to her. "Will you go fishing with us?" Donel asked, his cheeky young face freckled by the summer sun.

"I have no time for fishing, Donel, ask me tomorrow."

"You never have time any more," Corvild rebuked. "Tomorrow you will say 'wait until tomorrow,' as you did yesterday and the day before."

Aileen only smiled. Her time was fully occupied. She loved her brothers deeply but she had her own, more important, life to lead.

Cashal was indifferent to village gossip. Secure in the knowledge of his own prowess, he continued to go about life in Seandale as he had always done. Aileen was an extremely pleasurable diversion, he would even go as far as to say he cared for her, in a protective way. With her haughty ways and her deeply passionate nature, she added a touch of spice to his day; for the time being he was more than content to possess her.

He was enjoying, every bit as much as Aileen, the discomfiture the liaison was creating for Rory, who for too long had lorded over him in a most irritating fashion. His star was in the ascendant now, Rory was powerless to do anything but watch, pitifully aware that his marriage to Dvorvild had brought him nothing but a few nights of passion. Even Patrick O'Flerty, whilst recognising Rory's position as the chief of the

MacGillingrouths, was strongly drawn towards Cashal the Giant, whose popularity and charm won him the ear of everyone with whom he made contact.

It was therefore with great reluctance that Rory approached Cashal one day with another matter which was causing him concern. He strode into Cashal's dun, almost as though he expected to see Aileen there, and stood until asked to take a seat.

"Good day, brother," Cashal said, in his good-natured voice. "Please, sit for a while and regain your breath."

Rory had walked fast and was breathing heavily. His brow was beaded with sweat and he knew that he compared unfavourably with Cashal who was cool and sardonically in control whilst he, in contrast appeared uncouth and foolish. "I have heard," Rory said abruptly, without returning Cashal's greeting, "that Dermot McMurrough is back in Ireland. It is said – and this information came from O'Connor's agents in Dublin – that he has landed a large English army near Waterford, has seized the town and is now marching on Dublin itself. MacTilling is bound to join him – no doubt he hopes to reclaim these lands."

Cashal grinned, disparagingly. "Why worry? We've beaten MacTilling several times before, we can do so again. The High King will send help if we need it and we will drive the English into the sea."

Rory was dismayed at this cavalier dismissal. Cashal was a fool: perhaps he had forgotten that he, Rory, had already fought against McMurrough's earlier mercenaries and was well aware of their devastating efficiency. "Do you forget that Dermot's mercenaries are still in the country?" he said. "Scattered they may be, but active. And the Normans are now here in far greater numbers than ever before. I suggest you ready yourself, Cashal, for it is my belief that O'Flerty will be calling us soon."

"And I shall notify you, when he does," Cashal said, his blue eyes suddenly cold.

Rory almost choked on his anger at his brother's deliberate implication. It was a bitter reminder that O'Flerty was choosing Cashal as his confidant ever more frequently.

"At least if he does," he flung, raising from his seat and striding out of the dun, "you'll not be able to spare time for my daughter."

A few days after Rory's abortive conversation with Cashal, a party of men arrived from Patrick O'Flerty, summoning the men of Seandale to a hosting called by the High King. It was necessary to prepare defences against the Normans' forthcoming attack on Dublin.

Leading the party was the chieftain's eldest son, Murchad, eager to recruit the MacGillingrouth sept. Murchad was a strikingly handsome man: tall, with piercing blue eyes and profuse red whiskers. He arrived at the dun as Aifel and Aileen were preparing the mid-day meal and they stepped back to allow him to pass. Murchad greeted Aifel warmly, for he had known her as a young women but Aileen's striking looks had clearly made a big impression.

"Who is this, Aifel? I can't recall having seen her here before."

"She is my daughter, Murchad – Aileen."

"And I should have known her, for doesn't she take after her fair mother?"

Aifel blushed, she had grown unused to compliments.

Murchad looked at Aileen and smiled broadly. Despite her confident manner, she felt herself blush. The meeting had been unexpected and Murchad was uncommonly handsome. She recovered and smiled back at him, careful to throw her head back a little as she did so, well aware of the effect this gesture always had on Cashal.

"I must congratulate you on your daughter, Rory," said Murchad, as he passed into the darkness of the dun where Rory was waiting to receive him. "She has provided me with the most glorious vision I have seen for a long while."

His expression was lascivious and Rory suppressed a smile of elation. This was an unexpected turn of events, wherein lay not only the possible end to his daughter's infatuation with Cashal, but perhaps a closer involvement for himself in tribal matters.

Aileen couldn't hear anything of what was said inside the dun, for the men spoke in muffled voices and Aifel, her face glowing with pleasure, led her away to a quiet corner.

"What do you think of Murchad, Aileen. Is he not a fine-looking man?"

"Fine indeed," she replied, her eyes dancing.

"He seemed to find you fine also," Aifel said. "So fine he rapped his head on the door opening."

Aileen laughed. "No, mother, that was caused by my father, trying to push him back in my direction."

Aifel laughed with her and Aileen realised it had been a long while since she had seen her mother look happy. She took her in her arms and gave her a quick hard kiss on the cheek. Aifel laid her head on her daughter's shoulder. "Ah, you're a grand girl, Aileen, too fond of your body and its power, but a lovely girl for all that."

"Am I, mother – too fond?"

Aifel stepped away and considered her daughter's question seriously. "It can't hurt to use your youth and beauty when you can." She looked grave. "Once her looks are gone, there is little else to commend a woman, it seems."

"You are referring to yourself?"

"To myself, yes, but to you too, Aileen. You are right to want what you can take from life whilst it lies within your grasp, but I'm afraid of your feelings toward Cashal."

"Do you not like Cashal then, mother?"

Aifel hesitated before answering, Cashal looming up before her as clearly as if he stood there. "He seems right enough. He's strong and bold in battle and no more careless towards his women than others. But, Aileen," she looked at her daughter, whose heart was essentially good, and was filled with misgivings. "Can you not see that the blood which runs through your veins, runs through Cashal's too. If I were to condone your actions with Cashal, I may as well be prepared to close my eyes to the same relationship with Rory."

"Oh God, no, mother. It's not like that at all." Aileen felt horrified by the comparison.

"But it is. No child would be free from the desire of her father, or her brother – or her uncle, if the tribes were not to frown upon such relationships."

"I hardly know my uncle," Aileen said. She could see her mothers point of view but it was too late to leave Cashal now. The damage, if damage it was, had already been done and the cost of giving up such a prestigious relationship would be far too high.

Aifel raised her eyebrows. "Hardly know him?"

Aileen blushed, realising her mother had misunderstood. "Cashal has lived for a long time at the O'Flerty camp. Throughout most of my childhood he has been away fighting. I've not known Cashal as an uncle," with uncharacteristic modesty she lowered her eyes and blushed, "but I have known him as a man."

Aifel understood and felt compassion for her daughter's dilemma. No one knew, for she was careful not to show them, how much she hated her own lowered status, hated to see Dvorvild flaunting herself before Rory. She didn't want Aileen to suffer humiliation like that. But she couldn't condone her method.

"I would rather you leave him alone." she said, dogmatically. "Look instead at one such as Murchad. He can offer you more and will despise you less, in the long run."

Aileen couldn't help but consider the sense in this. From childhood Aifel had been a strong ally and she could remember when she too had flaunted her body. She hadn't always looked old and tired; this had happened mostly since the arrival of Dvorvild. Aifel had always spoken with great wisdom and Aileen had learned to heed her. But, for the moment, Cashal was far too important to let drop.

45

Turning to the idea of Murchad – well, she would not say no, for her mother was right, there was a great deal to be gained by such a union.

Matters came to a head for the MacGillingrouth sept when news reached Seandale that the Normans had invaded Dublin. The men knew that they must leave the following morning to join the vast armies of the Ard-ri.

Before leaving, Cashal kissed Aileen softly in a gesture she failed to understand. He had spent so much passion in their love making that it had taken the edge off his growing excitement over the battles ahead. Now, in the extreme chill before dawn, fingers of fear, a recognition of his own mortality, were plucking at the hairs on the back of his neck. He looked into Aileen's sleepy eyes and she smiled at him. She hadn't learned yet about tenderness, she knew only passion and power, pleasure and gratification.

Cashal too was aware that she neither loved nor cared for him beyond his ability to enhance her position. "Think about me when I'm gone?" It was half question, half plea, and he surprised himself in the asking.

"I'll think of nothing else."

To Cashal her voice was a symphony of seduction. She really didn't understand. Had it occurred to her that he may never come back? "If I die – ?" he started, yet found himself unable to articulate these alien feelings and the words tailed away.

She laughed, a surprised, rushed sound in the quiet of the night. "Die, Cashal? You are too big to die."

And he looked down at himself, his massive body suddenly seeming almost grotesque against her small frame; but her sentiments filled him with pride and renewed his courage.

When he left her she crept out of bed and climbed the hill which overlooked the village and the gathering men. She was excited: while Cashal's momentary doubts had failed to spill over onto her, his war-lust had. The long thin trail of men crawled through the valley away from Seandale and slowly, like blood issuing from a small wound, her childhood seeped away from her.

It had rained in the night. The clouds still hung low over the hilltop, the ferns, which dipped their heads as if drinking from the pools they edged, were decorated with tear-drops of silver. The long-coated, horned cattle which grazed the high ground left deep, dark green footprints on the milky grass. A pale mist clung to the tip of the uppermost rocks, softening their granite outlines. Bog cotton swayed very gently, despite the almost perfect stillness, giving its urgent warning in silence, and a tiny brook could be heard rushing through the deep undergrowth, plopping over the rocks and miniature cliffs which helped it on its tumultuous way.

Aileen stood shivering. The sight below her was as empty as death; henceforth, she felt, her life would be as devoid of colour as this pallid dawn. Now she understood Cashal's gentle kiss, the half-articulated question which had faded before the barrier of her ignorance.

Without its fighting men, Seandale was empty. Few men had been left on guard, and it was populated now only by women, children and old men. Corderg, along with Father Seamus, had charge of those remaining and there was every confidence that O'Connor, with his large army would be successful .

Aileen, perforce, returned to the dull routine of the pre-Cashal days, without even the older village boys to tease. She and Dvorvild spent many hours in idle talk, their eyes turning often towards the horizon, longing for the return of their men, and normality.

CHAPTER 6

On their way to Dublin, Dermot McMurrough's men scouted ahead of Strongbow's main force and discovered that the High King of Ireland was barring the way into the city from the south. Strongbow was deeply concerned at this news for it appeared that a bloody battle could not be avoided, the outcome of which would affect their long term success. Dermot, however, was more familiar with the surrounding countryside and laid a plan before Strongbow. Drawing with a stick upon the dust, he showed how, by circling through the Wicklow mountains to the north-west of the city, they would be able to approach from behind the awaiting Irish.

"It will take a little longer," he said, pointing out the route, "But it will save our men for future fights, and have the advantage of surprise."

Strongbow nodded his agreement to this idea, clapping Dermot heavily on the back.

The long march from Waterford to Dublin over poorly defined roads, and the tedious detour through the rugged Wicklow mountains, was taking its toll of Robert who, with the exhilaration – and the trauma – of his first battle behind him, had settled into the routine of a soldier's life.

The weight of his heavy chain mail, combined with the heat of the sun and the sudden soaking rains, had set Robert's body throbbing painfully. An ugly red rash crawled over his skin and the inside of his thighs and knees had grown rough and hard from the constant friction against his horse's flanks. The cut on his arm, which had been left unattended, had festered, the flesh raised, ugly and oozing pus; apart from the discomfort this gave him, he was continuously hot, even during the cold of the night and he found he could hardly drag his weary body from one day to the next.

Sitting around the camp fire, as the men talked of previous fights and showed the scars of old injuries, he fought to keep his eyes open. The flames before him blurred and swelled, and his head throbbed in pain.

" – do you not agree, Robert?" Someone nudged him and he jumped to attention. "Why, I do believe he was dozing like a baby," jeered Thomas.

Robert forced a smile. "Not sleeping, but dreaming," he said, winking at Thomas, who laughed heartily.

"And of what, pray tell?" he said, and jumped up, mincing about and thrusting out his chest, pursing his lips as he did so. "A fair woman, I've no doubt."

"If he's ever seen a fair woman at all," joked another of their party.

Too tired to dispute their arguments, or to brag about his conquests, he forced another smile and parodied a kiss toward Thomas, who laughed and returned the gesture.

The talk continued, with Robert careful to join in as far as he was able. He was reluctant to draw attention to himself; there had been many men injured at Waterford, most of them a great deal more seriously than he, and he was afraid of appearing weak. It was ever his problem: his father had disregarded him for so long that he was terrified of losing his well-earned respect in this most manly group.

The heat which had been in his body started to leave him, and he had to clamp his teeth together to stop them from chattering with cold. His arm throbbed and he thought longingly of his soft bed at home, which he would draw up before the great roaring fire and, covered by a thick sheepskin, sink into sleep. Sometimes, if he grew thirsty, his mother would bring him a hot posset to drink. He could almost imagine he was there now, with her gentle and concerned face leaning over him.

"Robert, have you gone to sleep again? You'll never make it to Dublin at this rate." The kindly de Barrie prodded him awake. "Does something ail you?" he added, noticing the pallor of his face and the twin high spots of colour on his cheeks. He reached over and touched Robert's face with the back of his hand. "You have a fever. How long have you been like this?"

At the mention of the word fever the camp fire became instantly deserted. Intrepid soldiers though the men were, their fear of disease was not unfounded: it spread like wildfire through the camps and often brought about more deaths than a battle. Robert felt too ill to recognise the courage of de Barrie, who stayed by him that night, as the others faded into the darkness.

"Have you any pain?" de Barrie asked. Robert's cut arm throbbed violently, the flesh pushing against his clothing. Even his fingers were hugely swollen, enveloping the rings he wore on his left hand. With his right, he indicated where the pain was, suddenly too weak to attempt to talk, too ill to care what anyone thought and totally oblivious to the fact that there was no one but de Barrie left to tend him.

De Barrie cut the sleeve of Robert's tunic with his knife, for the flesh was too swollen to raise it and Robert too cold to remove his clothes. "I see what the matter is," he said, his experienced eye quickly making out the festering wound. "We should find Silas, he knows about treating these things." Robert made no answer, and de Barrie threw a heavy rug over him, banking up the fire before leaving him to find Silas.

Despite his extra covering Robert shivered, drawing his knees up to his chest in a vain endeavour to keep warm. He saw a young girl walk towards him carrying a bowl of spring water and suddenly realised how thirsty he had become. He reached his hand out to take the water from her, smiling gratefully, and didn't even flinch as his fingers reached into the fire. The girl faded away, and he called after her, feebly. "Bring me water."

Silas, approaching him, turned to de Barrie. "It is the fever talking," he said and he too lent down to feel Robert's head.

"See this arm," said de Barrie. "It must have happened at Waterford."

"He said nothing about it," answered Silas, tersely, examining the suppurating wound. "But I have seen him hold it awkwardly at times, and he has looked unwell these past two days."

"What can you do?"

Silas looked about him; they were camped on a hillside, near to a small wooded area. Everything he needed to effect a cure for Robert was probably to be found growing here, but the night was deeply dark and he wasn't hopeful of finding anything 'till morning.

He thrust his knife into the fire, until the blade was glowing, and, without hesitation, laid the flat of the blade over the wound. Robert barely flinched as his skin hissed at contact with the red hot steel, but de Barrie jumped violently and tried to drag Silas's hand away.

"For the love of God, man, why did you do that?" he yelled.

"I have seen it done many times. The heat of the fire will burn away the bad flesh."

"Burn away the entire flesh, don't you mean?" De Barrie watched as the skin blackened and shrank away from the livid wound.

"Get me water and some linen," said Silas, forgetting momentarily that he was talking to a superior. De Barrie appeared not to notice and went to a pitcher which contained cold water. He returned with it, tearing a strip of cloth from a linen tunic.

Silas soaked the cloth in the water and poured the remainder over the wound; he then bound the cloth around Robert's arm. "At first light I'll go to the woods. There are plants there that can help him." Silas's gruff voice was unusually soft.

"At first light we must leave this place."

"We'll catch you up when we can," Silas said, "He'll not be ready to travel by the morning."

De Barrie was reluctant to agree to this. "I can leave you with the six men from Taffowey," he said after a moment, "and one of the Irish to guide you."

Silas nodded, gratefully. He too was uneasy in this unknown and wild terrain, and with a sick man to tend into the bargain.

At first light Silas looked down at the sleeping Robert. His fever had gone down somewhat and he appeared to be sleeping peacefully. As the army prepared to move on toward Dublin, now probably three day's ride away, Silas slipped away. When he returned he carried a bundle of greenery, and, placing some of it in a cauldron with some water, he boiled it down to a fine pulp. Using the blade of his knife he placed some of the pulp into the wound, pressing it down firmly and reserving the rest for later. He wrapped some large leaves around the packed wound and secured them with the linen; then he poured the liquid into a drinking vessel and held it to Robert's lips, forcing him to drink. Finally he covered him up again and sat by his side, patiently waiting to see what would happen.

Silas had learned this treatment from his mother, for they had had to survive for most of his early life in the woods and hills of Wales, and he had had plenty of unwelcome practice during his campaigns. He didn't understand, nor did he care to understand, how these things – fire, water and plants – could cure, but he had seen it happen and accepted it without question.

Robert was no exception, and when the sun touched the sky with ochre the following day, he was sitting lightly on his horse. Moving quickly, for they were few in number, they caught up with the marching army by the afternoon of the next day, within sight of the walls of Dublin.

Silas watched Robert anxiously as they rode.

"You worry over me like a ewe with her young," said Robert blithely, totally unaware of his narrow escape from death.

Silas smiled at him. "An odd looking lamb you make, sire," he said. But his master did indeed look well, better than he had done since he had left Waterford in fact. Silas had put his drawn expression down to battle fatigue and the unaccustomed lifestyle, admittedly surprised that Robert had not coped better. He had never suspected an injury to be the cause and had been shocked to see the extent to which the poison had crept into his system. Now Robert was his old buoyant self and Silas, observing him keenly, could see that he had grown in stature. He had killed and seen killing, he had been knighted, he had been injured, marched a quarter of the way across Ireland and almost died of his wounds. In all honesty, Silas could no longer view him as a young boy, still wet behind the ears.

In the months since he had first impressed Lord Henry with his skills, Robert had turned eighteen and had grown from a raw youth into a man. His face was bronzed by the unusually hot summer sun and constant exposure to the weather. The soldier's life had shaped him, remodelling his lean body, and he sat tall, muscular and strong upon his horse.

The citizens of Dublin, surprised by the army, immediately began negotiations for peace.

"It's a trick to keep us outside the city walls," said Raymond le Gros. Strongbow and Dermot, delighted with this sudden turn of events, looked at him in surprise. "They should allow us to negotiate inside the city, as a show of good faith," le Gros continued, warming to his theme. "Once inside they will be at our mercy, and will have no option but to surrender."

Strongbow turned and walked away from him; the idea was tempting and would diminish the bloodshed on both sides. He told Raymond he wanted some time to think it over.

Robert on the other hand was shocked. "What do you think of it, Silas?" he asked.

"I'm not here to think," came the typically non-committal response.

"It's devious enough to succeed," Robert went on, thoughtfully, "but we shall have a hard time living down our reputation if we go ahead with it."

"But we will live to live it down," rejoined de Barrie. "I'm all for the plan."

And certainly from a military point of view Raymond's occupation of Dublin was carried out with ease and proved to be a sensible move. Strongbow, whilst pleased to have gained possession so quickly, made a great show of disapproving Raymond's devious action: whether to protect himself against future reprisals or because of a genuine desire to be honourable, no one was really sure.

Robert, remembering the child who had died in his arms – as he was to do throughout his fighting career – remained torn between the honourable and the sensible. Perhaps le Gros was right, perhaps keeping down the bloodshed was the most important thing in the end; after all, the dead cannot be returned to life, no matter how honourably they died.

CHAPTER 7

With Dublin safely in their hands, the Normans felt considerably more secure, grateful for the protection of the city ramparts. The sudden seizure of the city spread dismay through the Irish ranks; so much so that O'Connor was unable to hold his men together, and was forced to watch his supporters melt gradually away, mostly to return home.

Inside Dublin, the Normans settled down, glad to exchange the rigours of the field for the comfort of the town billets. Their casualties, incurred by the slight resistance the shocked townspeople had been able to put up, were light, and the ease with which the campaign had so far gone served to confirm the contempt which most of them held for the Irish fighting ability. Apart from the initial storming of Waterford, and the injury to his arm, Robert and his men had experienced nothing more arduous than the long march to Dublin. Now, encouraged by McMurrough, Strongbow was pleased to move out into the surrounding countryside to conquer the lands of all those who refused to acknowledge Dermot as Lord of Leinster.

Those Irish who dared to defy McMurrough paid dearly. Their families were slaughtered or driven into exile; their homesteads burnt and crops destroyed. Attempts were made to introduce manorial control in the conquered lands and as time went by some Normans married Irish women, while others sought to curry favour with their native subjects by adopting Irish lifestyles and customs.

Reginald d'Evreux's followers were amongst the first in the scramble for land and fortune and Robert, with Silas by his side, spent days in the saddle campaigning on his patron's behalf.

"You've come a long way from the days when you were my page, Robert," d'Evreux told him one day.

"With your help, yes indeed. I shall be forever in your debt."

"No, Robert, not in my debt. You've worked well for me. This is a partnership of friendship, of equals. Perhaps it is time I let you loose – see how you make out on your own, eh?"

"If that's your will, I won't argue with it," replied Robert, clapping his friend firmly on the back.

Like many landless knights, Robert had long dreamt of building up his own estate and he now threw himself, with considerable zest, into the business of acquiring lands. In his campaign for this purpose he not only profited from the generosity of d'Evreux, but from the patronage of Dermot McMurrough himself. Robert's services on d'Evreux's behalf had brought him into contact with the Irish chieftain and as a result the latter had given him the assistance of Donal MacTilling, who was keen to recover the possessions which had been wrested from him by Rory MacGillingrouth.

Silas watched and inwardly blessed the foresight which had led him to throw in his lot with the uncouth young man who had approached him in Taffowey. Their relationship had changed subtly. With each subsequent victory Robert had grown more self-assured, had developed further as a warrior; but his underlying friendly nature and cheerful smile still shone out, redeeming the cold stare of his penetrating eye. Robert rarely sought Silas's advice any more, he made his decisions alone. Sometimes he asked for an opinion, but that was a different thing, and Silas felt it good that Robert had retained enough humility to do this. Two or more points of view on a tricky issue often helped find a satisfactory way through.

Autumn passed in a blaze of colour. The purple heather coloured the hills and was reflected in the lochs and gushing streams which ran full and lively down the mountainsides. Verdant Irish lands fell under Robert's eager sword but with the onset of winter the Norman troops were confined to the shelter of the walls and billets of Dublin. McMurrough returned from his incursions into Meath, bloated with loot and mindless of the homeless Irish, who were now condemned to a nomadic life in the face of an unusually harsh winter. He didn't remain long in Dublin, electing instead to retire for the winter months in the comfort of the great religious house of St. Mary's at Ferns.

Strongbow returned from Waterford to prepare, in the comfort of his winter quarters, for further conquests in the spring. The exceptionally severe weather brought any large scale campaigning to an end, providing a much welcomed breathing space for the Irish under threat in Leinster. The year of 1170 ended with Dermot McMurrough in the ascendency, and the O'Flerty septs confident that in the near future the powerful O'Connor would come to their aid.

The City of Dublin was an important trading centre, primarily a workingman's town, and Robert made his billet in a mud and wattle cottage with a thatched roof. There was a central fire where all the cooking was done, with a hole in the ceiling through which some of the smoke could escape. A little larger than the typical single-roomed abode, the cottage had been the home of a wheelwright who, having been moderately successful at his trade, had added an extra room to house his growing family. It was in here that Silas and Robert slept. The unfortunate wheelwright had been one of the few killed in the taking of Dublin, and his family had been left to fend for themselves as best they could.

Food, beer and wine were plentiful, for the Dubliners had always eaten well, with a diet mainly of corn, meat and bread cooked on the open fire. Robert found a woman to cook for them, and turned a blind eye when she and Silas disappeared behind the rug-like curtain which hung over one corner of the main room.

Winter passed in idle fashion, their days spent in keeping themselves fit in readiness for the fighting ahead, and their evenings round the fires, drinking the "Usque baugh" or water of life. This violently strong potion almost choked Robert when he first tried it and Silas even chose the thick, unpalatable beer – the sour drink of the poor of Dublin – over the whisky's fiery taste. Both preferred the plentiful wine which was brought to Dublin on trading ships from Bristol. However they accomplished it, they were often drunk and, readily served by the women of Dublin, Robert improved on skills other than fighting, which fully made him a man.

Winter stretched on into March, but the ground remained too frozen and the weather too inclement to enable Robert to leave the town. As March drew to an end, late crocuses and snowdrops finally forced their way through the granite-hard ground, and emerged, triumphant, to declare the arrival of spring.

As if in response to their prompt, Dermot McMurrough returned in high spirits to Dublin, heralding the beginning of a new season of conquest, and a new flurry of activity began.

Robert was outside, supervising the equipping of his men and horses for the coming forays, when Silas, breathless and grey of face, finally found him.

"Sire," he called, trying to make himself heard over the shouting of men and the whinny of horses.

Robert turned, smiling, to greet him. "Silas, why all the hurry?" he quipped. "Are you so eager to return to the open road? And who can blame you after the weariness of winter."

Silas didn't answer and looked sadly into Robert's face. Robert, finally noticing the man's demeanour, grew serious. "What is it, Silas – you have bad news, I think?"

"It's Dermot McMurrough. He's dead."

The words, coming so abruptly from his servant, took the breath, momentarily, from Robert's lungs. He visualised the big, lively Irishman; felt once more the hearty clap of his hand on his shoulder. It was impossible to imagine such a restless personality stilled by death.

Silas hadn't heard how the Irishman had met his end, only that it had been sudden and unexpected, for he had returned refreshed and full of life from his winter in St. Mary's. Nevertheless, the news was enough to dampen everyone's spirits.

"Who will be Dermot's successor?" Robert asked of de Barrie that evening.

The older man shrugged. "It should be Strongbow, my money's on him at any rate."

"But if not," Robert persisted, "How can we proceed without legal sanction or support from our King?"

"We'll have to wait and see, I suppose. This couldn't have come at a worse time – we'll be stuck here until someone makes a decision. We daren't risk our men, as you say, without full legal sanction."

Thus, Robert was forced to spend several days with his future uncertain. It would be a terrible blow if he were recalled to England before achieving his goal, just when everything had been going so smoothly.

"Don't worry," de Barrie said, "Strongbow is bound to be accepted. Remember he is married to Dermot's daughter, Eva. She's well-loved by the people of Leinster and they are fully aware that if they recognise the High King's claims they will lose their tribal independence."

His words proved to be accurate with even Dermot's son recognising Strongbow as his leader; but a new difficulty quickly developed. The English King, alarmed at Strongbow's rapid successes and feeling him to be beyond even his long arm, ordered his barons to come home to England.

"It is impossible," muttered Robert, to the impatient Silas. "How could we suddenly disengage now – even if we wanted to. The whole situation is ludicrous." He kicked the fire, sending sparks dangerously near to the thatch. Silas looked on, in complete agreement with Robert, for he was anxious to proceed and sick to death of kicking his heels in Dublin.

"What will Strongbow do, do you think?" Silas asked.

"I don't know. He's already sent Raymond le Gros to plead with the King and buy him with offers to hold all Irish conquests on his behalf. It may only be a delaying tactic. Who knows with Strongbow?"

Silas grunted his agreement and poured himself a flagon of beer.

In the event it was impossible for them to accede to the King's order, for McMurrough's death had provided the signal for renewed Irish attempts to drive them into the sea. Suddenly, and without warning, a huge Irish army appeared before Dublin, and Robert's time was fully taken up in trying to make good their defence.

"God knows how we'll get out of this," he said to a silent de Barrie, as they posted men and archers at strategic positions along the city wall. The siege had been going on for several days and was beginning to bite, a whole new aspect of the invasion, which Robert had never before had to endure. It was nerve-wracking trying to sleep at night, knowing that thirty thousand Irishmen were camped beyond the city walls, patiently waiting to starve them out. In his heart, Robert couldn't understand why they didn't try to force an attack, for although the walls were indomitable, the Irish army was large.

"Do you think they're waiting until we're too weak to counter their attack, or will they starve us out?" de Barrie said, and his face was white and drawn.

"It's the devil's own decision. Strongbow will have to do something soon."

"Aye, he will," de Barrie agreed, ruefully. "Have you noticed the stink?"

"How could I miss it? It's enough to make you want to surrender, without the hunger and the sickness."

The citizens of Dublin had been the first to suffer from lack of food, and many had succumbed to fever, caused by the inadequate sanitation of the city. The poor drainage system in Dublin had always been made more efficient by the scavenging animals which roamed the streets, but since all ships and tradesmen had been stopped from entering, food had quickly diminished in supply; driven by their hunger, people had killed and eaten all the chickens, pigs, dogs and cats which had lived on the effluent and scraps now left to rot and spread infection.

After six weeks things became unbearable and Strongbow tried to negotiate terms. He was in a hopeless position: to surrender would finish him personally and he dared not trust the Irish, who would more than likely accept their white flag, then turn on them. Why shouldn't they? He had done the same himself to capture Dublin.

Bitterly rebuffed, Strongbow returned to his men humiliated and angry. It seemed the only way out was through fighting and le Gros, newly returned from England, had re-entered the city by dead of night, and suggested they sally out in the same way. The Dublin garrison was promptly divided into three groups, each of which planned, if possible, to take the besieging Irish by surprise.

Robert, who was part of the contingent commanded by le Gros, was pleased to be on the move and new hope surged through him, so that he became expectant of a repetition of the Waterford victory. The natural fear of battle was superseded by the now familiar upsurge of excitement as he awaited the order to leave the city.

In the early morning, long before dawn, le Gros's men stood silent. Only the creak of harness and the clink of armour could be heard amid the expectant group. Robert prayed, as did all the other men, that the besieging host would remain unaware of their movements, and tension was high. Robert knew how vulnerable they would be on the march and his stomach turned over in anticipation.

The command to move was given silently. Hardly daring to breathe, the men coaxed their horses slowly forward into the cold darkness beyond the city walls. Mercifully they were undetected and after marching several miles they turned abruptly south-west to bring themselves behind O'Connor's vast army.

The closer they drew to the Irish the less afraid Robert became. He was elated at the prospect of the coming battle, now so neatly turned around. He glanced at the stocky figure of Silas riding beside him. The old soldier wore his typically impassive expression. Looking about him Robert saw the same expression everywhere. If they were afraid, his men didn't show it, nor were they ready, yet, to release the mounting excitement within them.

Growing weary, Robert began to wonder how much longer the march would take: several stops had already been called, the signal being passed silently down the columns of marching men, whilst scouts were sent forward to make a reconnaissance of the surrounding area.

Suddenly a loud shout went up, rippling through the marching men like a fearsome echo. As one, the army surged forward, bursting upon the sleeping Irish camp from three different directions. Men shouted and waved their swords above their heads as they bore down on the luckless Irish who crawled, bemused, from their tents. The swinging swords of the Normans were quickly turned red with their blood.

Robert galloped wildly into a group of men and they scattered before him. As they were unarmed he made little attempt to follow them but he could see that others of his men were less inhibited. The head of one soldier left its body in a huge arc, to land spurting blood at Robert's feet; his horse reared wildly and swerved and he stared briefly at the open mouth, stilled in mid-scream. He put the grisly sight from his mind and ploughed into the heart of the battle brandishing his sword. The sharp blade easily pierced the exposed flesh of men who fell, floundering, beneath his horse's hooves.

Heavily outnumbered, Robert knew that the Normans could afford no scruples and whilst it would normally have sickened him to slay defenceless men, the noise and ensuing chaos stirred his own blood and he felled several more of the Irish before they were able to regroup, to fight desperately for their lives.

The Welsh bowmen were mercilessly accurate as they fired into the seething mass of Irishmen. Robert, who quickly found himself engaged in hand-to-hand combat, shouted orders to his men as the resistance against them became ever more determined. Ahead of him he could see a large group of about a hundred men, led by an old chieftain whose white beard waved defiantly. The carcasses of the fallen were piling up before them, impeding further attack and Robert turned to call for assistance from his bowman. He saw Silas fall wounded, and quickly urged his horse to the rescue. As he was doing so, a huge Irishman came at him and Robert was knocked to the ground by the sweeping blow of an axe. His horse was mortally wounded and Robert lay winded and helpless on the ground, with only his long shield to protect him.

The two Irishmen fighting on either side of the old chief appeared invincible, one a giant of a man, the other distinguishable by his flowing red whiskers. The three seemed to bear charmed lives as their axes cleaved the bodies of those men and horses bold enough to approach them.

Robert watched as he lay winded and temporarily out of the struggle. He was aware of the fight surging around him. His helmet had been knocked to one side and he tried feebly to avoid the flailing legs of the horses as they galloped around him. He watched as a troop of knights entered the fight, forcing the courageous old man and his followers back. Robert craned his neck and tried to get to his feet, his head swam and forced him down again.

Gradually the furore around him diminished and Robert, using the side of his dying horse for support, managed to get to his feet. The few Irish who still milled around him paid him no heed; they had fought valiantly but for these men at least the battle was over. Riderless horses dashed aimlessly around and seizing one Robert scrambled onto its back and anxiously resumed his search for Silas amongst the corpses which littered the ground.

The noise and clash of arms was abating, but the tide had fully turned. The Irish host appeared to be in headlong flight and although the conflict still raged in the distance, where Norman horsemen were pursuing the fleeing Irish, Robert could see that the battle was over. Groups of men were dotted about the plain, searching as he was for their fallen comrades. Others foraged amidst the abandoned shelters, looting the bodies of dead and dying, of friend and foe alike. In one such shelter he came upon Silas, mercifully alive, although barely conscious and badly wounded.

"Has it been a victory, my lord?" Silas asked, his voice stiff with pain.

"A notable victory, Silas." Robert tried to smile, but the excitement of battle having left him, he was overwhelmed by the sheer carnage surrounding them. He signaled to a group of his men and, between them, they improvised a stretcher to carry Silas off the battlefield.

CHAPTER 8

As they made their laborious way back to Dublin, Robert was grimly reminded of the aftermath of battle. Everywhere he looked the scene was one of desolation, the ground littered with the corpses of the fallen, piled thickly where the fighting had been at its fiercest. Some of the dead lay peacefully, looking almost childlike, whilst others were horribly mutilated, the agony of painful death on their faces. The smell had already begun to pervade the air and haunted Robert long after he had reached the outskirts of the city. With irony he remembered his choice of words to Silas – "a notable victory" . The extent of suffering now coldly visible, he revised his opinion: it had been a bloody massacre.

Silas, lying beside him on his stretcher, looked up at his lord and smiled ruefully. "For me, sire, any sight is welcome. A victory doubly so."

Yet Robert was unconvinced and continued to gaze deflated and appalled about him. He could think of nothing else. Waterford and his forays through Leinster had done nothing to prepare him for this. So many wounded, so many slain. It was impossible to rid his mind of the spectacle. And there she was, in front of him, the wraith of the mutilated child of Waterford, pointing an accusing finger. So this was how it was to be, he thought, the pleasure and excitement of battle, the indescribable thrill of fighting and killing, but followed always by this numbing, disabling pity for the dead and dying, encapsulated by the eyes of an unnecessarily slaughtered child.

Silas, his tongue loosened by his narrow escape from death, seemed to sense Robert's unease. "Take heart, my lord. War is never pleasant, and this one was a massacre. What else could we have done? We numbered but five hundred men, whilst they must have had close to thirty thousand. It was an amazing feat and it's doubtful that O'Connor will be troubling us again for some time. Now at least we shall have some food," he added, reminding Robert that those same men would have happily starved them out of Dublin, had they been allowed to do so. "The Irish supplies will sustain us for several weeks."

"You are right as ever, Silas," responded Robert, his ghosts fleeing before him. He was overwhelmed by sudden gratitude that his man was safe and alive, and his eyes met Silas's with an expression of warmth which was briefly reflected before the older man slipped into a pain-filled sleep.

Within a few days Robert resumed his incursions into the Leinster countryside. Of necessity this was without Silas, who grew increasingly impatient with his slowly mending body, though Robert made it part of his business to keep him abreast of developments.

"The order from England that we must return home forthwith is most damnable nonsense, following our great victory," Robert complained one day.

"The order will be ignored, if I know Strongbow," replied Silas, who admired the earl greatly. "If King Henry wishes to make him comply, he'll have to come to Ireland in person."

As it transpired, it was Strongbow who decided to sail for England and plead with Henry, for he was conscious that his possessions in England and Wales were at the mercy of the King. Fortune once more favoured the Welsh earl, for he met with the King – accompanied by a large army – on the road to Milford Haven, intent on going to Ireland to discover exactly what his barons were about. The King was in a benign mood and, in return for the possession of Dublin and the east coast ports, he prepared to take Strongbow into favour. Thus Strongbow returned to Ireland with royal permission and resumed the consolidation of his conquests, leaving King Henry to sail for Dublin to receive the homage of all his subjects, Norman and Irish alike.

Robert wondered, somewhat anxiously, how this development would affect his acquired lands. In the event, the fact that Strongbow was now a royal tenant, and not an independent lord, meant that it affected the majority of the Anglo-Norman adventurers but little and they continued as they had always done to seize ever more lands from the Irish people.

Robert and Reginald d'Evreux were glad to have royal confirmation of all their holdings and sought to extend their conquests further west, sometimes acting together, sometimes separately. Friendship had grown between them during the months away from home, and they had become mutually dependent upon each other's judgement. Forays made with d'Evreux were swift and humanely carried out. The Irish, overwhelmed by the Norman superiority of arms and men, usually capitulated without a fight. Reginald and Robert were of like mind in the matter of looting homesteads. If they were to have proper stewardships of the lands they had captured, the people should suffer as little as possible, and the lands should remain intact.

Robert was appalled by the indiscriminate killing and torture inflicted upon the frightened people by his ally, Donal MacTilling, on whom he needed to rely heavily. MacTilling's tribesmen, motivated by revenge, were merciless. Riding through the sleepy villages, they would drag terrified people into the streets, sacking the village and often burning their homes.

On one occasion, Robert came upon a village which had recently been taken by MacTilling and his men. The single street was filled with weeping women and dead men, and a dreadful silence fell upon them as he rode through.

"What has happened here?" Robert asked one of the tribesmen.

"The MacTillings," – the man spat on the ground – "they rode through here, calling villagers to come out of their homes. They were afraid and barred their doors."

"Carry on," said Robert grimly.

"Donal MacTilling went to the chief's dun and appealed to him to come out. The chief asked if Donal would give him his word that his family would be treated well and the bastard said nothing – he had the door knocked down. Then he dragged the chief's wife and children from the house, saying they would 'learn to obey the MacTillings without question.'" The villager's voice filled with hatred and he paused. "The chief is a proud man and courageous in battle – he called him an Irish traitor. So Donal took his sword and ran it through the body of his eldest son, a lad of about twelve years. The chief was too slow to stop him, but his wife tried to. Donal had two of his men take hold of her, and watched while others raped her. She begged and screamed for mercy and they left her bleeding to death in the mud. Then they did the same thing to her daughters." Again the villager paused. "One of them was only nine years old," he said quietly. "The rest of the men rode through the village dragging women, from their houses. Any man who tried to stop them was killed." The villager's eyes ran with unashamed tears as he recounted his story. "Once their lust was satisfied they robbed our duns – no one dared stop them. When they finally left the village I could hear them laughing and bragging about their morning's work."

At their next meeting Robert, sickened by what he had seen and heard, turned on Donal. The light of friendship was gone from his eyes, leaving them grey and cold.

"What harm is done?" asked the Irishman. "Word will spread and we will meet less resistance in future."

"According to my information you received little enough today, and what kind of work can we expect from such people knowing the barbarity of your men?"

"Fear will make them work," argued Donal, unable to comprehend the young man's apparent weakness. He had seen Robert on the battle field and knew him to be a ruthless and courageous fighter, otherwise he would have thought him a soft-hearted coward. Respect mingled with dislike, and he eventually agreed to let Robert's soldiers take part in any foraging party, and in that way Robert managed to control the MacTillings' excesses.

CHAPTER 9

$C\!\mathscr{A}$ ileen walked through the sun-warmed main street, carrying water and herbs which she had collected from beside the stream. Seandale was unnaturally quiet with the men still away and life in the village seemed to be paused, breath baited, waiting for their return. News had filtered back of the dreadful massacre at Dublin and the women continually scoured the horizon for the first glimpses of their husbands, sons or brothers, none knowing who had survived and who had lost their lives.

Entering the dun, Aileen settled the water near the entrance and handed the herbs to Aifel, who wished to make medicine for Corvild. Some days ago he had developed a high fever, becoming delirious, and Aifel had watched him anxiously by night and day; this morning the fever had suddenly broken, and Corvild, fretful and listless, had called for her to bring him food and drink. Aileen looked at her little brother, now ten years old, with a newborn tenderness, remembering all the times she had refused to play with him because she was too eager for Cashal.

Aifel bent over him, holding a drink to his cracked lips and Aileen saw the marks of worry forged into the lines of her face.

"Let me do that," she said, taking the cup from her mother and putting a loving arm around her shoulders.

Aifel's eyes filled with tears. She was tired and easily overwhelmed by any show of kindness. With Rory and the other men gone, Corderg, Dvorvild, Aileen and Aifel had grown closer than they had been before, bound by a common cause and a common need for comfort.

"Mother, Aileen, come quick," Corderg's voice cut into Aifel's thoughts and Aileen jumped, spilling water down Corvild's chin. She felt a flutter of alarm, for Corderg rarely spoke so abruptly.

"What is it?" she said, going to where he stood by the open door.

"The Normans – we have had word they are headed this way. Father Saemus and I are calling everyone to the church."

"But why? We have done nothing to them, why should we hide?"

"Oh Aileen, you can be so foolish. Take my advice and come quickly." She turned to get her cloak and caught sight of Corvild, lying listlessly on his pallet. Aifel was bent over him, appealing to Corderg with wild fear in her eyes.

"I daren't move him, Corderg, he is too weak."

"Maybe the men are not headed for Seandale," said Aileen to her mother, hopefully.

"No, perhaps not, there's little enough left for them to take," agreed Aifel, wanting her to be right.

"I still think it would be better if you came to the church," Corderg persisted.

"What difference would it make," said Aileen, their helplessness hitting her slap in the face. "We're nothing but a village of old men and children, in the church or no."

"The Normans won't attack holy ground, Aileen. They are afraid." Corderg was torn between the need to move quickly, to warn the rest of the village, and his desire to see his own family safe. For the first time he saw something of his father's dilemma, the numerous problems of leadership. His mother was right: the boy was too sick to move – the Normans might even pass by the village.

"If you must stay, you must make sure you bar the door," he said. Corderg turned and ran off in the direction of the church, the light streaming in where the bulk of his body had recently stood.

Aileen shuddered briefly, feeling very alone; then with a swift movement she slammed the wooden door shut and dropped the heavy bar.

When MacTilling's men first approached Seandale, they thought it a deserted village, for nothing stirred. Then they sighted the pigs and chickens which wandered in the street and surrounding fields. The party, which was primarily a foraging one, quickly caught and slaughtered the animals, loading the edible parts onto their pack-horses and leaving the rest to the flies in the street. The main FitzAlan force was encamped some six miles away at the entrance to the valley where the Loge stream entered the Liffey, and the food would be welcomed by the men, who had been in the saddle for several weeks.

Several people had left their doors swinging open, in their anxiety to escape to the church, and the MacTillings, their task completed and still thinking the village emptied of people, made to return to camp. One of the soldiers, who had looked forward to some sport with the local girls, fired one of the cottages in a fit of anger, and the others, catching some of his mood, started to do likewise, galloping their horses up and down the street, shouting and putting lighted torches to the thatched roofs of the hovels.

The smell of smoke and the blood-curdling cries of the men reached Aileen and Aifel, who cowered into the back of the dark, smoky dun. Corvild slept peacefully, and, dragging him into the darkest corner, Aileen protected his small body with her own. She was shaking from head to foot; even her teeth chattered, and her tongue cleaved to the roof of her mouth, rendering her speechless. Mother and daughter stared at one another, the whites of their eyes gleaming eerily in the gloom.

The sound of horses' hooves vibrating through the ground suddenly stopped and Aileen strained to hear what was going on. She caught the sound of men's laughter and assumed, rightly, that they had stayed on to plunder the village. She gasped in her fear, the sound coming from her like the whimper of a puppy and Aifel put her hand gently across her mouth and placed a tiny kiss on her cheek. The familiar gesture was oddly reassuring and Aileen felt the worst of her terror drain from her. They waited, pressed against the furthest corner of the dun, for the men to leave the village.

When the door wouldn't open the three Irishmen outside looked at one another in grim delight. With a few swings, one of them axed through the door, splitting it from top to step. Shouldering it out of the way, they burst inside.

The noise and the sudden flare of sunlight made the women lift their hands in despair and, catching sight of the movement, the first man came threateningly toward them. His hair was long and straggly, as was his beard; his eyes, small and pig-like, looked out at them from below shaggy brows. The hot, unwashed smell of him filled the dun as he pressed toward them, axe outstretched, to gain a better view. The other two, unaware of the catch their companion had made, set about destroying the dun, turning over the stools, spinning wheel and tables in their haste.

The man with the axe remained perfectly still, his eyes locked into Aifel's. The other two men, growing accustomed to the dark, noticed the women cowering in the corner and with a whoop of delight rushed toward them, dragging them into full view. Corvild, still sleeping and hidden under the cloak Aileen had tossed over him, was left mercifully unseen.

Aileen fought wildly for her freedom as one of the men picked her up and dumped her unceremoniously in the centre of the cluttered room then knelt above her holding her arms above her head. He laughed as she struggled, watching her breasts as they moved against the taut linen of her tunic. Using his free hand he cut the tunic with his sword, exposing her naked skin. Delighted with his unexpected good fortune he fell upon her savagely, his hands bruising her body as he grabbed and kneaded it. A second man, having caught only a tantalising glimpse of her form before it became enveloped, threw his friend off.

Aifel shrieked and tried to reach her daughter. The third man grabbed handfuls of her hair and pulled her toward him, twisting violently so that she dared not move for fear of breaking her own neck. Throwing her face down over the up-turned table, her neck stretched agonizingly upward by his firm grip on her hair, he raped her brutally. The side of the table pushed into her, bruising her body, and as he grew more excited he pulled ever harder on her hair, causing her back to arch until it looked as though it might snap in two.

Aileen broke free and managed to reach the open door before the men caught her again, laughing with pleasure as she struggled and kicked. With every move her body grew more appetising to them. A sword pricked gently into her skin causing her to shriek and lunge back, a tiny trickle of blood wound its way over her exposed flesh.

Finally, unable to wait any longer the first man stood against her and raped her, whilst the other held her still. Aileen could see her mother over her assailant's shoulder and screamed out in pain and fear. Freeing one arm from the man's grasp, she hit back wildly, her fist striking him on the tip of his nose. In retaliation he punched the side of her head, almost knocking her unconscious. As she sagged, her rapist overbalanced, falling to the floor with Aileen beneath him. He seemed oblivious to his change of position, and his passion was quickly spent; but now the other man wanted his turn, and then, after letting Aifel's body drop to the ground, the third man stood watching until he felt ready once again.

Time stopped moving for Aileen, her pain-wracked body almost past the point of endurance. It seemed that the men, inflamed by an audience and by her beauty, would never cease.

Robert, accompanied by six of his men, entered the village, drawn by the wisps of smoke which, undisturbed by any breeze, lifted in tall plumes into the cloudless sky. The group of MacTilling men outside one of the huts caught his attention and, riding toward them, he heard a man's muffled grunting and the higher pitched moan of a woman. He burst into the dun in time to see the startled man roll off Aileen, trying to cover himself.

She lay fully exposed to his view, her hair wild over her face, her legs splayed out on the stone floor. Robert's gaze took in the body of the older woman who appeared to be unconscious and he went firstly to her, touching her gently, feeling for signs of life. Her heart beat was strong, and, ordering that she be covered for the sake of decency, he turned back to Aileen, who hadn't moved. He removed his own cloak and wrapped it around her before picking her up. She stiffened momentarily at his touch then grew limp in his arms and he felt the same pity for her which had so often caused him anguish after a battle.

Aileen cowered into the comforting folds of the cloak, and when nothing more happened she opened her eyes. His face was so near to hers that she screamed and flinched involuntarily back, hitting her head against the door, convinced that here was another man to torture her. Robert reached out a hand and stroked her cheek, trying to calm her, and she flinched from him again, her eyes looking through him, as though she would cut him from her vision.

The restless shuffling of his men disturbed his perusal of her, and he turned to tell them to mount up and be ready to leave. His eyes came to rest on the man who had been at Aileen on his arrival. Robert wore, if he but knew it, a similar expression to Aileen's. Both were utterly stunned, and both had withdrawn to a less painful place.

Misinterpreting Robert's expression for one of glazed lasciviousness, the Irishman smiled, showing blackened stumps of teeth between his red lips. "She's a ripe one, lord," he said, "more than ready for – plucking!"

Suddenly, infuriated beyond tolerance and without giving any thought to what he was about, Robert drew his sword and plunged it deep into the man's belly. "I only hope she was worth dying for," he said through clenched teeth. He was consumed by a white hot tongue of fury, different from the fire of battle, and a violent hatred for these uncouth, wild-haired mountain men who cared less for human life than for a crust of bread. "You have been ordered to keep your forays to the minimum. To provide food for the men and to leave the villagers alone, unless they offer violence." As he spoke, he walked slowly toward the second of the men, and pointed the tip of his sword into his chin.

"They did, sir, they attacked us – ," the man blustered, searching for a reason for Robert to spare him. Backing away he trod on Aifel's hand and she made a sound.

Robert looked down on her. "Take these women out of here," he said, his voice icy. The other men hurried to comply and for long moments Robert stood, his sword poised at the man's throat.

"What shall we do with the women, sir?" one of his own men queried, entering the dun. Robert lowered his sword, throwing a final look of contempt at the cowering Irishman. He turned and followed his man out of the dun to where the women sat, leaning against the wall of their home.

"Guard them carefully," he ordered. "I want no more harm to come to them," and he strode away, down the street, toward the church. He rapped on the door, and it opened slowly, revealing Corderg, white with fear. "Tell your people they may return to their homes." Robert looked unutterably weary and Corderg, sensitive to the feelings of men, detected the sorrow in his voice. He went back inside the church and shortly afterward the women and children sidled past him, blinking in the sunlight.

Robert continued his tour of the village, taking in the buildings which still smouldered from the firing, and the blood spilled from the animals in the street. Fortunately there was little damage which could not be repaired. No loss of life, at any rate. Cursing the mindless violence of the MacTilling Irish he returned to his men, still grouped outside the MacGillingrouth dun. The Irishmen had left, fearful for their lives, seeking the protection of their chief who shared none of the tender healthiness of this Norman knight.

"This is the MacGillingrouth sept, sire," said one of his men. "These women are wife and daughter of their chief, Rory MacGillingrouth."

Robert's decision was made swiftly and without consideration. "We'll take them with us," he said, mounting his horse. "Make ready to leave."

The man looked surprised but complied without question. His lord was just, but he had determination and disliked being thwarted.

Riding from the village Robert questioned his own actions. It was foolhardy to carry women with them and served no useful purpose. Yet he was loath to leave them. Aileen's face, shocked and crazed though it had been, was beautiful. He had never seen one more so and he realised that his decision had been made solely on the strength of the wish to keep her safe. For himself. Had she been a simple peasant girl he could have afforded to leave her in the village which was bound to become part of his swordland, but as the chieftain's daughter there was always the chance she would be secreted away to some remote part of the country, whilst her father continued to fight against them. He knew that his decision, made swiftly and without consideration, had been strongly influenced by hearing who she was. He hadn't wanted to lose track of her. It was as simple as that.

Robert puzzled over how best to avail himself of her. She was weak and too badly hurt for him to want to touch her now; he didn't want the girl to flinch from his touch – he wanted her to come readily to him. Suddenly he saw a solution, one which would enable him to complete his present campaign and postpone a decision about the girl. There was a monastery nearby and the prioress was a friend of his mother's. There, surrounded by nuns, the two women would be secure, and her father would be unlikely to guess their whereabouts.

The Priory of Whitley lay beside the Liffey, encircled by low hills and woods of oak and larch. It was a peaceful place and so far had escaped the ravages of war which for the past ten months had swept Leinster. Sister Martha, only recently installed as the English head of a community of Irish nuns, hoped that the peace of the establishment would be preserved indefinitely, now that the Normans were victorious.

Born and schooled in England, she viewed the steady advance of the Normans with the greatest pleasure. Although her nuns were Irish, she was held in high esteem, and had encountered little difficulty in carrying the whole Priory with her when she had introduced the new Romish ideas. It was natural that her interests should coincide with those of the foreigners, and the Normans had found Whitley worth supporting for the peace and respite it afforded them. Her arrival had been something of a triumph for Donal MacTilling, whose patronage had been restored as the Normans took over the O'Flerty lands. The Priory had moreover found a benefactor in Robert FitzAlan, who, grateful for his successes in the locality, was generous in his support – and because of her friendship with his mother, had welcomed her appointment to Whitley.

Officially, the Irish Church favoured the new ideas coming from Rome and a proclamation, recently issued by an Assembly of Divines at Armagh, had pronounced the invasion of the Normans to be a just punishment from God for the sins of the Irish people. The common sin, condemned by the proclamation, was the use of slavery, a trade which had grown up during the last decade or two between the Ostmen of the coastal ports and the merchants of Bristol. Curiously enough, the Priory of Whitley numbered amongst its nuns several ex-slaves of English descent who had found sanctuary there and Sister Martha was strongly opposed to the whole concept of slavery.

The Prioress was pleased to receive a visit from her most recent benefactor, when Robert and his small band rode into Whitley's courtyard.

"Welcome, Lord Robert," she said, smiling at the sudden memory she had of this warrior as a tiny child at his mother's breast.

Robert told her his reasons for coming, hiding the real truth with the explanation, "to allow the women to recuperate within the sanctuary of your walls."

Recuperate, the Prioress thought, shrewdly assessing the situation. This young girl, dirty and shivering though she may be, is outstandingly beautiful – less so and this dashing young knight would have been content to allow her to "recuperate" in the safety of her own village. She turned to one of the sisters standing behind her. "Sister Agnes, take care of these two women," she said crisply. Turning her attention back to Robert – "Whitley is greatly honoured by your visit. You'll stay the night, of course?"

"I would be most grateful, thank you," replied Robert, "But I must leave at first light. I came only to ask this favour of you."

"Which I can gladly grant. In exchange, favour me with the pleasure of your good conversation over food and wine," she said, smiling, and led him through the door.

By the time Robert and Martha had completed a discussion which ranged from the latest news from England to the prospects of Norman control over Leinster and the King's new-found interest in Ireland, it was growing late. Robert took his leave of her, to get some sleep before dawn when he must return to his camp. He hesitated, thinking to take a last look at Aileen before he left, but he shrugged the idea away and contented himself with the knowledge that she and her mother would not escape from this cushioned prison and would be there, waiting for him upon his return.

CHAPTER 10

"Aileen, you'll burn that bread if you're not careful," chided her mother. Aileen went half-heartedly to the oven and lifted the over-browned bread onto the table, where it crashed down like a stone. "Are you unwell?" she said, more gently, observing Aileen's lethargic movement.

"No, I'm well," came the unconvincing reply.

"Is it because of what happened?" Aifel prompted, wanting to help. Aileen looked at her, a faraway expression in her eyes.

"It's everything. I hate it here: the boredom, the quiet, the endless praying. How can you stand it?"

"I like it," Aifel replied and her glowing face gave testimony to the fact.

"But we're prisoners in this place, Mother, and that is what ails me."

"No, we're not in prison," Aifel replied. "Prison's a hateful place."

"Then why can we not leave?"

"We're to be kept safe, until your father returns."

"Safe. And why should the Norman wish the daughter and wife of his enemy to be kept safe?" Aileen's eyes flashed and the pallor of her face was replaced by a deep flush of anger.

Aifel didn't answer. The work was easy here and the peace and quiet acted as balm on the bruises she had suffered. The nuns showed her more kindness than her family had ever done and there was no Dvorvild, reminding her of what had once been hers.

Aileen, reading some of her mother's thoughts from her expression, took her hands. "Do you not miss Corvild and Donal?" she asked. She herself wondered and worried about them most of the time.

"Yes, I do miss them," Aifel replied slowly, sadly. "But they're growing up so fast. They don't need me any more. It's right that I try to find a place in the world where I may end my days happily."

"The world's a bitter, hard place," Aileen said, looking at her mother sadly. "I can't blame you for trying to find peace." The rape had frightened her badly and taught her a difficult lesson about life, but it had not made her wish to be safe if safety came at the expense of freedom. Had she a choice, she would have chosen to be like the hated Norman knight, strong and powerful, able to choose who could live and who could die. Free to fight battles, win lands and take anything he wished to possess. As he had taken her – of course – that was why he had taken her. He wanted her for himself. She was being kept safe for him. Despite everything a tremor of excitement thrilled her.

"The Norman means to make me his woman," she whispered.

Aifel widened her eyes. It wasn't news to her. She had already considered the possibility but Aileen hated the man so much she'd kept her ideas to herself. Yet, having come to the same conclusion, Aileen looked more alive than she'd done since they had arrived.

"The idea pleases you?"

Aileen's face was a picture of astonishment and shock. "It shouldn't do," she faltered. "I hate him."

"But you crave excitement," Aifel's voice was soft and gentle, "and hardly care how it comes. You're driven by your needs. It must be hateful for you to be here without men to manipulate."

Aileen giggled, and gradually Aifel joined in. Once started the laughter became impossible to control, and they ended up clinging to one another in a helpless dance around the kitchen.

When they had calmed down, Aileen tried once more to speak to Aifel. On the one hand she respected her views; on the other she wanted to reassure herself that Aifel had considered everything fully.

"Seandale is your home, our home. Why don't you leave here and come home with me?"

Aifel turned her back. Her eyes already ran with tears of laughter, they changed easily to ones of sadness. She had hoped Aileen could be as happy here as she was. She missed Corderg and their long talks into the night, but she had grown so close to Aileen recently that she had found compensation in her company. Now Aileen wished to leave. Wished her to leave. "No, I shall stay here, for as long as I can."

"And how long might that be?" jeered Aileen, her ready temper rising.

"As long as I live, if that pleases God." The words came unbidden and gave Aifel a strange, unknown comfort.

"If that pleases God," Aileen swept the loaf off the table. "Well, I shall please myself. No more bread-making, no more floor-scrubbing. I shall leave here and you can stay and please your God all you want to."

For six months Aileen railed at her mother and her mother pleaded with Aileen, but neither would back away from their own point of view. Aifel liked the life, with no men, and Aileen had no life without men. They could not agree.

Even the knight had not come back to claim her and she had begun to mistrust her instincts on that score. But if she were right, she must get away from this place and soon. The knowledge that her rapists had been not Norman, but Irish – MacTilling men – she put to the back of her mind. They had been together, she reasoned, therefore they must all be of the same mind.

One day a group of wayfarers, Ostmen and priests, arrived at the Priory. Led by a merchant named Sweyn, the Ostmen were hoping to find refuge in some Irish stronghold to the west and the priests were on route for the religious house in the town of Cashel. Sweyn had travelled by devious routes in order to avoid Norman raiding parties and was looking forward to a day's rest within the comfort of Whitley, as if it were a taste of heaven itself.

Sister Martha was glad for the chance to speak with outsiders, but she forbade the rest of the community to converse with them. Aileen ignored the rule and waylaid Sweyn in the Priory garden after Matins. Seeing him sitting on the stone bench, his cloak hugged close about him to keep out the cold January winds, she approached.

"Good day, Master Sweyn," she said, looking at him sideways through her dark-lashed eyes.

"Good day indeed," he replied.

"It's pleasant out here on a summer's day. But cold at this time of year," she observed, rubbing her hands up and down her arms as if trying to warm them. He followed their movement as they brushed over the swell of her breasts, feeling his breath shorten.

"It is cold, yes," he said in a low voice, feeling the sweat break out on his forehead.

"May I sit with you for a while?" She allowed a note of pathos to creep in. "I have so little opportunity for conversation, and," she paused and allowed her arm to brush against his, "company."

"Why are you here?" he asked, for she didn't fit in with the quiet nuns, who glided between the cloisters, never meeting his eye. She turned the full force of her green eyes upon him.

"I am the prisoner of a Norman lord." She spat the words at him, allowing the venom she felt to be clearly visible. "I was raped and beaten by his men and then he brought me here to await his ardour."

Raped and beaten – he felt a stirring in his own loins – and by the hated Normans.

She spoke again, standing up before him. "I'm the daughter of the MacGillingrouth chief. He would be pleased by anyone who had helped me to escape from this place. But there is no one who dares incur the Norman's wrath and lift a finger to help me."

He reached for her, taking her hand in his. She was young, beautiful and exciting to him, as was the mention of her father: the O'Flerty tribe could be a useful ally. "I would help you, if I could," he said.

"I couldn't ask you to take such a risk . . . " She saw the doubt on his face and instantly re-phrased her proposition, pausing dramatically, "But would it really be such a risk? The nuns can't stop me from leaving, and no one would know how I made my escape. They wouldn't connect it with you. You could leave openly and I could slip away after Prime and meet you." She gave him an adoring glance from under her lashes. "You would protect me. I can see you are a strong man and I – I would be your grateful friend." She allowed tears to form in her eyes and bravely wiped them away. As she lifted her arm her cloak fell back and his eyes lingered once again on her body. He was convinced.

Hurriedly they made their plans before she slipped away from him, planting a small kiss on his forehead. "I'll see you tomorrow," she whispered as she ran back into the Priory.

Aifel was in the kitchens as usual, singing as she baked bread. She looked up at her daughter, observing her heightened colour and the excited look on her face. Her heart lifted, for it was some time since she had seen Aileen so happy. Perhaps, she thought, the peace of the Priory is finally beginning to work on her. She kissed her warmly and was surprised to be enfolded in Aileen's strong arms and told, "I love you, mother."

Aileen hardly slept that night and rose before dawn, slipping on her dark robe. No one saw her leave; she had decided not to confide in Aifel, fearful that she would take action to stop her from going. She slipped, shadow-like, out of the Priory, running swiftly, hardly noticing the icy drizzle which beaded her cloak and hair, aware only of the growing exhilaration she felt at the prospect of returning to Seandale.

She waited for the Ostman as agreed, at the edge of the wood some distance from the Priory, and joined the travellers without incurring much more than a few surprised glances and whispered comments. Sweyn was delighted to see her and, ignoring the amused looks of his friends, took her up behind him in the saddle. Gritting her teeth she forced herself to lean against his sturdy back, pretending it was Cashal who sat before her.

They covered good ground through the day and towards evening made camp within striking distance of Seandale. Aileen lay huddled in her cloak, a warm sheepskin covering her, and looked up at the stars. Sweyn, maddened by the constant pressure of her body leaning against his back, followed her and sat down, his face looming palely out of the night.

"You are grateful to be going home?" he asked, his hand stroking her arm.

"Very grateful," she murmured, trying not to flinch at his touch. No stranger to the sexual needs of men, she had, so far, only encouraged the advances of those to whom she felt attracted. Sweyn was not such a man, with his filthy beard and overweight body, but he had been good to her. She knew that she could offer him gratification only if there was no other choice.

"I have been thinking of my father," she went on, turning her back slightly toward him. She allowed a tremor to enter her voice. "I have missed him so much. You remind me of him in many ways, Sweyn. Not many men would have helped and demanded nothing in return. My father is the kind of man who will appreciate that."

Sweyn stopped short. He had almost forgotten who her father was. But she was very desirable. His hand strayed to touch her and she turned further from him, so that he just brushed an uncompromising shoulder.

"I shall tell my father," she said, innocently.

Sweyn jumped. "Tell him of what?" he asked guiltily.

"Of your extreme kindness – what else is there to tell?" she asked, and her eyes glittered in the dark.

"I'll bid you goodnight then," he said, reluctantly.

"Goodnight then," she replied, stifling a yawn.

It was bitterly cold when Aileen awoke. The clouds hung low and menacing in a heavy sky and the trees pointed skeletal fingers in the direction of Seandale. Home, I'm going home, thought Aileen, and the ache fell away from her bones and the sleep fled from her eyes. She gathered her things and went to sit by the priests as they finished morning prayers. Their fire was hot and the smell of food welcoming.

"It will snow today, Aileen," said one of the priests, finishing his worship. He handed her a bowl of steaming broth. She wrapped her cloak round it to stop her fingers from burning and warmed her hands. "You'll be eager to be getting back home?" he said, his clean-shaven face kind.

Aileen looked into his twinkling eyes. "Yes, Father, I have been held prisoner at the priory of Whitley for six months. I miss my brothers and my father." She said it to impress the priest, wanting his approval, but as she spoke she felt genuine tears prick the back of her eyes.

"Have you had news of them, since you were kidnapped?" he asked, and she shook her head.

"My father and uncle went to fight the siege of Dublin. I've not seen them since. I don't know whether they lived or died." She paused and looked down at her feet. Why had they not returned from Dublin by the time the Normans had arrived to pillage and rape? The Normans had had no further to march and had probably stopped many times to destroy villages on their way. Would not her father have hurried straight home – if he could? "My brothers were at Seandale when I was taken," she resumed. "One was ill. I don't know whether they lived or died." She stared into space and the priest murmured words of understanding at her, which they both knew could do no good.

When she looked up the priest was watching her curiously. "Your food will be cold, child," he said. "What disturbs you?" He asked the two questions as though they were dependent, the one upon the other.

"Sometimes, Father, I feel an empty place – here," she indicated a point below her breast. "where there should be fulfilment. Sometimes in the night I want something – very badly – but cannot tell what it may be. And sometimes I feel a terrible fear that I will grow old and die without ever finding it."

She had never spoken in this way before, nor even been conscious of the feelings. Her homesickness, combined with the aura of compassion which surrounded the priest, had served to loosen her tongue.

"Father, is this the feeling which makes men want to fight, and others," and here she thought of Corderg, "and others to become priests or holy men? Are these the only ways of finding escape from the torments," and they were torments, the word was well chosen, "which hound me?"

"Yes, perhaps," the priest answered carefully. "And maybe when men spare the time to look into their hearts before they go into battle, they see something greater than their own needs and put their faith into that – which we call God." He looked at her, her strong face softened by some need which she was not yet able to define. He was aware his answer had fallen short, outside her comprehension. "Then, of course, there is love," he added in a shrewd voice.

"Oh, that," Aileen retorted. "Love has nothing to do with it, Father."

"Why not?"

She thought of Cashal and herself. "Love is when a couple take pleasure from each other's bodies," and then she thought of the ugly men, grinding their heavy bodies against her, "or when men force themselves on someone, in a way which brings pleasure only to them. But love has no place in what I feel."

"But those things are not love, Aileen, love is when your mind and body

78

want no more than to be with one person, and to be without that person leaves you unhappy and empty."

"Do you love like that, Father?"

He looked into her eyes, and saw no trickery there. "I once loved a woman like that. She died and I thought I would die, too."

Aileen wondered how this could be so, when there were women aplenty, more than a man could ever love in one life.

"Now I turn that feeling toward the Heavens and find fulfilment in my love of God," the priest added.

She had been foolish, wasting time in talking to this man who, despite his kindness, must surely be a little stupid. "Thank you, Father, you have helped me greatly," she said, copying the words she had heard her mother speaking to one of the sisters. She was impatient to be away and had half turned from him, the gentle, yearning expression leaving her face completely so it looked sharper, more selfish.

She wandered away from him and the priest saw Sweyn sidle up beside her, put his arm in a fatherly fashion about her waist, and allow it to slip so that it rested on her rounded rump, looking anything but fatherly. Aileen tolerated the embrace for a moment, although the priest observed how she hunched her shoulders, stiffening against Sweyn, before neatly sidestepping and taking her body out of reach.

"What time shall we reach Seandale?" she asked, her voice bright and childlike. "I long to see my father."

The priest smiled, she was clever; but would her cleverness protect her through the rough and ready life she would be forced to lead? His smile dropped. He had no doubt, having heard her opinion on love, that she would use her marvellous body to obtain her own ends and he could hardly blame her, but would it ever bring the fulfilment she was seeking? It was possible, but improbable.

Sweyn mounted his horse reached down and grasping her, wrist to wrist, swung Aileen up behind him into the saddle. Her legs screamed in rebellion, the muscles – unused to exercise after months of confinement – ached dreadfully and she could hardly swing one leg over the horse's broad back.

They rode in silence, bundled up against the cold. Curiously, as if it rose from the smoke of the recently doused fire, the Norman's face came to Aileen's mind. Strong and young with well-defined lips, light hair, not brown, not yellow, thick and crisp. Clean-shaven, with clear grey-blue eyes, which had looked upon her in tenderness.

He had not come back for her and thankful though she was at this reprieve, it was slightly insulting to have been forgotten. She shrugged her shoulders. More fool him: if he chose not to take what he had won for himself, then she would not complain. But the empty space was back below her breast, and her eyes raked the horizon in vain for something which she called home, yet meant more to her than home had ever done.

They crested the hill which overlooked Seandale in the mid-afternoon. The threat of snow had gradually faded and the sky was now a lighter grey, wrapped like a cloak around the village where it crouched down in its protected valley. Aileen watched eagerly for signs of life but could see nothing. I'm still too far away, she thought, but she was uneasy. From here she had watched the retreating backs of her father and Cashal as they had left for Dublin, nearly a year ago. Her eyes watered with the strain of trying to see and she passed her hand across them, squeezing them tight shut. When she opened them again she thought she saw smoke rising from the roof of one of the duns, but there was none. No people and no smoke. Seandale was obviously empty, and her heart sank as she imagined Sweyn's reaction.

They rode on down into the village in silence and in silence passed through the main street. It was unearthly with no livestock scratching in the mud, no bread cooking over crackling fires, no children running alongside the horses, looking for treats from the travellers. Her own home, as she passed it, was much as she had left it, the door rent in two. She shuddered at the ugly memory the sight induced.

"There's no one here," said Sweyn unnecessarily, and Aileen nodded although he couldn't see her. They stopped, grouped around the old church and dismounted. Sweyn talked to his men, their voices gruff and low and then returned to where she still sat astride the horse.

"Get down," he said, "we'll make camp for the night, and tomorrow head for Trigonnel's point. O'Flerty will be there – if he is anywhere," he added morosely.

Aileen nodded dumbly. Trigonnel's point, situated three or four days' ride from here, was the place most likely to succour the homeless septs; from there O'Flerty would assemble all local resistance and provide a secure place for his people into the bargain.

She slept near to the priests. It was clear from Sweyn's expression that he was growing impatient with her continued evasion of his advances, and, as he was by no means sure that her protectors were still alive, he was growing anxious not to pass up the rewards of her body. She dared not allow herself to become weakened by her misery, she realised, for if she did, her power would wane and he would sense it and use it to his own advantage.

Trigonnel's Point lay on the route to Cashel, and surrounded by marsh and forest, was just the refuge Sweyn's merchants wanted. Far into the west it was sufficiently distant from Strongbow's advance to promise safety for the immediate future. She sat stiffly in her place behind Sweyn, wishing she could change and sit behind her friend the priest – whose name she had learned was Thomas. She knew however that to insult him in such a way would be disadvantageous and she remained where she was.

The pace was slow, slower than she had anticipated and the weather, intermittently cold, wet and snowy, left her bones aching with cold. The days were short and the nights tediously long. On the night of the third day, Sweyn came and laid down beside her, whilst the Ostmen played around the fire and the priests chanted some strange dirge under the trees. She lay, stiff as a board, as he placed his hand on her hip and remained motionless whilst he considered his next move.

If he wanted to Sweyn knew he could force her, no one would try to stop him. The old priest would point a finger and condemn him to hell, but then, so what if he did? At least hell would be warm. He smiled. He might also lose his chance of finding favour with O'Flerty, which would be most unwise. Of course, neither he nor her father knew of her whereabouts; he could kill her easily if she caused him any trouble, or threatened him in any way and no one would be the wiser. He could throttle her now, whilst no one was about and they would discover her body in the morning and think she had frozen to death. On the other hand, if he treated her well, her father would be grateful for it.

"Aileen?" he said, his voice low. He'd never thought twice about taking a woman before; the situation was almost pleasurable in itself. If and when he did take her, it would be the culmination of many days of wanting – a novel experience and not one to be sneered at. But if he didn't, then he would feel she had cheated and humiliated him.

He pushed himself against her and she turned to face him. "You've been so very kind, Sweyn. I have a sister who is so beautiful it would take your breath away. Long blond hair and blue eyes. I've been thinking, my father has long wished to marry her to someone of suitable standing. I can make sure he sees you as such, Sweyn, and you would in that way be handsomely repaid for your kindness toward me."

He moved away from her and she sighed to herself. In future she would stick closely to the priests and in this way further discourage him. It was hard to tell a man, in the heat of his desire, to wait for the future. Had she allowed Sweyn any more liberties, he would have been unable to control himself. Then he may have felt the need to kill her, to keep her quiet.

She closed her eyes wearily. Her body was an asset, but it could be a trial at times. If she were less beautiful Sweyn would leave her be; but then, she argued, he would not have agreed to bring her home in the first place. Her lie had served her well: her imaginary sister had distracted Sweyn and she smiled to herself. By the time he discovered she had mislead him, he would be powerless to do anything about it. And she would see to it that her father showed his gratitude in some other way. She drifted into sleep, the smile still on her lips.

The dark wood had become for a while, a sunny copse, through which the sun dappled the ground with golden pools of light. The leaves of the trees, varying in colour from olive green to the lightest of translucent yellow hues, stretched above her head, forming a perfect archway, with the sound of birds singing and the chirrup of grasshoppers in her ears. She could feel the smooth movement of a horse between her legs and leaned her head on the figure in front of her, her eyes drooping in contentment. The horse stopped and dropped its head to graze. She felt herself lifted from its back, and enfolded in a pair of strong arms. She looked up into the face of a young man, the sun forming a red halo about his head. Lifting her face for his kiss she closed her eyes and pressed her body against him. He ran a finger around the contours of her face and she opened her eyes, impatient for his love.

"I have to go now," he whispered.

"But why?" she said, feeling tears prickle her eyelids.

"Don't cry. I shall return for you soon." And she watched as he remounted the great golden horse and disappeared into a misty haze where the sun's rays met at the end of the tunnel.

Aileen wiped her eyes. Dawn was breaking coldly, with no sun, no canopy of leaves: she had only been dreaming. But the dream had left the empty place again and more tears fell before she could control them fully. The priest had talked of love. Was that what it was like to love? She shook her head from side to side. Such a feeling had no place for her and she knew of no such man – and yet he had been familiar – she shook away her weakness and crept close to the fire.

When she went to mount up behind Sweyn he half turned his head. "Ride with him," he said tersely, pointing to the man behind.

She did as she was told. The journey had already taken six days instead of the four she had anticipated; the marshes were difficult to traverse, but they expected to be at Trigonnel's Point by nightfall.

The early cloud lifted and the sky became blue, although the sun lacked the strength to lift the frost from the ground. Sweyn, riding in front, suddenly drew his horse to an abrupt halt and, turning into the wood, he signalled for quiet. Dismounting, they led their horses into the shadows, hoping they would not be seen by the horsemen they could hear crashing through the trees toward them. Aileen's heart thudded. To be so near, and suddenly come under threat.

She had a clear view of the path and peered out at them as they passed

82

by. She could almost feel the white vapour which poured from the horses' mouths and hung in the static air. The leader of the horsemen, hearing sound in the woods, stopped his men and took hold of the sword which hung at his side.

With a loud yelp of delight, Aileen flung herself from the woods and stood before the troop of men. "Patrick O'Flerty," she cried, so overjoyed to see him that she forgot herself.

"It is the daughter of MacGillingrouth, isn't it?" said Patrick, a smile on his craggy face.

"Yes, indeed it is," another voice answered and she looked back to see Murchad, with his familiar flowing red whiskers, and his eyes as full of fun and lust as they had been when she had last seen him.

Sweyn and his men left the cover of the woods and Sweyn now congratulated himself for his restraint. The girl was too clever and he had, on occasion, doubted that she was Rory's daughter. She was talking now to Patrick O'Flerty's son, and, with a flash of resentment, he watched as she blazed her eyes at him, her body brazenly arched as she looked up into his face. Murchad's eyes were glued to her, and she showed him none of the cool detachment and childish innocence with which she had presented Sweyn throughout their journey.

"I had thought you dead, or captured by the Normans," Murchad said. "How delightful to meet you again, and looking so well."

"And you, Murchad, I had wondered if you were killed in Dublin."

He could read the genuine concern in her face and was gratified. He had almost forgotten her, but as she stood before him now he was filled again with the need to possess her. He even entertained the thought of making her his woman. His wife Tara would raise few objections and in truth he didn't care either way about her feelings. Rory MacGillingrouth would be a worthy partner.

" – and what of my father and my uncle Cashal?" she was asking. The order of her words failed to disguise that it was the well-being of her uncle which was uppermost in her mind.

Murchad remembered the tales he had heard: how she had displeased her father by throwing herself into her uncle's arms. "Both well," he said. "They'll be delighted to see you, I'm sure."

"And I them. We are headed for Trigonnel's point now."

"And we are riding out from there, on a hunting trip," he confirmed. "Who are your companions?"

Sweyn, seizing his opportunity, came over to where they stood. Keeping an eye on O'Flerty's back, he introduced himself to Murchad.

"So, we owe you our thanks for returning Aileen to us," Murchad said, shaking his hand. "Thank you indeed. Such a jewel has been sorely missing from the septs."

Aileen listened entranced to his flowery sentiments, so unusual amongst her kind. The old feeling of bridled power returned to her, along with her excitement at being near her own people. She felt the misery and worries of her journey leave her rapidly, replaced by a surge of energy which she could hardly contain.

"We must ride on," Murchad said to Aileen, as his father lifted his arm to give the signal. "But I'll see you on my return and you can tell me all that has happened since I saw you last."

"I shall look forward to it," she replied, lowering her eyes in mock humility.

She knew that talking was the last thing on his mind. It would be challenging to be confronted with two powerful men, both vying for her attentions. She wondered how she would handle the situation, and resolved to deal with it, if and when it arose. Cashal, after all, could be married by now and have long lost interest in her. Well, married or no, she was sure she would be able to re-arouse his interest. In fact the presence of Murchad would be enough to do it for her, without a doubt.

She remounted her horse and, sensing the new respect with which she was being treated following her obvious welcome from the chieftain, she rode triumphant, towards the stronghold of Trigonnel's point.

CHAPTER 11

In spite of the presence of women and children the camp was still very much one of war. The MacGillingrouth sept had moved there in its entirety and many others had subsequently joined. The two elements of daily life mingled strangely with one another. On the one hand there were obvious signs of family life with the pigs and chickens around; on the other, an enclosed area contained large, warlike groups of men practising their arms. The stronghold had been built on high ground and dominated the countryside, standing out high above the surrounding forest. A heavily stockaded perimeter had been erected, with sentries posted outside, as well as a look-out manning the highest point – a pencil-shaped hillock from which the encampment took its name – making Trigonnel's point a formidable stronghold. Patrick O'Flerty had chosen well and it was from here he meant to defy the Normans and halt the subjugation of Loswellery.

As Aileen and the Ostmen entered the stronghold, she saw Donel and Corvild amidst the large group of people who had come to investigate the visitors. Aileen flung herself from her horse, almost bringing down the man in front of her. Calling their names, she ran with outstretched arms to greet them. They had grown almost as tall as her and she took one in each arm, looking down into Corvild's face, which she had last seen in recuperative sleep before her ordeal in the dun.

"It's so good to see you," she cried. "I've missed you. How is our father, and – our uncle."

"Your uncle is well, Aileen," Cashal's familiar rumbling voice came to her ears and instantly she felt her pulse quicken and a flush come to her cheeks.

"Uncle," she smiled, her eyes half closing in a sensuous manner. "It is so very good to see you."

He picked her up, squeezing her tightly in his massive arms and held her high above his head. Lowering her to the ground, he kissed her passionately and the crowd cheered at his obvious enthusiasm. He swung her round like a cape and set her to her feet, where she staggered and had to lean against him until her dizziness passed. As it did so, Aileen saw Sweyn's face turn pale. She also caught Thomas's eye and saw that he dropped his gaze. He had heard her refer to Cashal as Uncle, had seen the passion of their embrace: it wasn't difficult to guess at what disturbed him and Aileen momentarily felt self-conscious.

Corvild re-emerged shortly from the crowd, followed by Corderg in his priest's robes. "Welcome home, sister," he said, a large smile on his face. "But where is our mother. Is she not safe?" He spoke the words quickly, in the only way he could force them out and waited, breath bated, for her reply. She looked at him and at the two young boys, Donel and Corvild, on either side of him; grimly waiting for news. She smiled, relieved that she had nothing bad to tell them.

"She is alive and well and very happy," Aileen said, seeing the warm glow which instantly spread upon her family.

"Where is she?" Donel asked, his face scanning the crowd.

"Not here." Aileen hesitated. Should she tell them that their mother had preferred to remain where she was, or should she say that she had been unable to escape? If she did that, it was just possible that Rory would send troops to "rescue" her. She could not afford to have that happen. What if Aifel refused to be rescued? "Shall we talk about this later?" she said, looking at Corderg. He nodded, a puzzled expression on his face.

Cashal put his arm around her waist and led her across the busy square to where her father sat, sharpening his axe outside a large wooden built hut. He looked at her without smiling: his old animosity toward his brother had not diminished since her disappearance and she could see the venom in his eyes. Cashal saw it too and took the opportunity to jibe at him.

"Aren't you pleased to see your daughter, Rory? Will you not kiss her, as I have done, to give her welcome?"

"Since you have kissed her already, brother, I will let it serve for us both," he commented drily, continuing in his work.

Aileen's heart sank. They had never been close, but she had been softened by their separation and expected him to feel the same.

"Well then, I shall kiss her again – for you," Cashal said and without further ado he took her in his arms and kissed her, his tongue parting her lips. This time Aileen felt uncomfortable and instead of closing her eyes as she normally would, she kept them open and saw her father's grim look of disgust. She tried to pull away from her uncle's arms, but he held her close to him, his legs braced against hers.

"Cashal, stop," she said, pulling her mouth from his.

"Then I will see you later," he said grimly, letting go of her so abruptly that she fell to the ground at her father's feet. Rory spat after his brother's form as he strode away.

"Father, will you not kiss me now?" she asked, in need of his approval. Rory hesitated for a brief moment then turned his head in a sulky denial. Aileen realised how difficult life was going to be for her if he maintained his present hostility. Without her mother's loving presence to protect her from the worst of his coldness she would be condemned to a world of silence, an art at which Rory excelled. In a household of people who were opposed to her relationship with Cashal, she would shrivel for lack of love. For the first time she recognised the enormous support she had always enjoyed from her mother, who, although she'd disliked the relationship between herself and Cashal, had never allowed it to come between them. Cashal had grown so blatant, flaunting his intentions in Rory's face that it had been humiliating.

With the adaptability of the young, and despite her fears, Aileen soon slipped into her new life, finding it little changed.

"What was it like at Whitley?" Dvorvild asked one day.

"Tedious!"

"Because Cashal wasn't there?"

"Because there were no men there at all."

"So did you not feel tempted by Sweyn's advances?" Dvorvild teased.

"No one could be tempted by Sweyn. He's a pig. He grunts and groans; he has no teeth and he stinks."

"Very tempting," Dvorvild smiled. "I missed you, Aileen. Rory's alright, but he's no fun. The boys have missed their mother and I've had no one to talk to."

"Nor I," Aileen said.

They worked harmoniously together at the household tasks, always chattering and laughing. One day, not long after her return, Aileen saw Donel sitting quietly in the corner, watching them.

"What troubles you?" she asked him, sinking onto her knees in front of him. She saw Dvorvild leave the room, tactfully.

"Why did our mother not return with you – really?" He had big round eyes and he turned them on her now in a heart-stopping stare.

"She wanted to come back, but she was happy with the nuns."

"Happier than she was with us?" He was too old to cry, but his lip trembled.

"I think, to make her perfectly happy, she would need to have you and Corvild with her. Would you like that, Donel?"

He paused and thought about it. His father was teaching him to ride and fight with an axe. His uncle Cashal was teaching him to hunt and fish. Corvild, he was sure, would never want to leave here, and he didn't relish the idea of leaving without him.

"Could I have my pony? Would I be able to go fishing? And who will teach me to fight?" he said.

"You might be able to have your pony, and you could fish. But you could never fight – it is the house of God."

"Like Father Seamus's and Corderg's." Following his father's lead Corvild had learned to disparage such institutions.

"Yes, but it's all women there." Aileen delivered her coup de grace.

"I think I'll stay here then. With Corvild."

"Mother will be sorry, but she'll understand. And she'll be happy, so long as you are."

"How will we know?"

"Because I'm telling you, and I've talked with her." She kissed him on his forehead and he leaned against her for a second, before pulling away. Donel turned to go, then thought of another question. At that moment Corvild, who was never far from his brother, sidled into the room. "Why wasn't she happy here, Aileen?" Donel asked.

"Well," she started, carefully. "Life was not always easy for her here –"

"Why not, she had us, didn't she?" Corvild interrupted, hotly.

"But she had Dvorvild too, and it made things very difficult for her."

"Why? Did she not like Dvorvild?"

"She would have liked her well enough, but for our father," Aileen said, struggling to explain. "Our father had to marry Dvorvild because she is O'Flerty's daughter, and so our mother was lonely without him."

"Is that why she stayed at Whitley?"

"Perhaps. And she was growing old – she is almost forty you know – the work is very light at the monastery and the nuns look after her."

"Will we see her again?" Corvild asked.

Aileen doubted it: it was unlikely she would ever wish to return, and the Priory was in Norman hands, inaccessible to O'Flerty men. But she couldn't hurt them with the truth. "Yes, one day. She thinks of you every night, you know, and asked me to tell you how much she cares for you."

The boy smiled. "But we can't tell her we want her to come home," he said, and his eyes glistened with tears.

"You don't have to, she knows that," said Aileen, taking them both in her arms. This time neither cringed away: they snuggled against her like lost animals.

Rory's large shadow passed across the three of them. "You'll make babies of those boys," he snarled.

"Don't be stupid, father," Aileen retorted. She stood up with her hands on her hips and faced him across the room.

"You'll not talk to me in that way and get away with it."

"I'll do as I please."

Rory strode over and hit her hard about the face. Corvild and Donel cringed away. They'd suffered at Rory's hands before and had no wish to be brought into any fight between their wild sister and angry father. Aileen looked at them, then back at Rory.

"I think, father, it's time I left your dun and moved in with Cashal."

"You'll do no such thing."

"He'd want me to. He's already asked me." '

"Over my dead body." Rory couldn't bear the thought of her doing as she threatened. There was too much talk already. It would damage his reputation beyond repair.

"Then don't hit me. Never hit me again." She took the boys by the hand and led them from the room. Rory watched them, open-mouthed. She had won yet another battle, he didn't know whether to despise or admire her.

Two weeks after he had met her in the woods on his hunting trip, Murchad approached Aileen. "I've heard tell you're Cashal's woman. Is it true?" he asked, his eyes serious for once.

"He is my uncle, as you well know," she said, trying to stall him.

"And more besides?"

Aileen hung her head briefly. Whilst her body rejoiced in Cashal's continued attentions, she could still remember the disappointed look in the priest's eyes. "Yes," she said finally, tilting her chin in defiance, "and more besides."

He surprised her by the sad look which he allowed to show on his face. "Does he please you?" he asked, and his eyes were so fixed on her body that she could not fail to understand him.

"He does please me, yes." she replied, experiencing a sudden thrill at having such a conversation, with such a man.

"But you could never marry him."

"I have no wish to marry," she snapped. Murchad felt a smile tug at the corners of his mouth. "Until my father forces me to," she added quickly.

"And is he about to do that?"

"He is cautious. He wants to make the best possible deal, and in his greed he could be encouraged to wait – indefinitely."

"So, you will remain – available – indefinitely?"

"Available?"

"Unmarried."

"I hope so," she said, and her look was as inviting as she could make it. This was her favourite of all sport: the tempting of the opposite sex, the sight of their wanting her, knowing her own power to reject them.

Suddenly he put his arm round her, holding her just long enough for her to want more from him. Then he held her away. "But you are Cashal's woman, I forget," he said, his eyes twinkling.

"I am my own woman, Murchad. Don't you forget." She flounced away, and he followed her movements, not bothering to suppress his delighted laughter which echoed round the copse.

For the most part, Rory, despite their arguments, was happy to have Aileen back. He was not oblivious to Murchad's obvious interest in her, which could be made to serve a purpose, and he knew that his daughter kept Dvorvild and the twins happy. Provided it was not flaunted before him, he tried to shut his eyes to her relationship with Cashal; in due course, he was sure, it would fizzle out. In the meantime he was more careful with her: Aileen's threat to live openly with Cashal was not an empty one and he knew that such an action could destroy his hopes for a liaison with Murchad.

He was pleased to hear Aifel would not be returning and strangely pleased to know that she was happy. Though he would never admit it, he cared for her well-being, provided it didn't impinge on his own, and her happiness was a small bonus.

90

CHAPTER 12

Patrick O'Flerty had constructed an enclosure defended by palisades of stone and timber in the centre of the camp; within this enclosure there was a dwelling constructed with more care than the other buildings. This area housed the chief and his family and from there, if it ever became necessary, it would be possible to stage a last ditch defence.

Patrick had encouraged all those who supported his opposition, irrespective of sept or clan, to gather, imploring them to forget other feuds and join him at Trigonnel's point. Constant appeals were sent to the High King, pleading with him to organise another hosting, but no reply came back. Rory O'Connor remained strangely quiet in the safety of his Connaught Kingdom, seemingly content to lick his wounds and recover from the humiliation of his defeat before Dublin. Lesser men, however, were more willing, and, unknown to FitzAlan, the numbers at the stronghold grew steadily.

Murchad was anxious to win back O'Flerty lands and was convinced that his father could not do so. He despised the ease with which the Normans had pushed his father back, dispersing their clan far and wide and creating long delays before they had been able to return home. Two of his three other brothers were equally ambitious and only the old chief's powerful domination kept them in check. Although O'Flerty controlled them with ease, there were those who forecast a bitter fight between his sons if he should either lose control, or die.

Murchad could not expect his claim to leadership to go unquestioned and only the youngest son, Liam, could be relied upon to support him; he was a poet and indifferent to tribal politics and Murchad had always been his favourite brother. Murchad now took the time to cultivate this fondness, listening for hours to Liam's work and talking with him about the things which interested him. It was not as difficult as he would have expected, for Liam had a grasp of life, a way of looking into the heart of it, which appealed to something buried deep beneath the warlike exterior of his elder brother.

"Love is the most important thing on earth," said Liam, explaining a piece of poetry he had written. "Love is the motivation for war and peace and the whole reason for our existence."

Murchad was silent as he listened to his brother, but when the latter had finished expounding his theories he let out a mighty roar of laughter. "If you used your sword as you do your pen, brother, the enemy would stand no chance of survival."

Liam bowed, in humble acknowledgment of the praise.

"Love of a woman can be a sweet thing, don't you think?" he said, when Murchad had stopped to gather his breath.

"I wouldn't know. Women are good for pleasure and for breeding, sometimes for politics – why complicate the issues with this love?"

"Why indeed, and yet it happens. We have all seen it happen from time to time."

"And when it does it wreaks havoc. I have seen great leaders crumble because of love."

"And some who have grown more powerful beside the right lady."

"Well, you could be right, but love is not for me. Now lust is a different matter. I lust after a lady right now, though she is proving to be rather evasive."

"What lady dare evade you?" his brother asked, genuinely surprised.

"Aileen MacGillingrouth, who flaunts her body at her uncle and flirts with me at the same time."

"And you stand for it?" Liam was amazed: it was inconceivable that his brother would allow a woman to dally with him.

"I do, for the time being. Cashal is my friend, and a giant into the bargain, I have no wish to fall out over Aileen. If perhaps she meant more to me – "

"Quite. And so you let her flirt with you. Let her believe in her power?"

"It excites me to do so. I spread my seed liberally amongst the other women of the septs, I enjoy the game with Aileen. When I am ready, I shall take the plunge," they both laughed at his choice of words. "Until then she is a pleasurable diversion, and, oddly enough, I like and admire her spirit."

"Well, as you say, if it were love you would fight to have her. Enjoy your diversion and her friendship, whilst you can," Liam said. "And when you are chief, will you make her your woman then?"

"If there is no pressing reason not to, I will. Rory MacGillingrouth could be an important ally."

O'Flerty's tribal numbers grew as his health diminished and with it there was a general air of restlessness. There was also a growing demand for action against the Normans and Patrick planned to end his chieftaincy with a great and ambitious scheme of reprisal.

CHAPTER 13

$\mathcal{T}$he castle at Gossard's Ford was the usual, hastily constructed type – a wooden tower surrounded by a palisade and a huge mound of earth. One of the initial attractions of the site, as far as Robert was concerned, had been this mound of earth, thrown up in a corner of land where the two rivers joined before flowing on to Dublin and the sea. It created a natural moat on two sides of the castle, leaving Robert with only the task of digging a ditch on the landward sides to keep the water in. Once constructed the castle would provide a commanding view over the flat countryside, and would form an ideal, and reasonably impregnable base from which he could control his domain.

Robert, having just inspected the progress made so far, stood back in admiration. He had made up his mind that the time had now come to cease further conquests and settle down, organising his lands so as to bring as much as possible into active production. Loswellery had been largely subjugated, and except for the peasantry, the dissaffected Irish had been driven out. It was now a question of holding the country down and of preventing any attempt on the part of the Irish to re-assert their old control.

It was now March and the hillocks were dotted with lambs and kids playing in the lush green grass. Robert sat amongst the wild crocuses, his horse grazing contentedly beside him. The sounds of carpentry and men shouting to one another in the castle to his rear were muffled by a gentle breeze. In time he would quarry stone and build his castle into a mighty fortress, more comfortable and more permanent, where he would bring his wife, raise his children and fulfil his lifelong dream of being lord of his own estates.

He wondered idly how his mother and father fared at home in Wales. He had had no word for several months. Despite the fact that he knew women were less intelligent than men, he had found much wisdom in his mother and missed her feminine outlook on things. Men were good for talk of war and killing; they were good for planning strategy and politics; but women had a softer and more long term way of seeing things – he supposed that was why they valued education so much for their sons and tried to instil upon them more gentle feelings. His close relationship to his mother during his formative years had influenced him more than he had at first realised. Destined for the church, Robert had been taught Latin by a tutor, read philosophical works and spent more time than most boys of his age in the company of women and thinkers.

And now he sat dreaming in a field, his own castle growing daily behind him, his lands, courageously won, laid out in panoramic splendour, before him. Silas no longer spoke to him as to a youth – no one did – they had fought together side by side, man to man and Silas had quickly lost his early scepticism, becoming a firm friend and loyal servant. Once the castle was completed Robert would have few dreams left to realise.

He turned his mind to the day when he had entered the village of Seandale and come across MacTilling's men savagely raping the young girl and her terrified mother. He had been unable to put Aileen MacGillingrouth out of his mind, and in tender moments she rose before him, as did the child from Waterford. He no longer needed to suppress the side of his nature which yearned for gentle pursuits, for he had proved himself an able warrior, earning the friendship of Reginald d'Evreux and the respect of the men he commanded. He'd had no time to return to the Priory of Whitley to collect her and make her his woman, but soon he would be able to do so. For months she had been in his thoughts and the soft roundness of her limbs, the thickness of her black hair, gleaming blue in the sunlight, had grown in importance for him until he was utterly obsessed by the memory of her. He enjoyed the company of women, the sighs of pleasure which his caresses could arouse. And Aileen – never, he thought, could a woman have been more ideally suited to him. He had seen her broken and dispirited, afraid and hurt, and yet he had also seen the fight she put up from the scratches and bruises on the bodies of her rapists. He could sense the passion of her nature from the shape of her body, the fullness of her lips and the depth of expression in her eyes. She would fit perfectly into his dream, provide him with healthy children and fulfil his sexual needs with equal ardour. He smiled as he dreamt about possessing her. She would probably put up a fight and the warrior in him revelled at the thought of conquering her, not through sheer force, but by breaking down her resistance through her own desires. He wanted her to want him, to come to him willingly and with eager anticipation. So his dreams wove themselves through his mind, a colourful tapestry, which no one but he might view.

Finally he got to his feet and, mounting his patient horse he returned to the castle. He collected his escort and started on the long ride to Dublin. They made their way over the flat lands where one day his own village would stand, and, after crossing the gorse-covered heath to the east of Gossard's Ford, entered the thick, dark woods that stretched for several miles on the route towards the capital. Here the men rode quietly, knowing that if they were to be ambushed, this provided the perfect setting. With their visors down and their long shields held before them, Robert's party rode steadily forward, the archers walking between the horsemen. The narrowness of the forest tracks made single file a necessity and each man was conscious of the need for caution. In this manner they penetrated deep into the wood.

The men entered a glade that skirted a large pool, the track weaving its restricted way between the trees and the water. Suddenly the air was rent by the sound of men shouting. Simultaneously, a hail of stones came hurtling from the tree tops and men, till now concealed in the branches, jumped down in the path of the horses.

Robert's horse stumbled and crashed to the ground, its neck almost severed by the ferocious blow of an axe from the hand of a gigantic Irishman. Robert landed on his feet and, regaining his balance, confronted the giant. He thrust with his sword, his long shield mercifully protecting him from another savage downward sweep of the giant's axe.

The two men engaged in a deadly duel, axe versus sword; Robert's armour providing protection, the other's lack of it allowing for speed of movement. So evenly matched were the two that they became totally absorbed in their own personal battle, regardless of the fight raging around them.

Amidst blood-curdling screams, the Irish, with their greater numbers and the surprise of their attack, beat many of Robert's men to the ground. The Welsh bowmen suffered particularly, deprived as they were of their traditional weapons and devoid of armour. Many had fallen at the first attack, their bodies now cluttering the narrow path and impeding the progress of the fight.

Silas, seeing his master fighting for his life, called out, his strong voice carrying over the noise of battle, "Back to back – use your swords, stand fast!"

His cry, ringing out midst the noise and confusion, had a rallying effect, putting renewed heart into Robert's flagging men. Very slowly at first, their superior discipline and battle skills began to tell, the assailants finding it increasingly difficult to make an impression. The mounted men abandoned their horses and fought alongside the remaining bowmen, calmly holding back successive assaults by the Irish.

Robert had never experienced such a fight before. Disposing of an opponent had always been a simple matter of kill or be killed and it was generally over in a few seconds. He was used to having many encounters during a battle but he realised that this time there would be only one. During the first ferocious moments he attacked the giant with all his skill, strength and energy, but his opponent didn't falter and Robert was hard pressed to deflect the equally fierce counter-attack.

The giant's axe scored several glancing blows and had it not been for Robert's chain mail his flesh would have been laid open to the bone. His massive broadsword was not intended for long duels, it was heavy and designed to finish a fight with one blow that could split a man in two – but first he had to hit the man. The giant was as agile as he was strong and, having dodged all Robert's swings, showed no sign of tiring. The impetus was now all his and as Robert staggered back from the whirling axe he felt his first real fear of defeat. The giant, sensing victory was near, pressed home his attack. Robert's limbs were numb with fatigue. He stepped back, trying to regain his balance but stumbled, falling heavily. He lay helplessly on his back and realised, with a sense of incredulity, that he had lost. That he was actually going to die.

The giant let out an exultant roar of triumph, discarded his axe, drew his short sword from his waistband and holding it with both hands above his head hurled himself at Robert's fallen body, his huge frame blotting out the sky.

During training Silas had forced Robert to split wood with a massive two-handed axe until he was weary beyond imagining; beyond the point where his body had used all its normal reserves of energy; until he had been forced to ask if he could rest. Silas' voice, part taunt, part sneer came into Robert's mind. "Tired are ye? Want to return to your books and your mother's kitchen? A warrior? Pah!" Robert snarled in rage at the memory and heaved his broadsword up.

Then it went dark.

Robert awoke to the darkness; there was a great weight over his entire body. They've buried me alive! was his first thought. Slowly he became aware that the weight and darkness were caused by the body of the giant. His bearded face was jammed against Robert's own and he was actually looking down the giant's throat. The yellow teeth and blackening tongue were exposed, the nose pressed against the side of Robert's face, squashing his cheek and half closing one of his eyes. Sweat ran through the dust and saliva on the dead man's face and mingled with Robert's. He tried to wipe it away, but his hands were clamped around the hilt of the sword and imprisoned under the dead man's body.

Now his armour truly came to his rescue. Without it he would have been stabbed by the hilt of his own sword, which even through the chain mail was digging deep into his diaphragm. He rolled his eyes and saw above him the white of the other man's eye, tinged with yellow; the blue iris, the dilated black pupil, even the tiny pink veins which criss-crossed it. Blood bubbled up and ran from the dead man's mouth into Robert's eye.

He couldn't breath, he couldn't move, he couldn't see. He was dying under the horrible carcass and he couldn't even panic. His cheek was numb and wet under the massive head. Waves of pain threatened his consciousness until he was unsure if he were the victor or had awoken in some special hell reserved for the vanquished.

Silas sliced across the wiry Irishman's throat, watching with interest as the skin parted and the blood gushed out. "Goodbye," he spat, and let the dead man fall to the ground. He looked about him and saw that Robert had killed the giant. He had tried to keep an eye on their combat, but had been, for a while, overwhelmed by raging Irishmen and unable to help. He was about to turn away when he saw a booted foot twitch. The giant's feet were encased in leather straps and both clearly visible.

"Jesus Christ," Silas gasped, as, with difficulty, he hauled the body off Robert, allowing him to take great gasps of cool, sweet air. Silas held out an arm to lift Robert up, who managed the smallest of smiles but didn't move a muscle, even to get away from his ghastly companion.

"Sorry, Silas," he breathed, "too tired – "

A few minutes later, still trembling with exhaustion, Robert looked around him, surprised to find that the fight was over. The steadfast discipline of his followers had prevailed but at a high cost. The bodies of men – some still locked together – littered the path, and the pool was stained with their blood. His proud archers were decimated and the survivors stared stupidly at their fallen comrades.

Riderless horses moved aimlessly about and groups of survivors leaned wearily on their swords or shields. A few men strove to recapture their mounts, while others went aimlessly from body to body. When, having made stretchers for the wounded, they finally set off toward Dublin, it was in a shocked and deathly silence.

CHAPTER 14

They were washing clothes in the small stream which fed the camp when the men who had left under Cashal's command to kill the hated Norman returned, the massive body laid out on a stretcher. Dvorvild saw them coming and ran over to see what had happened. The men were pale and Cashal, who had been deeply loved, was instantly surrounded by a host of anguished people. A kind of superstition had built up around him; his enormity, his joviality and his prowess had led them to believe he was invincible and to view him as a good omen. If it was possible for the Giant Cashal to die, many of them thought in numbed silence, it was possible for the whole stronghold to collapse.

Aileen was blithely enjoying the sharp March sunlight, watching the water as it splayed over the rocks and thinking, ironically, of the day she had first lain with Cashal beside the pool at Seandale. They had been together for many months since then and although she knew Cashal was not entirely faithful to her, she had remained his favourite woman. Aileen had lost no opportunity of feeding his jealousy of Murchad, despite the sharp blows this often precipitated, for it kept him wanting and men were powerless whilst they wanted. She had grown to care for him: his easy smile and strength of purpose, his casual approach to living. His booming voice and muscular body which had brought her pleasure after pleasure, had become an intrinsic part of her life. Her father had given up, finally, with his efforts to separate them, and Murchad had busied himself with his wife and other women, prepared to bide his time, although he still spared her the time to flirt and tease. Cashal and she were regarded as a couple. Her relationship with such a powerful man continued to bring her status; she had even stopped noticing it, taking it for granted that she would be held in awe by the younger girls and allowed to pass by the men, unhindered.

Dvorvild was weeping when she returned and Aileen knew instantly what had happened. She pulled away from the consoling arm around her shoulders and continued to stare into the water until her eyes misted over. She sat until the sun went down and on into the evening, until at last Dvorvild came back to get her. She hadn't cried, she had not uttered one word and she returned, docile, to the dun.

She sat where Dvorvild left her by the fire, and gradually her bare arms turned from blue to pink again and the heat put some colour in her ashen cheeks. Her eyes stared blankly out at the world, which had suddenly diminished in size.

"So, my brother has been slain," said her father, not unkindly. "He was a courageous man to the last. The struggle against the Norman knight was a long one, I'm told, but fair. The man who is strong enough to kill Cashal must be a valiant one."

So it had been him again. Her hated captor, the man who had stolen and spurned her. Now he had killed her lover. "Norman bastard," she spat venomously into the fire.

"A worthy opponent, even so," Rory reiterated, respect for courage and strength outweighing his natural hatred.

Corderg came to see her a few weeks later, his gentle face comforting. "You are unhappy, Aileen, naturally, but your relationship with Cashal wasn't right."

"Right doesn't come into this, Corderg. If right prevailed Cashal would be alive today and the Normal crawling with maggots."

"The Norman? Was it not he who saved you from the MacTilling men?"

She looked at him in surprise. She had been relying on her hatred to buoy her up; was Corderg trying to remove it?

"What did our mother think of him?" he asked, softly.

Aileen hesitated, thinking back to the conversation she had had with her mother, shortly after arriving at Whitley.

"Aileen, don't hate Robert FitzAlan, he saved our lives."

And she hadn't at first, but as the days and months passed and he hadn't bothered to return to rescue her from the place she came to see as her prison, she had allowed herself to grow bitter. It was degrading: she'd been kept from her family and her lover, and for no good purpose.

"Aileen?" Corderg prompted. He was watching the shadows pass across her face.

"I shall think about what you say, Corderg," she said, not answering his question and confusing him further. The only enthusiasm she had lay in the fires of hatred she kept burning. Now that Corderg had thrown water over them she was inexpressibly weary.

"Good. Remember, Aileen, I'm here when you need me, now you no longer have our mother to confide in."

She inclined her head and reached out her hand. It didn't quite reach his, but slipped down the side of his robe, to drop back in her own lap.

She never cried: crying would not bring him home to her. She reached out in the night feeling for his body and then withdrew her arm, remembering. She neither discussed him, nor refused to let others do so. She wanted no sympathy and received none. She walked the streets of the stronghold with her head high, so that even without Cashal's protection she was not accosted. She was, after all, the daughter of one of the most influential chiefs and respect for the Giant, Cashal, extended beyond the grave.

Rory had been sad when his brother was brought home, despite their lifelong animosity. He remembered him as a young child, always running behind on sturdy little legs, calling, "Wait for me, wait for me." But Cashal had ever been a thorn in his side, and had kept him from finding greater favour in O'Flerty's eyes. It had not escaped Rory's attention that on that last mission, of the greatest importance to O'Flerty, it was Cashal who had been placed in charge. But with Cashal out of the way now, Rory was more often called upon in the councils of war to give his opinion; and without Cashal's sneering face to dissuade the wavering factions, it was more often complied with.

Murchad was in a similar position. His brothers had often used Cashal's influence to win O'Flerty over to their point of view, and although Cashal and Murchad had remained friends, Murchad had sometimes felt himself displaced in his father's affections. This in itself had not been a serious matter, for Cashal was not a direct threat to the chieftainship; but with the political wrangling between his brothers and their allies, any favoured warrior could influence important decisions. With Cashal gone the strength of Murchad's position was now indisputable.

Murchad took to visiting Rory at his home, where they could talk undisturbed into the night, and where he could observe Aileen from close quarters. She showed little sign of the grief she was experiencing, other than for the fact that she no longer flirted with him. He treated her kindly, patiently waiting for her to return to normality, and before many weeks had passed he noticed her silently observing him, listening from the shadows as he talked of the revenge they would take on the Norman who continued to rule their lands. It was still O'Flerty's wish to capture the Castle, which was now the centre of much Norman activity, but with the King of England remaining in Ireland they were afraid to strike, and had to satisfy themselves with talk of revenge and the plans to carry it out.

It was not until the King had left Ireland that plans began to take more form, and Aileen listened with great interest to the details of how O'Flerty's men would burn down the castle and kill its inhabitants. More and more Aileen's attention was drawn toward Murchad, and she began to await his appearance in the dun eagerly, taking a greater interest in her clothes, combing her hair and tying it back with rawhide and waiting on him as he talked to her father.

"What do you think of Murchad?" Dvorvild asked her, eyeing her knowledgeably.

"That he is a great warrior and the man best-equipped to oust the Norman knight from power," was the quick retort.

"Do you not find him attractive, Aileen?" for Dvorvild did, comparing him to the older and less formidable Rory.

"My father would welcome any relationship between us," Aileen replied carefully, but Dvorvild saw her eyes glisten and knew the ice was melting.

"And do you not miss having a man to keep you warm at night?" she said, her blue eyes roving over Aileen's form.

She did. Her body, now used to loving, missed it sorely, and she had begun to wake frustrated in the night. She regretted the passing of Cashal, but she craved the living. She no longer stepped out of Murchad's way as he passed her in the narrow doorway; instead she held her ground, forcing him to brush past her. It was an old trick, but it worked. She no longer avoided his gaze, but met it full and square, meeting him eye to eye, and tilting her chin back proudly.

When she wasn't thinking about Murchad, disturbing memories filled her mind. She had begun to dream of the day the MacTilling men had raided Seandale, the details subtly changed. Hopeless and helpless she relived the experience, watching her mother almost hidden from view as the filthy man attacked her. She would stare fixedly, her own ordeal becoming secondary as she saw her mother growing weak under the attack which went on and on. Her mother was dying – the rapist continued his assault – she fought and screamed to get at him – to save her mother's life. The noise became overwhelming, her screams, the groaning of her mother, the rapist's laughter echoing in her ears with the special quality reserved for nightmares. Then suddenly the door – which was restored – flung open, and a harsh silence filled the dark room. The men were frozen and her mother's face turned toward the light. Time seemed to stand still, then

Aileen turned her head in slow motion to see the body of the Norman knight, in full armour, standing in the doorway with the light behind him, his sword raised.

He walked calmly over to her mother and, impaling the Irishman on the end of his sword, picked him up and flung him from the dun. He repeated the action, killing the remaining two men and then tenderly, as if he were handling a baby, he picked up her mother and wrapped her in his cloak, laying her down before the fire. Then he turned to Aileen, bent over and kissed her. She pressed against him, not wanting him to leave her, desperate for more.

Suddenly she was in the Priory at Whitley and her mother was telling her that Robert was their protector, their saviour, swearing him undying allegiance. And she was invariably filled with a dreadful yearning to kiss him again, her body aching for him, until she felt utterly desolated that he was not with her.

Her dreams of desiring the Norman conflicted terribly with her waking plans to seek revenge and she dared tell no one, not even Dvorvild, of her suffering. The desire which the dreams had awakened was redirected toward Murchad; she replaced FitzAlan's face with his, pretending that it was his body she craved and not that of the man who had killed Cashal, the man whom she hated with every fibre of her being.

She went out late one night to walk around the stronghold, too restless to sleep, her body aching for love. As usual she made her way down to the stream. Murchad, on his way home late after drinking with his men, spied her as she crossed the street and followed. He watched in silence, much as Cashal had done long ago, and he felt a rare tenderness as the moonlight played upon her face.

The idea of their coming together still held for him a dream-like quality which he was never able to put out of his mind. He walked slowly toward her, expecting the usual flirtatious behaviour, the final rejection, but she looked up at him and he saw tears in her eyes. He bent over and, with one finger, brushed them away. Then he kissed the place where they had been. The feelings which swept over him were totally new and unexpected and he hesitated, but Aileen, whose desire was overwhelming, pulled him down toward her and he was surprised at her obvious readiness for him.

"You hate Robert FitzAlan as I do," he said, as they lay quietly together, satisfied and dreamy in the moonlight.

Her mother's words, and Corderg's too, flashed through her mind, and she was surprised at the sudden denial that rose to her lips. She pushed it away, disgusted with herself at the disloyal emotion. She couldn't tell Murchad that while he had loved her, surprising her with his tenderness, it had been Robert's face she had imagined above hers. "Oh yes, Murchad, I hate him," she said, all the more vehement because of her doubt.

"Then I will capture him. I will make it my personal quest to do so," he said, "And you will know that I am doing it for you."

She had to turn her head, for this idea filled her, not as it should have done with joy, but with an empty, sinking feeling of dread.

"Murchad," she said, in agony at her confusion, "I will live for that day."

CHAPTER 15

⟨T⟩he High King and those chieftains secure in the North and West remained silent; and, as far as Leinster and the neighbouring provinces were concerned, the superiority of the Norman arms and the Welsh bowmen was so overwhelming that there was very little resistance against them. Only in rare cases did whole septs, such as the MacGillingrouths', flee in order to regroup and continue in the defence of their lands. The majority of belaghs seemed not to mind about their change of master. In many cases this proved to be the substitution of a stronger, often more kindly stranger, for the familiar chieftains, who had frequently been unable, or unwilling, to protect their homes – a question also, of exchanging lives of constant fighting for ones of comparative peace.

Life for those peasants under the control of Robert FitzAlan or Reginald d'Evreux, both renowned for their humane treatment of their men and workers, offered great compensations and Gossard's Ford Castle, nearing completion, promised them protection for the future.

Robert was relieved to be free from his constant campaigning and decided to pay his long-awaited visit on Aileen. No sooner had he reached this decision however, when he received word from Reginald d'Evreux, requesting his help in conquering lands further to the west.

This additional campaigning successfully completed, Robert had time again to think about Aileen. Feeling unusually light-hearted he hurried home, planning to go immediately to Whitley and claim her. Strongbow, however, had plans of his own, which inevitably involved Robert and his men, and further weeks of campaigning ensued, delaying his plans still further.

Disturbing news from Dublin indicated that the King was still suspicious of Strongbow; he refused to make the Earl his representative in the more recently conquered territories, and instead promoted the interests of Hugh de Lacy in neighbouring Meath as a counter-poise.

Henry of England, ensconced meantime in a palace built for him outside Dublin, spent his days over Christmas feasting those Irish kings and chieftains who came to the capital to acknowledge his overlordship. The feasting continued into the New Year and Henry imagined that all Ireland was truly his, the alliance with the native kings being, he thought, the perfect check on the appetites of his Norman Barons. This royal opinion was further enhanced by the Irish bishops, who, meeting in Cashel, pledged their support to the English King and his reforms upon the church. These reforms, as it happened, proved to be his greatest success, for contrary to his belief, Henry's presence in Ireland had had little effect in firming up his hold on the country. The Irish, outwardly amenable, merely paid him lip service and saw, in their agreements, a promise of support against the Norman baronage.

Disaffection at home in England, especially among his own sons, caused Henry to curtail his Irish adventure long before he was able to complete his work. Assuming that his presence and the size of his army had ensured his hold on Ireland, he decided to return to England. He marched to Wexford, embarking on Easter Monday after first appointing royal constables to guard the lands handed over to him by Strongbow. Robert himself was little affected by these politics, having received royal approval on all his holdings.

By the beginning of the New Year, King Henry realised, to his dismay, that Ireland was not united under his rule. Another visit was necessary, but affairs in England and on the continent demanded his attention and a further Irish expedition had to be postponed indefinitely. Thus Ireland had to be left to the Norman barons and this meant Leinster continued under Strongbow's rule.

Left in comparative peace, Robert was able to complete his work in Loswellery. The castle at Gossard's Ford was soon finished and he settled to the life of a local magnate. He had learned from a travelling priest that Aileen had long since left the Priory of Whitley and determined to visit Aifel as soon as he could, hoping to glean some news of her.

Aifel was surprised to hear the visitor in the refectory had come expressly to talk to her and fear left her tongue-tied as Robert greeted her in friendly fashion.

106

"I've come to discover the whereabouts of your daughter Aileen," he said, his mannerly approach softening Aifel. She regarded him seriously and found herself pleasantly disposed toward him. Still young, he was moreover handsome and powerful and she wouldn't ever forget that it was he who had rescued Aileen and herself from almost certain death. She remembered too the care and solicitude with which he had brought them to Whitley and in so doing, given her a new lease on life. Whitley was a Norman refuge and, separated from the venom with which her kinspeople still regarded it, she now viewed Normal rule as inevitable and largely benign. All of which influenced her to look kindly upon the young man seated before her.

"May I ask, my lord, why you seek my daughter?" She looked at him coolly.

"I need a wife, your daughter suits my needs."

A wife! Aifel looked up at him, astounded. How strongly her daughter was able to influence the most unlikely of men.

"Why Aileen?" she continued, emboldened by his manner. She noticed, with another small shock, the way his face softened as he thought about her question. Why, he loves her, she thought, delighting in the knowledge. She had known what it was to love and be loved, long ago, when she was fourteen, but Rory had wanted her and her father had wanted him as a son-in-law; her lover had died later in a fight against the MacTillings. She had never forgotten the warm feelings he had awoken in her, and was forcibly reminded of them by this powerful lord.

"She is beautiful, why not?" he said, in answer to her question.

"Aileen escaped from here over a year ago," Aifel told him, "she was going to return to Seandale. I heard she finally met up with her father at Trigonnel's Point and as far as I know they're still there." She thought with nostalgia of her sons, who would be nearing their thirteenth year by now. Grown up without her. And Aileen at seventeen, how did she fare? She realised how much she missed the close relationship which had sprung up between them during their time together at Whitley, and thought that if this lord was being honest with her, there was a good chance she might see her again.

Robert rode home thoughtfully. Trigonnel's Point – of course she would be there. But the mention of this stronghold had alerted him to other problems which he had been meaning to deal with for some weeks. Emboldened by the return of the King of England to his own country, the Irish had shown signs of rising against their Norman oppressors. Many of their raids had been made from Trigonnel's Point, where it was now known that many dissenting Irish were gathered. It was perhaps time to launch an attack on the stronghold, securing his lands once and for all. In the process he would recapture Aileen and fulfil what was rapidly becoming an over-riding ambition with him.

From a small seed of interest, a strong sapling of desire had taken hold, fed and watered by his continual dreaming and the barriers which had prevented Robert from having Aileen.

CHAPTER 16

For several weeks Robert had kept a vigilant look-out on the surrounding countryside, expecting an O'Flerty attack at any time, but it never came. He left the castle one fine morning to take a walk. The vast expanse of sky was lilac, the long grass swayed in a gentle breeze which turned its tips to silver, a skylark soared above his head and broke into glorious song. All around him seemed peaceful and drowsy.

A small herd of swine grazed at the edge of the wood and Robert observed them with detachment as they moved amongst the trees, a vague unease niggling at the back of his mind. He looked back up at the castle, suddenly aware that his armour and sword were there and he was armed only with a short sword. With the intuition of the soldier, he tried to identify the source of his discomfort, turning his eyes once more to the pigs rooting in the wood, then to those nearer. Something was definitely wrong, but he could not pin-point it. Robert stepped backwards toward the castle, his eyes still searching for a clue and it hit him, at the very moment they broke cover. The shapes in the distant wood were far too large to be pigs, why had he not seen this immediately?

His preparations at last complete, O'Flerty had led forth his men. Knowing the countryside he had lost no time in passing through the forest and marshlands that separated the Irish stronghold from the grasslands of Gossard's Ford. By keeping to the high ground and marching only by night, he had avoided contact with any who might possibly warn the enemy. And in this manner the Irish force had been able to come to within a short distance of the castle, their approach effectively masked by the trees surmounting the heights of Meath. With no indication that they had been spotted, the prospects for success looked good.

They burst from cover in a wild, whooping mass, the pale sunlight shining on their spears and on the helmets and occasional coat of mail purloined from Norman casualties in previous conflicts. Unnoticed at first, they quickly scattered those who stood in their path, cutting them down ruthlessly, indifferent to the fact that many were native Irish, their own people, some from the MacGillingrouth sept itself.

The sea of Irish swept onward, their objective to forge the dyke which separated the palisades from the open fields; and this they did with very little resistance. Once over the dyke they began to meet stiffer resistance as the guards finally grouped under the massive attack and sought to stem the advancing forces. The archers, from the height of the tower-top, shot deadly accurate arrows into their midst, while the Irish put lit torches to the wooden structure in an attempt to set fire to the castle.

Robert, once he had realised that the O'Flerty men were almost upon him, turned to run for the castle, dreadfully aware that he was too far away to reach safety before the castle gates were shut against the Irish. He joined with the other jostling and screaming bodies who, like himself, were unarmed.

The Irish, excited by the anticipation of victory, swarmed over the bretsche, some engaging in hand-to-hand fighting with those of the castle guard who were defending the outside walls. Their torch-bearers continually hurled torches upon the tower and already small fires were breaking out, the smoke rising in spirals to the sky.

Robert reached the gate just as they closed behind the guard and for a moment he hesitated, at a loss to know what to do. He was forced into action by a horse and rider coming straight for him and Robert froze. He stood, with his legs slightly bent, his short sword in the air above him, waiting until the last moment to see which way the Irishman would lunge and to be near enough to usefully parry any attack. The horse was almost on top of him and he saw the sword lifted ready to be brought down on his head. Robert still stood his ground and as the sword fell he ducked and swiped viciously with his own weapon. It met, with a sickening crunch, against the man's lower leg, which immediately gaped open showing the gleaming white of his shin bone, before blood spurted out, masking the wound. The man screamed in agony and fell from his horse. Unimpeded by his armour, Robert quickly mounted in his place, dragging the sword from the wounded man's hand as he did so.

He wheeled the horse around, to be faced by a horde of screaming

Irishmen. He felt a wave of desolation wash over him as he realised the extent of the attack, unaware that things were already turning in the castle's favour. The men on the tower had had little problem in putting out the fires and had now boiled huge cauldrons of water, which they were tipping onto the Irishmen below.

The Irish were disordered and Patrick O'Flerty rode to the head of them, trying to rally his men. Murchad, riding just behind him, felt a surge of pride and affection for the valiant old man whose voice was having such a rejuvenating effect on his troops as he rode through the thick of battle, one arm raised high, his fist clenched. Murchad saw the arrow coming. With devastating accuracy it hit Patrick in the eye and he collapsed instantly. Murchad watched in horror as the men fell silent then began to panic. He looked around for Rory, but couldn't find him. In desperation he turned his men back towards the shelter of the wood.

Robert, growing weary in the face of the opposition, fought bravely to make some ground, but a violent blow from a well-aimed club felled him from his horse and he landed almost at Murchad's feet. He heard the Irishman shout, "Take him alive," before a glaring red light infused his vision and he fell back, unconscious.

He came to, his whole body shrieking in agony, and opened his eyes: the pain in his head was so overwhelming that he closed them immediately and quickly blacked out again. When he once again regained consciousness, he raised his hand to his head, very slowly, and felt a huge lump. Taking his hand away he saw that blood stained his fingers.

Fighting down waves of nausea he heard the sound of birdsong and men talking. He was lying on grass. Eventually daring to open his eyes again he saw the branches of a mighty oak above his head and assumed that he was in the woods west of the castle. He could hear Gaelic voices around him, lamenting their defeat and the death of their leader and for a moment he rejoiced, thankful that his castle had been saved.

A man sauntered over to where he lay and looked down on him. He kicked him with the toe of his booted foot and Robert moaned in pain. "He's awake," the man shouted, and others grouped about him, their bodies looking long and threatening from Robert's supine position.

"Murchad wishes him kept alive. Give him water and watch him closely."

Robert wondered in a confused fashion why they should wish to do so, but thanked God for his redemption. The man held a drinking vessel to Robert's lips and watched as he drank greedily. When he'd finished his captor turned Robert over with his foot, tied his hands behind him with a leather thong and sat watching him dispassionately.

Soon he was bundled unceremoniously onto the back of a horse, his head throbbing dreadfully as it bounced with the animal's movement. After an agonizingly long, slow and dejected march they arrived at Trigonnel's Point.

Robert was aware of the large group of townspeople who immediately surrounded them and of their despair at learning their leader had fallen. He could make Murchad's voice out, above the rest.

"Did Rory MacGillingrouth return?"

The huddles of people grew quiet, turning their heads to look at one another.

"Did anyone see Rory MacGillingrouth?" Murchad repeated, his voice ringing out clearly over the camp.

"My father has not returned, Murchad, and I see yours has not either."

Robert recognised her distinctive voice easily and turned his head painfully to where she stood. She was dressed richly, wearing a flowing robe, and with some kind of carved jewel in her hair. Murchad dismounted and went to her. She put her arm around him and kissed him tenderly. An empty feeling filled Robert, died and filled him again as he watched them walk away from the crowd, arm in arm.

Eventually Robert was dragged from his horse's back, half led, half carried, to a small hut amongst a group behind a wooden fence, and thrown inside. He sank gratefully to the floor, incapable of any emotion other than relief that his journey had now terminated, so he could shut his eyes and block out the searing pain.

Robert was puzzled. After some days of imprisonment, during which he had remained confined in the semi-darkness of the hut, there had been no indication of what his fate was to be. The Irish were well-known for their summary and drastic treatment of their prisoners and yet he still lived. He wondered about the intentions of his captors, arriving at the notion that they must intend to hold him hostage for some reason; though ransom was not a practice of the Irish they must have some sort of barter in mind to continue to hold him in this way.

His imprisonment was uncomfortable in the extreme: he remained bound hand and foot and was untied only to enable him to eat his meal – if meal was the right description, for he often gagged in trying to swallow the food. The days passed by slowly. He was bored and afraid, uncertain of his future and in a great deal of pain from his wounds, which were exacerbated by his bonds.

When he could manage to keep conscious for long enough, he questioned his guards about Aileen. Some were taciturn, some brutal in their response, but one young man, obviously besotted by his leader's woman, gave him a very clear picture of her situation. Aileen had become a person of great importance, he explained. Prior to the battle her father Rory had achieved more status than of recent years: due largely to her influence he had become Murchad's right hand man, for Murchad was deeply enamoured of her. Everyone had been amazed that such a man could be so obsessed with one particular woman. And yet, the guard sighed wistfully, she was possessed of a strange power over men. Even the Giant, the mighty Cashal who had the strength of ten men, had fallen for her – perhaps courting danger and hostility had enhanced their relationship, for he had had opposition.

Robert pieced together the story, realising that the man he had killed must have been this Giant – Cashal – who had become a legend in his own right, and Aileen with him. He tossed and turned in fevered sleep, and often thought of her.

Murchad and Aileen occupied two rooms of the household and Tara, his wife, rarely saw them. His sexual appetite was seemingly more than serviced by the passionate girl. Before Aileen, Tara had already shared him with two concubines, though as far as she could see he had not since visited any of his women, and Tara found it in her heart to be grateful that he had never made herself the object of such desire.

"Good morning," she said as Aileen emerged, flushed and tousled, from her rooms. Tara was baking bread and handed Aileen a piece, which she accepted with a pleased smile. Pouring herself some water, Aileen went to the door of the hut to eat and drink. She looked down at the village below her, almost lost in a fine drizzle which fell persistently, merging the fresh green of the trees with the rich hues of the grass and the violet of the hill which dominated the stronghold and gave it its name. The mighty boulders of granite which lay scattered indiscriminately on the ground appeared woolly, like lost sheep, and Aileen found herself wondering how they had come to be there. Had some mighty giant, busy with the creation of Ireland, found himself left with these boulders and flung them into the air, to stay forever where they landed?

Tara observed Aileen as she stood deep in thought, and wondered what bothered the girl, for despite Aileen's vivacity, she often gained the impression that she only pretended happiness and that some deep problem occupied her mind.

"Are you thinking of the Giant?" Tara asked, out of the blue. Aileen jumped, wondering how on earth Tara had so accurately read her mind.

"Why yes," she said, whirling around in surprise. As she did so she realised that Tara referred not to her idle daydream, but to Cashal.

Tara walked solicitously over and put her arms round Aileen. "Was he

113

so important to you?"

Aileen didn't know how to answer, for in truth she had already forgotten her sorrow at his death. "No, please don't be concerned, I'm very happy as I am." Some quirk infused her words with a hint of pathos and Tara, she was sure, interpreted this as a brave front.

The pathos came not from Cashal the Giant, but from her memory of the young Norman knight dragged into a hut and forgotten many days ago. Seeing him helpless beneath Murchad's guard had softened any remaining anger. She had started to view him as her mother did, as a man who had successfully interceded to save her life. Now she wanted to do the same for him. She was unwilling to see him die and to feel herself indebted; her pride demanded that she repay him in kind for his treatment of her.

She knew that the only reason he had been kept alive was to use as barter in the event that the Normans were holding her father. More frivolous demands were being made as well, such as the return of his Loswellery lands, but no one seriously thought these would be met; and so, on the news of Rory's death, or in the event of his walking back into the village, Robert would be tortured to death.

Aileen knew that she would have to tread carefully. Murchad had become increasingly possessive and jealous, and she was wary of appearing to be interested in other men. She had thought at first about pleading for Robert's life, but quickly shelved the idea, remembering how vehemently she had originally professed to Murchad her hatred of him.

Last night, tentatively testing the waters and careful not to appear concerned about the outcome of the conversation, she had broached the subject. They had been lying passive, his arm protectively around her following a wild lovemaking which had pleased them both immeasurably, and she said idly:

"How is your prisoner faring, Murchad?"

"He is still alive, but barely," was the casual response.

"Have you news of my father?"

"No news, we still don't know if he is being held at the castle, or if he was slain during the fighting. I had the knight beaten, to get him to give us information but he was obstinate," a note of grudging respect crept into his voice.

"Information?" she said, "On what? He cannot know any more than we do."

"He can tell us who runs the castle, but he chooses to remain silent."

"Perhaps our men were overly enthusiastic in the beating and failed to make clear that it was for his own good."

Murchad laughed, knowing the hatred his men bore the Norman: this was quite likely.

"Would you like me to try – after all, it is my father we are trying to save," her voice wobbled tearfully, "and I can do no worse."

"You are fond of your father, aren't you?" he said gently, "And I have been remiss with regard to your feelings. You've said nothing on the subject before."

"Because I trust your judgement and I wish only to serve both you and my father."

"Then why not try?" he said. "Go tomorrow and see what a pretty face can achieve, which a cudgel can not." He squeezed her salaciously and kissed her. She pressed her body against him, making him forget anything but his desire.

Aileen was eager to help with the household chores that morning, nervously delaying the moment she must approach Robert. Her dreams made her feel uncomfortable about being anywhere near him and for this reason she was acutely embarrassed at the thought of facing him.

The drizzle had turned into heavy rain by the time she set off, and she pulled her cloak over her head, running through the mud to the hut where he was imprisoned.

"Let me in. I have to talk to the prisoner," she said to the guard. He looked anxiously at her. He had orders to let no one in, but this was the chief's woman. "Come on, man, I don't have all day," she said imperiously.

"I'll have to check with Murchad," he said apologetically. She stamped her foot but the man, a stickler for rules and probably chosen because of this, remained adamant. He called for another guard before going to find Murchad and she went with him, furious at being thwarted in this way.

"Murchad, this man will not allow me to see the Norman," she said, forestalling the guard. "I have gone all that way, and in the rain, for no apparent reason." Her eyes flashed in fury.

"You told me to watch him and let no one in," the man said, his voice surly.

"And what did you think I was going to do – walk out with him under my cloak? Do you not trust my word when I say Murchad has asked me to talk with him." She looked from him to Murchad, her attitude uncompromising.

"Let Aileen in," Murchad said curtly, annoyed at seeing Aileen so distressed. "And in future, there is no reason why her word should be doubted, remember that."

They walked back, the rain now seeping through her cloak and running down the back of her neck.

"I'll come in with you," the guard said, as she made to push past him.

"No. I shall go in alone." He started to demur but she again stamped her foot. "Don't make me return, in the rain, to seek permission I already have," she said threateningly and the man warily opened the door and stepped back for her to enter.

The hut was dark and smelled foul, for Robert hadn't been allowed out since his confinement. She could hear the sound of flies buzzing angrily. It took some moments for her to detect him: the window was designed to let in air, not light. When her eyes had adjusted to the gloom she saw him slumped against a wall, a beard disguising his formerly clean-shaven face, his hair tangled and lousy. She drew her breath sharply, surprised that anyone could have survived for so long in such conditions. He was staring at her, his eyes demented. She drew her cloak closely round her body and backed away, suddenly afraid that he had lost his mind.

He had paid little attention to the movement outside his hut – women often brought the guards their food, so he was used to the sound of their voices. His bruises, which he had received at the hands of three of the guards, were sore, and his arms and wrists hurt abominably from the leather thongs which still bound them. To keep himself sane and to try to alleviate some of his sufferings, he had turned to spiriting his mind to faraway places. He often thought about his mother or imagined he was riding his great war-horse into battle. He thought of his castle and the little river which meandered past its walls, through the sweet, heather-scented fields of Loswellery. And he dreamed of Aileen.

He looked up now and saw her face shining palely in the gloom. He tried to spring to his feet but was far too weak; his legs bent lifeless beneath him so that he leaned against the wall and pushed himself up, his progress slow and painful – humiliating too, beneath her unwavering stare.

She waited until he was standing before she spoke. Her voice was compassionate. "Are you well?"

"I am imprisoned, with all that that entails," he said.

"And they have hurt you?"

"I'm improving, thank you."

"You get enough to eat?" It was obvious he didn't. Where was the mighty lord who had ridden to her rescue? This man would be pitied by the peasants in the fields.

"I get all I can eat," he amended. He was unable to eat more than enough to keep him propped against his wall; the food must have been rejected by the swine before reaching his hovel.

She regarded him levelly, noting the inference without comment. They fell into pained silence. There was both too much to say, and too little. She appeared to him a shining angel, her face and body healthy and even more

116

beautiful than he had dreamed; and he to her so poor and pathetic a relic of his former self that her heart was turned to pity and she desired nothing other than to see him freed and restored to his former glory. Then her obligation would have been met and the old score evened out.

"I've come to try and help you," she said.

"For what purpose?"

"Because you saved my mother and took her to a place where she has been happy. She wanted you to know her gratitude."

"And you?"

"I was unhappy and escaped." She by-passed his meaning, preferring to keep her feelings buried.

"I saw your mother."

"And was she well?" – So, he had returned to Whitley for her.

"She told me where I might find you. I believe she thought I'd make a good match for you."

"You are Norman, and I, Irish. You have conquered my people and stolen our lands, how would I wish to make a match with you?"

"Because I'm the conqueror, Aileen," his voice was filled with pride, but then he looked ruefully at himself, stinking and wizened, and laughed briefly before continuing. "And it is not unheard of – many Norman knights have taken Irish women to be their wives."

"I am already a woman of power. Murchad, who is chief here, is my man and I have all I want." Returning to the reason for her visit, she said, "But I owe you a debt of gratitude and if I can, I'll try to help you."

He wanted to thank her but the words stuck in his throat. He said nothing and she stood a long while, waiting for a response, before she continued. "Do you know why I am here?"

Robert didn't answer.

"My father is Rory MacGillingrouth. He fought in the Battle of Loswellery – he has been missing since then. They think he's being held at Gossard's Ford."

"And your powerful chief Murchad sent you to find a way of securing his release." Robert sounded bitter. He closed his eyes and leaned wearily back against the wall. Aileen was offering him her help, it now seemed futile to withhold his any longer. "You'll need to talk to my servant Silas Strongarm, but he'll want evidence that I am here."

"Then be careful they don't cut off your ear as proof."

"He knows my ear no better than yours, it would prove nothing."

She smiled despite her hard resolve and he thought how much it enhanced her already exceptional looks.

"I must go. If I can I will return. You are safe for the time being, so keep well."

117

"Keep well, Aileen." His voice was wistful, she didn't know why.

Robert watched her leave the hut cool and unaffected, clearly only interested in fulfilling her obligations and repaying her debt to him. She was a woman of power, proud and emotionless, save for that one tiny smile.

He had a chance, he had a chance. His heart leaped at the thought of freedom; his blood raced with the now unaccustomed thrill of having something new to think about. But the exhilarations passed quickly and left him wilted. He sank to the ground.

"Murchad," Aileen said as she passed him a platter of food. "The prisoner talked."

"And – "

"And I know who you should contact at the castle to obtain my father's release."

"Good, you've done well."

"But, if you continue to abuse him as you are doing, he will die, and you will lose your bargaining strength."

"What's wrong with his treatment?"

"He's been beaten and starved. He's still bound hand and foot and he looks as though he will lose his mind."

"It's not easy for a man of action to be imprisoned, but madness is perhaps the best he can hope for."

"And no more than the bastard deserves," she said, "but we must not let him die, Murchad. Forgive me, but I fear for my father."

"See to it then that he has better treatment. Keep him alive, while I start further negotiations with the castle."

She kissed him, put food into his mouth, poured wine down his throat and laughingly made him forget Robert FitzAlan. But later that night she dreamt of him and awoke as she had used to do, filled with desire. She stood at her window looking out at the slumbrous night with its deep purply-brown skies. It's only during the night that I think this way, she persuaded. Then she forced herself to think of Robert as he now was, humiliated and humbled by his captivity. Yet still able to say, "I am the conqueror," and laugh.

CHAPTER 17

People were talking in huddles about her influence over Murchad. His brothers, seeking to belittle him and thereby obtain power for themselves, called him the MacGillingrouth Puppet; but other factions admired Aileen, for she kept the MacGillingrouth interests at heart – and she had been the Giant's woman. Cashal had greater influence on the tribes now than he had done during life, with many a young man seeking to compare his own achievements with those of the Giant, whose heroic exploits had grown beyond the abilities of any mere mortal.

As a mark of his affection and to remind others of her special position, Murchad had given Aileen a slave of her own, Lys, an English girl from the Bristol area, who was intended to serve as companion and maid. Captured while still a child, Lys was fully prepared to devote herself to Aileen's service, preferring the life of comparative comfort to which she was now introduced to the drudgery of her previous existence. She was an intelligent girl and within weeks a strong bond of affection had developed between them.

Murchad meanwhile spent increasing amounts of time with his fellow chiefs. Despite the failure of the attack on Gossard's Ford, the damage to its village which had been growing alarmingly and the capture of FitzAlan, had boosted his reputation, enabling him to hold his own against those who criticised his rule. Large numbers of men, however, had come to Trigonnel's Point to assist in the assault on Robert's castle and these now presented something of a liability. They continually frustrated the smooth running of the chieftaincy, opposed Murchad's apparently incomprehensible reluctance to execute FitzAlan and added fuel to the dissension which simmered beneath the surface of the Irish camp.

Robert's lot had altered rapidly, following Aileen's visit. His food had improved, both in quality and quantity, and his bonds were left off. At first he thought they had forgotten to re-tie him, but when they brought his next meal and still made no move to tie his hands, he himself loosened the thongs around his ankles and no one paid any attention. The following day he was taken from his hut into the fresh air and allowed to exercise for one hour. He ignored the jibes and taunts of the men and women who passed by, pleased only to see the light of day once more and feel his cramped muscles stretch. He was frequently taken around the encampment during his hour of freedom and he made a mental note of its layout, his dreams of escape embellished by the new regime.

Back again in the confines of his solitary prison, Robert's thoughts naturally dwelt on the woman who had been responsible for these changes. With nothing to occupy his mind during the long hours of semi-darkness, he recalled again and again the first time he had set eyes on her, comparing her to the woman she had now become. He longed to possess her and fantasized fiercely throughout his hours of sleep, so that dawn each morning found him unrested and frustrated almost beyond endurance.

As week succeeded week however, any hope of exchanging Robert for Rory diminished and Murchad's other desire – to gain repossession of the Loswellery cantreds – came to nought. Silas, under considerable pressure from the Leinster baronage, found it impossible to follow his natural inclination to help Robert. Indeed the outcome of the whole business served only to inflame and renew foreign aggression. D'Evreux and the others refused outright to negotiate and there were rumours of an assault on the Irish stronghold, a retaliation against their attack on Gossard's Ford.

In the circumstances Murchad yielded to the general demand for the death of his prisoner. Robert's fate was sealed as soon as the decision had been made, and as if to endorse this Rory reappeared at the camp, limping heavily but grinning broadly in his pleasure at having come home.

"Rory, for the love of God, where have you been hiding, man?" said Murchad, delighted to see his friend.

"My leg was smashed in the fighting. God alone knows how, but I managed to get back into the woods. I was delirious by then, wandering around absolutely out of my mind. One of the belagh's found me," he winked at Murchad. "It pays to spread your seed, I've always found. She hid me, took care of me until I was fit again. We dared trust no one with the news I was still alive."

"Then you were never the captive of the Norman bastards?"

"Never. Why?"

"They let us believe you were. We held FitzAlan here in return for our lands, and for yourself."

"They'll never let go of our lands. And as for myself – here I am, hail, hearty and thirsty for Norman blood."

"Then let him die at first light," grinned Murchad.

Aileen came into the room at that moment and flung her arms round her father's neck and kissed him. She had overheard what Murchad had said and though she was pleased to see that Rory was alive, she now doubted her ability to save the Norman. Desperately she racked her brain for her next move.

"Your daughter has served you very well, Rory. She's been a fine substitute for you."

"A pity she wasn't born a boy," said Rory, grudgingly.

"No, indeed it is not," said Murchad, squeezing her affectionately. Rory laughed.

"Shall you be coming to bed early tonight, Murchad?" asked Aileen, after her father had left to be reunited with his sons.

"No, I daresay we'll be late. We have some serious talking to do now that Rory is home."

Aileen sighed with relief – serious talk, maybe, but accompanied with serious drink. Irish whisky was strong, and they would soon be oblivious to everything around them.

Pretending to be asleep, she waited for a long while until the men were ensconced in their council rooms and only when she was sure the household was settled and could hear Lys gently snoring in the other room, did she go to the guard outside Robert's prison.

"You see my father has come home," she said conversationally. The man was a MacGillingrouth and smiled at her in pleasure.

"And the Norman bastard will die tomorrow," he spat in disdain.

"Murchad and my father are talking right now about how best to dispose of him and I feel at a loss, for I have no one with whom to share my great relief at my father's return."

The man looked at her fine body, her full breasts and welcoming eyes.

"Here," she said, " will you not take a drink with me, to welcome him back?"

"I will indeed," he felt flattered to be thus approached.

Aileen watched the guard as he grew steadily more drunk and more careless. When she next handed him a drink she brushed herself against him and let out a moan of pleasure. He forgot himself and fondled her breast and she raised up for a kiss. He needed no more, and pulled her to him.

"Oh, God," she said, "I had forgotten what an attractive man you are. But we daren't, for if Murchad found out he would kill us both."

"He'll never know from me that you have even been near this place," he said, his breath coming in short gasps.

She handed him a drink. "Let's sit quiet for a while, until the village sleeps, and then – "

" – and then," he said, laughing and taking another drink from her flagon.

Soon, having drunk too much in his anticipation, he fell to the floor and started gently snoring. She poked and then shook him to see if he was likely to awaken. He grunted and turned away.

She burst in on Robert, who was asleep. "You must leave now, whilst all the men are busy planning how you will die."

He was jerked awake by the urgency in her voice, her words sinking in slowly at first, then with a rapidity which brought him hastily to his feet. "Aileen!"

"Wake up, quick," she cried, seemingly unaware he was already standing. She was shaking from head to toe, knowing that if she was caught her relationship with Murchad would not save her. Only God knew how he would react to her treachery. But it was too late now, and she was as confident as she could be that tempting the guard to make advances toward her had created a sure accomplice.

"I'm awake," he said, his eyes alert in the light of the torch she held low to the ground.

"My father has returned. Tonight they are drinking and planning – tomorrow you will die," she repeated, her voice studiously calm as if she were talking to a young child.

Robert hurried to the open door and looked around cautiously: the guard slumbered on. He turned back to her, his eyebrows lifting, questioning.

"Drunk," she explained, "now goodbye, just get out of here."

He ran once more to the door and she saw his form disintegrate in the dark. She put her hand to her heart, feeling its steady thump, thump. She felt sick.

"Aileen?" the voice made her jump, terrified at being discovered in that place; but it was Robert.

"Please go," she said, her voice conveying for the first time her acute fear.

He took her face between his hands and looked into her eyes. Then he bent and kissed her, gently at first, then with a fire and passion which made her legs tremble. She was reminded forcibly of her dream for it was being enacted now, in reality.

"Thank you," his voice was only breath in her ear, and she was suddenly cold and alone for he had gone.

Once outside, Aileen drank in huge mouthfuls of the pristine air, feeling it fan her flushed cheeks. A fine rain fell on her and she lifted her face toward the heavens, letting their peace still her fears. Then, on feet which made no sound, she ran home. Lys was peacefully sleeping, just as she had left her, and she crept into bed, pulling the sheepskin around her comfortingly.

She slept eventually, once her fear had fully left her and once she had stopped re-enacting that final embrace to which she had responded so readily. When Murchad returned, unsteadily climbing into bed, she embraced him fiercely and cried out, with tears in her eyes, for him to love her.

"What's wrong?" he asked, pleased and surprised, the room spinning around him.

"Nothing at all, now you are here and my father is home safe." She held him tightly and his weight on her increased, for he had fallen into a drunken sleep.

CHAPTER 18

Robert stood on the edge of the forest looking back at the camp. He was grateful that he had had the opportunity to learn the layout during his exercise periods; without that he could have blundered about in the darkness and risked recapture.

He breathed freely for the first time since he had left his prison and a feeling of elation almost overwhelmed him. He could still feel the pliancy of Aileen's body, held all too briefly against his, but more importantly he had felt her response, given spontaneously, before she had had time to think.

He wasted no more than a few moments to regain his breath, before plunging on into the thick of the trees, determined to put as great a distance as possible between himself and Trigonnel's Point. Pursuit, he was sure, would not start until after daybreak.

It was too dark for him to follow any direction. He could only hope he hadn't turned back toward the stronghold, but he was horribly aware that he could be running in circles. He tripped often on the undergrowth and his arms and hands were soon covered in jagged cuts. As the first hint of dawn broke, he settled for a short rest in a disused badger's set, pulling leaves over his body for warmth and concealment. It was a basic shelter, but he did sleep briefly.

As soon as he woke up he continued his journey, his stiff limbs slowly loosening as he ran – then walked – following the direction of the rising sun. He stopped often to drink water from the many streams which wound through the trees, and searched the bushes for berries but could find none. Although he saw many rabbits he had no weapon with which to slay them. In any case he had no way of lighting a fire.

Nothing except the noises of unseen animals in the undergrowth disturbed the silence and he felt utterly alone, moving in a world of semi-darkness, for the day was dull and the foliage thick above his head. As the day crept on Robert's hunger grew. Kneeling by a stream he saw a bunch of wild cress and quickly devoured it. It did little to appease his hunger and he spent a good deal of time staring into the rapidly flowing water, looking for fish. He plunged his hand in and although he touched the scales of one, it was too quick for him and darted out of his grasp.

Desperate, not just from that day's hunger, but with the knowledge that a long journey lay before him, he sat to consider his situation. Though he had walked for hours he had no way of knowing if he had always travelled away from Trigonnel's Point, although he couldn't see the beacon. He realised with some dismay that he would have to subsist on those roots and plants which he could identify as edible until he reached his own lands. A man could survive on water alone for several days, he thought, but he'd have to conserve energy as much as possible and concentrate on the position of the sun to check his bearings if he were not to waste precious time going round in circles.

Soon the twilight darkness deepened. The night sky, filled with stars, blinked at him from between the tree tops, and finally, lodging himself between two large rocks, he slept.

Thus, sleeping by night and walking by day, he made slow progress through the forest, certain he was lost, despairing of ever reaching home. He was weak and disorientated from lack of food and had to rest often until his head cleared, for he was plagued by dizzy spells. Sometimes when he stopped he was sure he heard leaves crackling behind him, as if someone were following in his tracks, and he tried to convince himself that this was another tedious effect that hunger was having upon his senses. This didn't fully pacify him though, and he found himself continually turning, expecting to see something loom up at him out of the bushes. He trembled with an indefinable fear, brought on by isolation and dread of the unknown, which drenched him with perspiration and left him despising his craven weakness.

Robert finally came face to face with his demon when he looked around at dusk for somewhere to sleep. A man, clad in furs and carrying a stave, was staring out at him from the protection of a bush, his eyes wild and furtive. Robert jumped back, and would have fallen but for the trunk of a tree which supported him. When he had pulled himself together he looked up into a pair of strikingly blue eyes set in a leathery, weather-beaten face, which was almost consumed by a huge shaggy beard.

Robert was overwhelmed by a feeling of relief to see his demon was no more than a flesh and blood man and felt laughter tugging at the corners of his own mouth and bubbling in his chest. The man smiled back at him, seemingly unsurprised by this unusual welcome.

"Thank God you are real!" Robert said, then more formally he added, "Peace be with you."

The man smiled broadly at him. His answer was slow and careful, as though he were unaccustomed to speech, and Robert had to listen hard before he could decipher it. "Who are you?" – the words were punctuated by expansive gestures.

"My name is Robert." He too spoke very slowly, looking all the while into the man's eyes. "I'm lost – a trader – looking for the Norman Castle at Gossard's Ford."

"Gossard's Ford," the man repeated.

"Can you help me find my way back?" Robert instinctively liked the man and was pathetically grateful for his company. The other nodded again, his head moving exaggeratedly. They communicated in this way for some time and eventually laid down for the night.

Robert woke in the morning, just before dawn had lightened the sky, to smell food roasting. For a moment he thought he was delirious again; his stomach growled and lurched and he tasted bile in his mouth. There was a fire burning, he could feel its heat on his face and hear fat spitting and hissing amidst whisps of blue smoke. Rising stiffly from the ground he walked over to the man who had so quickly become his friend and took the piece of rabbit which was offered. The meat was so hot it sizzled as it touched his skin and his mouth watered uncontrollably. He ate ravenously, heedless of the blisters which rose instantly in his mouth. When he'd eaten that he ate more, until his stomach ached from the food he'd consumed, then finally he washed it down with water from the stream which flowed past them.

After they had doused the fire Robert followed the stranger hoping his trust was not misplaced; his eyes automatically scanning in every direction in case he had been tricked into returning to Trigonnel's Point.

They talked, painfully at first, but Robert soon realised that he had no need to speak slowly, for the man, whose name he learned was Cormac, clearly understood and the more he spoke, the easier it became to understand him. He told Robert his story, as they tramped shoulder to shoulder through the trees.

"My brother is Donal MacTilling," he said, and Robert, on hearing the name, at once realised the similarity in their eyes. "When I was a young man I fell in love with Donal's wife, and because of this, and because Donal was afraid I would steal his position as chief, I was driven into exile." He swiped angrily at a branch with his stave. "I witnessed Donal's defeat at the hands of Tiernan O'Rourke and then became a mercenary, selling my sword to anyone who would pay."

He went on to talk of his war deeds. "I fell into disfavour yet again, through some misunderstanding with the Ard-ri himself and no one would talk to me at all after that. Eventually I returned to Leinster and have lived as an outcast in this forest of Thore ever since. I observed the Norman advance with pleasure. I watched as the new castle was built, and rejoiced. I saw old man O'Flerty killed in battle and as he's an old enemy of mine, I rejoiced again. There is little else for me to do, outcast in these woods." He laughed – he evidently had a great capacity for enjoyment.

Robert listened, without interrupting. He never doubted that he was hearing the truth, for the man had developed an air of simplicity over the years of his exile. He told Cormac his own tale and the man's eyes shone out at him from under his shaggy brows.

"Well, I knew you were Norman, of course," he said. "And I am glad I can help Robert FitzAlan."

"Why so?" Robert said, smiling, yet mistrustful still.

"For something to do and to hurt the O'Flerty's," he replied, clapping Robert on the back and almost knocking him to the ground.

Cormac, once he'd grown used to conversation again, proved to be an eloquent and prolific speaker, filling Robert's head with tales, old and new, of life in and around the forest. He knew a great deal of local history and legend, which he passed on with aplomb and the walk seemed neither so long, nor so tedious as it had before their meeting.

Robert had wandered way off course and it took them a further five days of travel to complete their journey, during which time he learned a great deal from the Irishman's resourcefulness and grew fond of him for his open cheerfulness and refusal to be daunted. The time passed swiftly and when they were within a day's walk of the castle, Robert made a decision.

"Cormac, do you wish to remain living in the forest?" he asked.

Cormac shrugged.

"I would like you to come back with me. I can find good use for a man such as yourself, and," Robert paused, unused to blandishments, "I wouldn't want to lose a good friend."

"Then I will come with you," Cormac replied with gratifying alacrity.

They were making their way slowly and carefully across the treacherous Sheen Marshes. Robert knew Cormac considered the Normans were here to stay and was pleased by his happy acceptance of this fact. Many of their Irish allies were reluctant ones, who had joined them as the lesser of two evils and Robert was always on his guard against treachery.

He had, along with the other barons who had burnt their bridges and come to settle in Ireland, little intention of ever returning to England to live, so a loyal Irish friend was of immeasurable value. He had come to love the green Loswellery countryside and despite his efforts to deny it, even to himself, he didn't want to leave the place where Aileen lived.

It was another full day before they reached the grasslands of the Loge Valley and came upon signs of habitation. Soon after this they were within the domains of the castle and Robert saw people he knew. With the familiarity born of long absence he welcomed them warmly, and by and large his friendship was reciprocated although they were clearly shocked at his unkempt appearance and by the fact that he was still alive. It had been late winter when they'd last seen him and now summer was taking over from spring.

Robert borrowed two farm horses from one of his tenant farmers and he and Cormac covered the last part of their journey in style, and at speed. They were greeted with surprise and great joy as they cantered through the castle's stockade gates, and word quickly reached the castle itself, bringing a grinning Silas out to greet them. Robert, having spent so long in solitary confinement before his strenuous journey through the forest, was almost moved to tears by the warm grasp of Silas's hand, and even Silas's eyes seemed suspiciously bright, although Robert dismissed this as having been caused by the sun, which was setting behind his back.

Robert had tubs of hot water brought up to him and he scrubbed off the grime and stench of months of deprivation, noticing for the first time the many scars and lumps which had become part of his once unblemished body. He cut off his beard with great relish, rubbing his hands carefully over his face, enjoying the feel of its contours beneath his fingers. When he met Cormac later he was surprised at the man's appearance, for he too had washed and changed, and trimmed his enormous grizzled beard, albeit with great reluctance.

"Sire, it's good to see you back in your rightful place," said Silas, holding up his wine cup in a toast. "I despaired of seeing you again. The Irish believed they could regain their land through holding you ransom, and they seemed to think we had the MacGillingrouth chief here. I bluffed them, but they grew tired of waiting and the barons refused to deal."

"They had no choice in the matter. One man can't be held to ransom against all the lands so grievously won – I would have done the same in their place."

"And how did you escape from that hell hole?" Silas asked, stuffing bread into his mouth, as if it were he who had been starved.

"Silas, you have changed not one wit. Your stomach is still your greatest love," laughed Robert, poking at him with his knife.

"And your love, sire, what is now your greatest love?"

Robert laughed and looked toward Cormac, who knew a little and had guessed a great deal of his feelings toward the O'Flerty chief's favourite woman.

"My castle you refer to? It is good to see her again, to find her still faithful to her master."

They laughed some more.

"Your escape, sire?" reminded Silas, and Robert, assisted by Cormac, began to fill him in on the details. Silas remained silent as they talked, but his hand was gripped to the hilt of his sword and his eyes were cold, the tension in his face deepening the lines which filled it.

It took no more than a few weeks for Robert to fully resume his old style of life. A tour of inspection of his lands convinced him of how effectively Silas had conducted his affairs during his imprisonment. Much of the destruction inflicted by O'Flerty's raid had been dealt with; the cattle that had survived looked sleek and the herd replenished; the work of restoration was moving swiftly and the cultivation of his lands, so rudely interrupted, had re-commenced; the life of Gossard's Ford had very quickly returned to normal.

Robert was fully occupied in riding around his territories and often chose to take Cormac with him, their friendship growing stronger daily. Initially, Silas and some of Robert's oldest supporters resented this, but Cormac's exceptionally open and friendly nature soon won them round, so much so, that Silas and Cormac soon became fast friends themselves. Later, when Robert made Cormac his steward, Silas was the first to support the choice. Cormac had changed his appearance beyond all recognition; the wild, unkempt and bearded figure of the woods was now indistinguishable from the rest of the castle's household. He adopted the short, Roman-style haircut of the Normans and his face was clean-shaven.

Robert never had cause to regret making Cormac steward, and he quickly became popular with the Irish workers, showing them understanding and sensitivity, which boded well for the future harmony of his estates. Silas retained command of the Gossard's Ford garrison, and despite his age remained active and alert, fully capable of acting as Robert's lieutenant whenever the need arose.

All in all, Robert considered himself well served, and his life, rich and full. Nevertheless, and to his great shame, he was unhappy. Aileen's image filled his mind night and day, underlying his actions and invading his dreams. He vowed to seek her out at the first opportune moment, but said nothing of this to anyone, fearing still – a remnant from his life in Wales – that he would become an object of ridicule.

PART TWO

1173 – 1180

CHAPTER 1

$\mathcal{L}$ife for Aileen at Trigonnel's Point was not without its worries. Despite the watchful care and protection of Murchad and the attention of Lys, who had become a devoted friend, things were not running as smoothly as she could have hoped.

The first few months of Murchad's chieftainship had seemed idyllic, with Aileen as royal favourite, queening it over the rest of the household. The hostility which had been building around Murchad since the Robert FitzAlan episode had not really affected her and in many ways she was happy.

Gradually she came to realise that there was a more disturbing feeling of discontent aimed against Murchad's chieftaincy and that she was generally held responsible for his faults: his growing love of comfort and his apparent irresolution. The idea of the barter had never been popular and Murchad's treatment of the Norman captive, the knowledge that Rory had not even been held by the Normans and the lax security which had allowed FitzAlan to escape – all had served only to add fuel to the fire. The whole issue had become a black mark against Murchad's ability to rule. Criticism was widespread, with Murchad's own brother, Turlough, at the very centre of it.

Aileen, once she was faced with the reality of her decision to help Robert escape, was torn between her pleasure that he had not been recaptured and a deep sense of disloyalty. She tried to assuage her guilt by giving Murchad all her love, lavishing it upon him freely, and in her own way she loved him truly.

Turlough had collected a considerable following of discontented tribesmen around him and had grown increasingly arrogant and hostile, his relationship with Murchad turning sour as a consequence; and the two were frequently at loggerheads in the war council. Another of their brothers, Murrough, surreptitiously sided with Turlough and secretly lusted after Aileen. She was uncomfortably aware of this, hating his devious nature.

Murrough and Murchad were deep in amicable conversation one night, sitting before the fire. The wine ran freely and Murrough's speech was liberally laced with words of affection for his brother. He was pleasant to Aileen throughout, including her politely, and smiling, almost fawning, upon her. His sugary manner didn't fool her: Murrough was making her feel increasingly nervous.

"Murchad," she said carefully, watching as Murrough's form disappeared into the darkness.

"Yes?"

"I worry that you are being taken in by your brother's duplicity. He wears two faces, you know. Are you not aware that he is one of your greatest opponents?" Her brows were closely knit, in concern.

"You have nothing to fear, Aileen," he said, his voice tender, though not hiding his evident amusement.

"Murchad, listen to me, this is no joke. Murrough is dangerous for us. You don't see the way he looks at me when you're out – you don't hear him talking in corners, but I'm telling you, he does. Turlough is not your only problem. Can you not see that what I say is true?"

He stared into the flames of the fire, his shoulders hunched, so that she couldn't read what was going through his mind. "Please, Aileen, enough talk. You must trust me to know my own brother."

She dared not say any more, but her anxiety was in no way alleviated, for she was sure he hadn't taken her seriously. Despite his apparently open manner, she knew that he invariably kept his real thoughts to himself. She shivered involuntarily, trying to brush off the cobwebs of fear which had draped themselves about her. She went to leave the room but Murchad took her arm and pulled her around to face him. He kissed her and his lips were tender; the kiss spoke more of friendship than of passion.

"Aileen," he looked into her eyes. "I shall let no harm come to you. If you hurt, I hurt also."

His sincerity brought tears to her eyes, for she knew that she was responsible for much of his trouble. In her earlier pursuit of men she hadn't realised that some who seemed so unassailable, whose interests appeared to lie only in the conquering of lands and the subjugation of women, could feel anything as tender as the emotions which both Murchad and the Norman, and even, to a lesser degree, Cashal, had shown her. Maybe love didn't enter into the picture where marriage was the goal, but between some men and some women, love crept in. It had crept in for Murchad, she was sure.

She spoke equally tenderly when she at last answered him, pulling herself away from his embrace to look him in the eye. "I know that, Murchad, I know." Choked, she could say no more. She kissed him lightly and left for her quarters. The weight on her shoulders was such that she could almost feel it bowing her back.

"What ails you, Aileen?" Lys asked her a few days later.

The weight had not lifted, and Aileen still felt listless. "Do you feel a change, Lys, as if something were happening?"

"In the very air around us. Something is going to happen, I am sure of it."

"And there is nothing I can do. I've talked to Murchad but he won't listen. Yet Murrough continues to look at me in a way which makes me afraid. And he touches me at every opportunity. When Murchad is there, he treats me as a well-loved sister, but the rest of the time, there is something in his look – " She didn't finish her sentence for she had nothing tangible to pass on, but Lys understood her mistress fully.

"He's a revolting man. I've seen the way he is with you. But Murchad will look after you."

"Whilst he is here. But what of when he's away?" There was a resigned note to Aileen's voice. Lys didn't answer – there was no answer.

Murchad was growing morose and short-tempered; as time went by even Aileen was afraid to approach him. Yet she stayed by his side, trying to support him: if he collapsed it would mean her certain downfall.

Turlough now treated her with open contempt, a sure sign that he sensed Murchad's end was near, but Murrough remained the same as ever, chillingly the same.

One evening they were eating their meal alone by the fire. Murchad ate in silence and when he had finished he pulled Aileen down to the floor and gently stroked her body. It was a rare occurrence these days and Aileen felt new hope rise within her.

"I'm leaving at first light. Will you miss me?"

Her heart thudded, the hope died. Miss him? She would remain in terror for her life until his return.

"Yes, I shall miss you," she replied calmly. He smiled and kissed her.

"Where are you going?" she asked a little later, "how long will you be away?"

"Oh, two days, maybe three. FitzAlan has hopes of building a monastery now. He has a band of masons coming from Dublin, accompanied by an escort of soldiers. It should take no time to dispose of them. You'll have Lys to keep you company, and men to guard you. Don't worry."

"No, of course not, I'll just look forward to your return." She said no more about her fears, but there were no men, apart from those he was taking with him, whom she fully trusted to remain loyal to Murchad.

He kissed her swiftly, his huge beard tickling her face and body. They hardly slept at all that night and yet he left in the grey dawn looking vital and refreshed.

Aileen hurried back from waving him off. She found Lys washing clothes in the large tub behind the dun. "Lys, what's the gossip amongst the slaves?" It was well-known that the slaves knew most about the politics in the camp: their masters often seemed to forget they had ears and talked without fear of disclosure.

"About what?" Lys lifted dripping arms from the water and wiped them on her apron.

"Murchad?"

Lys hesitated before answering, but there was little to be gained by prevarication. "It could go either way, but if they turn against Murchad, I fear for your safety."

"I have so few friends?"

"You would be well-liked but for the power you have held. There's jealousy surrounding you – belief that you rule Murchad. I'm afraid if they rebel, they'll not spare you."

"Then you believe Turlough is about to strike?" Aileen showed no sign of her alarm, and her voice was low-pitched and strong.

"If it's not too late, you must urge Murchad to act immediately upon his return." Lys spoke in a whisper.

"Do you think you're in any danger yourself, Lys?"

"I'm only a slave, slaves will always find masters." She shrugged philosophically.

Aileen left the room, determined not to show her trembling hands. Lys was right: Murchad must deal with this immediately upon his return. If he did return.

The day passed slowly, although she and Lys had enough to occupy themselves with cleaning and repairing clothes. By nightfall they had heard nothing to worry them and Aileen was feeling a little more relaxed. She went to bed, aware of Lys's comforting presence outside her door. The big bed, normally so fully occupied by herself and Murchad, stretched emptily away from her and despite the warmth of the night she shivered.

She didn't douse the torch which was burning in its sconce on the wall, but lay staring into its flame, trying to keep herself calm. She prayed that Murchad would quickly despatch his duties and return safe on the morrow. It was unrealistic. He had said two to three days and he had only left that morning.

The torch began to flutter as it burnt itself out and, watching the flickering patterns on the walls and ceilings, she grew drowsy. As her mind wandered in a world of half-sleep, half-wakefulness, Robert's face drifted before her eyes. He looked as he had done when she had first seen him – a conquering hero; then the image dissolved, showing him again as a pitiful wreck, painfully trying to raise himself from the ground, and finally, she saw him as he had bent his head to kiss her.

She fell into a deeper sleep. She dreamed she and Murchad had been condemned to death by Turlough. Murrough and Tara were present: he, sword in hand, she, strident in her abuse as Aileen had never seen her in reality. Murchad, with the vagary of dreams, drifted from the scene and Robert appeared, holding out his hand to pull her onto his great horse's back. She awoke with a start, wondering what her dream could possibly mean. She had dreamed before of the Norman kissing her, deeply, and in its own way that dream had come true.

As she regained her senses she felt uneasily that she was not alone. Panic stirred within her. She strained, listening for the slightest noise. The torch was almost out, leaving a dull red glow which did little to illuminate the room, but she was sure she saw a shadow looming in its meagre light. She fixed her gaze upon it and it seemed to move toward her. She told herself it was her own imagination, right up until a hand was clamped down over her mouth, almost cutting off her air supply.

Now he was close and her straining eyes had adjusted to the dark, she could plainly recognise Murrough. "Get out of my chambers," she commanded, as he removed his hand.

"Quiet!" he ordered, his voice a hoarse whisper, "and I won't hurt you." He held her pinned to the bed and she wondered, despite his words, if he meant to kill her. His intentions soon became clear when he took his hand from her mouth and threw off the bed covering, exposing her half-naked body. He handled her roughly, inflamed by her struggling.

"Murchad will have you killed for this," she spat at him.

He laughed. "By the time Murchad returns, he will no longer have the authority to do anything." His voice, now he had let the false good humour drain from it, was ugly.

Aileen had always feared Murrough, more than she had been able to understand. An instinctive hatred, which made her flesh creep when he was near. She flinched as he threw his leg across her thighs to prevent further struggling, and made renewed efforts to break free. Despite her struggles and threats, he raped her. It was clearly intended as punishment for herself and Murchad, as well as gratification for him.

Throughout she expected, prayed for, Lys to wake, but nothing disturbed Murrough and he left – laughing at her tears – undetected.

CHAPTER 2

She lay awake for the rest of the night, not daring to move, expecting at every moment to see Murrough re-enter her room. When the sun rose, painting the trees with colour and throwing the village into sharp relief, she got off the bed and crept to the door. She waited a long time before daring to open it, and when she did she jumped violently as she saw the unmoving shape of her maid lying in the doorway.

"Lys," she cried, fearing the slave was dead. Lys stirred and groaned and Aileen bent and shook her, hard. "Lys, Lys, wake up," she urged, checking behind her all the while, expecting Murrough or Turlough to appear.

Lys groaned again and finally came to, her eyes sticky and unfocused.

"What's the matter?" Her voice was muffled, still half-asleep.

Aileen fetched some water and spilled a little over Lys's face, then gave her a drink, holding the cup to her mouth with an unsteady hand. Gradually Lys recovered her senses enough to realise that something was very wrong.

"What's the matter?" she asked again, coherently at last.

"Murrough came, last night. He raped me."

"Oh, dear God, are you hurt?" Lys's eyes were dark in her pale face and her heart beat uncomfortably; she'd been expecting something like this. The dread had been like a fast undercurrent in unruffled waters.

"Thankfully no, not really, but Lys we must do something. I have been too afraid to leave the dun and wake my father, but we should do so now.

This could be the beginning of an uprising."

"I don't know why I didn't wake up," Lys said as she struggled to her feet. She tried to remember going to sleep the night before and failed. The evening before had vanished from her memory, leaving only a handful of shadows.

"It doesn't matter now – perhaps you were drugged. But we can't dwell on what has already happened, we must do something now to try to prevent what's about to happen." Aileen was suddenly aware of how her night of passive inactivity may have cost Rory his life. "Dress quickly, Lys, we'll go together to see my father," she said, returning to her room.

They had dressed and were leaving the dun when they heard shouting and the unmistakable sound of horses' hooves. Aileen froze, sure that this was the beginning of the revolt, but then she heard Murchad's voice, strong and unbelievably welcome, rising above the rest of the noise.

She ran out, fleetingly aware of the startled expressions on the faces of those she passed. Murchad caught her flying body and held her against him, smiling at her wild welcome.

"You see," he was saying over the hammering of her heart. "I promised that I would return as soon as I could. As usual we were thwarted by –" he stopped suddenly aware of the expression on her face. "– Aileen?"

"Come inside, Murchad, I must talk to you most urgently."

He followed her in and she gave him a full account of what had happened. His face paled and his eyes grew cold as he listened to her.

"If I had not returned early they would have already taken over the village. They were going to ambush me." His lips were stiff, the words stilted. "And, by God, if I had not gone –," he couldn't finish, his anger was so great. He caught Aileen to him and she was suddenly afraid of the repercussions the night would bring. He released her suddenly and strode from the room.

Aileen stood where she was for a short time, but curiosity got the better of diplomacy and she ran outside to see Rory and a grim-faced Murchad striding up the street, followed by a large group of armed men. They gathered on the green near the front of the main homestead and there was no sign of any indecisiveness from Murchad as he rapped out orders, sending his men in different directions.

A few moments later the men returned, with Murrough, Turlough and twenty white-faced men herded like worried sheep into a bunch. Turlough walked with his head held high, his expression defiant, but Murrough had to be dragged by six of Murchad's men, his screams echoing in the surrounding hills.

People started to emerge from their doorways to see what was going on, and the street was quickly filled with curious onlookers. Murchad, once everyone was gathered, stood before them and in a loud voice bade them be quiet. He had his brothers brought before him, the one stoic, standing as if frozen, the other still writhing. Murchad kept his eyes on them as he gave the order for a fire to be lighted, and a sigh rose from the crowd. Murchad waited for silence, his eyes cold as he gazed upon his people.

"Who supports my brothers in their respective claims to leadership?" His voice rang out strong and firm in the chill morning air.

The silence was profound. No one said a word, afraid even to breathe, lest any sound be taken as positive response.

"What, none here present wish to change the hand which wields the power?"

None appeared to.

Aileen licked dry lips. A baby cried and was hastily shushed; a toddler ran, chasing a butterfly into the open, and was quickly restrained. Murrough's raspy breathing filled the silence, reminding Aileen of his lust-filled gasps of the previous night.

Turlough spoke, he too sounding strong and fearless. Aileen felt a pang of regret: together he and Murchad could have been invincible. "Speak up, those who have offered me support. Those who have found my brother an inadequate leader." His look was challenging as he stared into the eyes of the twenty or so men who had been hauled in. When they failed to respond a cynical smile curled his lip. He looked into the crowd. No one acknowledged his gaze. "So will no one speak for me?" Turlough said, and contempt for them all was plain upon his face. His pride and courage moved Aileen almost to pity, but she was aware that she would have been shown no mercy had Murchad not returned at such an opportune moment.

Murchad waited, allowing ample time for any answer. He would not be accused later of rushing this thing through. Tension built by the second. Finally, raising his arm, he ordered Murrough and Turlough to be taken before the fire. A great roar rose from the crowd as the tension finally broke and even Turlough flinched, knowing his fate was sealed. The formalities were adhered to by the reading of a long list of allegations, each one painstakingly covered. At each alleged crime the bystanders were invited to refute the claims, but at each point silence fell, like a shroud, over the scene.

Finally Murchad spoke, proclaiming the sentence. Upon his orders a large man, holding branding irons in his hand, plunged them into the fire. Turlough was dragged to the fire and held down by two men.

He saw the red hot iron come towards his eyes and still he made no sound, but as it was forced down onto the delicate skin he screamed and jerked violently, almost dragging the men who restrained him to their knees. A smell of roasted flesh filled the air and was dispelled by the light breeze. The crowd flinched with him and a heavy groan filled the emptiness which followed his scream. He slumped, unconscious, to the ground.

"Bring Murrough forward," said Murchad. If he felt any sorrow at what had happened to his brother he showed no sign of it.

Murrough was dragged over, screaming for mercy. His eyes met Murchad's and Aileen saw a tremor run through the chief. As the executioner went to put his brands back in the fire, Murchad held up a hand to stop him. Murrough sagged with relief, believing his brother had relented, pitifully grateful for the vacillation for which he had only yesterday condemned him. The crowd seemed to hold its breath.

Murchad's next orders, given quietly to the guards beside him, passed unheard by Murrough. The guards marched forward and took hold of Murrough, stretching him out on the ground. The smile of relief which had lightened his face died, and a look of shock, almost comic in contrast, replaced it.

The guards stripped him and held his legs and arms so that he laid spread-eagled before the spectators, suddenly pathetic in his vulnerability and fear. Only then did it dawn on Murrough what Murchad had planned for him. He did try to scream, but the sound died in his throat, as horror shrank his vocal chords and drew the moisture from his mouth.

Aileen, realising at the same moment exactly what was to befall, stepped forward involuntarily, the very fact of her extreme hatred of Murrough adding to her instinctive denial. He saw her move and his eyes, the only part of his body which he could still move, glared wildly in her direction.

"It was her, Murchad, it was her. She begged for it. She has pursued me at every opportunity. She came to me last night and – she begged for it."

Aileen didn't speak, her face drained of colour and she felt nausea turn her stomach. But Murchad took her gently, lovingly, before them all, and placed his arm about her shoulder, showing he knew his brother to be a craven liar.

The executioner held his knife high, ceremoniously, in the air, then bent with icy precision towards Murrough's crotch. Despite the men holding him, Murrough writhed wildly, arching his back and twisting away from the inevitable. People craned to see what was happening; the smell of his fear was tangible in the heavy air. Dust rose in billows, obscuring his flailing limbs from sight. The executioner's knife rose, descended, cut.

Murrough's scream was thin and short, but its impact stilled the crowd as his shouts had not done. The executioner raised his knife a second time No one moved. The executioner's knife was stayed, suspended in the air above Murrough's unconscious form.

Murchad sighed heavily, the only sound in the tense, waiting silence. Aileen held her breath.

"No more," Murchad's voice was a hoarse whisper.

The executioner turned slowly and met his eye.

"Enough. There has been enough bloodshed!" He turned away, his arm still around Aileen's shoulder and the crowd parted before them.

His final words hung in the air and the executioner lowered his knife.

CHAPTER 3

"Murchad, you're not happy. Won't you allow me to help you?" asked Aileen.

"No, I'm alright, I'm alright," he said, forcing a smile. It soon slipped however, and the expression of morose sadness – which was becoming habitual – settled back, lifting the youthful impression from his face.

When he wasn't feverishly working outside with his men, she would observe him as he sat gazing into the fire, his shoulders hunched. She knew he was worrying about the way he had treated his brothers, particularly proud, independent Turlough, who now wandered sightless about the village. The children who had once dogged his footsteps and lifted adoring eyes to see his face, now jeered at him and put the dead branches of trees, or other pitfalls in his way, laughing as he floundered. He had become totally dependent on the goodwill of those men he had once led.

Although Turlough couldn't have known, Murchad couldn't bear to look upon his brother's face. He felt he had given leniency to the greater offender and often wondered how Turlough would have fared had he not been the first to receive punishment.

When Murrough was fully recovered, he was brought before Murchad. Aileen, despite her reluctance, was present at Murchad's request.

"Murrough," said Murchad, "I've spared you much suffering because you are my brother."

Murrough, thin and bowed, his spirit broken, said nothing.

"But it pains me to see two of my brothers wandering about the village, a perpetual reminder to me, to trust no one."

Aileen wondered anxiously if this was a jibe at her, but Murchad gave no sign that it was.

"And for Aileen to have to see you, to know how you defiled her, to be constantly reminded that I did nothing when she warned me of what was coming, this is too much to bear." Murchad waited to see if his brother would answer; his voice, which had been low and reasonable, now became harsh; Aileen knew it was because he wanted to hide his sorrow. "Murrough, have you nothing left to say?"

The broken man stared at the ground and shook his head slowly.

"Then I must tell you that you are to be exiled. You are never to come near the settlement again. You are no longer my brother, no longer to call yourself O'Flerty." Murchad looked again for response, but could see little of his brother's face: it was bent and shadowed. His own was pale, even his piercingly blue eyes were grey, all colour drained from him. "I shall make orders that if you are seen nearby, you are to be chased away. No one may give you food or shelter. If you enter the encampment you will be put to death."

Murchad's voice had lowered and Aileen knew he was fighting to control himself. He tried one last time to force his brother to respond, but Murrough remained silent. Still and silent. He was led from the room and passed Aileen without a glance in her direction. She saw the light gleam off his cheeks. He had cried, soundlessly, and although she hated him for what he'd done, Aileen felt compassionate tears prick the back of her own eyes.

It was unlikely that anyone would ever again accuse Murchad of indecision; his actions had shown him to be both decisive and capable of compassion and he had grown in stature in his people's eyes. No one realised what his impulsive action had cost him.

For the first few nights after the punishments he'd been passionate, almost brutal, in his love-making to Aileen, as though she were nothing to him; but after that he seemed to lose all interest. She wondered as time went by if he was going to others of his concubines, but had no way of knowing. She couldn't ask Tara, whom she hardly ever saw any more; Murchad had moved her out when Lys had moved in and Tara's veiled hostility had been added to that of the other dissenters. She made an effort to be polite but Aileen felt this was out of fear, rather than friendship.

"What do you think Murchad will do with the prisoners, Lys?" she asked as the girl combed and braided her hair.

"Oh, I don't know," she said, thoughtfully. "Your Murchad's a hard man to read."

"What do the people want to see?"

"I think they're disinterested, but on the whole they have seen Murchad can act justly and perhaps it would be a good chance to prove he can also act mercifully. In that way he would show them another facet of his personality. Keep them guessing. It may not harm."

"No, indeed," Aileen replied.

Making a swift decision, she had Lys fill her bath, and she washed herself thoroughly, her hair swimming on the water like black seaweed. When she had bathed she stood and let Lys dry her until her whole body was red and tingling. Then she rubbed sweet smelling herbs into her skin and hair and Lys braided it again, looping it up on top of her head. She dressed in one of the beautiful gowns which had been brought from Bristol to Dublin, and which the passing traders had sold her at a good price, hoping to win the approbation of so powerful a lady. It was low cut, showing the swell of her breasts, and edged with gold braid. She pinned on a beautiful Celtic brooch made from gold and enamel and decorated with precious stones. Then she placed a gold torc, brought from Wicklow, around her neck. Murchad had acquired it on one of his numerous raids and given it to her early on in their relationship; she hoped it would evoke memories of happier days.

She looked beautiful as she posed before Lys, her skin lustrous, her eyes the deep green of a shaded pool, holding a promise which Murchad could not fail to read. Her hair, partly braided, partly loose, shone with azure lights and fell softly down her back, enhanced by the rich blue of her gown.

Aileen placed cushions on the ground and laid upon them in front of the fire, aware of how its gold and orange hues brought her skin to life. She had a flagon of wine, bread, cheese and a bowl of freshly picked blackberries set out on the table.

When Murchad returned home he saw her, seductive in all her finery, and for the first time in a long while his blue eyes twinkled. He sat down beside her and tried to take her in his arms.

"Not yet, Murchad," she said, smiling. "First, we must eat," – she reached over and took the bowl of berries, popping one into his mouth, – "and then, we must drink," – she handed him a full vessel of wine, sipping from it herself before she offered it.

They ate and drank, and as they did so she brushed his lips with hers. She fed him with tiny pieces of the bread and cheese, held wine to his lips and laughed, a light airy sound, as he tried to take her in his arms. When they had finished eating she placed the rest of the food within his reach, and laid her head on his lap. He stroked her hair very tenderly and looked into the fire, thinking for the first time in ages how good life was.

"Things are much easier for you now, are they not, Murchad?" Her voice was a whispering caress.

"How, easier?" he said, amused as always by her interest in his affairs.

"With the uprising so successfully stopped, your chieftainship unchallenged and the stronghold, at least for the time being, prosperous and at peace, it seems things must be easier."

"Yes," he agreed thoughtfully, and Aileen was certain he had not even looked at the positive aspects, so lost was he in his private world of guilt and doubt. She allowed him time to think before continuing.

"You have shown such great courage and qualities of leadership, Murchad, yet perhaps only I know and understand the grief you have suffered."

He looked at her soulfully and she could imagine what he must have been like as a child. Her feelings toward him were mixed, both sensual and maternal. She took one of his hands and laid it upon her breast so he could feel the steady, soothing rhythm of her heart, the comforting softness beneath his calloused hand.

"You could have acted no other than you did, and everyone knows this." She didn't mention Turlough by name, afraid of jarring the harmony she had created. "The chieftaincy belongs with someone capable of putting the welfare of his people before the ties even of close family. You have proved your courage in battle and in leadership; your people love you, and I," – she gave him a melting look – "I, who have always loved you, have grown to respect and trust you beyond all others." She felt deeply moved, for she meant what she said. Though she possessed a highly developed sense of self-preservation, she preferred to speak with honesty wherever she could.

"You speak in flattering terms," he said, but a great black cloud had been lifted from his mind and he felt, for the first time in weeks, light-hearted and sensuous. He smiled, and the smile was his familiar, teasing one.

She smiled back at him. "I expect you have already decided what to do with your prisoners?" she said, her expression became adoring, so she seemed to be hanging on his every word. She didn't allow him to answer yet. "I too have been thinking about it, and I would like to have your opinion, to see if I have learned my lessons well under your tutelage."

He nodded benignly and she began – falteringly at first – building in confidence. "As I have said, you have shown yourself to be strong and wise. The imprisoned men have families in the camp, people who walk now in fear – and rightly so – " she added quickly, "for those men did a great wrong. They have walked in fear for weeks now and look towards you for the final judgement. Expecting the worst they cower before you, wondering what you may do next."

"Go on," he said, his voice low.

"By rights you could exile the men, or have them blinded. But as I see it, you have another option. You could show another quality of leadership, one which I know you possess:" – the hold of her eyes on his was hypnotic – "the quality of mercy. Now they know what you can do, if you choose, those men would be too afraid to turn against you yet again, and having suffered the agonies of waiting and wondering what their fate will be they could be made into your most loyal servants by one benign gesture. Am I right, or am I wrong, Murchad?"

"You would, in my position, release those men?"

"No, Murchad, I could never begin to envisage myself in your position, for I don't posses your fine qualities, but having observed you – intimately – "she put her hand over his, where it covered her breast, " it is my opinion that you will release those men, and in that way secure their loyalty and the goodwill of all their families – and of the rest of the stronghold as well."

He laughed. The sound, deep and rumbling, echoed through her head where it lay on his lap. "How right you are, Aileen. How clever you are. You have learned well. Very well indeed. And accurately read my mind. I was going to announce tomorrow my intentions of doing just that. But enough of eating, drinking and talking," he pulled her up so that he could kiss her. "We have other business, sadly overlooked, to attend to."

CHAPTER 4

$\mathcal{D}$uring the months following his escape, Robert spent a good while campaigning, albeit reluctantly – under his feudal oath – for le Gros, now one of the foremost Norman leaders. He had grown increasingly weary of fighting on the behalf of others and where possible sent Silas instead, for Silas was only truly happy when he was away on campaign.

Robert's presence was sorely needed at Gossard's Ford, for the raids from the tribe of Murchad O'Flerty were continuous and increasingly ferocious. Always fearful of another major attack upon his castle, Robert was determined to organise his men properly for an all out assault on the Irish stronghold, and this needed careful planning.

He had strengthened the castle walls and continued with the construction of the large religious house, which he was erecting on the site of the old village of Seandale. Such houses were valuable assets, providing central points from which grew villages and markets, encouraging trading, and enabling people such as Robert to sell produce on their own doorsteps. More importantly they bound the community together, creating a parish from the dissected family groups under their lord's protection.

The Irish Church, convinced that without Norman support the Irish people would slip from one abomination to another, was eager to support Robert's project of building a new Cistercian monastery. A visit from the Archbishop of Dublin, Laurence O'Toole, was an outward sign of ecclesiastical interest and spurred the Irish labourers to greater efforts, so that Robert grew confident enough to send to England for the Anglo-French Ranulph of Caen who was to be the first abbot.

During the month of March 1174, there was a great deal of coming and going at the castle, and Silas – returned from the wars – and Cormac, spent many hours in conference with their master.

"How are the men shaping up, Silas?" asked Robert.

"The sixty foot-soldiers from de Puissey – under command of their senechal, Charles of Ghent – and the MacTilling men are all ready for action. D'Evreux forces will arrive by the beginning of April, and will need no further training."

"And none know what is afoot? Secrecy is of the utmost importance, I always mistrust the MacTilling men. What do you think, Cormac?"

"That the MacTillings are compliant and keeping their big mouths shut," he said with great relish.

"Then, with such a respectable army, and aided by the secrecy of our attack, we can be hopeful of ridding ourselves of the O'Flerty irritant," Robert said, smiling. At the back of his mind, securely locked away from sight, lingered the image of Aileen. "Cormac, you have completed your route plan, and know which way we should march?"

"Yes, of course." He explained the route he had decided upon and Robert blessed his intimate knowledge of the area.

"When we arrive we shall raid at first light, as usual," he said, "and I want the MacTillings held in reserve."

"But is it wise to withhold men? Surely if we attack with full strength, we can't fail?" said Silas.

"Yes, why risk a defeat when we can ensure success?" agreed Cormac.

"You are right, of course, but there are reasons for my decision. Firstly, the MacTillings are unnecessarily bloodthirsty; more importantly, I still can't completely trust them. If they are held in reserve, I'll feel easy in my own mind. If we need more help, I'll be prepared to risk it – I shall have no other choice." He looked at his men and they nodded their agreement.

"Is there anything else?" Robert asked. The two soldiers shook their heads. "Well there's just one point I'd like to make. Should I be otherwise detained – injured, or killed – I want you, Silas, to take over the command of our men. De Puissey's and d'Evreux's will be taken care of. It may be up to you to call in the reserves. I shall leave it to your judgement."

"Yes, sire,"

"And that is all I have to say, except good luck, and God be with you."

Silas and Cormac left Robert, still sitting, planning at his table.

"What do you think?" asked Silas of Cormac.

"Think? About what?"

"'If I am detained – injured or killed.' What did he mean by detained?"

"Fighting?"

"No. He would have said that, as he always has before."

"Then what?"

"Which is exactly what I asked you. He has spoken at length to you of his affairs."

"So?"

"So?"

"Silas, you are playing games with me. Out with it, man."

"Have you ever thought that Robert has other things on his mind. A distraction which stops him from being content with his lot?"

"I'm sure he has, Silas."

"Have you considered it may be connected with his escape from the O'Flerty?"

"The woman?"

"The woman!"

"And she is within the stronghold."

"And he says 'if I am otherwise detained.'"

"Good luck to him, if he is fool enough to waste his time on a woman," Cormac shrugged.

"Yes, indeed. If he is fool enough," smiled Silas.

The small army set off within a few days, with no idea of where they were headed. The secrecy had been maintained and only the leaders knew the identity of the target. There was much speculation and a great deal of excitement.

Murchad had changed, become warm and jovial, his back straight once more, his head held high, his sexual appetite had returned – increased – and Aileen was satiated by him, absorbed and overwhelmed by his confident virility.

They laughed and talked together; they fought and played like children, to fall, breathless, on their massive bed. She stroked the scars which crawled like snail tracks over his body, tracing them with the tip of her finger, then with her tongue. They learned together to prolong the joy of loving.

He loved her as he had never loved another woman. As he had never known a man could love. He brought her his problems and doubts; he bared his soul before her and revelled in the new horizons which opened up before him. He saw new sights through her eyes; he recognised that part of her which was selfish and self-seeking, determined upon survival at any cost, and he loved her for it. She found he was tolerant and humorous, and grew to love him for it.

Robert's army reached the outskirts of the O'Flerty camp just before dawn on a blowzy, scented morning in May. Concealed within the abundant forest greenery, the men crept forward and, as the first rays of the sun filtered through the trees, lending golden haloes to the leaves, they charged the sleeping stronghold.

The Trigonnel guards were sleeping and Robert's men were upon them before they could raise the alarm. The Welsh, Flemish and English soldiers penetrated the outer limits of the encampment easily, with the Irish contingent cooling their heels at the edge of the forest. As the men burst upon the town, the ground vibrated beneath the horses' feet, white dust flew and the first full light of the sun was masked.

Robert, drawing a few men off, rode away from the tumult and, with his knowledge of the camp, quickly found the area of the chief's homestead. He pin-pointed the largest dun amongst the royal buildings but they were immediately confronted by an armed guard. Robert's men were outnumbered, but not seriously, and the two factions stood still for a few moments, taking stock.

Robert lifted his arm, commanding the attack. He led the charge, slicing through the first of his adversaries with a dream-like ease, but the fight that followed was as fierce as any Robert's men had previously encountered; Murchad's home guard had been selected for their size and ferocity and fought with both sword and axe. But as soon as Robert was reasonably certain of victory he called his men to fight on and ran into the dun.

Immediately he was confronted by Murchad, sword in one hand, axe in the other. He came at Robert savagely, recognising him: the cause of so much anguish; the root of the dissatisfaction which had led to his brothers' disgrace; the same man who had killed his friend Cashal, and kidnapped Aileen. The first mighty swing of the axe caught Robert unawares, but the younger man was lithe and, although unbalanced, he dodged easily and the axe dug deeply into the wood of the door, which cracked and split.

Murchad let go of the axe and swung round with his sword. Robert, low to the ground, trying to recover, swept at Murchad with his own sword. Murchad felt the blade sink deep into the exposed flesh of his leg and stop against the hardness of bone, yet he felt no pain. He bore down, his sword in line to slice through Robert's skull. Again Robert parried the blow and Murchad staggered, following the trajectory of his swing. They stood simultaneously, then lunged at one another in a hard fight between two equally matched protagonists, but Robert had the protection of his armour and Murchad did not. Finally, Robert got in a deep thrust, which entered Murchad's stomach and he doubled over, dropping his sword. For one brief moment Robert hesitated, and Murchad's blue eyes looked into his, without entreaty, without hope. He died, unsurprised, from another deep thrust into his chest, with Aileen's name upon his lips.

She hadn't even heard them. The night had been long and she had drunk a great deal of wine before eventually falling asleep. Cocooned in furs and sheltered from noise in their room in the centre of the building she had slept undisturbed. The fight had been fierce: the battle fitting in with her dreams, a nightmarish reminder of the day the Norman had rescued her mother and herself from certain death, and at the end of the dream his mouth was on hers, as it always was.

She opened her eyes and Robert was there. In her confusion she held out her arms to him – inviting – and he stepped toward her, his sword dripping blood. Their eyes locked, held, recognised and a message flew between them, but the blood on the sword distracted her, and she woke up fully, to see half a dozen men fill the bedchamber, their eyes lustfully upon her body. The sun shone in through her window; she could see the dust motes flying aimlessly in the shaft of ochre light, and stretching fingers of warmth onto her bed.

"Murchad?" she called weakly, unsure, disorientated, her dream again merging with reality. "Murchad," she screamed in pain. For she knew, in that instant, that it was his blood on Robert's sword; and it was she who had helped Robert to escape. The two realisations hit her simultaneously, accusingly. She sat up in bed, her heavy breasts unashamedly bared. "Robert FitzAlan. I hate you, by God I hate you," she cried. He said nothing, and one of the men behind him broke the silence with an uneasy laugh.

"Get out. Get out of here," he said, his voice as they had never heard it before. They backed out and he went over to her, trying to talk, to tell her he meant her no harm.

"You've killed him," she repeated, over and over, drowning his attempted platitudes. She leapt from the bed and threw herself at him, her legs curled around his back, her nails raking his face. He caught her arms easily, and became suddenly fully aware of her, clinging to him, naked and venomous. Taking his breath away.

"I should have let you die," – and the hysteria was gone. She was suddenly without fear, without feeling of any kind, absorbed by her utter hatred of the man who had killed two of her lovers. He had no more to say, his lips gripped together in a thin line. He took the coverlet from her bed and wrapped it around her. Sword in one hand, the other holding her securely over his shoulder he left, followed by his men.

Murchad's blue eyes stared without seeing Aileen as she was bundled from the dun. She screamed his name; the sound pulled from the depths of her being, and then fell silent.

The erstwhile stronghold was a bloodbath. It had done precious little good to keep the MacTillings in reserve, to try to protect the people. In the light of the fact that this stronghold was the one which was most fiercely hated by his men, Robert cursed the fact that he had given no orders for clemency. Accordingly they had shown none. Dead children lay sprawled on the ground, covered in a film of white dust and congealing blood, their rounded, tanned limbs heavy and distorted where they had fallen to Robert's men. Children – everywhere Robert looked – dead children. And dead dogs and cats. And dead women and old men, and yet more dead children. Aileen stopped struggling in her horror at what she saw. He forgot he held her. He saw two of his men brutalising the body of a young girl, younger than Aileen, and darkly pretty. One held her; one raped her. Armour was cutting her body, but it didn't bleed, she was already dead. Her mouth was open, her lips frozen back showing her teeth in a perpetual snarl.

Aileen saw Tara and two of her children, faces down in the dust. The Normans had hacked her down as she fled before them, and she still held her children's hands in hers.

Dead.

Dead.

Aileen had played with them, listened to their gurgling laughter. The little one used to take her cheeks between his fat little hands and kiss her mouth. The wound in his back had split him almost in two. The Normans had a reputation for leniency toward the villagers they'd captured: the Irish were supposed to be the cruel ones, Aileen thought. But she saw no Irish men, no MacTilling men: only Norman and English and others whom she didn't know.

She felt Robert pause as he passed the first of the children and the tremor which passed through him. When later they rode together away from the stronghold she said, "A good job, well carried out, my lord," and he flinched but didn't answer.

154

CHAPTER 5

He had to go back. In his heart he knew it was pointless, the damage had been done, but he had to return. He left Aileen with the MacTilling men who still waited at the edge of the copse, warning them that not one hair of her body must be harmed.

She sat on the ground, ignoring the hooves of the horses which milled about her, and looked coldly at the smoking ruins which had been her home and the home of her family. She hadn't seen Rory, or the twins, or Dvorvild, but their homestead was in a different part of the stronghold and she wouldn't have expected to. She tried to pray for their safety but a cold hard void prevented her. God could have stopped this without her prayers, if he'd had a mind to. She spat on the ground and turned her eyes to the virgin blue of the skies, thinking about Robert FitzAlan.

She had been attracted to him; she had dreamed of his kisses and of having his arms around her, even as she had lain with Murchad. She had freed him from his prison and saved his life, and in that way repaid any debt she might have owed him. And now she was free of that encumbrance. Free to hate.

Murchad was dead, her home was gone and she was the slave of the Norman bastards. But she was alive. And while she lived she swore she would never let the Norman own her, and with all the power in her body she would reject his love, if love was what he sought.

Tiny white streaks of cloud floated idly past her line of vision, oblivious of the suffering below. Aileen wondered if Tara, Murchad and the other people who had been slain drifted by too, on their way to heaven. Her eyes filled with tears but she rubbed them away with her knuckles, grinding painfully into her eyes until she had herself under control. She could do nothing for any of them, nothing, but remember her vow.

Robert hurried back to the encampment where men were still fighting in isolated patches. The major part of the battle had lasted no more than an hour, hardly longer than it had taken Robert to slay Murchad and his guards and capture Aileen. He thought, guiltily, of how he could have prevented this bloodbath, had he not been "otherwise detained".

"I tried, sire, to stop this," Silas's voice, gritty, came through a mist. "It was hopeless. Whatever they saw they killed. Perhaps they would have listened to you." It was the first implied criticism Silas had ever made. Blue eyes met blue eyes, and Robert's dropped first.

"Perhaps they would have done," he said, staring out over the dead encampment.

A young soldier galloped past, excited, filled with a joy for life and the new sense of power he had discovered this morning. "A thorough victory, m'lord," and he smiled, thundering off once more.

"A thorough victory – strange words," Robert muttered, the skin on his face taut with the dust which still dimmed the sunlight. But apt ones, for the stronghold was razed to the ground, its inhabitants dead, dying, annihilated. He was too late to be of help. As he had known he would be.

He called his troops, almost complete, almost undamaged; and, too sickened to chastise them, he led them from what had been, until dawn this morning, Trigonnel's Point.

Aileen watched him return. He rode out of the dust, the sun making a golden light around him and his men. He led the column, a majestic vision on his grey horse, red caparisoned, his banner flying gaily, and her stomach churned. All dead. All Gone. All because of him.

Robert's men waited at the edge of the wood and the sound of trumpets filled the air, calling any straggling troops to join the mass. They came, driving cattle and sheep before them, laden with food, clothes, arms, even some jewellery. Loot – for a good morning's work. They drove, too, a pitiful group of captives, remainder of the hundreds of O'Flerty supporters, and Robert stood before them.

"Go home, go back to your homes and live in peace." His voice sounded thin, his words meaningless. They didn't rejoice, but turned and walked wearily back into the smoke and dust.

"Oh great and magnificent lord, what a priceless gift you have offered them. Their lives and their homes." Aileen spoke, her eyes on her people.

He looked down into her face and felt sick at the hatred he saw there. "Would you have preferred them to become my slaves? Would you have me kill them, too?"

"I would have had you remember the life you had restored to you, in this place. By these hands." She lifted her hands, which were brown and strong. "I would have had you spare them torture and offer them only a noble battle."

"I have spared you, who saved me."

"You intend then to let me go?" She would not compromise.

He shook his head. "To that place? You could not survive. All the men are dead."

"Yes, and all the children, too," she said, knowing his weakness. "But, as you so rightly said to my people, it is our home."

"I can offer you a great deal. More than you have ever seen."

"Can you offer me freedom? The only thing in life worth owning?" Her stare was challenging. He couldn't answer her, for he had no intention of letting her go. Then it would all have been for nothing. He wheeled his horse round, rearing, to face his men, leaving her standing, her blankets clutched around her, amongst the horses.

"Take her up," he cried to Silas. "We'll return to camp. Find her clothes. Take care of her." He rode away and she watched the large clods of soft forest peat fall from his horse's hooves, until he was swallowed up amongst the green of the wood.

Silas took her unceremoniously behind him and she refused to cling on, forcing him to slow his pace, lest he lose his precious burden.

"You'll fall, if you don't hold fast."

"No. You're wrong. I am already fallen," was her bitter reply.

Silas shrugged. She was the reason for the massacre which had sickened even his war-hardened heart and if it were not for Robert's orders he would have liked to see her fall and be trampled.

They stopped at the camp which had been erected by the retainers during the morning. Silas smelled the roasting meat and his stomach rumbled in anticipation. Aileen saw the tents pitched in a large circle around the field. They looked so cheerful, billowing in the soft wind, bright under the hot sun. Red, blue and gold, with banners flying crisply in the breeze. And encircling them, the rich, full trees of summer, magnificent, reaching into the sky as if searching out the sun, creating at their feet, deep purple shade, where the horses were tied and watered. Behind them the lilac and soft blue tones of the hills stretched away, and away, to Dublin, to Waterford, to the coast. The marvellous lush green grass, unique to Ireland, reached between the mountains, creeping up to the banks of fathomless, icy lochs, feeding the cows and sheep which all belonged now to the invaders.

She remained seated as Silas dismounted, making it difficult for him to move. She wanted to crawl away into a dark corner and cry until the aching loss melted a little, but she would not do that. She sat, statuesque, staring into the distance until Silas, who was hungry and exasperated, pulled her to the ground. The bed cover she wore draped around her, slipped, revealing her shoulder and right breast, and she did nothing to prevent it, but looked at Silas to see what he would do. He turned his head and pulled the cover back over her and she smiled at his discomfort.

"I'll get you some clothes."

"You are too kind," her voice dripped with sarcasm, lost on Silas, who wanted only to get rid of her and eat. He went away and returned with a bundle of clothes.

"Come with me." He could have been calling a dog.

She followed him. The faster he moved, the more slowly she did, until he was forced to pull her resisting body along behind him. He stopped outside a bright red tent. "In there," he indicated. "I'll wait."

He waited. He jigged from foot to foot. He sat down and drew a pattern in the dust with his booted toe. He lay, looking up at the sun through half-closed eyes, his stomach rumbling and gurgling. Finally he entered the tent to see her fully dressed and seated demurely.

"I've been waiting for you to come out," he said, exasperated.

"I've been waiting for you to come and get me," she said, sweetly, patiently.

"God's teeth," he swore, wondering if he would get to eat that day.

"Quite," she agreed, inclining her head.

He took her arm and pulled her rudely from the tent over to where men were dishing out bowls of thick soup and large hunks of venison and bread. Silas took two portions and, ignoring the ribald comments of his comrades, he dragged Aileen beneath the shelter of an ancient oak tree.

"Do you want food?" He was abrupt.

She took it, although her stomach heaved at the thought of eating. She felt ill, her head thumped and thudded with every move of her eyes and body, her face felt clammy and her mind was filled with graphic memories of the morning. But she ate, to show him she didn't care, to show him she hadn't been that badly hurt, and she forced the food to stay down by sheer will-power.

Silas watched her without speaking, shovelling food into his mouth and chewing voraciously.

"I may have some privacy, I assume?" she asked, rising. She could hardly speak: vomit had forced its way up and was settled now at the back of her throat. Her face had turned green and was beaded with moisture.

He led her into a thicket of bushes and stood with his back turned, listening to her heave and vomit and giving her time to recover. He gave no sign that he understood her discomfort as she walked out of the thicket. She was so pale that her eyes seemed to fill her face, yet, smiling brightly, she held her chin high.

"I'd like a drink," was all she said, and he went to fetch her one. When he returned she was leaning against the trunk of the tree, her eyes closed. She opened them immediately and took the water he offered, thanking God that it was water, for she could not have stomached ale.

Silas watched her sip. She would not bend or show him how ill she was, and he wouldn't have wanted to tell her that he knew. A hard core of respect for her resilience and her spirit grew inside him, to stand beside the dislike which matched it. He understood her, and not wanting to witness her suffer the indignity of a collapse, which he was certain she would soon have to do, he dragged her back to the red tent, telling her he had orders to keep her there until morning when they were to start the march back to the castle.

She entered the tent nonchalantly, her shoulders back, but when she saw he hadn't followed she laid down on the sheepskin and closed her eyes. Her head spun immediately, the pain flared up and then subsided. She thought she would never sleep, but she slept quickly and deeply, her body intent upon healing.

When she woke she forgot where she was for a while and reached out for Murchad. She touched only the spiky field grass and smelled the warm sun-drenched tent, and she pulled back her fingers and stuffed them in her mouth to stop the involuntary sob.

Silas brought her more water and some bread, which she ate and drank gratefully. She sank her small white teeth into the coarse bread and chewed delicately with her mouth shut as she had been told the English ladies did; but when Silas had gone she tore hunks of it and stuffed it into her mouth, then drank thirstily, in great gulps, burping loudly afterwards. Silas heard her and laughed, his chest moving as he clamped his mouth shut to hide his mirth.

She felt better. According to the sun, which was very high in the sky, she must have slept for hours and her headache was mercifully gone. She drank again from the large pitcher Silas had brought; the water was cool and slipped between her parched lips like silk. She was dressed in men's clothing, probably belonging to a dead soldier; the garments hung off her slight body making movement awkward, and she turned back the sleeves and legs of the linen trousers.

She heard Robert's horse as he returned.

"Where is she?" he asked.

She could see the shadows of men's bodies outside the tent, watched him dismount and hand the reins to someone who led his horse away. He parted the cloth which covered the opening and stepped inside, filling the tent with his presence.

"Silas found you clothes?" He looked weary, dust-covered, his face drawn.

"As you see," she said, pirouetting before him, knowing she was ugly in her borrowed clothes.

"Good." He paused and she realised he was trying to find something to say to break the silence. She had him at a disadvantage. "And food – you've eaten?"

She nodded.

"And drunk?"

She nodded again.

"Good. Good." He stared at her and fiddled with the hilt of his sword, and she, knowing his discomfort, stared back at him. He wasn't with her, his mind was elsewhere and she waited.

He had spent the time since he'd last seen her back in the stronghold with a group of surprised "volunteers". They had given food and drink to the survivors and helped them in their grisly task of stacking the dead bodies. The survivors looked upon him with sullen eyes, not understanding why he should wish to see their grief, wondering what was on his mind, and he'd left them at last knowing he was unwanted, knowing that anything he could have done to save their pain should have been done before the battle had started.

D'Evreux had approached him as he rode back to camp. "Where have you been?" He could see Robert was distressed and kept his voice light whilst Robert gained control.

His friendly smile was lost on Robert. The sun slanted through the leaves of the trees above them, gold and green, leaving speckled brown marks on their skin. Robert explained where he had been, his voice dull.

D'Evreux was perplexed. "Why?" he asked, "all supplies have been removed from the camp."

Robert nodded his agreement, but didn't answer. They rode on without speaking for a short time.

"It was an astounding victory, praise God. A pity more lives weren't saved, don't you think?" Reginald struggled to find the right words.

Another nod.

D'Evreux ploughed on regardless. "Not something one likes to see, but there, the O'Flerty have ever been a thorn in our flesh. We need not fear

160

them in the future. There is no O'Flerty any more."

"Not any more. Did we ever, truly, fear them?"

"They took you, Robert, and held you prisoner for several weeks – can you say you were not afraid?"

Suddenly Robert was back in the dark hut, starving and bruised, bored out of his mind, helpless. Hopeless. Terribly afraid; until she had come and given him food and heart and finally the way out of there.

Still he only nodded.

"How did you get out? I never did hear the truth of that."

"Someone helped me."

"So I heard."

"A woman. I intend to marry her."

"Marry, Robert? From gratitude – you made her a promise?"

"No. Not gratitude, no promise."

"Then for what purpose? Is she O'Flerty?"

"She was the chief's woman. I killed him. I killed another of her lovers, too. In another battle." His voice was dull, as if he were talking in his sleep.

"And she saved you, after that?"

"Yes. Even after that. For the sake of her mother, I believe."

Reginald was intrigued, he had heard none of this before. Robert's handsome, sensitive face stared stonily ahead, but Reginald felt he needed to unburden.

"Tell me," he said, and Robert did, from the beginning when he had first seen her, leaving nothing out. It was a penance for him and yet instead of punishment, he felt cleansed afterward, whole.

"So! You love this Aileen MacGillingrouth."

"I desire her."

"Ah no, Robert. Desire is easily dealt with. Many a good woman has served my desire. When only one will do, that is love."

"Then, perhaps I do love her. I owe her my life in any event."

"Yet you are unhappy for a man who has just won his love. Marriage is no problem – many knights have married Irish girls. It seems to work."

"She hates me."

Reginald looked at Robert in surprise. Of course she hated him. He had stolen her lands and killed her people; he had kidnapped her. What did he want?

"So what?" he said, "You can love her hard enough for two, can't you?" He laughed, "Or die trying."

Robert was not amused, but he smiled and urged his horse into a canter. Reginald kept up with him. "When can I see her?" he asked.

"When you want to. I shall take her back with us. You'll see her then, if not before."

"I'll wait with impatience," he said, "I must return to my men. I shall see you at sunrise."

"At sunrise," Robert nodded and waved as they parted company: Reginald to go to his troops, camped a mile south of Robert's men.

Aileen still watched him. Her hair, dishevelled and lustrous, fell over her shoulders, her green eyes were fixed on his face.

"I've been at Trigonnel's Point," he said, stupidly. The pain which ripped through her – the images – were suppressed, to be dealt with later.

She smiled, brazen, proud. "You'll have missed most of the sport whilst you were fighting at the chief's homestead. Was there anyone left to amuse you? Anything left to pillage?" She kept her tone conversational. Its blandness stabbed him like a blunted knife.

"Many died this morning, Aileen." He looked at her, begging forgiveness.

He said nothing more but she knew. If he had been her lover she would have loved him, cradling his head on her breast; it was so easy to comfort men. But she wanted no comfort for him. Just pain, and more pain, until it reached and surpassed that which he had caused her. "Perhaps you know my father Rory MacGillingrouth? Or his wife, she is flaxen-haired and very beautiful. Or my two brothers, about twelve years old they are, with freckles on their faces. Did you perchance see any of those people and give them God's speed from me?" He flinched and his grey face turned a stranger colour. "And I have a servant, a loyal English girl, her name is Lys. Did you see her in my dun, this morning, when you came calling?" She stood, hands on hips, legs apart, her voice like ice, her face like thunder. "What, you don't answer? Perhaps you fear some ill has befallen them? No matter. They are Irish. They are of little account."

He ignored the tone of her voice. "I don't believe I saw anyone like that. I know Rory MacGillingrouth, I don't think I saw him."

Hope sprang within her. If what he said were true, she might yet be rescued. It was fleeting hope, she knew. Rory would never be able to amass a force large enough to invade the Norman stronghold. Still, perhaps he was still alive. And Dvorvild, Corderg and the twins. She closed her eyes and for a moment only looked vulnerable. He lifted his hand to stroke her cheek.

"Don't touch me – sire. I'll thank you not to touch me." She moved her chin, so his hand caressed the nothingness between them. He left her. She had won their first engagement and he was defeated, already weary of the fight.

She wondered if he would come to her that night, and was surprised when he didn't. The only disturbance came from Silas, who brought her a warm cloak and another sheepskin, for the night was growing cold. The cloak was fur-lined, and she held it against her cheek, feeling the unfamiliar softness combined with the thick wool. It was a luxury she had not known before. She wrapped it round her, feeling the warmth settle on her body, and when all had grown quiet she contemplated escape. She was reluctant in many ways to try. She felt she was safe here, whereas out at night in the woods she could be killed without anyone ever knowing. Still, she thought she should try. She poked her head out of the tent and peered about her. The man, Silas, snored by his fire. She crept further out and stood upright.

"Would you like company or are you alright?" Silas hadn't moved as he spoke.

"I need to visit the wood again, I fear," she said.

"Then I have given you too much food and drink, and will remember that in future," he said, surly at being disturbed. He took her to where the trees met the field and waited. She wasn't long and returned shivering.

"There are wild boar and wolves in these woods, aren't there?" he asked, knowing that there were. "I pity anyone who has to travel without light, without weaponry and without company in this wood."

"I'm cold," she said quietly. "Can we go back?"

That night she dreamed of Cashal as he had first come to her on that boiling day by the pool. She saw the laughing, jealous faces of her friends, heard again her mother's disapproval, Corderg's warnings and Rory's ill-hidden fury. She talked with Dvorvild, pretty Dvorvild, from whom she had learned so much about the working of her body and the way it could be used. She saw Cashal's mutilated body carried into the village as she washed at the stream; Murchad coming to claim her when she had pretended he was the Norman knight. She cried, and slept on.

They broke camp as the sun started to climb in the sky, promising another fine day. By the time its warmth had driven the dew from the ground and lifted the swathes of mist from the tree-tops, they were on their way. Robert had found a horse for Aileen and rode beside her, sitting tall and straight in his saddle as his horse jogged and threw its head in the air, snorting and raring to go.

Aileen stared ahead of her, ignoring him, and out of the corner of her eye she could see him turn his head every now and then to look at her.

"You are comfortable, Aileen?" he asked her once. She turned her head away from him, declining to speak. "We make slow progress, I'm afraid."

She cut in on him. "Please don't apologise for the speed at which we are forced to travel. You and your men are sadly encumbered by the spoils from my home. Perhaps it is I who should apologise?"

He flushed, and she noted the startled look in his eyes. He said nothing and they continued in silence.

Later he went to have a look at his men who were, as Aileen had said, slowed down by the livestock they were driving and the loot, which in some cases weighed their horses down to a pace no faster than a slow plodding walk. The long lines of men marching single file through the undergrowth were soon able to double up as the path widened, trampled underfoot.

The return journey was taking twice as long as the initial march had done. Aileen, sitting in her self-imposed prison of silence, ached for the arms of Murchad; his lively humour, his open adoration. She missed Lys dreadfully: her idle chatter, her open warmth, the girlish jokes they had shared. There was nothing girlish in the way she must behave now: she couldn't smile, nor laugh, nor chatter. She daren't flaunt her body to tease the men who cautiously looked in her direction. Instead, she maintained the frigid demeanour of the captured princess she felt herself to be: noble, dignified and so dreadfully lonely.

Robert rode, sometimes beside her, sometimes spending several hours away with his men. She saw how his deceptively kind face would lose any lingering smile as he approached her; he drew a curtain over his personality, through which her barbed responses could not penetrate. She rejoiced in his discomfort and, to pass the tedious hours, planned how she would play her part. If joy had been removed from her life, then she would make sure that she did everything in her considerable power to take it from his. His suffering was her only pleasure, she must learn to make do with just that.

After several days of discomfort, for it was impossible for such a large army to erect their tents in the dense forest, they arrived at the Sheen Marshes; and the MacTilling Irish branched off to the hill country where they had settled, taking with them their share of the captured cattle and plunder.

The three Norman contingents proceeded cautiously through the marshlands and Robert kept a close eye on Aileen, concerned lest her horse should stumble and sink in the treacherous ground.

The mud spattered her but she never once lifted her hand to wipe it away, and he watched helplessly as a runnel slid down her face. It moved him, for some reason, and he wanted to enfold her in his arms. Not for the pleasure of her body, but to offer her some hope. Instead, he ordered Silas to watch over her and cantered ahead, selecting half a dozen men to accompany him.

"Robert, hello," Reginald greeted him, as enthusiastic as ever.

"We should ride ahead, Reginald. Have you seen Ghent?"

"He's already gone on ahead." Reginald gave orders to his men, picked a handful to accompany him, and fell in beside Robert. They met Charles of Ghent, who also picked some men from his troops; and so, accompanied by about twenty guards, they rode on to Gossard's Ford ahead of the main body.

Aileen, unhampered by Robert's presence and flanked by Silas, allowed herself to unbend a little and once, when Silas's horse slipped to his knees, almost pitching him to the ground, the surrounding men heard her laughter ring out in the muffled wastes.

Robert arrived at his castle several hours before she did, and went immediately to the quarters he had picked out for them. Large wooden coffers lined the walls of her bedchamber and a beautifully worked tapestry, depicting a hunting scene, hung from floor to ceiling. The hay on the floor was fresh-mown and clean, and despite the warmth of the day he had a large fire built; it crackled in welcome. His eyes strayed to, and lingered on, the wide bed, with its carved headboard and silken coverings, and rested there; then he turned heel and left the room, his boots thudding on the wooden floors. He almost ran into the red-faced woman he had chosen to be Aileen's handmaid, and she flushed and curtsied.

"Is all ready for your mistress?" he asked her, abruptly.

"I have boiled water for her to bathe, and will lay out her dressing robe. The sheets and linen are scented with lavender. I hope she will find it all to her liking." The maid was anxious to please her new mistress, who was something of an enigma amongst the servants, and she waited for some comment from Robert.

"I hope so, too, Marie," he said, and continued on his way.

She thought him rude and unapproachable, and couldn't understand why his men thought so highly of him. She watched from the narrow window across the arable plains to where the Sheen Marshes met the home woods and eventually she saw movement, like an immensely long snake, coiling its way through the trees. The smell of roasting meat drifted on the air, indicating that preparations for a celebration banquet were well under way. Marie placed cold water and cool wine on the serving table before the window, and prayed that her mistress would be less taciturn than her master.

The three leaders sat in the great hall, a long room filling almost the entire ground floor of the three-storied castle. Wide stairs led to a balcony above where the bedchambers were, then wound carefully to the upper floor, which led out to the ramparts. Stone was already being quarried to rebuild the castle, but its new timbers were dry and sound, and the castle felt impregnable. Straw covered the floor, freshly laid, sweet and dry. Hounds lay panting in the hearth, ready to prowl beneath the men's feet when the banquet started and drag discarded bones into the recesses of the room. Dog fights would add to the clatter and noise. But for the present, d'Evreux, Ghent and FitzAlan talked in muted tones over their ale.

The loud clatter of men and horses filled the courtyard and Robert went out, standing at the top of the steps to welcome Aileen to her new home. Ignoring the men surrounding her, he stood at her stirrup and helped her to dismount. She looked as if she would spurn his help, then, deciding against it, took his arm, and landed, dignified and unruffled at his feet.

He smiled, encouraged by her acquiescence. "Welcome home," he said, and the wind rifled through his hair, giving him a carefree look.

"Home?" She looked deliberately, back in the direction she had travelled, and his heart sank. He took her arm and led her up the steps and into the hall.

"Would you care to see your chambers?"

"Indeed, yes," she replied, cool as alabaster. He led the way, thinking how different this homecoming was from the one of his imagining. He had thought to bring her flushed and happy to her bridal suite; had imagined countless times how he would kick the door closed behind them and sink with her on to the feathered mattress. Instead he left the door ajar and showed her in, much as a servant would have done.

She pressed past him, going to the window and looking out, so that his arm, spread out to indicate the coffers – which contained new clothes brought from England – went unnoticed, and he spoke to her uncompromising back. "You will see I have had more suitable garments laid ready."

"Thank you."

"I've found you a hand-servant. You'll let me know if she doesn't please you?"

"I'm sure she will." But she thought painfully of Lys, wishing she was here to share in the wonder and the luxury spread before her.

"If you are comfortable, I shall leave you to rest."

"I shall be comfortable once you have done so." She kept her back to him.

He hesitated for a moment, anger coursing through him at her continued aloofness. "Aileen."

She sensed his mood and tensed. "Yes?"

The woods in the distance blurred; she wanted to turn and face him, but resisted, hoping he wouldn't come up behind her. It was the first time they had been alone together. Murchad would have dragged her to the bed if she had responded in this way to him. As would have Cashal, but the Norman was more reserved. He turned and left the room, slamming the door behind him. She heard his voice, cold and hard, the lighter tones of a woman, and seconds later there was a gentle tap the door. She ignored it. It

166

was repeated, louder, and when she still didn't respond, she heard the door open slowly.

"Madam?" The voice was hesitant. Aileen responded to its Irish lilt, and the fear it held. She turned, lifting her brows in a silent question.

Marie looked at the woman who stood framed in the light from the window. She was tense and stood proudly unbending, although she must have been tired from the long journey. She was dressed in men's clothes, far too large for her and spattered in mud, her hair hanging in rats' tails, tangled and filthy. Marie's heart sank. Her dreams of serving a great lady, with delicate manners fled: the woman before her was no more than an Irish peasant. It gave her confidence, and she introduced herself without waiting for her lady's orders. "I am Marie, I am to serve you." She let some of the contempt she felt show.

"How do you intend to do so?" Aileen had been unfriendly for so long, she didn't even notice she was doing it.

"In whatever way you desire, m'lady." Marie was both surprised and annoyed at Aileen's reaction. She longed to slap her face, but she feared to do so. Her master would have seen her flogged.

"All I desire, Marie, is my freedom." Aileen felt her eyes fill with tears: the woman looked kind and motherly, reminding her of Aifel, but she had somehow angered her, and increased her isolation.

Marie stood still, lost for words, while Aileen wiped her eyes. "I don't know the ways of the English lords," she said. "I don't know what I do desire."

"Perhaps a bath, a change of clothes. I have had water boiled for you."

Aileen's face lit up as she looked down on herself, saw the filth, remembered the man's attire. She smiled and Marie warmed to her. "Yes, a bath, a change of clothes. I have no clothes of my own, though."

"Yes you do, madam. Coffers full of them." Marie went to one and opened it, and the rich colours filled the room.

"These are my clothes?" Aileen went over to the rest of the coffers, all of them filled with cloaks and robes of silk and soft wool, cotton and velvet. She put her arms into one and lifted some of the contents: they smelled of spices from the East, rich in colour and beautifully decorated. "How shall I know what to wear?"

"Whatever you wear will improve your appearance," smiled Marie. She had now seen a side to Aileen that no one else in the castle had done: lost and frightened, needing support. Marie responded to her need with pleasure. If her mistress needed her services her job would be ensured, and if they got along well together, it would be all the better for that.

Marie had a hip bath brought to the room, and cauldrons of hot water, the men who carried it arrived panting from the kitchen. Marie ordered them about, telling them to place the bath near to the fire. Finally, all was ready. Aileen, from behind the curtain which separated her dressing room from her sleeping quarters, emerged naked once they had left, and Marie helped her into the hot bath. She lay back, luxuriating in the refreshing heat, and Marie poured oils into the water and rubbed them into her body. The smell was heady and pungent, dispelling the foul odours of the long journey. Afterwards, clean and slick, she stood by the fire as Marie towelled her dry. She then rubbed more scented oil into her skin and hair and placed a fur-lined robe about her shoulders. Aileen sat at a low stool as Marie painstakingly pulled an ivory comb through her tangled hair.

"Ouch!"

"It must be done," chided Marie.

"You sound like my mother,"

"I expect so. Who is your mother, may I ask?"

"Aifel. I am the daughter of Rory MacGillingrouth. I was Murchad O'Flerty's woman – until FitzAlan killed him."

Marie had heard of Aileen MacGillingrouth. Most of the people from hereabouts had done. Of her beauty, and her magic, and her proud defiance. She knew of her relationship with the legendary Cashal MacGillingrouth. The woman had known power – and Marie had thought her a peasant.

"I think I met your mother once. You have a brother in the priesthood?"

"Corderg, yes," Aileen was delighted. She felt less alone, warm and sweetly scented, wrapped in luxury.

"Corderg, that is he. He's a good man. When my village was raided he helped me. My husband was killed by the MacTilling raiders. Corderg gave food and protection, and through the Prioress of Whitley found me this position. I owe him a great deal."

"My mother is at the Priory – if she's still alive," said Aileen. Talk of her family made her homesick and she had to blink away tears.

"I'm sure she is," said Marie, kindly. "What's happened at Trigonnel's Point?"

"Everyone was slain. Almost all are dead. The stronghold has been burned to the ground and sacked." Her voice was dead-pan as she stared straight ahead into the flames of the fire.

"The work of MacTilling, no doubt," spat Marie. She hated the MacTilling men and their mindless violence.

"No. The work of our gentle lord, the chivalrous FitzAlan."

"But I had heard he is lenient towards villagers."

"Then you have been misguided. He killed Murchad before my eyes. He carried me through streets which ran with the blood of helpless children. He let his men take all the livestock and burn all the homes." She paused, allowing her words to sink in, remembering how Robert had trembled at the sight of the dead children. "He has kidnapped me, and brought me here against my will."

"He has treated you kindly?"

"He hasn't raped me – yet," she said.

"He means to marry you, so it is said."

"Perhaps. He'll find his wife unresponsive."

"But clean and beautiful." Marie ran her fingers through the wet hair, which now shone like smooth polished silk. "Turn around and let the fire dry your hair," she added practically. "Would you like some wine?" Aileen nodded, and Marie handed her some in a pewter goblet. "May I advise you?"

"You may give advice – I may not take it."

"Then, be careful. It is said that Robert FitzAlan is kind-hearted, but like all men he has a temper. He is very powerful. You could gain much by earning his compassion."

"I care not for his compassion. I live only to ruin his easy life."

"Then take care you don't ruin your own as you do so." Marie was practical, and sensed the same trait in Aileen. The woman was consumed by her hatred at present, but to have become as powerful as she had done – some said she had ruled the O'Flerty tribe through her lover – she must have a strongly developed sense of self-preservation. Aileen remained silent, and Marie carried on combing through the thick locks of hair until it was dry.

The combination of wine and warmth and the scented luxury of her rooms had relaxed Aileen. She looked up with a smile as the door opened. Marie, who looked up also, saw the answering smile light his cold eyes, and warm his face. She looked back at the woman seated at her feet. What a powerful hold she must have on men. It was clear that Robert FitzAlan was bemused by her. His smile died, as Aileen's did, leaving him looking cold and unapproachable once more. Marie dropped her gaze. It wouldn't be expedient for her to witness his shame.

"Leave us," he said, not even looking in her direction.

She sidled past him. It would make her life very difficult if her mistress persisted in treating FitzAlan in that haughty fashion. It would be his servants who took the brunt of his anger.

"You look better. When you have finished dressing, we'll go down and eat. We have prepared a victory banquet."

"A victory banquet? So you want to parade the spoils of war before your men."

"I wish only to have you beside me."

"For what purpose. To gloat and brag? The great Lord FitzAlan with the woman O'Flerty loved on his arm."

"Were you loved by him?"

"Oh yes, FitzAlan. He loved me, and he was a man who knew how to love." Her blow struck home.

"Did you return his love?"

"Vehemently. Passionately."

"I knew you would be a passionate woman." His voice was deep and low, his breath ragged. "Yet, loving him, you helped me to escape?" He took two strides across the room and stood with his chest against hers. "I remember I kissed you."

"Did you? I forget."

"No, you don't forget when you risk your life for a man."

She had made a mistake and she knew it. He was right, she could never have forgotten such a thing.

"You returned my kiss."

"No."

"Like this." He put his arms round her and held her against him, then he kissed her. She remained like stone in his arms until he released her.

"Like that? Murchad would not have considered such a response worth mentioning." Her mouth was dry with fear at her temerity. She lifted her chin; she would not let him see her afraid.

He wanted to hit her. "But Murchad is no more," he said through gritted teeth. His arms tightened, and she was forced to bend back. "And you did kiss me, Aileen. You will kiss me again like that."

"It will never happen."

"Yes. You were made for loving. Eventually you will give in."

"By which time you will be old and impotent."

"Then perhaps I won't wait for you to want me."

"Why should you? Rape, murder – they are all you know."

They were growing heated. Outside the door, Marie listened, unsure whether to smile or frown at what she heard.

He threw her on the bed. Instantly she raised herself on her elbows. "Come on then, brave knight. See how Murchad's woman shows her love."

"Don't talk to me again of Murchad."

"Why not? I love him. Can I not talk of the man I love?"

"Loved, Aileen. He is dead."

"Not in here, he isn't," she whispered. "Not in my heart." She thought of the queasy sickness which had disturbed her journey. That last night she'd not had time to take the herbal preparation she used to ward off unwanted babies. The warmth of Murchard's body had scarcely left her before the invasion had started. Perhaps he lived on in more than her heart. She wanted to taunt Robert with this, but she was too afraid he'd harm the baby. If there was a baby.

"You can rape me, you can humiliate me, you can do what you want with me, FitzAlan. But you can't make me love you, and you won't make me want you." She let her robe fall open; saw his reaction to her semi-nakedness. "This is the body which Murchad loved to touch," she said. "Every time you touch it, you will know I am wishing it were he."

He stayed looking at her from the foot of the bed. He could not have taken her then, even if he had tried. He was white and trembling.

"Be ready in ten minutes. I will take you to the dining hall."

"Certainly – sire." She made no move to cover herself, although her heart hammered with fear.

Marie entered as he left. "God's teeth, mistress, you play dangerous games," she said to Aileen, whose eyes glittered as she watched Robert's retreat.

"Dangerous games are alright, while I continue to be the victor."

"You unmanned him."

"I merely offered myself to him."

"Yes, you are as clever as I had heard." Marie had never heard a woman speak in that way to a man before. And she knew that Aileen couldn't have carried it off if Robert hadn't loved her. "He's in love with you," she said.

"Of course."

Marie didn't know how to answer. Her mistress was too clever, too proud and too sure of herself, and yet she was vulnerable, too. Marie had seen that, but, she now realised, it was only because Aileen had let her.

"Marie?"

"Yes, madam."

"Call me Aileen. I dislike being called madam or mistress."

"I dare not. It is forbidden."

"In private, then. When we are alone." And she dropped her proud facade, and reverted to the lonely friendless woman who hadn't known how to order her servant. She got up from the bed and put her arm round Marie's shoulders. "I need a friend."

"Alright, Aileen. In private."

Aileen squeezed her affectionately. Marie hugged her, not sure if this was another of Aileen's games. "And what shall I wear for this 'victory' feast?" Marie sighed – her mistress changed subject more quickly than the Irish skies changed in hue. Together they rummaged through the first coffer and pulled out a midnight blue, velvet gown, trimmed with gold, the cloth falling in soft folds to the ground. They also found a gold-embroidered surcoat which Marie shook out and held up to the light. Aileen gasped: it was exquisite.

171

Marie helped her put the gown on, and quickly braided her hair and veiled her. Then she stood back and surveyed her protege. Aileen was almost too beautiful to be true and, dressed in such splendour, Marie suspected that even the King of England would desire her. "Put on the surcoat," she said. It fitted perfectly secured by a wide belt, the gold cloth setting off the deep blue of her robe, and the rich darkness of her hair.

"Be careful he'll not be able to resist you," warned Marie, thinking it would be a good thing if he didn't try. They were a splendidly matched pair, if only Aileen would unbend.

"Let him try to do otherwise." The smile left Aileen's face as if it had never been, and a cold mask of hatred took its place. Just in time, for the door opened again and Robert re-appeared.

"Good. You're ready."

"Certainly I'm ready. Were those not your orders?"

He ignored her sarcasm and took her arm to lead her to dinner. Pausing at the top of the steps, he allowed her time to marvel at the great hall below, now filled with men. Huge haunches of venison and wild boar filled the table, and freshly baked fine bread, flagons of wine and bowls of apples jostled for space. The hall was ablaze with candles and a pall of blue smoke hung above the table. The noise was deafening as the men laughed and shouted to one another, but the room fell silent as Robert walked with his lady down the wide stairs.

"See how the Irish whore looks dressed in English women's clothes," whispered one indiscreet young soldier, already drunk. His neighbour wisely ignored him.

Reginald d'Evreux stood gallantly and pulled out Aileen's chair. He stooped and kissed her hand. "You would grace the table of the King himself," he said. She smiled at him, showing a small dimple in her chin. But she had seen him in his scarlet robes at Trigonnel's Point, deep in combat with one of her father's guard. His bluff manners hid a man as cruel as FitzAlan; she would not be deceived by them.

She sat bolt upright like a queen at Robert's right hand. Although he turned several times to talk to her it was noted that she answered as briefly as possible, and never smiled or looked directly at him. "Why does he allow it?" a drunk man asked.

"He'll beat her later."

"If he has time – for beatings."

"I'd not waste my time," the man laughed, and lifted the wine to his mouth, tipping his head back to drain the cup. The wine spilled down his face and onto his robe and he spluttered and choked, almost tipping backwards off his chair.

"You fool," laughed his friend, "You cannot keep a-top of your chair, let alone a woman such as that."

"Only give me the opportunity to try," he said.

Aileen watched the men, eating, drinking and laughing, just as the men had done at home. They were all alike. She was surprised at how alike; only their strange appearance, their unbearded faces and short-cut hair set them apart. They sounded as her father and Murchad had done after battle. She pushed the unwelcome memories away and watched Robert and Reginald as they grew progressively more drunk, whilst she sipped her own wine carefully.

Robert stood unsteadily and lifted his wine cup. The room fell silent. "A toast to you all, for the tremendous victory," he said, and Aileen swore she saw him look at her. The men rose, but she remained seated. All eyes turned toward her. "And thanks be to God for delivering us safe and unscathed."

"Thanks be to God," the men roared, still looking at Aileen.

Robert was drunk, fool-hardy. He pulled Aileen to her feet. "It is customary to stand and give thanks to our Lord, following a victory," he told her. "Perhaps amongst your people this is not so?" His voice was loud and clear, for he was determined to show his authority over her.

Her answer also rang loud and clear, to every man present. "It is customary with my people too, of course. But I have seen no victory."

The room fell silent. Robert seemed lost for words. Aileen sat down. He pulled her to her feet again and she felt a hot flush burn her cheeks. "Drink to our victory." He handed her his cup. She took it, looked into it, and tipped the contents over the table.

"Lick your victory off the floor – my lord. Like the dog you were when you won it."

He lifted his arm to strike her, furious and humiliated, but years of indoctrination stayed him, leaving his arm raised stupidly in the air as the heat burned his cheeks. She sat down again.

"Will you stand and drink, for victory?" He hid the tremor in his voice and spoke through gritted teeth.

"Yes, I will stand and drink for victory."

He hadn't thought she'd be so easily subdued, and thanked God. He had recognised his mistake in challenging her openly in front of all his men as soon as he had made it, but he knew no way of backing down without losing face.

"To victory!" she cried, loud and clear. "To the great victory when all Ireland is cleared of bandits and murdering Norman bastards."

He was thunderstruck. No women he had ever met would have dared to speak to him in this way. He'd been taught chivalry, he adhered to its principles. But it left him without recourse. Trembling, he took her by the arm and pulled her from her place. He took another goblet and held it out to her.

"Drink!" he commanded. He held his breath, as did the men around the table.

She refused to take it and stood brazen in the middle of the floor, a taunting smile on her face. "I'm tired. I shall retire," she said.

He took her wrist and forced the goblet into her hand, holding it clamped within his own. He forced the cup to her lips and tipped it. Wine ran down her chin and stained the blue robe.

"Well done, my lord," she said, scathing in her contempt of him, "You are indeed a very strong man." She turned, leaving him open-mouthed, and made her way up the stairs.

The stunned silence followed her, every eye was upon her. Robert hurled his cup across the room, followed by a wooden platter. The dogs pursued it, fighting over possession. The waiting tension mounted, with no one willing to invade its territory.

"She's a proud lady, and worthy of you, my friend," said d'Evreux, "I say we drink to this proud lady and to all the others who grace this earth." He stood and raised his goblet and they drank. The tension was broken. Robert went to leave but Reginald detained him, speaking low. "She's clever and without fear. A rare woman – handle her with care if you want her to love you." The noise around them had built once again and his voice was audible only to Robert.

"Should I beat her?"

"Would it help, do you think?"

"You see the way she is."

"Then, don't beat her. It'll not change her. And if you break her spirit, you won't love her. Take care. Don't try to humiliate her publicly again, and she'll not humiliate you. You have the upper hand, but only just. Keep it, Robert."

"Odd advice. I've never seen you treat a woman like that."

"I've never known a woman like that," Reginald replied.

CHAPTER 6

She waited for him in her room, fully expecting him to follow, and bolstered her courage with the memory of Murchad's strength: he would not have given in to weakness. She tried to imagine what he would have wanted her to do in this situation, but succeeded only in conjuring up his twinkling eyes and his easy laughter. The memory twisted something deep inside, made her feel bereft, for she had condemned herself to a life devoid of laughter, of any emotion, except the cold, bitter hatred with which she armed herself.

After a few moments, Marie came in and put her arms round her. She was surprised to feel Aileen tremble, for she looked poised despite her anger. "Whatever has happened – Aileen," she hesitated over the name.

"He told me to drink for victory. When I refused he forced me, in front of his men." She showed Marie the stains on her gown. "I thought he would hit me."

Marie was surprised. She had never met Robert before yesterday but the servants in the castle and the families who farmed his lands found him an amiable lord, friendly, concerned for their welfare. His men-at-arms respected him also, and she hadn't heard a word against him during the three weeks she had been at Gossard's Ford, despite the fact that he had been away for much of the time, leaving ample space for dissent.

"My head aches," said Aileen, and she sounded tired and dispirited.

Marie wrung a cloth out in water and held it firmly against Aileen's face. Aileen lent back on her cushions and shut her eyes, a small vein throbbed in her temple.

Marie was pensive. Her mistress was a fiery-tempered woman and she had already seen how well she could provoke Robert; she knew too how Aileen must have felt about attending a victory banquet in celebration of the massacre of her own village. But it would be foolish to get caught up in the middle of this warring couple, so she pursed her lips and held her tongue.

Aileen welcomed the cold of the cloth against her skin, but not the sudden cooling in Marie's attitude. True, she had taken Aileen in her arms, but it had been an empty gesture, and she'd had little to say. How Lys would have raged and chattered and sympathised. Aileen closed her eyes; Marie's warm and motherly body gave comfort even if her pursed lips did not.

"You should go to bed. You must be tired."

"Not yet."

"Then at least let me help you into your night-robe."

"Later."

Marie stood, uncertain of what to do. She wished fervently that she had a mistress who knew how to behave. Women who fought men inevitably lost. Their servants were more often than not held responsible, made to suffer. Marie had suffered a great deal in her life. Though she liked Aileen, the little she knew of her, she was afraid of her. She sat down in the corner of the room where the light from the sconce barely reached, and, watching over her mistress with concerned eyes, began to doze.

Aileen too slept a little, but fitfully. She was uncomfortable where she sat, but felt reluctant to be found lying vulnerable in her bed when Robert came up. The first tenuous fingers of light reached out over the horizon before she raised herself and went to lie down.

When Marie woke, stiff following her night's uncertain rest, she got up and lit the fire, throwing a coverlet over Aileen. She did indeed look vulnerable as she lay, as crumpled as the clothes she still wore, and Marie tentatively touched her cheek. Aileen stirred but didn't wake.

Robert opened his eyes, his head throbbing painfully, and tried to remember what had passed to leave him feeling so overlaid in gloom. As the memories of the preceding night returned, he struggled to control the desolation which swept him. He had been humiliated by Aileen, and in his turn had tried to humiliate her, not for the sake of doing so but because his temper, usually slow burning, had temporarily taken him over.

He had been confronted with a situation with which he was totally unfamiliar, and was pleased that his father had not been present to witness the scene. If his own mother had acted as Aileen had done, she would have been flogged, but in any case he found it impossible to imagine her doing so. Reginald d'Evreux had taught Robert a great deal about chivalry when he had been his squire, but little about handling a woman who failed to respond to it.

He turned and punched the feather bolster. Burying his head in it he tried unsuccessfully to go back to sleep but finally gave in to the inevitable and roused himself. He poured cold water over his head, shaking himself vigorously and spraying droplets over the floor; he slipped on them as he left the room, and hit his head on the bedpost. Angry and sore, he crashed from the room and out through the great hall, still littered with the sleeping bodies of his men and dogs after the night's excesses.

The absolute still and calm of the early morning eased his bad humour, and, as he often did, he looked out over the huge vista, his own lands of Loswellery, which he had fought so hard to win. The air which moved over these lands was pure and clean, a gentle caressing touch that cleared his head almost instantly. The small cottages which had sprung up almost overnight emitted tiny plumes of white smoke which dissolved gently in the white blue of the sky.

Going to the stables, he had his horse saddled and jumped on its back. He wore no armour, took no weapons other than his short sword, for who was now left to waylay him? He galloped out of the courtyard. The guard who opened the gate called out his welcome, and Robert lifted his arm in greeting.

The horse's long mane lifted, its neck stretched out as it reached forward, enjoying the freedom from its stable and battle harness, just as Robert appreciated the feel of the wind against his skin. When at last the horse began to flag, Robert allowed it to slow down and trotted past a small group of cottages whose doors were open to the morning air.

A tiny child, with long, curly hair as bright as the morning sun, was playing in the dust. She had picked a bunch of wild flowers: blue columbine, with its pink blush; dog rose, its pink leaves exposing tiny yellow seeds; violets; yellow and purple foxglove, and white campion with its silver-grey borders. He paused beside her, dwarfing her already diminutive form. She looked up at him, completely unafraid, and smiled, showing her first little white teeth as she held the flowers up toward him.

He dismounted, enchanted by her beauty and the beauty of the setting, and took her up in his arms. To his surprise she kissed his cheek, her lips as soft as the petals of the flowers she held. She strained in his arms to reach the horse and he took her over to it so that she could pat the animals warm grey coat; her touch was so light that the horse twitched, thinking a fly had landed, and the child laughed in delight.

A woman came to the door and looked out anxiously. She froze when she saw Robert holding her baby and opened her mouth, but she neither spoke nor screamed.

"Your child is beautiful," he said, smiling at her. His head was bare and without his armour he looked less imposing than usual; she managed to smile stiffly back at him, her eyes riveted on the child in his arms. He had wanted to take the baby on his horse's back and walk around with her, but the anxiety in her mother's face prevented him. He handed her back and the mother hugged her closely.

"What's your name?" he asked the woman.

"Mary, sire." In her fear she could barely move her lips.

"And the baby?"

"She is Siobhan, Lord." She pronounced the word "sheevorn" and looked warily at him all the while, afraid he would take the child from her.

He wanted to linger, to fill himself with the normality of the morning, but the woman was too afraid of him. He thought of the mangled bodies of women and babies, no older than this one, which he had left behind him in Trigonnel's Point, and was not surprised.

Mary saw a sad look creep into his blue-grey eyes, which had smiled so kindly at the baby, but failed to understand it. She would talk boldly of his visit for days, but she was afraid of his presence.

Robert remounted his horse and cantered slowly away. The baby waved after him and buried her face in her mother's hair when he drew out of sight.

It was the first time the thought had ever occurred to him, but he knew now he wanted children of his own. He knew he should want a son, several sons, to take over the lands after he was gone, but in his heart he craved a little girl, with dark hair and liquid eyes which would light up to see him, as Siobhan's had done. A little girl who looked like Aileen, with her spirit and courage, but who would love him and let him teach her to ride and swim in the river which bordered the castle.

He turned his horse back toward the castle. His impetuous ride into the morning mists had provided him with an answer. He might not be able to make Aileen love him, but her children would. He would marry her as planned, and give her babies, and eventually, ensnared by her children and the luxury of her life style, she would have to grow to love him.

He handed the horse – which was sweating lightly and snorting its pleasure at the easy ride – back to the groom, and went indoors. The great hall was cleared of most of its inhabitants, and servants were sweeping the straw back against the walls, picking up the half-chewed bones and replacing the burnt-out candles. He stroked one of the hounds as it sidled up to him and it followed him to the foot of the stairs, looking after him as he ascended.

He knocked gently at Aileen's door but didn't wait for her to answer before pushing it open.

"Oh, it's you," she said, and averted her head.

"As you see." He smiled, moving so he was gazing directly into her eyes. His look was intent but warm and she found it hard not to return his smile. In her effort her face grew stony and Robert felt some of the morning's magic leave him. He too fought to hide his feelings and the smile remained, both on his face and in his eyes.

"It's a beautiful day, warm, sunny. Why do you not walk with me and enjoy it?"

"What for?"

"For the pleasure it would bring you." He took her hand in his; it felt small, but strong and capable. He remembered its feel from the days of his captivity.

"Walking with you would bring me no pleasure."

He swallowed but kept his tone light. "Then walk alone, or take a horse. You would like to ride, to see your lands?"

"My lands? I thought you had won these lands for yourself."

"And my lands will also be the lands of my wife, and of my children."

"I wish her luck of them, then." Aileen whisked away from him and looked out of the window.

He had meant to be kind, gentle, sensitive, but now that he was before her he couldn't withstand her jibes and felt anger rise in him. "You know that you are to be my wife, Aileen. The mother of my children." His voice rose and he controlled it with effort. "I know you hate me now – that I have caused you distress – "

"Distress – is that what you call it when you obliterate my home and steal my lands and kill my people? Is this what causes English ladies distress?"

"Your leaders would have done the same, Aileen. Was Murchad such a gentle soul? Did he never kill, nor sack, nor burn down the homes of his enemies?"

Furious with him, she bit her lip. "I'll thank you not to mention Murchad's name."

"Words I spoke to you, only last night, if you remember."

She did remember. She turned to face him, her green eyes blazing in her white face. "You have no right to talk to me of marriage, of children, and of the man I loved."

"I have the right to do anything I please. These are my lands, this is my castle, I am the lord." He gripped her shoulders as he spoke. "You never

179

loved Murchad, you used him, Aileen. As you used Cashal before him, for your own ends."

"That's not true, but if it were – so what?"

"You don't know how to love. You don't know how to feel. You're a cold woman. You'll grow old and your beauty will fade. You will have nothing to offer a man, if you cannot offer him your love."

"What do you know of love anyway?" she said, more disconcerted than she cared to be. His words were mad, she didn't understand them.

"I know about love." He let his hands fall to his sides and a bleak expression grew in his eyes. She watched him intently, curious to know what he was thinking. "I know what love should be. And I know what love is. And perhaps I was wrong, perhaps it would be better if I had never loved."

He looked so sad she was tempted to touch him, to ask him to tell her about his love, but he smiled and drove the grey from his eyes.

"So about that ride. You must have a palfrey of your own. Choose one from the stables. If there isn't one to your liking, tell me what you require – I'll provide it. As my wife you shall have all you want. All you need."

"As your wife, I shall have nothing of what I want or need."

The tender moment had passed. They were sparring again. She had been saved from a gesture she would have regretted and she smiled slightly in her relief.

"Too bad. It changes nothing." He had grown arrogant, she had left him no other choice. "Reginald d'Evreux leaves within the month. When he is gone, I shall arrange for our marriage."

"And there is nothing I can say or do to stop this?"

"Nothing."

"I could kill myself, rather than be your wife."

He looked at her shrewdly. She had the courage, but not, he thought, the desire.

"No. I don't think so. You are full of surprises, but you love yourself too much to die." He laughed, genuinely amused at the shocked look his observation had provoked. For once she didn't answer, and he left the room quickly whilst he was still the victor. She had hurt him, as she always did, but he was growing slowly used to her evil tongue and the blood was singing in his veins now, much as it did during battle. She might hate him, but she would never bore him. A pretty girl passed him in the corridor and smiled, lowering her eyes modestly. She resembled Aileen but her eyes were violet – and kind. "Like Aileen, but not like her," he muttered, and the girl turned her head.

"Sire?" she asked in a timid voice.

"Nothing, be on your way – no, wait." He turned to face her and she looked up into his face, expectantly. Aileen had filled him with vigour, with passion; he burned with it. Yet a kernel of fear inside told him that if he tried to force her he would instantly be rendered impotent, and the fear kept him from her bed. He stared at the servant girl for a long while. He could ease his desire with her, for she would never dare to defy him. But he thought of the great knights of his dreams. Perfect, pure and chivalrous. Courageous in battle and gentle. If he didn't have his ideal he had nothing; and if he couldn't have Aileen, he would have no one.

He sent the confused girl away and clattered down the stairs out into the courtyard. Instead of the loving he would have liked to indulge in he busied himself with his men, making sure that any wounded soldiers were receiving proper treatment.

Later he rode out with Cormac in the bright, breezy afternoon, to survey the crops of grain now growing sturdily in their well-drained fields, and to look over the livestock and the outlying farms. He knew that if it were not for Aileen's influence, he would think his lot a happy one: he was more than satisfied with Cormac's stewardship; the weather had been kind that year; the animals were fat and glossy; the people content and well fed.

"You had a great success at Trigonnel's Point, I hear?" Cormac asked easily.

"We turned a thriving stronghold into a slaughter-house," Robert replied bitterly.

Cormac looked at him, surprised by his tone. He had been regaled with stories of the victory, of men running craven through the streets, and of plunder heaped to the skies. Now he understood the quiet with which Silas had greeted him. "I had wondered what ailed Silas," was all he said on the matter. "And what of O'Flerty's beautiful woman?" Of course, he had witnessed the debacle of the previous night, but, like so many others, had been too drunk to take in what had happened. The scene had fled to places in his mind where he stored the inconsequential.

"She is a bad-tempered witch," Robert replied, and Cormac looked at him again, expecting to see anger, or even sorrow in his face, but Robert was smiling. "She has a sharp tongue and is unlike any woman I have ever met."

"Irish women are less humble than your Welsh ladies," Cormac said, and Robert could hear the hint of pride in his claim.

"Humility is a trait that Aileen MacGillingrouth would despise."

"As would all MacGillingrouth – they are a proud and ambitious people. It is said that you intend to marry her."

"Oh yes. Soon we will marry."

"She'll be pleased to have made such a conquest, I dare say," Cormac was sure of no such thing, it was the way he liked to talk.

"I dare say," replied Robert, "in due course, she will be very well pleased." He laughed out loud. The day had been a good one: the tender moment with the child, a battle won with Aileen, a battle won with himself, and a rewarding afternoon with his friend and steward. He had a great deal to be pleased about.

CHAPTER 7

For two days Aileen kept to her room, until some of the anger faded from her heart. She slept little and dreamt sadly when she did. She had Marie bring food to her room and when the woman reverted to calling her Mistress, did not correct her. There was a coolness between them. Aileen missed Lys and the friendship which they had shared; whilst Marie, despite her maternal feelings toward Aileen, was uncertain of how to behave, so remained withdrawn. It was an unhappy state of affairs. Robert didn't visit once during that time and as Aileen didn't leave her room, she didn't see him.

She was driven out on the third day by boredom. Marie brought food to her in the solar, which was a pleasant room hung with rich embroidery and furnished with carved wooden seats, padded with thick cushions. A small fire burned merrily, for despite the warmth outside it was cool within. There were fresh rushes on the floor and the window looked out to the side of the castle, over the stable block. She stood there, as she ate, watching the activity below, and stepped back slightly as she saw Robert emerge from the shadows. He stood out from the rest of the rabble. His noble, upright carriage and the proud tilt to his head, often softened by the ready smile on his face. As she watched, she heard his laughter ring out, followed by that of the man beside him. They took their horses and rode away, obviously in deep conversation. Robert was liked by his men, and she had learned from both Cashal and Murchad, and to a lesser degree her own father, how important and how difficult that was to achieve. She bit her lip, disliking the direction her thoughts were moving. She could allow no affection for this man to dull the edge of her hatred: to do so would be disloyal to Murchad's memory and to the rest of her people.

Knowing he was out she slipped down to the stable block, taking great mouthfuls of fresh air as she did so. Except during spells of rare illness she had never spent so long indoors, and she craved activity.

The men watched as she passed, but none talked to her until Silas eventually saw her and stopped polishing his shield – which had merely provided an excuse for him to rest himself in the sunshine – and went to see if she needed assistance.

"I was told I might choose myself a palfrey," she said, half expecting a swift denial.

"Yes. Whichever one you wish. Come and I'll show you." He led the way to where the riding horses were stabled. "Pick from any of these. I'll let the groom know."

"Are you leaving me then?" she asked, and he stopped, surly man that he was, at the unusual timbre of her voice.

"I'd stay if you wanted."

"Yes – stay." She was among strangers and his was the only face she knew. Suddenly she smiled and Silas felt warmed by it, as he had been by the sun before she had come. Their eyes met in sudden wordless understanding.

"There is a mare here which I like especially," he told her, and they stopped by a beautiful horse who watched them with dark, intelligent eyes. Aileen opened the stable door and slipped inside. The mare nudged her, her nose soft and warm against Aileen's hand. Aileen blew in her ear and patted her neck, making friends, whilst Silas fetched a halter. The horse was silver-white, finely built, bred for speed. Her mane and tail were long and of the purest white; they glittered in the sunshine.

"Would you like to try her?" Silas asked.

"I must borrow some men's breeches," she said.

Silas raised his eyebrows, and immediately Aileen's happy expression became thunderous. "What? What ails you?"

"Men's breeches, mistress?"

"Men's breeches, master."

"Women ride in their riding habits."

"No. English women ride in their riding habits, Welsh women ride in their riding habits. But Irish women ride in breeches. I have none, I shall have to borrow them. Please arrange it for me." He had to turn his head to hide a twitch of mirth. She thought he was angry and stamped her foot. "And I want no side-saddle, I ride as you do, astride, it is all I know."

"As I do, yes, Madam." He had to leave, the twitch was becoming overwhelming. He called a groom to saddle the mare and Aileen returned to her rooms.

"Marie," she called. The woman hurried to her side. "I'm going to ride. Silas will be here shortly with a pair of breeches for me, please bring them as soon as he gets here."

"Breeches?"

"Breeches, sure to God you'll not object to me riding in breeches, you, an Irishwoman?"

"You, the wife-to-be of an English lord?"

"Marie, I'm an Irish woman."

Her tone brooked no argument and Marie hastened to meet Silas. He was at the top of the stairs. She recognised him by the linen trousers he had over his arm. "You must be Silas, the mistress sent me to fetch these." She smiled, taking in the rugged features of the man before her. A real man, she thought, stocky, well-built, his face deeply scored by life, and weather-beaten. He bore himself with pride, but he was a man of the people.

He, too, looked and liked what he saw: Marie had a happy, rosy, uncomplicated appearance, and made him think of good food. "She is a handful, your mistress, I'll be bound," he said, his eyes twinkling.

"Too much of a handful for me," she retorted, "she'll lead me into trouble."

His eyes strayed to her ample bosom. "And you're too much of a handful for me, it seems," he smiled, "And I too could lead you into trouble." His hand lifted as if to follow the direction of his eyes and she slapped it away but her rosy cheeks had become vermilion and her smile struggled for precedence, though she tried to look stern.

"Will you come and sit with me, while she rides?"

"Maybe. Maybe not."

"You'll find me by the river, under the beech tree – when you're ready."

She took the breeches from him and returned with them to Aileen, who looked at her shrewdly.

"You've been blushing, Marie."

"No, mistress."

"Yes. I'm neither blind nor stupid. You have an assignation. Who with?"

"I have not," Marie sounded indignant, but she blushed more furiously than ever and turned, placing the breeches on the bed, to hide the fact.

She helped Aileen undo her robe and lifted it carefully over her head, watching as she put on a linen shift and the breeches. Her lips pursed but Aileen took no notice. Marie, she had learned, pursed her lips a great deal, but nothing ever seemed to come of it. Anyway, she seemed more human now that Aileen had seen her blush.

When Aileen returned to the stables the mare was ready for her, dancing on hooves which seemed hardly to touch the ground. She mounted easily and without assistance, and, accompanied by the groom who insisted he was acting under orders, she rode away from the castle.

As soon as she came to a flat area of grass, littered with dandelions, she urged the mare into a canter, and then into a gallop, delighting in her speed and responsiveness. The ground flashed beneath in a blur of yellow and green.

"If you only had wings, I could fly you away from here," she whispered, and the mare twitched her ears. "But then, where would we fly to?" The wind brought tears to her eyes and she was forced to concentrate to see where she was going. But the feeling of flying stayed with her. She had heard of the great winged horse called Pegasus, but he had been a stallion, she thought. "Then I'll call you Peggy," she said out loud.

She felt crazy with joy as the exhilaration of the moment wiped the fear and anger of the past week from her mind. It was childish to talk to a horse, to be so elated over finding the animal a name, and yet, with so little to feel happy about, she desperately needed some diversion.

She turned her head to find the groom, whose horse was heavier and blundered behind them losing ground. It could gallop in this way for many miles, carrying a fully armoured knight, but when it came to sheer speed, was no match for Peggy. The idea of escape flickered into Aileen's mind, and just as quickly out. Trigonnel's Point was at least six day's ride away, and she had no food, clothes or real chance of survival. And what was left for her there, anyway? Life here was too comfortable to motivate her to risk so much for so little. For the time being.

Feeling Peggy begin to pant, she pulled her in and cantered at a more sedate pace along a cart track leading to the small village she had seen from her room. The groom fell in beside her and they rode through the village, the people turning curiously to watch her. She saw them out of the corner of her eye, huddled together gossiping, and wondered what tales were abroad and in what form they would finally travel from homestead to homestead.

She was aware that her name was already becoming legendary, linked as it had been to the grandeur of the MacGillingrouth sept, the O'Flerty tribe, Cashal and Murchad. Now she was the prisoner of Robert FitzAlan. Would she be hailed as a heroine or spurned as a witch?

She speculated idly, comfortable with the situation, for it was one she had grown accustomed to over the past two years. In fact, she ruminated, she would have it no other way. If no one ever talked about her, she would almost feel she didn't exist. And one thing was for sure, Aileen MacGillingrouth most definitely did exist.

They had passed now beyond the village into a field of vegetables where men and women weeded and dug, sweating in the heat of the sun. She was reluctantly impressed by the order and efficiency which was abundant in the farming of Robert's lands.

The people were fat and happy; no hollow cheeked babies, or men and women bowed beneath the weight of their travail. These people obviously worked hard, ate well, and sang at night in the village green, drinking whisky and beer and talking, talking until their jaws would move no more. Aileen had heard their refrain from her bedchamber and longed to join them, dance a jig and throw a glance filled with promise at the best-looking man in the village. Instead she had sat alone and listened and planned cold strategy, which brought only fleeting satisfaction to her hot and passionate nature.

She drew Peggy to a halt and sat quietly for a moment. The groom saw a sad look mask her face, and felt inexplicably sad himself. Then she turned and trotted very slowly back the way she had come, giving the village a wide berth. She rode by with her head averted, not wanting to feel like the outsider she was. The groom wondered what it was that had so displeased her.

Once the village was behind them she cheered up; the groom saw her pull her shoulders straight as she urged Peggy on again, cantering alongside the river, dazzled at times by its sparkling waters which reflected a myriad rainbows.

She stopped at a place where the grass sloped gently down to the waters of the Loge and dismounted, pulling the reins over the horse's head and leading her down to where tiny waves lapped the shore. Peggy drank thirstily, then surveyed the horizon, an intent look in her eyes, water dripping from between her lips. Aileen took off her soft shoes and waded in, pulling Peggy behind her, and they paddled, waist high, the horse splashing as she tried to lift her feet clear of the water. Then Aileen clambered onto the horse's back again and, holding on to her mane, swam her into the centre channel of the river where the water ran deep. Peggy stretched her neck and blew water from her nostrils noisily, her tail streaming behind her like silver weed.

The groom led his horse to the bank and watched, his eyes wide in surprise. He'd never seen a woman behave in such a way.

Peggy lurched out of the water, found her feet and shook wildly, almost unseating Aileen, and spray drenched the surrounding area. The noise made Silas look round from where he sat gazing into Marie's bovine face. He chuckled and pointed while Marie pursed her lips and tutted.

"Do you not like her?" he asked.

"She would be my friend if I let her," replied Marie, her tone bumptious.

187

"Would she indeed? Then why do you not let her?"

"I am not merely her servant, you know." Colour filled her face again, and Silas stifled a smile. "I serve the master, too. And how can I serve him by conniving in corners with her against him."

"But Sir Robert would be displeased if he thought you were displeasing his lady."

"You have no idea of the way she goads him,"

He remembered the victory banquet and had a very good idea. "She is a brave and unusual woman," was all he said.

"Oh, brave and unusual is it? And I, I suppose, am dull by comparison?" The corners of her mouth drooped sulkily and he remembered that no woman cares to be compared with another.

"I prefer women like yourself, with the wisdom to hold their tongue and the experience to please their man." He kissed her hard on the lips and squeezed her ample body. When he drew away from her she smiled.

"I'll agree the maid is young and inexperienced," she conceded.

Silas smiled inwardly, careful to hide the truth. He had never said Aileen was inexperienced. "Then you should try to help her, guide her. I'll warrant Sir Robert would thank you for it, in the long run," he said. She looked doubtful. "Look at it this way, if all around her is hostile, it will make that emotion all the more easy for her. But if all is soft and friendly, she will melt. The sooner she melts, the best pleased will be your master. So you will, in that way serve both."

"You know a lot about the ways of the world, it seems," she retorted, but she was softening.

"About Robert FitzAlan's world, yes I do. I have shared his hopes and dreams and seen him grow from youth to man. He loves your mistress and would wait for ever for her approval."

"Wait? For ever?"

"English knights are like that. They can love a maid from afar for long years, and she would never know it. "

"It sounds strange to me," Marie said peremptorily. "What a waste of virile manhood."

"They don't see it as a waste: for them it is a part of life. Robert FitzAlan would see this as a challenge, to be overcome. I, on the other hand, see no point in wasting my virility." He grabbed for her lasciviously.

"Oh, you are a devil, Silas," she squealed, then fell silent.

Before Aileen left the horse, she kissed her nose gently, and gave her a turnip.

"Will she suit you, do you think, mistress?" the groom asked.

"Very well. She is perfect." He smiled at her, and she thought what a nice face he had. "Her name is Peggy," she called over her shoulder as she went to change her wet clothes.

Marie was nowhere to be found and Aileen asked a young maid busy cleaning the passageway to help her with the fastenings of her dress, which was made of yellow silk, cut low, and belted across the hip with a narrow chain which hung almost to the ground. The maid did so gladly, pleased to have something more interesting to pass the day than sweeping up rushes and replacing candles. She asked, diffidently, if her lady needed help with her hair, and Aileen nodded, feeling languorous following her ride and not inclined to sit alone staring at the walls.

"What's your name?" Aileen asked. The girl was slim and dark, like her, and had a pretty face.

"Shelagh," the girl answered shyly.

"And have you worked at the castle for long?"

"A fair while, my lady," she said.

The door opened, interrupting their conversation, and Robert walked in. He looked from Shelagh to Aileen, and Aileen saw the expression on the girl's face. Shelagh blushed hotly and looked at him in adoration before lowering her eyes, to look at her feet. Robert barely seemed to acknowledge her presence but Aileen had seen the small jolt with which he had initially recognised her.

So that's the way the land lies, Aileen thought and a wave of anger swept over her, dulling the pleasure of the day.

"What can I do for you – my lord," she said, as facetiously as she could.

"I heard you had been riding, I wondered if you'd enjoyed yourself?"

"It was alright," she said, yawning. "Rather tiring, I shall take a rest. Leave me," she said to the maid. "I daresay you too are ready for your bed," she then said, looking from Shelagh to Robert and back again. Her tone was heavily suggestive. Then she flounced away into her dressing room, pulling the heavy curtain across.

The maid left the room, flabbergasted by the sudden change in atmosphere. Aileen hadn't seemed in the least tired before the lord had appeared. And why should she, Shelagh, be ready for bed – it was only mid-afternoon, and the lady herself had just changed into day clothes. She shrugged and loitered in the passage, hoping Robert would catch her up. A door banged behind her and she looked round. It was him sure enough, but he looked furious and brushed past her almost knocking her to the ground.

"Excuse me, sire," she said timidly.

He turned and looked at her impatiently, then hurried away. She hung her head disconsolately and resumed her sweeping. It was clear he couldn't be bothered with her, and yet, that other time, he had looked as if he might be interested.

As soon as she heard the door slam shut, Aileen emerged from behind her curtain and paced the room, her gown sweeping the floor with an angry hissing sound. "Damn you, Robert FitzAlan," she swore, not understanding where her anger lay, aware only that some of the sunlight had fled from her day.

She looked from her window, to where life still continued without her in the world outside. Two figures walked close together, not touching, from the direction of the river, and as they drew closer she recognised Marie, in her red gown, talking animatedly to Silas. She heard him laugh and he put his arm around her waist, as if sharing a joke. She smiled at their obvious pleasure in one another, but the smile soon faded: their closeness emphasised her own isolation.

FitzAlan was in the great hall talking to d'Evreux when she trailed down the stairs on her way to the solar. It was too late for her to turn back, and she lifted her chin and tried to sweep past them.

"Good day, Aileen," d'Evreux's charming voice made her pause.

"Good day, sire," she replied. She gave him a friendly smile, half turning her face from Robert.

"Will you join us? Our afternoon would be enhanced a thousandfold by your company."

His flowery words were balm to her ears. She pouted her lips and threw back her head, in the old way. "Would the company of a mere woman not stop your important conversation?" she said, perfectly aware that it would not.

"On the contrary, it could only add a sparkle where dullness prevails."

"Nevertheless, I shall take my sparkle into the solar – with your permission. You may join me there when you have finished being dull." She left them, and d'Evreux laughed heartily.

"She has more than a fair share of audacity – 'You may join me there', indeed."

"She has more than a fair share of everything which is bitter and cold," Robert said, trying to smile and succeeding only in looking sullen.

"Then you must make it your duty to make her sweet and warm. If you don't care for the job, perhaps I – ?" His sentence tailed off, the implication hanging in the air.

"You only say that because you know I wouldn't wish her upon you," Robert commented drily. "But I wish I could do as you suggest. No matter how hard I try, she remains cold."

"That much anger at least shows that she can feel," d'Evreux remarked. "She may play the part of a cold woman, but I'll wager she is only acting."

"She acts remarkably well."

"She is remarkably clever."

"So you keep telling me. Perhaps I should let you take her back with you. You champion her most ardently."

"And you are most jealous. No need – it is you she loves to hate, Robert. I am just an amiable foil to arouse in you the very emotion you are now feeling." He patted Robert on the back, sympathetic to the torment Aileen had put him in. "I shall be leaving soon, and you will marry."

"I shall ignore her jibes until then."

"Play her at her own game?"

"At which she is the master, and I, only the apprentice."

"As I remember it, you learn quickly and well."

"I have had expert tutelage, Reginald."

"No less so now," he laughed.

They turned to other matters, and Aileen waited in vain in the solar. She tapped her foot impatiently, then sank into a chair, taking up some needlework, but she was clumsy at it and it was quickly spotted with blood. She hated Robert and Reginald and everything they stood for, but they provided stimulation; her sparring with Robert made her blood sing in a way she had not encountered since the early days of wooing Cashal. She pricked her finger again, and tears pricked her eyelids. She was infuriated at being left here alone: bored, frustrated, and demoralised at their obvious dismissal of her. Was she not beautiful enough, clever enough, to hold their interest? Obviously not, she thought, flinging her needlework away from her in disgust.

She flounced from the room, intending to pass them with her nose in the air, but again she was frustrated because the hall was empty except for the wolfhound which came and sniffed her curiously. "At least I'm beloved of animals," she said with acrimony. Nevertheless, she fondled the be-whiskered beast gently, feeling his wiry coat beneath her hand. "Come on," she said and walked to the main door, but the dog held back, watching her with a puzzled expression in its eyes. "Come on," she wheedled again, bending forward to entice it, rubbing her fingers together as if she would offer it food. The dog stared blankly, cocking his head to one side.

She left him there, revising her original opinion. "Not even beloved of animals," she thought, ruefully.

She saw Robert stride into the courtyard and was nearly knocked over as the great creature rushed past her to follow his master, adoration illuminating his soulful eyes.

HAPTER 8

$\mathscr{F}$or three weeks Aileen had been waking up, her mouth dry and her head aching dizzily. As soon as she raised herself from the pillow her stomach heaved, and when she was eventually driven from her bed, she stood retching over a bowl in the corner and wishing she were dead.

Marie watched her quietly, her eyes knowledgeable. "How long has it been like this, mistress?" she said, wiping Aileen's glistening face with a damp cloth.

"Since the taking of Trigonnel's Point," gasped Aileen, retching again, pitifully unable to bring anything more up.

"And you know why?"

Aileen turned to face her, a worried frown on her brow. "I have my suspicions," she said cagily.

"Is it our lord's child?" Marie asked her. To her knowledge the relationship had not been consummated.

"No. It is Murchad O'Flerty's," she announced with pride. Marie was reminded once again of the prestige her mistress had possessed, even before she had come to Gossard's Ford.

"Then he is not to be forgotten," she whispered, and there was an expression of awe in her tone.

"No, Marie, he'll not be forgotten." And suddenly she was joyous, her sickness receding. "If he's a boy, I'll name him for his father."

"It will never be permitted," said Marie, gasping at her mistress's effrontery.

"Who's to gainsay me, pray?" she said, her expression haughty. Marie declined to answer. She had learned the value of holding her tongue at some of Aileen's more preposterous utterances. It was obvious FitzAlan would stop Aileen from doing any such thing and Marie saw no advantage in telling her so.

"Will you tell him?" she asked.

"Perhaps. When I am ready."

"Your wedding is less than a week away. He should know before that."

"I could make it my wedding gift. After all, he has given so much, and I, so little."

Marie wasn't deceived by the sarcasm as once she might have been. "It would be a cruel present." Her association with Silas, which was flourishing, had shown her many a positive side to their employer's character. She valued Silas's opinion, and Silas held his master in the highest regard.

"No more cruel than he deserves."

Marie sighed and folded the cloth carefully. There was no reasoning with her where Robert was concerned. It must be lonely for Aileen, she thought suddenly. No family, no friends around her, and full of hatred for the man determined to keep her. Marie rarely looked at things from Aileen's point of view, it was too uncomfortable for her. She too had lost her home and many of her family at the hands of the invader, but she had given in to the inevitable and allowed herself to be swept along by the tide of events. In her case, as with others who worked under Robert's patronage, her standard of living had improved. Aileen had more than most, but none was less satisfied. Part of Marie respected her strength, part resented its implied criticism of her. "But you are Irish," Aileen had often said when Marie fell too squarely on Robert's side of the fence. The words made her flinch for they had no answer, and spoke to a part of her which she preferred to keep buried. The last time Aileen had said this, Marie had ignored her, and Aileen flared up. "No? Well perhaps you are no longer Irish, after all!" she'd taunted, and Marie had had to fight the tears which threatened to overwhelm her. She didn't tell Silas: he could not have understood, and although she pretended indifference, to herself as much as to her mistress, she still awoke with a sodden pillow the next morning.

Aileen looked at her. "What are you thinking?" she asked, for Marie's face was a picture of different, fleeting emotions.

"That you are in for a difficult time."

"Why, you think me unfit for delivering babies?" said Aileen, frightened suddenly.

"Ah, no. Your baby will be born with the greatest of ease," she said, smiling as she eyed Aileen's well-rounded figure. "No," and the smile faded, "I was thinking of this battle you persist in fighting. It'll not be so easy once you have a baby to look after."

"What do you mean?"

"You are careless of your own welfare. You can afford to be defiant when it is only you who will suffer the consequences."

Aileen interrupted. "But with a baby to think of I will be more vulnerable?" She spoke slowly, "Yes, you're right. I must put up some sort of truce with FitzAlan. And yet, I should miss our battles if I did."

"Miss them?" asked Marie. Her mistress was a constant source of amazement.

"Yes. But never mind, the time is not yet. I have seven months or more in which to decide how I will deal with this. In the meantime – ," she broke off as the door opened. A maid brought in some breakfast and settled it on the small table, near the window.

She ate in silence, her sickness leaving her hungry as usual. She planned to ride that morning and wondered idly if it would harm the baby. Somehow talking about him had made him a reality. However, if he were Murchad's child, and of course he was, then he would take no harm from a gentle ride in the country.

The stables were busy. Reginald d'Evreux was leaving in the morning and his men were making ready for their departure. Aileen led Peggy from the stable and waved at Cormac who was lurking nearby.

"Will you be riding this morning?" he asked, his ready smile growing when he saw her. He was always one to state the obvious. He loved to talk, if only to hear the sound of his own voice. Marie said it was because he had spent years in silence, but it was a typically Irish trait all the same.

"As you can see. Will you be joining me?"

"Indeed, indeed I will."

Robert had urged – without any great difficulty – that Cormac spend time with her. To keep an eye on her, he had said. Cormac sensed there was more to it: that Robert wanted her surrounded by people whom he felt to be his loyal friends; perhaps he hoped their feelings would rub off on her, or perhaps he wanted to keep abreast of her feelings. Whatever his reasons, they dovetailed exactly with what Cormac wanted to do. He liked what he had seen of Aileen, who loved her native lands as much as he did. He liked her spirit and her sense of humour. He had no cause not to. For Cormac she had smiles and endless chatter. For Robert she had only sour looks and her words were terse and always solicited. Cormac was saddened by this: he imagined they would do well as lovers, if only Aileen could see it, and Robert dare believe it.

Aileen itched as they rode along to tell Cormac about the baby, but held her tongue. She had constantly to remember that he was devoted to Robert, and she wanted to keep this particular gem until she was ready to impart it. She acknowledged that she was afraid to tell Robert, for she couldn't foresee his reaction. She was already beginning to see that Marie was right: her responsibilities would be overwhelming once the baby arrived.

As they rode from farm to farm the people came out to see them, and to talk to Cormac. They had already started to turn to Aileen with some of their problems, finding her sympathetic to their needs; and her early love of children had flourished recently, perhaps because of her isolation. They ran to greet her and she chattered to them happily, their laughter mingling with hers. Often she rode home with tired bunches of flowers they had gathered for her, and these she tenderly placed in water to brighten her room. Sometimes, as she sat and looked at the children, she cried for her brothers and for her father, wondering what had become of them; and she thought too of her mother still at the Priory. But time began to dull the memories and the pain, and her life drifted onwards.

Robert rarely called to see her any more. She thought he had lost interest. The girl, Shelagh, was often to be seen, like a shadow in his wake, and Aileen felt uncomfortable in her presence. Marie, if she had known all this, would have presumed her jealous, but Aileen would have strongly denied it. It was a matter of pride, she convinced herself, that was all. This was her first experience of being usurped by a younger woman. She was forcibly reminded of Aifel and Dvorvild and of Tara and herself. Poor Tara, her body last seen lying in blood and dust on the ground, still clinging to her babies' hands: a death she had not deserved to suffer.

Robert came to see her on the eve of their wedding. He looked relaxed and smiled appreciatively at her. She was dressed in a simple white dress which clung to her body, showing it off to its full advantage. Her dark hair was partly braided around her head, with the rest hanging to below her waist; it gleamed in the sunlight which streamed through her window.

A sharp knot of desire brought a lump to his throat. "How are you, Aileen? You look well."

"I'm as well as can be expected."

"Considering the ordeal which lies before you," he finished. Like Marie he had learned the way her sharp tongue worked.

"Quite so," she replied, and he swore he saw the faint glimmering of a smile lift the corner of her mouth.

"Is there anything you need? Anything more I can do for you?"

"Apart from giving me my freedom, you mean?"

He inclined his head, not deigning to answer.

She looked around her at the room which spilled over with all the luxury any woman could need. No trader passed by Gossard's Ford without being first taken to Aileen, or Robert himself, who bought her expensive or inexpensive trinkets alike and had them sent to her room. Despite herself, she couldn't help but be excited when she saw one go by, knowing that some delicious item would soon find its way up to her. She swept the room with one expansive gesture. "What more could I ever need?" she said, forgetting to sound sarcastic. It was the baby, she thought, which was making her soft. She'd noticed in other women that their tongues lost their edge in the early stages of pregnancy.

"If you're happy, I'm happy," he said, but he was thrilled at the apparent softening in her attitude. It augured well for the future. They looked at one another for an extended moment, their arms hanging limply at their sides, and Aileen found when she looked away that she had almost forgotten to breathe.

After he had left, she had to force herself to think of Murchad, of his dead eyes staring blankly whilst she was bundled ignominiously out over Robert's shoulder. Instantly she felt the seething core of hatred spread throughout her body, to such a point that she was forced to calm it for fear of damaging the baby. She had no illusions. Whether she wanted to or not, Robert FitzAlan was determined to marry her; all she could do was make sure he lived to regret the decision.

She went to bed early, wanting to look her best, having first considered arriving at the chapel in a state of disarray, straw in her hair, and in an old linen shift which she would have worn in the old days at Seandale for tending the swine. She had even considered arriving naked, but even she would not dare do that, and she was dubious as to the results such an action would bring. If it were to alienate Robert enough to call off the wedding, it might also humiliate him, leaving him no choice but to incarcerate her somewhere to be forgotten, or have her publicly flogged. It was always possible, probable, that in either case she would never be allowed to reach the chapel, but returned ignominiously to her room and forced into putting on something more seemly. Ultimately she'd decided to show herself at her best; she would be silent and cold and as beautiful as Marie's skill could make her. That way Robert would desire her all the more, making her rejection of him all the more painful.

Marie came to see if she needed anything before going to her own bed.

"No, thank you. But wake me before dawn, I need to recover from my sickness before the ceremony. Heaven forbid that I should be ill during the ceremony."

They laughed together but Marie swore she saw a speculative gleam in her mistress's eye. "You wouldn't?" she said, accurately reading the look.

"No, but I'd like to," was the reply.

It was a cool morning. Aileen was up early and Marie washed her hair and braided it and laid her finery out on the bed.

Aileen went out to see Peggy, who was grazing contentedly in a paddock near the river, and stood talking quietly to the mare. She shivered in the fine mist which lay in a pall over the low-lying fields, obscuring the water. Beyond it she could hear the beating of duck's wings, their deep-throated cries drifting eerily out at her: a surreal, unearthly sound. The scene was as unreal as the commitment she was about to undertake: as though she had stepped outside herself and was watching proceedings from afar. It was an uncomfortable sensation, forcing her to think, not allowing her to feel.

Peggy wandered away, leaving silvery imprints in the soaked grass, and merged quickly into the mist. Aileen was left isolated, abandoned and lonely.

"How did I ever come to this?" she cried into the void, but her words sounded thin and without substance so that even her pain was a mockery. She stayed until the sun started to force the ground-mist away and noticed, with a start, that autumn had already tinged the trees with gold and umber and the heather on the hills was turning purple. Would she one day sit as an old woman, perhaps at this same spot, and reflect on her life? Would it still bemuse her then? Would she, like the trees had done, age quietly, without awareness, then look back in surprise at the years spread about her like fallen leaves upon the ground? And what would she have to reflect on? for she could see no way out of the life which was being thrust upon her. She would have a horde of children about her, no doubt. FitzAlan's children, whom she would love as he would. Their destinies would be irrevocably entwined if this were the case, and her grand-children would know little, and care less, about the circumstances which had led her here today.

She shrugged the uncomfortable idea away as the sun burnt off the last of the mist, revealing acres of golden grain. Then she walked briskly back to the castle – ready to do battle.

Robert, too, woke early – ready to do battle and had never felt so afraid. He couldn't protect himself from Aileen's barbs by putting on a coat of armour, he couldn't parry her jibes with his sword, or set his Welsh archers upon her. And to make things worse, he had chosen this war, with nothing at all to be gained from the attack. He was predestined to failure, and yet he could do no other. He loved Aileen and he couldn't allow himself to fail: she had to return his love. But if she didn't, she would have to bear his children, she would have to be his dutiful wife – he would have to accept second best.

Angrily he took up his sword and stared at it, as if it held all the answers. Should he be a man who cared less than nothing for the desires of his wife, or should he be a knight, and put her honour above all? "And, by God, I have done so. I have honoured her, and kept from her bed. I have given her luxuries she has never known. And I shall marry her, and nurture her dubious honour. What more can a man do?" He could almost hear her reply:

"You can give me my freedom. I haven't asked for this. I saved your life, and you took Murchad's in return. Let me go, and honour me in that way."

He brought the sword down with a crash, hacking into the thick wood of the table. "No, damn it. I won't ever do that," he shouted into thin air. His manservant cringed in the corner: he'd never seen his master act in this way.

It was a tight-lipped couple who met in the nave of the chapel, where Arnulf, the castle's chaplain, performed the wedding ceremony. Aileen made her responses at the last of every possible moment, stretching the tension to unendurable limits.

They looked beautiful, the tall muscular knight and his lady, but there was nothing beautiful about the atmosphere which permeated the chapel and Arnulf crossed himself as he watched them leave.

They walked in silence back to the main hall, mocked by the glory of the day, and Robert thought how hollow a victory could be when the opposition was unarmed. He was buoyed up by his anger, for they had both forgotten that brief tender moment in her bedchamber where their eyes had met and held. That one small moment of shared humour, before the cold had descended to encompass them again.

"I should like everyone to drink a toast to my lady wife," Robert said when they were seated, and Aileen saw with dismay that his smile was forced and his hand shaking. He's not afraid, she thought, so he must be angry. And angry he was, for he was remembering that other toast when she had shamed him.

"To the lady Aileen," – the response was ragged, but they drank with gusto. She sat, unsmiling. Those who knew her best wished she would show the laughter and the sparkle which they knew was her; others thought her sullen and wondered why he should want to marry such a one.

Marie and Silas looked at each other; Silas shrugged and grimaced, and Marie smiled and nodded her head in silent communication. It was good to have a man in her life again, she thought, and Aileen was a fool to regard it so lightly.

The banquet went on and on, until Aileen thought she would be unable to endure another moment. She could, and knew she could, have ended the ordeal at any time, but that would have brought the dreaded confrontation closer, when they would finally meet, alone, as man and wife.

As the feast dragged on for the married couple, it heightened in enjoyment for the other guests. Miming, tumbling and music took place around the boar's head, the centrepiece of the table, and there was drink and food in unlimited quantities. The noise in the hall soon became deafening. Robert looked time and again at Aileen's unyielding profile and let his anger mount, as did his desire.

Eventually, Aileen rose and turned a face which looked pale and haggard toward her husband. "I have had enough. Will you let me retire?" she asked him. She'd never asked his permission for anything before, but he didn't notice. He did notice she looked ill, but was too drunk and too angry to care: it seemed another effrontery and one could never tell with Aileen if she were playing games or not. He watched her walk away from him, savouring the almost unconscious sway of her hips, and the way the men's eyes followed her progress.

The hall was heating up with the dancing, swirling bodies of his guests and the suffocating smoke from the hundreds of candles which lit the room. He watched and the drink he had taken merged all the bright colours and sensations into one whirling mass, and the mass was the essence of Aileen, hot and vibrant and full of life. He followed after her. There was nothing for him in the hall now she was gone. Why drag this out any longer? Silas whistled and cheered as he saw the departing figure Robert turned and gave him a smile.

Aileen was met by her women who huddled about her, giggling and making ribald comments, undismayed by her lack of response. But Marie was surprised by Aileen's appearance: she seemed broken.

"Is it the baby. Are you sick?" she whispered.

"A little queasy – it's nothing," she replied.

"Then what ails you?" Marie was startled to see tears fill Aileen's eyes.

"The futility. The helplessness. My own disloyalty," she replied, and her voice was flat, empty.

"You've not been disloyal," Marie said, not understanding.

"I am married to the man who has carried out atrocities which I cannot even number. And I loved the man he killed, Marie. Is this how I avenge his death?"

"Did you?" the maid asked. "Did you love Murchad?" She wanted to goad Aileen, to buoy her up, but Aileen was too dispirited to react.

"Perhaps I did, perhaps not," was all she said, anxious to terminate the discussion. She just didn't have any fight to spare.

When the women escorted Aileen from her own chamber to the bridal one, she was actually shaking with nerves. They removed her beautiful white velvet gown, her barbette and veil, and combed out her hair until it hung down her back like fine black silk. The bed was strewn with flowers and they laughed, delighted as women are at weddings, to see so beautiful a bride. But she lay white and shivering, ignoring their chatter.

"Please leave me," she said finally to the women. "Go and enjoy yourselves, for God's sake."

They left her, putting her temper down to the obvious "first night" nerves which had left her trembling. And when Robert came in he found her like that: pale, white, shaking in his bed, and was completely taken aback by her.

"Aileen, for God's sake, what is wrong with you?"

She sat up abruptly, and looked him full in the eye. "You have me here, so why ask me what is wrong? You are the winner. I, the loser. I wish you joy of me." She was so vehemently angry that she surprised even herself; her words caught on a sob, and all her fine plans of cool ridicule fled. Weeping women did little to discourage ardent men – she had not lived for twenty years without finding that out.

"I have no wish to win, not in the way you mean. I want only to love you, and for you to love me."

"I'd sooner have married one of my father's pigs," she cried, and he stepped back as if she'd slapped his face.

"By the time I have finished with you," he said, tearing off his clothes, "You will wish that."

She scratched and bit him as he threw himself upon her, but he wasn't deterred. He held her in his arms and looked into her face, which was twisted and almost ugly with the hatred she felt.

"I've always wanted to hold you like this," he said. But the words were not tender, not as he had dreamed of saying them; they were cruel and taunting.

She tried to lift her knees and push him off her, but he was strong and she was imprisoned. "And I have always dreaded the moment."

He kissed her to shut her up and as she arched her back to fight him a long shudder of desire swept through her and she pressed herself against him, ardently returning his kiss. It was unexpected, entirely involuntary; she was swept away by a tide of emotion which she couldn't stem.

"Ah God, Aileen," he breathed, and she responded, whispering:

"I love you, I love you." It came naturally to her, as if she'd said it many times before. Suddenly she heard herself, her dreadful words, and they rose again, the spectres which haunted her sleep, and waved their skeletal fists at her. Her body was so hot with the passion she felt, it took all her will-power, every ounce of courage she possessed.

"Oh Murchad, Murchad, love me," she groaned, and pushed herself against his body, delighting in the feel of it, even as she did so.

It didn't register at first. She felt his ardent response, the hardness of his body as he pushed ever more strongly against her and then he realised.

He hit her. He had vowed he never would, but the pain was so intense, so confused with his passion, that he couldn't help himself. The blow wasn't hard, and he left her in the bed, to jeer and mock and tell her ladies later how Robert FitzAlan had been unable to consummate his marriage.

CHAPTER 9

$\mathscr{T}$hat year, 1175, had been a momentous one for the Norman barons, forging new lives and lands upon the defeat of the Irish people. On the first of June, Strongbow died. A leg ulcer, treated too carelessly, had lain him low and, cursing both his condition and the heat of the summer, he had quite unexpectedly expired. Even as he lay dying, however, further Norman successes had been reported to him – most notably that the popular Raymond le Gros, after a brilliant campaign, had captured Limerick, thus finally and irrevocably confirming his master's hold on Leinster.

But what would happen now that Strongbow's strong hand had been removed? What would Henry of England do without the independent-minded Welshman to frustrate him? Surprisingly, Strongbow's demise had little effect upon the country. Peace and ever-growing prosperity was widespread – in itself a measure of all that the great man had achieved – and men like Robert FitzAlan continued to govern their lands without too much interference. Nevertheless, men were saddened by his death and continued to worry about the future. In England the news came as music to the King's ears: he had been planning to make his favourite son, Prince John, Lord of Ireland and was pleased that the troublesome baron would no longer be able to oppose him. Henry, therefore, re-asserted his power by once again appointing a royal representative in Dublin. In the meantime Leinster's lordship had fallen to Strongbow's infant daughter, Isobel, although to the baronage generally this made little difference. Largely ignoring royal dictates from Dublin they continued to enjoy the comparatively quiet times that followed on from Strongbow's pacification.

Unlike many of his contemporaries, Robert, his thoughts centred upon Aileen, had not been tempted to take up the cause of any warring Irish sept. Instead he busied himself with the affairs of his estate, aided always by the inexhaustible energies of Silas and Cormac. The English and Flemish settlers who augmented the original belagh families lent an air of civilised standing to the village which was rapidly growing up outside the castle's perimeter. Robert should have been a very happy man, but instead, following the debacle of his wedding night he'd been dogged by an underlying sense of failure.

When Robert left Aileen on the night of their wedding, he had gone to the stables, woken the surprised groom to prepare his horse, then galloped into the darkness. He had returned three hours later and gone to his old bedchamber, its cold bleakness suiting his mood. By morning time he had himself under control: whatever he was feeling he hid it well, putting on his smile as he did his cloak.

He went to Aileen early, entering her bedchamber – their bedchamber – with a nonchalant expression which was lost on her, for she was doubled up over a basin in the corner of her room and retching violently. Marie, standing with her arm around Aileen's shoulders, looked up guiltily and, meeting his eye, blushed and turned her head.

He knew then, exactly what was going on. Heartsick, he watched Aileen try to hide her condition. He noticed her shape, her breasts which were fuller than they had been, her more rounded face, the emotional swings. He'd seen the same thing with Katherine d'Evreux when she was pregnant.

None of them spoke until Robert, aware he must do something, strode over to Aileen. She looked up at him, steadying herself on the table; he resisted the urge to support her.

"When will you have the baby?" he asked.

Too sick to prevaricate or twist the situation to her own advantage, she avoided his gaze. "Spring next year, I think."

"Then we must start making preparation. Tell me if there's anything you require." He wanted to be genial, but instead he sounded stilted and formal. She nodded and he could see tears in her eyes.

She lifted her arm to wipe them away. "This wretched sickness makes me cry like a baby," she said, then flinched at the analogy.

"Of course," he said. "You must take care of yourself. Rest more. Don't become over excited." It was a way out for both of them, he thought. A way of excusing him from her bed, which instead of being a source of pleasure had become the cause of his emasculation; of achieving some middle ground without losing face. He left the room, for there was nothing further to say, and Aileen looked at the closed door with a haunted expression on her face.

They met again at breakfast and talked politely about the weather, the farms, the livestock, anything but the subject which was uppermost in both their minds. As she wiped her mouth with a napkin and moved to leave the table he detained her gently, putting his hand on her arm. She paused, half sitting, half standing, then sank back into her seat.

"I need to know, Aileen. Is the baby – ?" He couldn't ask, and floundered stupidly.

She rescued him. "Yes, Murchad's baby. There has been no one else."

He nodded, gratitude and jealousy vying for precedence. Her tone had been compassionate, more gentle than ever before and he detained her again, as she was about to leave. "Is there anything more I can do? Anything you want which will make your confinement more pleasurable?"

The expression in his eyes as he looked into hers was too intense; she felt consumed by him and it was with difficulty she looked away. There was something she wanted very badly. She awoke every morning and could have cried for lack of it. For lack of her. She didn't want to ask him for anything, or to feel in any way indebted, and yet – . "There is something." This time it was she who was hesitant, he who came to her rescue.

"If it's within my power to help, I'll do so." That look passed between them again, constricting her breathing.

"I had a slave girl – Lys. She was very dear to me. Can you find out if she was killed?" She didn't mention Trigonnel's Point, for fear of the ready anger the subject inevitably roused.

"I can try," he replied thoughtfully. "You would like her here, of course?"

"Above all things," she said and although she spoke quietly he could see how much it meant to her, and how much it cost her to ask.

"I will try," he said, to reassure her.

"Thank you." He didn't detain her again and she went up to her room, to lie on her bed for a few moments. Her heart was beating furiously and although she tried to convince herself that this was due to her excitement at the prospect of having Lys with her – if she could be found – she knew it wasn't that alone.

When she went down to ride Peggy she saw Cormac and Robert talking earnestly in the stable block. Robert called her over and Cormac smiled at her in his usual welcoming way.

"Greetings to you, my lady,"

"And to you, Cormac," she said.

Robert saw her eyes light up as she spoke to him, so that they appeared a lighter green, like the inside of a wave just before it breaks, he thought, and smiled tenderly.

"I've been talking with Cormac about your request, Aileen." Robert explained.

"Can you help?" She turned back to Cormac, all anxiety and excitement.

"If anyone can, I can."

"You sound very sure. I hope your abilities match your beliefs." Her tone was bantering and Robert felt left out. Why could he not have such a relationship with his wife? He would have valued it above all things.

Cormac bowed comically and winked.

"When will you be ready to leave?" Robert asked him. "As you see, my wife grows impatient."

"Tomorrow, at first light. I'll go back to Trigonnel's Point and start my search from there."

"You'll take care, Cormac?" Aileen said. "I'd not want you hurt on a mission on my account."

And she meant it. Robert watched the sap green of her eyes darken to olive and worry lines creased her brow. "You were going to ride, Aileen?" he asked, keeping his voice light to match theirs.

"Yes, I see no reason why I shouldn't at this stage."

Cormac looked from one to the other with beady eyes, detecting a slight nuance in her voice.

"Then let us all ride together," Robert replied jauntily. She was surprised at his suggestion and could do no other than comply.

He was surprised at her knowledge as they surveyed the home farms: she had taken the time and trouble to learn the names of the farmers and even in the rapidly growing village, people seemed pleased to see her. His own mother, back at home in Wales, could not have faulted her and he felt great pride as people congratulated them on their marriage. He watched as she took baskets from her saddle and administered the potions and bandages with a strange compassion. She worked easily, side by side with Cormac, conversation almost superfluous between them.

"I see I shan't miss my steward while he is gone," he commented, "for I have a good one in my lady wife."

She flushed with pleasure, then despised herself.

They stopped and ate with one of the farmers, whose wife bustled around, delighted at the privilege of serving their lord. It was a good day. Cormac's informal and friendly personality infected them all and temporarily obliterated the cold wall which so often came between Robert and Aileen. Robert found himself unwilling to return to the castle and kept suggesting that they just ride here, or look over there.

Finally he remembered his wife's condition and a black bear of misery settled on his back. All the day's pleasure was clouded by the memory and as they entered the castle gates he was once more overcome by a dejection which reflected in the set of his shoulders and the clipped nature of his conversation. He allowed himself to be distracted by Silas, who rode away with him to oversee a problem which had arisen in the lists.

Cormac and Aileen watched him leave. "'Tis a shame, lady," Cormac said, "that your lord doesn't have more time for pleasure."

"Why so?" she asked, sensing his sincerity.

"He's a good lord. None better. But he works too hard, rests too little and takes little pleasure from his achievements."

"Has he always been so?" she wanted to know. It seemed that no one other than herself could fault Robert and yet he had been responsible for so much carnage.

"No, he used to be light-hearted and easy going. Proud of his lands and of his achievements. The massacre at Trigonnel's Point caused him a great deal of unease."

"Go on," she said, as Cormac paused, fearing he had said too much.

"He hates unnecessary bloodshed. Silas has heard him, call out in his dreams, after a battle and seen the horror on his face in the aftermath of fighting."

"Yet I have heard he is a great warrior." – And he had killed both Cashal and Murchad. Both strong men. No weakling could have done that.

"And so he is. He's valiant during battle, but that doesn't mean he is war-like in his nature. He wants nothing more than to farm his lands in peace with a good lady by his side." Cormac looked at her shrewdly. "He would have stopped the massacre in your homestead, if he could have done. He berates himself for failing, for turning his attention at the crucial time."

"To killing Murchad and abducting me. Do you suggest I should simply forget that?"

"No. How could you? But do you think Robert could have allowed Murchad to live? Would Murchad have given Robert his life, had the situations been reversed? And would he have left so beautiful a woman behind?"

Robert had said something similar – "Murchad would have done the same as I have done," he had said, or words to that effect. And she had turned her mind from the reality, because it weakened her.

"I am still part of the O'Flerty tribe. How could I, of all people, condone their chief's murder?"

"Because you can do no other. Because you are with child and need your lord's protection. Would Murchad O'Flerty have cared so well for Robert's baby?"

He would not have done, she was sure. Robert had surprised and softened her by his selfless actions: indeed, she had never encountered such chivalrous treatment before.

"How did you know about the baby?" she asked.

"I didn't, but I do now," he said, and his eyes twinkled.

"My God, but you are devious. I should have you flogged," she said, but she laughed as she did so. "And you seek to warm me toward my husband because you care for him. But I have an obligation to my family and my people. I dare not soften." Her voice became deadly serious.

"Otherwise?" he said, and he looked fully at her, deep into the window of her eyes.

"Otherwise I should not be able to call myself Irish. Do you not think it would be easier for me simply to comply with my lord's demands?"

"Easy? No, compliance is not a trait I had noticed in you. Forgive my frankness."

"There! You have learned something this day," she said, tossing her head. "Compliance is inherent in all women, is it not?"

"If you say so, my lady." He chuckled as she flounced away, but beneath the banter, he fervently hoped she would consider what he had said.

They ate their evening meal quietly, both thoughtful, surrounded with the normal clatter and laughter. After such a pleasant day in Aileen's company, Robert was questioning his own behaviour. He couldn't help but remember the sensations which had spread throughout, not only his body but his whole being, when she had grown passionate in his arms. The insult, the terrible, shocking loss which had taken its place when she had called him Murchad could not be overlooked, and yet? And yet he had done so.

He had offered to find her friend and spent time with her. Time which he had enjoyed and during which he had found new facets of her personality that he had never dreamed existed. She was kind, she was thoughtful and she was bright. She understood about growing crops and rearing livestock and talked knowledgeably, so that he could almost forget she was a woman.

He had swallowed the pain he had felt when he'd discovered she was carrying Murchad's baby, feeling that in all honesty she couldn't be blamed for her condition. Yet she seemed not to appreciate anything he did for her and still maintained her polite distance, whilst talking, very merrily, with Cormac, who had given her nothing.

And taken nothing from her.

He was damned and weakened by his ability, which his father would see as a disability, to see every side of the situation. But he must act as he saw fit, without perpetually looking over his shoulder to see what his father would have done. He knew Aileen wouldn't have lasted for many hours under his roof, with her arrogant ways and cruel tongue, but it was very hard to imagine his bluff old father loving, or even caring, more for a woman than he did himself. And that was how he felt for Aileen. He'd rather have her with him, and vitriolic, than not have her at all.

He ate and drank some more and laughed at a joke without even hearing what it was about. Aileen looked at his profile and couldn't help but wonder where he travelled, for his mind seemed many miles away.

Perhaps, he thought, if the slave could be found, Aileen would soften towards him. She must be lonely, cut off as she was from everyone she'd ever known, and pregnant too. He would try to love her child – at least he would try not to hate it, but he did fervently hope it wouldn't be a boy. It always seemed there was more of its father in a boy and having a little Murchad in his nurseries would be adding salt to an already stinging wound.

The memory of Murchad filled him with a sudden rage and he gripped his hand until the veins stood out in his forearm. He would deal kindly with Aileen and with her baby. He would take care she had all she needed – but – he would no longer attempt to make her love him. She had done too much, gone too far, to push him away, and finally she had succeeded.

Shelagh paused beside him and topped up his cup. He was resolved, and tossed back his wine. The decision, once made, lightened his load and he entered into the laughter and ribaldry which surrounded him with gusto.

Aileen too was thinking as she sipped her wine. Her ladies had tried to give her buttermilk – for the baby – but she hated milk, and Murchad had, so she could see no reason to give it to their baby.

When Robert had left her bed the night before, her body had taken a long while to let go of the longing he had aroused. She'd convinced herself that it was only natural that she should need the love of a man: Murchad had been demanding and she had grown used to it. So why had she cried herself to sleep, and why, every time she tried to conjure up Murchad's face, did she see Robert's, in all its guises? That she had hurt him badly, she was well aware, but instead of that knowledge bringing her satisfaction, she felt ashamed and sorry for what she had done. It was perverse and stupid to feel so badly, and due, she was sure, to her condition, which was making her soft and vulnerable. She felt sure that when Lys arrived she would be strong again. But would even Lys be able to drown those words which she had masked by calling Murchad's name? "I love you, I love you" She doubted it. She had heard their echo long after he left her.

She couldn't stop thinking of Cormac's words either, and of the people who depended upon Robert for their livelihood: they all liked him. It was hard to maintain the cold indifference with which she had always treated him, under such a barrage of good will. Perhaps she should soften, weaken – for the sake of the baby. If he approached her again, he would find her more compliant. Far more compliant.

When she left the table she smiled at him briefly, but he didn't notice and the smile died on her lips. She lay on their great carved bed, wrapped in her fur-lined dressing robe, for a long while before she finally gave up and crawled under the blankets. She woke before dawn and knew he hadn't come to her. She waited for the flood of relief but there was none and she shivered, drawing the covers more closely round her. At least, she thought, she'd have been warm with him there.

It was late when next she awoke to see her ladies bustling around and the dreaded buttermilk beside her. She looked militant, but nothing else was forthcoming. "What's this?" she demanded finally.

"Buttermilk," Marie replied.

"I won't drink it."

"Sir Robert says we are to give you only buttermilk."

She drank it because she was thirsty, hating the rich creamy stuff, and immediately brought it up again. That, Sir Robert, is what I think of your orders, she thought, as she heaved.

CHAPTER 10

ℭormac left, as promised, early that morning, accompanied by five men. Robert had chosen him because, being Irish, it seemed he stood a better chance of success. For the same reasons his companions were also Irish, well armed, but not seeking to do battle. In case of trouble Cormac proposed to pose as a merchant dealing with the import, sale and distribution of slaves.

They made good time and arrived five days later at Trigonnel's Point, only to find it desolated. As Robert had surmised, there were still a few families who had lingered on, living in those dwellings which had survived the worst of the Norman torches. These duns, patched with turfs and wood from other buildings, housed those who had chosen not to accompany the bulk of the survivors into the far west.

It was to these folk that Cormac initially addressed himself. It was a slow business but conversation eventually elicited the fact that their leader was none other than Father Seamus. His wife having died, the old priest had chosen to stay to look after the remnants rather than start a new life elsewhere.

Seamus was willing to talk and Cormac rapidly established good relations with him, so much so that he felt it safe to reveal that he was really no merchant, but an emissary from Aileen.

"And what is the news of Aileen?" Seamus asked. He could vividly recall the arrogant set of her chin, her ready tongue, and he softened at the memory of her beauty and charm.

Cormac told Seamus of the marriage between Aileen and Robert.

"Dear Lord. Forced to marry the man who caused her people so much grief." The old man's face was lined and sad.

"He's good to her. He loves her, Father," Cormac said. "In fact that is partly why I am here. She is expecting and wishes to have her old servant by her at this time."

"Lys?" asked Father Seamus. Cormac nodded.

"She's alive, I hear," Seamus said slowly. He looked at Cormac, liking what he saw and decided to confide in him. "Have you heard tell of Murrough O'Flerty?" he asked.

Cormac shook his head. "No, I don't think so."

"He was brother to Murchad. Before your Norman overthrew my people there was a threatened uprising here. Murchad's brothers Turlough and Murrough tried to take over the chieftainship of Trigonnel's Point."

Cormac had heard gossip about the subject, it had never really interested him. Except for one bit he had never been able to verify.

"Go on," he said, encouraging the old man to speak.

"Murrough raped Aileen," the priest's eyes were shrewd. "He was severely punished for it – although as it turned out, not severely enough."

"You intrigue me," said Cormac. He'd heard of the rape but never had it confirmed. "I believe I know what you are about to tell me. He was gelded for his trouble, was he not?"

Father Seamus looked at him, full in the eye. "He was a bad lot. A sly, evil man, who wanted the chieftaincy for himself and Aileen with it. He is now the chief of a new tribe, comprised of remnants of the old tribe and other stragglers. They have made a sept over towards Limerick."

"Led by a man who has been unmanned – surely not!" Cormac said. Shock at what he was hearing vied with belief. "No tribe would take such a man as leader." He felt the priest was trying to make a fool of him and was surprised that he would attempt so obvious a lie.

"He was not unmanned." Seamus held up his hand to silence Cormac, who tried to intercede. "Oh, we all thought he would be, even though the job was only half done."

"Surely not, how could – ?" It was impossible to imagine such bungling.

"I don't know how, I know only that to prove his manhood Murrough had a slave brought before him. He raped her in front of the whole village to prove himself. She had been a virgin," the priest frowned in disgust. "There was no doubt of penetration."

Cormac's hand went to his sword. That such a man could live to rule was an abomination to him. He wondered how Aileen would react and decided to keep this piece of news to himself. "You were telling of Lys," he said, remembering why he was there.

211

"Lys was one who was taken from here. She lives now with that sept. As far as I know she is alive and well."

"Would you help Aileen? In her loneliness she needs friends around her."

Seamus looked doubtful.

"The child is Murchad's. She could lose it if she continues to mourn. Lys could help her to get over her loss."

"Why should I help?"

"For her sake. For Murchad's. For your own. My lord has built a monastery near Gossard's Ford. It needs men like yourself to run it. It is new and thriving and I believe you could do yourself a great deal of good by helping Sir Robert."

Cormac had little difficulty in convincing Seamus that Lys must be found and to his relief the priest volunteered to lead a small party into the west. He had managed to convey such a rosy picture of life at Gossard's Ford that Seamus also agreed to do his best, upon his return, to persuade his fellows to seek protection from the Normans there. Existence at Trigonnel's Point had become steadily less bearable and the idea of ending his days within the confines of Robert's new monastery was most attractive.

Cormac, satisfied that he had done all he could, returned to Gossard's Ford to await the outcome of his efforts.

Seamus's party didn't have to go further west than Limerick, for there, almost by accident, they made contact with what was left of the O'Flerty's, still grouped together under the leadership of the exiled Murrough, who was actively supporting the Thomond king in his war against the foreigners.

After a journey fraught with hardship, Seamus and his men gratefully accepted the welcome and hospitality of their old companions, although they were sorry to see the town in turmoil. It had recently been the scene of bitter fighting between the Normans and the Irish, and Seamus arrived not long after the town, abandoned by Raymond le Gros, had been handed back to Donel O'Brien, the Thomond king.

Seamus was drinking with an old friend when Murrough came upon them, his face tense.

"Greetings, Murrough," Seamus said, rising to shake the younger man's hand.

"Why are you here?" he growled. He had little cause to like Seamus.

"I came merely to visit with friends, to see how things are going with you."

"And to hide your old bones during the winter, no doubt."

Seamus smiled and offered Murrough a drink. "It is excellent whisky,

Murrough, drink some, forget the past."

"I would that I could," Murrough said, and drank heavily.

"It's good to see you alive, with so few old friends left living," Seamus said. "Do you remember young James, with his axe bigger than his whole body?"

Murrough laughed, his tension leaving him slightly. They lapsed into a reminiscence of the past, liberally interrupted by the whisky Seamus had carried with him.

"You've done well, very well indeed," the old man said. He had stayed sober, unlike Murrough, who'd become morose with all the talk of the old days.

"How so?"

"The tribe, what there is left of it, has flourished under your ministrations."

Murrough laughed and poured another drink.

"Why," said Seamus, warming to his subject, "I think Murchad – God rest his soul, would have done no better."

"Devil take his soul, I say," growled Murrough. "And look what happened under his leadership."

"You're not wrong, no, you're not wrong at all," Seamus weaved over to Murrough and patted him warmly on the back. "By God, but you have been wronged, Murrough. You'll not mind my saying that?"

"No, I'll not mind, Father. Have another," Seamus held out his goblet and Murrough filled it. "In fact, I'd say it's good to hear you come round to my way of thinking."

"I'm deeply hurt, Murrough. Did you think I was against you, back in the old days?"

"I thought you were, yes," Murrough's words were slurred together and he leaned on the table.

"But you were wrong, so wrong. Oh, I know I had to support the man. We all made pretence of that. You only have to see what happened to anyone who tried to oppose him." Seamus paused dramatically, and Murrough's eyes filled with maudlin tears.

"It was a terrible thing, Seamus. A terrible thing he tried to do to me. And it destroys a man, more than you could ever know. Then to be cast out into the woods – I almost died there, weakened as I was,"

Seamus nodded his understanding and poured him another drink.

"Have one yourself, Seamus. Have two – ," Murrough said, taking a drink, " – but in the end I was the victor. They failed in what they tried to do. My wounds healed, my manhood is intact. Anyway, I was not sorry when FitzAlan destroyed the lot of them. Only the best were left, and myself, chief of them all. A ragged bunch they were too, until I saved them."

"What do you think of this bit of news, then?" asked Seamus, leaning towards him conspiratorially. "Aileen MacGillingrouth lives. She is now FitzAlan's wife."

"The whoring bitch," Murrough slammed his drink down onto the table.

"Wait though. You're a clever man. FitzAlan wants your slave girl, Lys. He thinks to soften Aileen's heart with her."

"He'll be lucky. She's got no heart."

"You know that, I know that. But FitzAlan is ignorant of the fact. This can work to our advantage."

"How so?"

"He'll pay well for Lys. You'll be able to buy food for the winter. And drink too," he added, pouring another.

Murrough gulped it back, half spilled it down his shirt and, in trying to brush it off, almost fell off the chair.

"Whoops, steady now." said Seamus. "If you sell her, you will gain from FitzAlan, and lose nothing of value."

"Why would I do that? If it makes the whore happy, it makes me unhappy."

"Two reasons. Of course, you have cause to hate Aileen, but stop, think. She was only a useless pawn, a mere woman. It wasn't she who had that terrible thing done to you. Don't waste your hatred on someone of such little import."

"If not against Aileen, who then?" Murrough said. But he didn't hate Aileen. He desired her still. She represented success. She was beautiful, she was strong and she had been his brother's favoured woman. Having Aileen for himself would confirm to all men who still doubted it, that he was every bit as much a man as his brother had been.

Seamus was answering him, he turned back to the subject. " – FitzAlan. That's who. Was it not because of him we were driven, sept against sept, brother against brother?"

"Yes, it was that Norman bastard who caused all this." He gripped his goblet tight, imagining it was the Norman's throat he squeezed.

"Now, you're a clever man," Seamus pressed his advantage, "you don't need me to tell you how to get at FitzAlan. But I will, I'm old, let me indulge myself – it's not often I get to talk with a great chief." He smiled, deprecating, at Murrough, who stared back at him with drink-sodden intensity. "This is how I see it. FitzAlan is so besotted with the girl that he wants only to please her."

"Yes, so you've already said, man. Get on. Get on."

"But Lys is a devious bitch, like her mistress. With Lys to help her, Aileen will make his life hell. Already they say he is a wreck, a ruin. You

214

know yourself how she can destroy a man."

"Too well, by God."

"He is already almost there. Lys will give Aileen the final coup de grace. Then – and this is the whole beauty of the plan – once he realises what she has done to him, he'll have her locked in the dungeons and starved to death. He's already almost had her flogged, you know. But she got round him that time."

"Pity. I would have liked to have seen that." And if he couldn't have her himself that was what he'd like to see. But he would have her someday. How much easier it would be to get her if the Norman lost interest.

"You can be instrumental in both their downfalls, and be paid for it as well."

Murrough's eye's lit up, seeing the sense in what he heard. "How much?" Seamus lent over and whispered. The chair, which had been steadily tipping, finally gave up and Murrough shot backwards. He made a feeble attempt to rise but, hopelessly drunk, gave in and snored peacefully on the floor.

Seamus put a small mountain of gold on the table and hastened out, tipping his full goblet over as he left. The liquid ran down the length of the table, to drip onto the floor beside Murrough's inert head.

He found Lys and had the men saddle up. "Tell your master I must make haste. I've paid him in full. Remind him of the harm he is doing FitzAlan with this clever move." The men stared after him, bemused. Murrough snored as they left town.

Once out in the bushes, Seamus started to rock with laughter. Lys – who had been quietly sitting by her fire when Seamus urged her to drop everything and come with him – looked at him in surprise.

"What is it, Father?"

"Do you know where I'm taking you, child?"

"No, Father,"

"To see Lady FitzAlan, that's where."

"Who may she be, sir?"

"She may be Lady Aileen FitzAlan."

Lys smiled, then laughed, as the full realisation dawned on her. "How did you get him to give me up? Murrough hates Aileen," she said.

"Not as much as he'll hate me when he finally wakes up." And not as much as he'd have us believe, he thought to himself and chuckled with delight. The return journey proved uneventful and they managed to maintain a steady pace, with few unnecessary halts. The group arrived tired and triumphant at the castle approaches, having taken exactly four weeks since leaving Limerick.

CHAPTER 11

𝒯he sickness passed. Aileen woke up one day, steeling herself for the onslaught and it didn't arrive. Marie smiled to see her dancing around the room with her arms above her head, laughing and happy.

"It seems you are feeling better," she said, picking dropped items of clothing off the floor. But Aileen didn't answer and stood frozen to a spot before the window. Marie, lost in her own daydreams, failed to notice her sudden lack of movement. It wasn't until Aileen screamed, making her jump and drop the pitcher of water onto the floor, that she recovered.

"Dear God," she exclaimed, rushing to her mistress's side. But Aileen brushed past her, pulling on her dressing-robe as she went. All that was left of her were a series of wet footprints leading out of the bedchamber and into the hall.

Marie watched from the window, bemused. She saw Aileen, bareheaded and barefooted, race down the steps into the courtyard and her hand went to her mouth in horror, convinced at every step that the girl would fall. The people she passed turned, following her headlong flight with their eyes, to an old priest heading a procession of ragged, travel-weary strangers. The priest lifted a hand in greeting, but Aileen ignored him. One of the young women jumped onto the ground, leaving her pony to wander at will, and Aileen threw herself into her arms.

Robert hurried to where Aileen and Lys stood crying and heedless of the open-mouthed stares they were receiving. He had been talking to Silas when Aileen rushed out, immodestly dressed, to greet the newcomers, and immediately hurried to protect her. Covered from head to toe though she was, she still received the critical stares of men who had never seen a lady of the manor attired in nothing but her dressing-robe.

"If Lady FitzAlan could see that one," said Silas, "she'd have a thousand fits."

"What's she like, then?" asked Cormac, his eyes on Robert.

"Welsh, refined, modest. She knows her place and keeps to it."

"A real lady."

"Oh, a real lady."

"Then it's queer how our Robert has found himself caught up with the Lady Aileen, Irish, unprincipled. rebellious."

"But yet there is only one real difference between them," mused Silas.

"What's that?"

"One's, as I say, a real lady, the other, a real woman."

Cormac grinned appreciatively.

It was several minutes before Robert could calm the two women enough to lead them away from what had effectively become an amphitheatre. He took them into the solar.

"Aileen, I must talk to you soon, when you've re-acquainted yourself with Lys," he said, and smiled at them as he left the room. Aileen nodded impatiently and returned her attention to Lys.

"I thought you were dead," they spoke together and laughed. Lys hesitated, Aileen had grown so grand since she'd last seen her – the wife of a knight, no less – that she was almost afraid to speak once the hysteria had died away.

"I've missed you, Lys," – it was the umpteenth time she'd said it, but now Aileen spoke with quiet sincerity and Lys saw a wealth of pain behind the simple words.

"What's been happening with you, Lady Aileen?" She emphasised the last bit with a flourish.

"I've married, as you see,"

Lys interrupted her, "And to such a man." She rolled her eyes heavenwards.

"So you like my husband?" Aileen asked, and again, Lys was surprised at the new seriousness.

"I like what he looks like," she said, unusually careful. "But I sense there is something troubling you."

"He killed Murchad. He killed Cashal."

"He had killed Cashal when you helped him escape from Trigonnel's point," Lys reminded.

"It was the way the slaughter was carried out at Trigonnel's Point. You were there, you know how it was."

"It was the same when Murchad raided the English stronghold where I lived with my family." Her eyes grew troubled at the memory. "No worse."

Aileen had never asked Lys about her life prior to the time when they had met. But of course, the girl hadn't been born a slave.

"No worse than that, you say?"

"War is a terrible thing. People do things in battle which they would never otherwise do. I learned to forgive the Irish and I learned to care for you."

"Although to you, we were the oppressor."

"Just so."

"Was it difficult for you to give me your loyalty, Lys?"

"Never. I loved you. You've been good to me."

"But our cases are different."

"Different, but similar, I think. How does your lord treat you? Does he beat you?"

Aileen laughed. "I've given him cause. He's only ever treated me with kindness."

"Someone went to a great deal of effort to bring me here,"

"That was Robert," said Aileen, "when he knew I was pregnant,"

"You're pregnant?" Lys's voice lifted in a high note of surprise. "Is it your lord's baby – my lady?"

"No. Murchad's," she said. "Lys, please, don't become formal with me. I was a royal princess at Trigonnel's Point and you still called me Aileen. I can't bear for anything to change the way we were."

"When will the baby be born?" Lys looked over Aileen's body and noticed for the first time that her normally flat tummy had rounded, but she couldn't be very far gone yet.

"In the spring. I've been afraid, Lys, but having you here will make so much difference."

"Don't you have a maid?"

"Marie. She's afraid of me. She'd like to be a friend but she thinks I may lead her into the dungeons."

They laughed together.

"She purses her lips at me when I displease her and frightens me half to death."

"Never. You've never been afraid of anything," scoffed Lys.

"Its easier to remember that now that you're back with me." Aileen smiled and hugged Lys, hiding the tears welling in her eyes.

Robert and Cormac went to welcome Seamus, having first summoned a servant to see to the travellers' refreshment.

218

"I'm grateful to you for bringing my wife's slave," said Robert, impressing Seamus by coming to see him personally. "I believe you want to live at the monastery at Seandale?"

"Seandale was my home for many years. It would be pleasant for me to spend the few I have left there."

"And your fellow travellers, will they make their homes here?"

"Mostly here, sire. Providing you can fulfil the obligations which Cormac here made."

"Peace, prosperity and plenty of work?"

"Precisely."

"As long as I have those things, your fellows will," replied Robert, and again Seamus was impressed by his simplicity.

They talked for a short while and Robert bid Cormac find a comfortable bed and some proper food for their guests, then he went to find Aileen and Lys who were still in the solar. They looked a little startled as he walked in. He had the feeling that he'd been the subject of their conversation.

"I hadn't wanted to interrupt," he said.

"We've said all we have breath for," said Aileen and he was weakened by her generous smile and the warmth of her voice as she spoke. He looked at Lys.

"I hope you'll make my wife happy. She has fidgeted from morning to night worrying about your coming."

"I thank you, my lord," Lys said, "for bringing me here. I was desolate to think I would never see my mistress again. I believed that she was dead. Now I've not only found her, but am amongst the English once again. Something I never believed possible."

"And now that you are among your own people, I assume you are still willing to serve your mistress?"

Lys nodded. "Of course, sire."

"I'm glad we were able to find you. Now that you're here, you can no longer be a slave and you must consider yourself a free woman in every way. Your only duty will be to serve your mistress – my wife."

"Thank you," Lys whispered breathlessly. Aileen remained silent but Robert noticed that her eyes brimmed with tears. He turned away, happy to have been able to do something which had finally brought pleasure to his wife.

Aileen insisted that Lys share her room, although she had long since given up expecting Robert to come to her; it seemed a safe insurance, if an unnecessary one.

Within weeks of Lys's arrival Aileen no longer felt as though she were a captive, and she thought more and more often of Gossard's Ford as her home. Her pregnancy was easy – so Lys and Marie told her daily – but impatient woman that she was, she chafed at its restrictions. Her wild, tumultuous rides had to be curbed, but she refused to stop altogether. Instead, Lys and Cormac took gentle rides with her, the boredom alleviated by their lively chatter and Lys's irrepressible laughter. The two were very similar: both had a twinkling eye and an active tongue and neither remembered, very often, to treat Aileen with the respect which was her due. Thank God. Aileen had in Lys all that she had missed with Marie, and now she did have it, she learned to appreciate Marie's more cautious, motherly approach to her.

Lys liked Marie, and she worshipped Robert. "How can you resist him?" she asked, as Robert left the room one day, following a visit carried out for the sole purpose of ensuring that his wife had everything she needed. He did so several times a week, and Aileen, although far more friendly than she had ever been, was still overly polite towards him.

"As easily as he does me," she replied flippantly.

"He only wants a nod and a wink, you fool." Lys was nothing, if not honest.

"I'm perfectly happy with the way things are," Aileen assured her.

"Huh!" Lys turned away in disgust.

"How dare you turn your back on me. What have I done?"

"If you don't know, I won't tell you," Lys said, and she left the room, ignoring Aileen's demand that she stay.

Aileen was left railing uselessly, with Marie tutting in the corners of her rooms, but refusing to be drawn into argument.

"My mistress is becoming more like a spoilt child with every day that passes," she muttered to Silas later.

"But easier for you to handle, I think."

"How so?"

"A cold, dignified lady must be harder to handle than a spoiled child, and more unhappy, perhaps?"

She thought about it carefully. He was right: Aileen was happier, despite her frequent outbursts. Perhaps because of them. She was passionate by nature and the icy veneer she had wrapped around herself had served to keep her in, as much as to keep Robert out. A lonely, miserable igloo of an existence it must have been, which the fires of her personality had now melted. And she was by no means always cross: she could be sweet and considerate, or even boisterously happy.

"You're right as usual, Silas. And few women are reasonable all through their pregnancy."

"Few women are reasonable, I'd say." He received a playful smack across the face for his pains.

CHAPTER 12

$\mathcal{S}$he laboured throughout the night and, as morning broke, with the sun illuminating the daffodils and snowdrops in the fields, Ishtilde, named after Murchad's mother, was born.

She was a vigorous, black-haired baby, strong and lively from the start, and a perfect replica of Aileen. Lys washed and wrapped her in the little robe which had been Aileen's first fine needlework achievement and laid her in her mother's arms.

Aileen, who, once free of the seemingly never-ending pain, wanted only to sleep and forget, felt her heart lurch when she looked at the tiny figure, whose lips were pursed and ready to suckle. It was a joyous moment negating all her suffering. She was swamped with love for Ishtilde, looking into the un-focussed violet eyes with an expression of adoration. The baby waved tiny hands in the air and let out a huge bellow of anger.

"She's like you, mistress," said Marie, her voice softened by a beaming smile, "she must have everything, just at the very moment of wanting it."

Lys became Ishtilde's devoted slave – it seemed Robert had freed her unnecessarily – and she was blissfully content to spend her days petting and caring for the baby. Surprisingly under the circumstances, Robert, who had cause to detest her, also found the child fascinating and often came to inspect the nurseries.

The whole episode of Ishtilde's birth had served to reinforce the admiration and respect which Lys had already acquired for Robert FitzAlan: not only had the Norman given her a new lease of life as a free woman, but, since arriving at Gossard's Ford, she had enjoyed a style of life far superior to any she had previously known. Without it affecting her deep devotion to her mistress, it had become clear that the English girl had become a doughty champion of FitzAlan.

By the first days of April, Aileen was completely recovered, and ready to resume her rides. Lys preferred to stay behind with the baby, almost resenting the abundant love Aileen showered on the child. She had hoped Aileen would be an indifferent mother, but, as with all things, she either loved or hated with verve.

It was a relief for Aileen to be able to get out. Cormac and she enjoyed long hours of conversation about the estate, as they had always done before Ishtilde's intervention. Much as she loved the baby, Aileen did find some of the more mundane chores of motherhood irksome, and happily left them for Lys to perform.

Robert, seeing her slim and beautiful, settled at last, yet at the same time vivacious and provocative, was nearly overpowered by his desire and driven almost out of his mind by longing. He had the greatest difficulty in controlling his emotions. It made it harder to realise that Aileen now found him more acceptable, because hope was perpetually followed by despair when she continued to show no interest in sharing his bed.

They still quarrelled occasionally. She would grow openly rebellious then, in a fit of angry pique, confine herself to her quarters. On such occasions, Lys would let her stamp her feet and vent her spleen and then, slyly, make remarks about hate being akin to love. Such teasing would only throw Aileen into a tantrum and looking at Lys she would spit out, with ill-concealed venom, "Don't be ridiculous – I could never love that man. I'm wedded to him by force and wish I were free. I wish I were miles from here." Lys held her tongue, but continued to smile to herself, indicating clearly that things were a great deal better than Aileen was prepared to admit.

When Ishtilde was old enough to travel Robert waylaid Aileen one morning and told her to prepare to make a journey, in two days' time, to visit Aifel at Whitley. "I have to go to see Sister Martha," he explained, "and I know you'd like to show your mother her granddaughter."

Aileen made no effort to hide her delight and Robert smiled at her. Despite everything, he still derived a great deal of pleasure from pleasing her. Lys had told him she'd been thinking a great deal about her mother recently, wondering what she'd make of the baby .

Robert and Aileen left, accompanied by an escort of mounted soldiers, several servants and Lys, with the baby in a carrier on her back.

Aileen, as she always did, rode astride. It intrigued Robert that Aileen never rode side-saddle, as most ladies did. He admired the barbaric way in which she appeared in the now famous linen trousers, which had been the cause of considerable comment at Gossard's Ford, fascinating all those who witnessed her daily rides. It was clear that her skill in handling the lively Peggy would have been seriously handicapped had she adopted the more decorous mode of riding. Robert found her almost scandalous behaviour just another endearing trait, try though he might to disapprove.

Watching her from the great height of his war horse he realised how much he longed to win her total acceptance. Life without her love was quite empty, the glimpses of friendship increasingly tantalising.

It was perhaps as well the journey was a short one. The weather was warm and the mild, dry nights meant that no hardship had to be endured as they slept, side by side, on the forest floor. The moon was bright, the stars shining and Robert found the whole scene idyllic. In comparison, his isolation, with Aileen so close, was compounded, leaving him empty and unfulfilled.

Arriving at the Priory, Robert was quickly closeted with Sister Martha, but not before he had arranged for Aileen to spend some time in the gardens with her mother.

"Aileen," Aifel cried, as she came into the garden to find her daughter. Great tears of happiness filled her eyes and, despite the passage of time, she seemed younger than Aileen remembered her.

"You've become a nun," cried Aileen, thinking of all the words with which she could have greeted her mother. The surprise at finding her a postulant had whipped them out of her mind. "Why? Now you can never leave here."

"I never want to," replied Aifel, smiling from ear to ear. "I love the peace here, and I thought all my family were dead." She cried again, and clung to Aileen as if she would never let her go.

Robert, gratified to see the expressions on their faces, spent longer than he needed to do with Sister Martha as they reviewed the political developments of the world outside Whitley, the financial needs of the priory and the story of all that had happened since Aileen had made her escape from there.

Aifel saw Lys standing nearby with the baby in her arms, and Aileen called her over.

"Meet Ishtilde, your grandchild," she said, and Lys handed the baby over to her.

Aifel peeped inside the wrapping which confined the baby and sighed with pleasure. "She's so like you were, Aileen. My grandchild." She thought of her other children, not knowing if they lived or not, and was torn between her great joy of the moment, and her great sorrow. "Is this

FitzAlan's child?" she asked, and saw Aileen's face cloud over.

"No, Murchad's. Conceived on the night of his death." She told her mother the whole story of the fall of Trigonnel's Point, but left much out of the relationship between herself and Robert, seeing little point in distressing Aifel any further.

Before leaving the next morning, Robert was stopped by Aifel in the secrecy of the small chapel. "I beg you to take care of my daughter and of my granddaughter," she said.

"You have my word, Aifel."

"She is lucky to be wed to one such as yourself," she told him, and he smiled, wishing Aileen could be persuaded to see things in this light.

He rode beside his wife as they left the Priory. "How did you find your mother?" he asked.

"I found her much changed – happier than I had imagined." She looked down to where Peggy's mane lifted and fell as she strode along. "Robert, I owe you a great debt of gratitude. For my mother's happiness, and for – other things." She had been about to say for her own but couldn't bring herself to make such a confession.

He was surprised but pleased. "If I can do anything to make your burdens lighter, Aileen," he said, "I will do so." They said little more, but an inner glow warmed him for many hours. He galloped ahead of the slow moving party to select a suitable spot to make camp and as he rode he considered what she had said and what he was sure she had been about to say.

Later, as he looked at her in the fading light of the spluttering camp fire, he echoed something Aifel had said to him long ago on his first visit to Whitley. "May she come to love you, too," and he added a prayer to the sentiment. He observed Aileen's dark beauty, her well-formed body in the bodice-like garment she wore above her trousers and her long black hair blowing about her face, and was filled with an aching desire. So near and yet so far away, he sighed, yet perhaps getting nearer?

Controlling his emotions with difficulty he asked quietly and in a voice which he hoped reflected his consideration: "You must miss your mother dreadfully?"

Aileen nodded dumbly.

"You know she doesn't have to stay at Whitley. There's room for her if you want her to come to Gossard's Ford."

She didn't reply although she had obviously heard him; instead she looked searchingly at him, her green eyes misty in the firelight. Finally she did speak, her voice husky with unshed tears.

"She wouldn't come. But thank you." As she spoke the tears escaped and ran down her face and he left her for a while. He'd never made her cry. Not in anger, not in sorrow, but these tears were for another reason; he was sure the ice was beginning to melt.

The remainder of the journey was made in companionable silence, Robert continuing to ride alongside Aileen. Each seemed immersed in private thought. From time to time though, Aileen glanced at the man beside her, as if she were about to speak. His face which could look grim and thoughtful, would smile at her, and light up his handsome features in a way which was entirely new to her. She felt intrigued.

In this manner they drew near Gossard's Ford, the scenery around them growing increasingly familiar.

He looked at her. "Don't forget, if you wish me to talk to Sister Martha and your mother, my offer still stands."

She nodded and he winked at her but said no more.

CHAPTER 13

$\mathcal{R}$obert had to go to Dublin in answer to a summons to consult with Hugh de Lacy and, since Cormac accompanied him on this occasion, all the day to day running of Gossard's Ford was left in Silas's hands. Robert thought of leaving this to Aileen, the normal practice whenever a Norman baron was away from home, but despite the rapid growth in their relationship, it had not yet reached quite such a high point of trust.

He left in foul weather, which kept Aileen a prisoner for several days chafing to get outside. Eventually the day dawned when the sun shone strong and warm; coming after days of chill winds it was particularly inviting. Aileen, restless and only too willing to leave Ishtilde in Lys's care, went to the courtyard. She was irritable at having to ride without Cormac, but unfortunately the captain of the castle guard, who normally deputized for him, was also absent, having left as commander of Robert's escort. Silas was loathe to let her go alone, yet couldn't spare her anyone at that precise moment. Imperiously she ordered Oswald, the day's captain of the guard to provide her with an escort, but he too refused to order the preparation of her horse unless she would go escorted. Such thwarting of her wishes made Aileen see red and, assuming her most haughty and domineering guise, she brushed Oswald aside and saddled her horse herself.

She then turned to a nearby groom – a young inexperienced soldier named Culpeper and ordered him to saddle up and join her. He made to protest, thought better of it and hastened to obey. Confident of his abilities to protect her, he was flattered at this chance of spending time with his lord's beautiful wife. Oswald considered stopping them as they left the castle, but aware of her wicked temper, thought better of it.

As soon as he was approached by a worried Oswald, Silas grew concerned that he had fallen down on his promise to take care of Aileen, but there was very little he could do. Even if he succeeded in finding her he was loathe to force her to return – far better to let her continue with her ride in peace. He shrugged his shoulders and returned to his quarters – though not without a prayer that all would end well: FitzAlan's wrath should anything go wrong would be too terrible to contemplate.

An hour later, Aileen pulled her horse to a halt at the edge of a small copse surmounting a hill. As she looked back over the relatively flat country across which she had ridden, she was struck by its peace and prosperous appearance. There was a good deal to be said for Robert's administration – everything was so different from the wild and turbulent countryside it had once been. Before her, round the side of the copse, she could glimpse to the south and east the vast Forest of Thorn, and below it the Sheen Marshes. She reminded herself that somewhere beyond that barrier lay her old home, Trigonnel's Point. Memories flooded back to her – and she realised with a shock that they were no longer painful, or particularly nostalgic.

She had moved more quickly on Peggy than Culpeper on his weighty mount, and he drew up with her, his horse's flanks heaving.

"Not so fast next time," he begged, anxious that something might happen to Aileen whilst under his protection.

Aileen tossed her head and dismounted, handing the reins to Culpeper. "We'll rest a while," she said. He looked at her thinking – as he had done many times before – just how beautiful she was, and thanked God for giving him the chance to be her escort. He immediately forgave her the wilfulness that had led her to race ahead of him and, aware of the admiration in his eyes, Aileen smiled.

They gazed around at the breathtaking views, Culpeper still sitting on his horse. Suddenly, out of the blue, the groom fell forward, clutching hand to head, whilst his horse, startled by shouts from the surrounding trees, reared and unseated its rider. A stone, flung with great accuracy, had found an easy target in the unfortunate man.

Aileen, taken by surprise, was helpless as some half a dozen men burst from concealment. Within seconds she was seized and carried roughly into the trees. Meanwhile, another man caught the bridle of her horse and dragged it after her. Back in the copse the group collected their own horses, lifted Aileen onto hers and, at a word from one of their number, set off down the hill towards the Sheen Marshes.

Aileen's kidnappers were in a hurry to get away from the area, and to cover as many miles as possible. For an hour or more no halt was called to the mad pace at which they travelled and no word was spoken. Aileen tried to distinguish her individual captors: some seemed vaguely familiar and she was certain that they must be members of the O'Flerty tribe. She had no idea what they wanted from her, but she was sure that none of the people she recognised had been strong supporters of her father or Murchad. The knowledge left her with a growing sense of unease.

A halt was eventually called when they were through the marshes and had entered the forest. The men were obviously grateful for a chance to pause and take a much-needed drink. Aileen sat on her horse waiting for someone to bring water to her, but no one paid her any attention and eventually, driven by her thirst, she went over to the brook. As she bent to drink she could sense some of the men watching her and fought to ignore the uncomfortable feeling this gave her. When she'd drunk she wiped her mouth with the back of her hand and turned to get up. She caught the eye of the man next to her and was immediately filled with horror. The shock of recognition sent a chill through her and she gasped involuntarily. Murrough looked back at her. He stared but didn't speak and she backed away from him, returning to Peggy, clinging onto her familiar body as to a lifeline. She could hear men jeering and laughing behind them.

She had last seen Murrough as he had been sent into exile, maimed and pitiful, when she had thought never to see him again. She shuddered, remembering the night he had raped her. He had wanted her badly enough then. And he had wanted her more than just as a means of satisfying his lust; raping her had been his way of proving his superiority over Murchad. He had frightened her even before the rape. Now, unable to understand his motives for capturing her, she was even more afraid. He was the one man she felt unable to deal with and she was at his mercy.

None of the men spoke to Aileen; they watched her covetously and sometimes she heard her name mentioned, followed by laughter. But there was little time for talking, for Murrough evidently had only one concern at this stage: to put as many miles as possible between himself and his pursuers, who would surely start out before long. As the journey progressed the feeling of isolation began to be oppressive and instead of being relieved Aileen began to wish someone would talk to her.

When they stopped again for a brief rest and Murrough was seeing to his horse, she dismounted and walked confidently over to a couple of men whom she recognised from the time of Murchad's rule at Trigonnel's Point. They looked up as she approached them and then at each other.

"I want you to tell me where we're going," she said, her voice imperious.

"Then you must ask our leader," the taller of the two answered. His companion sniggered.

"I'm asking you," she said, looking him in the eye. Neither man answered, but stared insolently at her. "You," she said pointing at the tall man, "You were one of my father's men, were you not?"

The man nodded, slightly shamefaced.

"What do you think he'll do when he finds out how I'm being treated?"

The two exchanged glances, then the shorter man spoke. "What could a dead man do to us, mistress?"

She felt the breath leave her body and stood for a moment trying to gather herself. The men watched her without compassion. "My father is dead? Was he killed at Trigonnel's Point?"

"No. His son Donal died there. He was killed later in Limerick."

"And my other brother Corvild?"

The tall man shrugged. "Dead too. Killed fighting for O'Brian."

She felt tears burn the back of her eyes and for a moment she thought the men looked sorry. She didn't want their pity and lifted her chin proudly, her eyes cold and her lips compressed.

"They died for Ireland then. Whereas you two follow that maggot Murrough who would do nothing for anyone."

"He'll do something for you, I dare say," the tall man said looking at her with a leer.

"He always wanted you for his woman. Even when you were lying with his brother. And what our chief wants, he gets." He laughed cruelly as her face grew pale. She turned away from them abruptly, horrified and confused by everything she'd heard.

As they resumed their journey, Aileen had plenty of time to consider her fate, and that of her family. She had to control the tears which threatened to overwhelm her as she thought of her father and brothers, and she realised that their deaths meant she could assume no protection from Murrough. She yearned to be back at Gossard's Ford with Lys and especially Ishtilde, who left an aching, empty place in her arms. It was only now she had been taken from it that she realised the place had truly become her home. Robert, ironically, was the only one who could help her now. Eventually the pain of hopeless dreaming became too much and she forced herself to clear her mind and concentrate on where she was going.

Murrough rode up beside her and let his leg graze hers. Peggy flattened her ears and bared her teeth as the strange horse jostled against her and Aileen understood how she felt. She vowed she would ignore Murrough, not give him the satisfaction of knowing how much pain he had already caused her, but he made no effort to speak. She found his silence disconcerting, another facet of his personality which she couldn't understand and when the path grew wider she moved Peggy away from him. Again, without a word, he caught hold of the mare's bridle and yanked her back. Peggy threw her head up in pain and Murrough laughed. The sound was like the blade of sword being dragged across stone and Aileen winced.

Towards nightfall the men set up camp, lighting a large fire and sitting around it telling jokes and stories, many of them at Aileen's expense. Murrough watched her as a vulture watches his prey, and ate greedily when the cook placed a platter of food in front of him. He made sure that she received no food until he had finished his, then he sat and watched her eat, silently mocking her until she felt tears of humiliation sting her eyes.

In her primitive bed on the forest floor, Aileen lay wide-eyed, believing Culpeper was dead and that no one would know what had happened to her. Suddenly the hairs on her body raised and she grew tense. She looked up and saw Murrough, standing silently above her.

He lay down next to her and stroked her hair. She could scream or run or fight him, but no one would heed her call, no one would come to her aid, and there was nowhere for her to go. Her mouth dried and her heart hammered, leaving her legs and arms like the trunks of fallen trees, dead weights pinning her to the ground. She could smell his breath, feel its warmth on her face. His eyes bore into hers and locked so that she was compelled to return the stare.

"What are you going to do with me?" she said finally.

"For now I'm content just to look and savour and plan for the future. I've wanted you for a long time, Aileen. I wanted you before my brother made you his, and now that you're mine I want you still," he replied passively.

She could think of nothing to say, something in his demeanour told her there was no point in saying anything. He was mad, crazed, and wouldn't listen to her. Still, the fact that he had spoken at last somehow brought life back into her. The adrenalin was pumping through her veins, lending her courage.

"I'm not yours, Murrough, I never was and I never can be." Her cheeks burned in the darkness.

"No? You think not. You think my brother saw to that. And yet, there are more ways than one to skin a rabbit. Have you ever noticed how a trapped rabbit struggles to be free, its eyes staring? So easy to make it scream, with the power to kill or release it – so much power over one tiny rabbit?" His face was incredibly ugly and the fear stopped the breath in her lungs.

"Tell me what you want." He couldn't want her as his mistress, she was more confused than ever.

"Pleasure, little rabbit."

"You could not pleasure me," she taunted, then wished she had held her tongue. She was at this man's mercy. When would she learn to control her temper? He didn't reply and his eyes gleamed at her in the dark. Then, moving very slowly, he grabbed her arm just above her wrist and held her. His strength was quite incredible, he had always seemed such a weak man – but that was because of the way he acted. Always wanting to prove himself. Always ingratiating towards those with the power. Only now he was the one with power. Slowly, his eyes still boring into hers, he pulled her hand towards his crotch. She was dumb with shock, not understanding what he could be doing. Then she felt him. She snatched her hand away and her pupils were dilated, her mouth open in surprise.

"So you see, I could pleasure you, my little one," he said.

She was too terrified to retaliate. Her head span with half-formed questions. He rubbed her with his bristly cheek and she flinched away from him. "Goodnight, Aileen," he whispered suddenly, turning on his back. His sudden loss of interest, after what she had discovered, was incomprehensible and she lay awake for hours after he fell asleep, listening to his heavy snores and trying to keep her rising fear at bay.

Throughout the next day she grew increasingly demoralised by Murrough's arrogance. He ordered her about, much to the amusement of his men, and watched her almost continuously. It was as though he were playing a game with her, and her skin crawled as she waited, waited for him to spring – as she knew he would.

He came to her again that night.

"For God's sake, Murrough, what are you doing here?" she asked, when once again he made no move to rape her. He only laughed and the realisation that he wasn't going to do anything – yet – left her more cold and disturbed than she would have been if he had simply taken her there and then. She couldn't understand it. How could Murrough be as he was, and yet not take her? It was blatantly obvious he could be excited by her, but what excited him was apparently something more than just her body. She wondered if he came to her at night merely to impress his men – that would be typical of him. He had always been sly. But how much longer would this be enough for him? She wondered how much damage had actually been done to his manhood by Murchad, for she had seen it happen and knew that he must have suffered something. The O'Flerty men had always thought highly of their virility – and of their sons. Murrough probably had no remaining family, and must surely be incapable of fathering children. She thought again of Ishtilde, his niece - perhaps his only living relative. Aileen knew she was in danger. Eventually Murrough would grow tired of playing games. And she knew that no clever words would assist her. No tantrums. Any reaction she offered would bring him joy, in his perverted way. She tried one last argument, a final appeal to a better side of him which might still exist, in the hopes she might touch something in him which was still capable of tenderness.

"Your family are all dead, aren't they?" It was half-question, half-statement.

"Probably."

"Did you know that I have a child, and that you are her uncle?" If she had sought to win his pity by telling him about Ishtilde she'd failed. She saw that as soon as she had spoken.

He waited to see if she had more to offer, then shrugged. "Congratulations," he murmured drily. He saw tears creep into her eyes and gave her a hideous, cruel smile before pinching her cheek roughly. "I hadn't thought to see you cry," he said "It's an unexpected bonus for me."

She tried to stop but the tears, having finally found an outlet, wouldn't dry up. He watched as they continued to fall. When she had regained control he laughed at her. "We may fetch her, too. It would be good to see how the mighty Aileen MacGillingrouth could be brought, begging, to her knees." He picked up a twig and snapped it close to Aileen's ear. The sound coming out of the darkness made her jump.

"I lied – there is no child," she said hastily.

"I don't think so, Aileen." He left her trembling on the ground. Murrough's words were a threat she could not ignore. A weapon to get at her which she felt she had unwittingly brought to his attention. She was suddenly painfully aware that he had a hold on her through her child, and that through her own stupidity she had added to his power.

The next morning she stopped him as he was about to mount his horse. "What do you want from me, Murrough?"

"Well, that's a question I thought I'd already answered. I want pleasure from you."

"Then why have you not taken your pleasure?"

"Oh I am doing. Every day. You're afraid of me, aren't you? He looked into her eyes and once again she found she couldn't look away. "And you do so love your child. It is in my mind to take her away from that Norman devil and bring her to you. I too could derive a great deal of pleasure from having her here."

Aileen's mouth dried so she could hardly speak. "You wouldn't hurt my baby, Murrough. She's part of your family."

"'Family' didn't prevent Murchad from having me gelded. And I didn't see you rushing to my rescue."

"So it's revenge you want?" She battled to keep her voice strong and failed. "You would harm Ishtilde to hurt me."

His lip curled. "Perhaps I would. What's a girl-child worth, and a bastard at that?"

"Nothing at all, Murrough. Not worth the risk in trying to capture her."

"But to you, Aileen, she's worth a great deal. And you have something I value."

"My body?" her question was hopeful. Giving her body to this man would be easy if it would save her daughter.

"Your complete and total submission to me."

She was about to retort to this, then bit her tongue. The old Aileen would have fought him, the new one answered very differently, to protect her child. "I can give you that, Murrough, you have it, if you promise not to harm Ishtilde."

"No. If it comes that easily it's not worth having. I shall send men back to Gossard's Ford to take Ishtilde and show you every day just how much power I have. And I will watch you beg and plead for mercy for your child. Now that is what I call pleasure." He swung himself onto his horse and looked down at Aileen who was white-faced. He urged the horse forward and as it drew away he turned to her. "How long would your child survive, I wonder? It would be interesting to see what we could devise to make our pleasure last. I hear, Aileen, that you are expert in such things."

Aileen had not had an easy life, she was no weakling, but something evil in Murrough frightened her more than she could say. She felt the life drain out of her as he leered into her face. He was like a vampire bat, sucking her blood. In cold dread she prayed to the god that Corderg worshipped and to the ancient gods of Ireland, that they would save her and protect her child. But she could not truly believe in any of them and felt herself to be utterly alone.

After five days' hard riding they arrived at Trigonnel's Point. It was late afternoon and the sun was casting long shadows across the almost deserted camp. The days were growing colder and the air was sharp; Aileen drew her cloak around her and shivered. She watched as a few women and young children crept stealthily into the street to welcome the visitors – once they were sure they were safe. Their shouts of greeting filled the air, but no one greeted Aileen.

She waited to see what she should do, but for once even Murrough wasn't watching her and she slipped away, making her way to the centre of the stronghold to where the chief's household had been.

Her home was gone. Some of the wooden railings which had made up the barricade remained, but the buildings it had contained were gone – as if they had never been, and try though she might she could not imagine them whole again. She stood still, then staggered drunkenly, searching for something, anything, which would prove that she had once lived here with Murchad. But there was nothing.

She sank to her knees as a wave of desolation hit her. Where, she wondered bitterly, was the strength which had carried her through so much suffering. She bowed her head, clasping her hands together as if in prayer. If only you were alive, Murchad, she thought. Though Murrough evidently wanted her as his woman, she knew that she would mean nothing to him. And to those remaining of the O'Flerty tribe she was no more than a discarded relic of the past. No one had spared her more than a second glance, no one was interested in what became of her. No one but Murrough, and he was chief, his word was law and his law regarding her had not yet been revealed.

"What? Aileen MacGillingrouth on her knees?" Murrough's voice was disdainful and Aileen jumped to her feet. He had come to taunt her again. "No doubt you were remembering my dear brother and the time when you ruled this place through him?"

She tried to ignore him.

"How the mighty have fallen," he jeered.

"If I have fallen as you say, Murrough," Aileen said dully, a shadow of her former defiance rising up again, "beware that I am not on my way up again."

"You may have further to fall yet. In fact, my *lady*," he said sarcastically, "I can assure you that you have." He turned from her and walked away and she could hear him chuckling softly to himself.

She had thought they were going to stay at the camp, but after a day of rest they moved on. She refrained from turning for a last glimpse of the stronghold, knowing it would please Murrough to see her do so, but she was swept with a wave of lonely sentimentality and said a silent farewell to Murchad.

She rode behind Murrough trying to keep a good distance between her horse and his. Sometimes when she was forced to draw closer to him he would allow heavy branches from the over-hanging trees to swing back into her face. Once he caught her unawares and a branch knocked her to the ground. He ordered the rest of the company to ride around her, leaving her bruised and humiliated in the dust, cowering away from the horses' milling hooves on the narrow path.

At night she dreamt of Ishtilde and longed to have her again in her arms, but then she would wake up, feeling empty and alone as she struggled to remember where she was and what was wrong. She grew used, but never resigned, to waking up to see his eyes fixed on her face, and she became thin and pale through lack of food and sleep.

One day she came across a baby rabbit helpless and abandoned in the wood. She picked it up and held it to her with tears in her eyes as she thought of Ishtilde. A tear dropped and lay glistening on the animal's tiny back. She looked up to see Murrough standing over her and dropped the rabbit quickly, watching it dash into the cover of the wood.

"I have decided I will bring Ishtilde here for you, Aileen," he said. "A mother should not be separated from her child." His voice was cold and hard.

"Robert would never let you near her."

"Is he then so enamoured of Murchad's child?" He chuckled. "I doubt it. And in any case it was easy enough bringing you here. Why should your baby present me with any difficulty?"

"What would you have me do? "

"Suffer, Aileen, that is all I want you to do."

"Murrough, I beg you – don't hurt my baby."

"So the proud Aileen MacGillingrouth now begs, does she? See how much I have already achieved through my little niece. Well, I have sent men back to fetch her already. She'll be with us soon."

His laughter filled the woods as he walked away from Aileen, who stood helplessly staring after his retreating form.

That night she dreamt of Ishtilde again. She was cuddling the baby who looked at her with large violet eyes. As she looked back at her, Ishtilde's image dissolved and it was a baby rabbit she cradled. Murrough's voice filled her ears. "Have you ever noticed how a trapped rabbit struggles to be free, its eyes staring? So easy to make it scream, with the power to kill or release it – so much power over one tiny rabbit?" His voice faded and she was back at Seandale watching the MacTilling men as they raped her mother, and Murrough was there, laughing with pleasure at her helplessness. Aifel begged Murrough for mercy and he picked up a twig, holding it in both hands high above his head. The gesture was ceremonial in its execution; he paused for a while and then with a callous expression he flicked his wrists, breaking the twig. The man who held Aifel, taking this as a signal, put his knee in the small of her back and wrenched her hair. Aileen heard a sharp crack as her mother's spine snapped under the sudden pressure.

Then she was back in the wood. Murrough had Ishtilde in his arms and stood as if waiting for a sign. There was no sound, no movement, and Aileen held her breath, waiting in terror. She saw a man come towards them out of the darkness. His foot rose and fell in slow motion towards a small twig on the ground and she opened her mouth to scream at him but could make no sound. Murrough gripped the baby tightly and smiled in a parody of tenderness as Ishtilde whimpered in pain. Aileen's eyes went from the twig to the baby and in wordless horror she saw the man's foot fall. "Don't kill my baby," she screamed, jerked out of her inertia as a sharp crack filled the night.

The night was dark, leaves rattled in the breeze and glittered in the occasional light of the moon as it moved through swathes of heavy cloud. A vixen wailed, her cry haunting and Murrough watched Aileen toss fitfully. He could see the beads of sweat gathering on her forehead and she muttered incoherently in her sleep.

"Don't kill my baby," she cried suddenly, and her voice was filled with a mindless terror. She sat up and her face came to rest only inches from his. Her eyes were level with his own and he noted her fear with pleasure.

For seconds she seemed to hover between sleep and consciousness. He heard the vixen cry out again, the sound eerily like the sound of a child's wail. He paid it no attention but Aileen started violently as the wail grew into staccato screams which pierced the night. Like a woman possessed by devils she jumped up from the ground and fled wildly into the trees, tripping and stumbling heedlessly through the undergrowth. Murrough remained still, shocked by the rapidity of her action.

She could hear Ishtilde screaming and blundered towards the sound, desperate to reach her child but confused by the trees and bushes which impeded her progress and masked the direction of the cries. Murrough chased after her and caught her easily, gripping hold of her arms. He threw his head back and laughed for joy while she scratched and clawed at him hysterically.

"Give me my baby. Please God, don't hurt Ishtilde," she screamed, and her eyes were blank – the eyes of a sleep-walker.

CHAPTER 14

The young soldier, Culpeper, had not been killed as Aileen supposed. Struck, suddenly on the forehead he had indeed been knocked from his horse and dragged semi-conscious by the animal. Some distance from the hillock, however, the horse had stopped, wild-eyed and nervous. Bruised and battered by the rough ground over which he had been dragged, Culpeper had somehow managed to extract his foot from the stirrup and lain for several minutes beside his horse, until he had recovered his senses.

He returned to the top of the hill to look for Aileen, but found nothing but trampled grass, indicating several horsemen had been nearby. In the distance he could see a party of horsemen making for the Sheen Marshes. He mounted painfully and returned to the castle to raise the alarm.

Robert, returning the following evening from a largely pointless visit to Dublin, was greeted with the news of Aileen's disappearance. Tired from his journey though he was, he set off in pursuit almost at once, having ordered a fresh horse for himself and twelve men-at-arms to accompany him. He surmised that her captors were O'Flerty stragglers, heading possibly for Trigonnel's Point, judging from the direction in which Culpeper had seen them ride.

They took as few rations as were necessary, and, riding hard, were well into the Thorn Forest by nightfall. They rested for only a few hours each night, travelling until well after dark and rising before dawn, and in this way covered the distance to Trigonnel's Point in only four days. Once they'd arrived there, they found that Murrough had left only the day before, headed west.

Lys had talked to him about Murrough, briefly. He'd summoned her to his side as he prepared to leave, and seen the fear in her eyes when he'd asked her what kind of man he was.

"Did he treat you badly, Lys?"

"Neither well nor badly. He is obsessed by 'owning' Aileen, though," she added. "I think he only used me as slave because I had been hers." She didn't tell him of the dire threats Murrough had made whilst drunk, of what he would do to Aileen if he ever got her under his wing.

"Then he will surely make her his woman," Robert said, and she saw an almost fanatical light in his eyes.

"I fear he will, sire. He seems determined to prove his manhood." She told him of what had befallen Murrough and Robert felt a cold hand grip his heart.

He had to rest that night: there were no fast horses at Trigonnel's Point, and his own were exhausted. He didn't sleep at all, but spent the night in futile fear, worrying over what Murrough had planned for Aileen. He hoped she would be compliant for once in her life. If she fought other men, as she had done him, she could expect little mercy.

In desperation he went out walking and his aimless feet brought him to the area in which he had been imprisoned. His "cell" had been destroyed, but he stood where he had stood then and imagined Aileen was in front of him, her face pale in the darkness. Echoes of their whispered conversation buzzed in the air and he sank to his knees and prayed, as he had never prayed before.

It brought him a peace of sorts and he suddenly understood how Aileen must have felt to have been made prisoner and taken from her home. He vowed that if he found and rescued her, she might have her freedom, realising finally, that if he truly loved her he must allow her to make her own life. But it would never stop him loving her, and it would never prevent him from offering her his protection.

When he finally raised his head, the dark sky was stained with a pale silver glow. He had to make a guess at their destination, and plumped for Limerick; before the sun was fully up, they were on their way. Late the following day the scouts he had sent ahead returned with news that a small party of Irish were within striking distance. Robert decided to make camp, and went with a companion to spy out the enemy position. He reached them as the sun was beginning to set and making a glorious red glow over the wide glen, reflected in the still loch by which Murrough's men had pitched their camp.

Murrough had taken few precautions: his fires smoked and burned merrily and they could smell food cooking. Robert prowled around the perimeter and found only one sentry posted. Clearly, Murrough expected no hostile visitors this far into Irish territory.

Greatly relieved by the casual set up, Robert was not long in working out a plan. His main concerns were for Aileen's safety during the attack, and the wide expanse of unsheltered ground over which his men would have to travel. Neither could he be sure that as darkness fell Murrough would not post further sentries.

He waited until the sun was fully set, and, leaving his sergeant behind, returned to camp where he immediately gave orders for his men to follow. They returned to the glen, keeping to the trees which bordered it, about half a mile from the enemy camp. Leaving their horses in the shelter, his men crept on foot to where the sergeant lay in waiting for them. "As far as I can tell," he told Robert, "Murrough has only posted one additional sentry, but," with a grim chuckle, "I've already disposed of the first!"

The moon was bright and by its light they were able to creep right into camp, where they could easily make out the sleeping forms of its inhabitants. They circled quietly until they found the place where Aileen lay sleeping, slightly removed from the main body of men.

It was over very quickly. The Irishmen were killed without even waking from their sleep. No sound, except one quickly terminated scream, disturbed the night.

Aileen woke up as a rough hand went over her mouth and opened her eyes wide with shock. Robert felt her jump violently. She seemed not to focus on his face but stared blankly at him, whilst large tears drenched her cheeks and his hand. He felt her fight against him and as he moved his hand away she screamed for her baby. The sound rent the night.

"Aileen," he shook her, for she seemed not to know who he was. "Aileen it's me – Robert."

"Robert, Murrough has Ishtilde. Save her, you've got to save her."

Robert swallowed, suddenly aware there was something wrong with the way Aileen was reacting. She had spoken his name but still seemed not to recognise him.

"Murrough is dead, Aileen. Ishtilde is safe at home with Lys."

"No. No, Robert, you don't understand. Murrough has my baby. I've begged and begged to see her but he won't let me."

She was beginning to frighten him: she was not herself and seemed unable to take in his explanation. "Come with me, Aileen," Robert said, lifting her to her feet. He led her to where Murrough lay – as if still sleeping – with his throat cut. As she looked at him great sobs wracked her body and a spark of recognition ignited then died in her eyes when she looked again at Robert. Robert tightened his hold on her as the tension seeped from her body and she grew limp in his arms.

He took her up behind him on his horse, for she seemed incapable of riding, and she clung on to him pathetically. He could feel her flinch and tremble at every sound and often he had to turn to reassure her. Whatever Murrough had done to her had been extreme, for Aileen had always been defiantly courageous under attack.

"Why are you so afraid?" he asked at last, but she didn't answer, except to mutter incoherently about rabbits and Ishtilde.

"Ishtilde is safe," he said over and over, but she couldn't seem to grasp the fact. Her tears, which had started to fall when they made camp, were still unabated when she fell into an exhausted sleep.

He woke before the sun had risen and looked down on Aileen's face. She had slept fitfully during the night and several times she had screamed out, startling Robert out of his shallow rest. Eventually he had taken her into his arms, cradling her warmly until she calmed.

As the sun lit the sky Aileen stirred softly at first, then jumped up from her bed with such a jerk that Robert was knocked sideways. Her long hair was loose and dishevelled about her face and she looked like a madwoman. And like a madwoman she fled through the sleeping camp, disturbing Robert's men who sat up and watched her tumultuous dash in shocked silence.

Robert ran after her and caught her in his arms and she struggled and fought him until she fell to her knees. "Please take me to Ishtilde," she begged and her hopeless sobs wrenched at his heart, bringing tears to his own eyes.

He led her back to her pallet and cupped her cheeks between his hands, looking intently into her eyes. "Aileen, listen to me. You musn't worry, you'll make yourself ill."

She stared at him listlessly.

"Trust me. I have killed Murrough. Don't worry about anything, don't think about anything. Ishtilde is safe. Let everyone else do the worrying for you from now on. Let me take care of you."

She seemed at last to understand him, for she nodded dumbly and allowed him to guide her back to the camp. She was compliant after that and seemed to need Robert to do everything for her. Her eyes followed him about as he moved, and so long as he was within sight she remained calm.

When the men had broken camp he carried her – for she was still limp and lifeless – to her horse and rode with her in front of him so that he could support her trembling body in his arms. Gradually, as the day wore on, she seemed to come out of shock and began to sit straight. They stopped to water the horses and he and Aileen sat side by side on the bank of a busy little brook.

"Are you feeling better?" he asked and wished she would make some retort. For so long he had wanted her compliance, but now he had it, he wanted the old Aileen back, to spit and scratch and show him she was still alive. He remembered Raymond d'Evreux telling him that if she were broken, he wouldn't love her. Was she broken now? If so, Raymond had been wrong: he did still love her; broken or whole, she had all of his heart. He wished he could find the words which could offer her comfort.

He talked then, and for a long while after they had resumed their journey, of Gossard's Ford, of Cormac and Silas; repeating old anecdotes, trying to make her laugh. He talked about Marie and Ishtilde and of Lys, but she responded very little, and continued to flinch at every unexpected sound. At night when they made camp she sat and stared into the fire, but when he left her side her eyes followed him. She seemed unable to relax at all without him with her. Her need of him should have been a source of happiness, but he was too worried to rejoice.

It was a long journey. He had thought at first she would recover her buoyancy, but as day flowed into night and back to day again she toiled on, her face a blank.

"We'll soon be home," he said one evening. "I'm sure you're anxious to see Ishtilde?"

She nodded and gave him one of her pallid smiles.

He gave her ale to drink and had almost to hold it to her lips, the liquid trickled down her chin as if she were a baby and when he left her to go and fetch some food she looked as if she was going to cry. He took her hand and held it between his two. "Don't be afraid any more, Aileen. I don't know what he did to you, but Murrough is dead."

She closed her eyes at mention of his name. "Yes. Murrough is dead. Ishtilde is safe."

"And I've been thinking. You have never loved me and I was wrong to try to make you. I was wrong to marry you against your will. Things will be different once we return. I won't bother you again." He squeezed her hands. "Whatever you want, you shall have. Your freedom – anything." He looked into her eyes: the green was smooth and without depth. Blank. "Do you hear me?"

She nodded without conviction and laid down to sleep. He slept close by her and awoke later that night to see her sitting, petrified, at his side. He touched her arm which was ice cold and he pulled her under his cover, wrapping his body around her. He stroked her head until her breathing calmed, and eventually she slept.

At dawn the sun fell upon her face and illuminated it. He sat and stared at her for a long time, a deep sadness almost overwhelming him.

They reached Gossard's Ford that night, and Lys ran out from the castle with Ishtilde in her arms. The child was screaming, having been awoken from her sleep, and Lys was laughing with pleasure at seeing Aileen safe once more.

Robert helped Aileen from the horse and she smiled blankly at him. "See, it's Lys and Ishtilde," he said. He had grown accustomed by then to talking to her as if to a child, but Lys froze with horror.

"What's happened to her?" In her distress she forgot who she was talking to but Robert ignored the oversight.

"Show her the baby, Lys."

Lys placed the screaming infant into her mother's arms and Aileen stood still, holding the baby carefully. "Ishtilde is safe," she said, and a smile brightened her eyes for a moment before the familiar blankness settled back.

"Take her inside. I'll be there soon," Robert told Lys, and watched as she took her mistress's elbow and guided her into the castle.

He walked slowly and pensively to where his men were already settling their horses, and was greeted by Silas.

"Congratulations," Silas said.

"For what?"

"Were you not completely successful?"

"Completely," he grunted, and a vision of Aileen as she had been on the day she had ridden with Cormac and himself came back to him. Smiling, alive, full of her own importance – and independent. Then he remembered her as he had just seen her: being guided back to the castle by Lys, not heeding the screaming baby in her arms. "Completely," he repeated.

He wandered away, leaving Silas scratching his chin.

242

CHAPTER 15

The grey haze which surrounded Aileen prevented her from taking in the enormity of her release. Safely ensconced in the castle she heard and responded and did as she was told. She fed her baby and patted her back to bring up wind. She rode Peggy, accompanied by Cormac, and she ate and drank whatever she was given. She remained impassive as her ladies dressed her hair and pushed her into one set of clothes after another.

Time passed monotonously and brought no change. People started to talk of the way Aileen had been, as if she were already cold in her grave.

Robert came to see her at every opportunity and sat and talked with her. She answered his questions without feeling. He kissed her cheek when he arrived and again when he left, and she learned to lift her face to receive the kiss, but she never responded.

Lys cuddled the baby and loved her as her own, and Aileen watched, her green eyes devoid of any expression. She learned to hand Ishtilde to Lys whenever she cried, finding it impossible to calm the child; it had become an automatic gesture, made without words, like everything else.

"I never thought I'd say this," remarked Marie to Lys one day, as Aileen gave the baby to her, to change, "But I miss her tantrums."

"And her laughter," reminded Lys.

"And her wilfulness – she was so fond of getting her own way," Marie added. "Perhaps it would have been better if Murrough had killed her."

"And yet, I believe there is still something there," reflected Lys. "If the master is late she sits looking at the door, like a devoted hound, until he arrives."

"But she does nothing to welcome him."

"Nor anything to discourage him either. I still have hope." Lys finished dressing Ishtilde and turned to where Aileen sat quietly sewing.

"Will you take her, Aileen?"

Aileen laid down her sewing and reached out her arms, and Lys handed the baby into them. They sat in the light of the window, Ishtilde a tiny replica of her mother, her little hands waving as she played with the dust motes in the rays of sunlight. Aileen paid her no heed, and sat looking out of the window.

Ishtilde, who had just started to grab everything in sight, reached out for the sewing on the little table and picked it up. Lys and Marie were talking in the corner and didn't see when the baby, finding the needle, pulled it out and stuck it into her mouth. She screamed as the point bit into her and Aileen turned slowly and looked down on her, a bemused expression on her face. She held the baby – still screaming – out for Lys to take.

Lys saw the needle, which the baby had almost swallowed, and sticking her fingers into the baby's mouth she pulled the needle out just before Ishtilde could swallow it. Hugging her to her bosom, she cried with relief.

"You stupid, stupid woman," she screamed at Aileen. "She could have died for all you cared. You nearly killed your own baby." And in her fury she slapped Aileen hard across her face.

They stood, Aileen, Marie, Lys, as the baby screamed in Lys's arms, and slowly Aileen lifted her hand to her cheek. It was white, except for the livid hand-print striped across it.

"I'm sorry, I'm sorry," Lys cried, still hugging the baby to her.

"Give her to me." Aileen's voice was firm and cold. Lys obeyed automatically.

Aileen took the baby and all she could hear was Lys's voice – "she could have died for all you cared." Then she saw the rabbit, which in her dreams had always turned into little Ishtilde screaming helplessly, whilst Murrough laughed and Aileen begged on her knees for him to show compassion. Finally she saw Murrough, his throat cut and gaping, dead on the ground.

It was over. The firm hold she had taken on her emotions was released. Cracked open by the shock of Lys's blow and the realisation of how close she had come to losing Ishtilde.

"Ishtilde, Ishtilde," she wept, cradling the baby close to her heart.

The door opened and Robert walked in, taking in the shocked expressions on the women's faces, and Aileen and Ishtilde crying over by the window.

"Aileen," he ran over to her and took her in his arms.

"Oh, Robert. I thought you were never coming," and she leaned against him and cried as though her heart would break.

He didn't know what had happened, but the woman who cried in his arms was alive. He could feel her, gripping onto him and he motioned for the women to take the baby. They did so, leaving the room quietly and closing the heavy door behind them.

As she held him she remembered, as though their whole lives were reflected in a slow moving stream, all they had been through, and she saw his kindness reflected clearly, cleanly in front of her.

"Do you love me still Robert?" she asked, and he hesitated, remembering his vow, made at Trigonnel's Point. She must be free.

"Not as I did once," he said carefully, and she pulled away from him a little, her tear-stained face infinitely sad. He didn't know how to tell her that his love had become selfless, that he no longer wanted anything which didn't bring her happiness.

"Then it's too late. I've waited too long."

"You can have your freedom. You can do whatever you wish, I'll never stand in your way."

She walked away from him, looking at the sunlight playing on his strong face and felt a pain like a knife go through her. She didn't know what to say. He no longer loved her, and now, too late, she recognised the love she held for him.

He left her when she had calmed down and returned to his bedchamber. He had to leave, for her close proximity was inflaming his desire to the point where he could hardly contain it.

She joined him that evening for the main meal in the great hall. "I owe you so much," she said, looking straight at him.

"As I do you," he replied.

As they ate, she recounted her ordeal over the past few weeks, her mind now able to fill in the blank void and understand how Murrough had tricked her. He paled as he listened. "But you're alright now," he said. "We thought perhaps you would never come back to us."

"It was Lys, shouting at me, telling me I'd killed my baby," she explained. She watched as he took his jewelled goblet and drank from it, gazing at the strong hand with its long tapering fingers. She fought the urge to take it in her own and kiss it. Now was not the time to remind him that she was his wife.

The people around the table were quiet that night as they watched their master and his wife in animated conversation. Robert and Aileen left the room together and walked side by side up the steps to the gallery.

Robert walked with her to her room and left her there. It was a tender moment, at least for him it was, and he desired nothing more than to take her cheeks between his hands and kiss her. She swayed towards him and he tore himself away, superstitiously afraid of what might happen if he forced his love upon her.

After he'd gone she stared at the door which separated them. Sighing wearily, she undressed and prepared for sleep.

Robert awoke with a tremendous start, sensing something moving towards him in the darkness. He gripped his short sword, which he always kept close to his side and waited for his eyes to adjust to the gloom.

He could make out her form although her long black hair was invisible in the darkness and, dropping the knife, he watched as she made her way slowly towards him. She laid down beside him on the bed. She touched his cheek, stroking gently, then ran her fingers through his hair. As she leaned over him he could feel her breasts grazing his chest; and he was overwhelmed by a passion which he'd never known before.

She kissed him gently, then more forcefully and he opened his mouth and kissed her with equal force. Her hands were gentle but firm on his body, and he pushed towards her, certain that he must be dreaming. Determined to prolong the dream for as long as possible, he responded with a passion he'd only ever imagined as she nibbled his ear and he could feel her hot, sweet, breath. He felt her body, which was shapely beneath his inquisitive hands. He touched her full breasts and ran his hand down to her waist, following the curve of her full hips, and he knew it was no dream.

"Aileen?" he asked, stupidly, bemused by what was happening.

"Lys told me you would never come to me, my lord," she whispered, touching him in a way which took away his breath. "But I couldn't sleep, for thinking of you."

"What were you thinking?"

"That whether you love me or not, I am your wife, and I owe you my life."

"And is that why you're here?"

"Yes. And because I love you."

He didn't answer, except to pull her ever closer to him, until they were both overwhelmed by their emotion.

In the morning his manservant opened the door and was sent away. The couple didn't leave the bedchamber until the afternoon, when they rode out together, their horses touching as they went. Marie and Lys, who were watching from an upstairs window, turned to face each other and smiled.

"I always knew she loved him," said Lys, her smile triumphant.

CHAPTER 16

$\mathcal{T}$he year 1178 was one of some importance to the FitzAlan family. It marked the beginning of their fortunes, the start of one of the great Anglo-Irish families destined to play its part down the ages, in the turbulence of Ireland as well as in the more prestigious story of her sister island, England.

Politically it was a quiet year with little interference from Dublin in baronial life and still less from local conflict. Robert's fiefs were large so that the peace throughout the Leinster countryside enabled Robert and his lady to give them their full attention.

Aileen had grown accustomed to being the lady of Gossard's Ford, despite the fact that she had never been brought up to do so. As an Irishwoman she became a very popular figure, and she found a ready and sympathetic acceptance from the native belaghs who quickly credited her with an understanding of their needs.

At the end of 1179, Aileen was brought to bed – much to Robert's delight – with an heir whom they named Richard after Strongbow. Later this was followed by the birth of their daughter, and then a second son. Robert's cup of happiness was filled to overflowing.

Whilst Loswellery basked in the sunshine of contentment and growing prosperity, Norman settlement was extended and intensified. Castles – the symbols of Norman power – appeared everywhere to mark the foreigners' advance. No longer the hastily constructed wooden fortresses that Robert remembered so well, but solid structures of stone. In many places settlers, drawn in the main from Wales and the English West Country, came to serve their masters on the new Irish lands. By and large the Irish chieftains came to accept the Norman presence, particularly in Leinster, Meath and along the eastern coastline, but elsewhere an unquiet peace can best describe the conditions that existed.

Irish resistance, especially in the West, continued spasmodically and without any firm direction. Norman lords frequently took sides in the many local squabbles that characterised Irish life, thereby at one and the same time, extending their power and antagonizing the Gaelic population. Irish anger, though bloody and ferocious, was never national and therefore ineffective.

Like many of the Norman adventurers who had come to Ireland with Strongbow, Robert FitzAlan remained resentful of royal attempts to curtail his freedom of action. It must be admitted, too, that under the influence of Aileen, he grew increasingly Irish in his ways. He was careful not to provoke the Dublin authorities; courted the patronage of his feudal overlord, William Marshall, and so remained comparatively undisturbed.

Thus, young Richard FitzAlan grew up in peace, typical of the first generation Anglo-Irishmen, popular with Irish peasants as well as with his father's tenants. Although he looked towards England as the ultimate support of his father's power, he did not, like his father, regard Wales as his homeland. To him, it was a foreign country.

Corderg returned to live with Aileen and Robert, and took up the running of the monastery after Ranulph's death. He had survived the slaughter at Trigonnel's Point, having left by then for training at Cashel. He loved the children and Aileen found it a great comfort to talk with him about the many doubts which continued to beset her throughout her life. It helped them both to grow in wisdom and Robert turned to them often for advice.

On a star-filled, moonlit night, Aileen and Robert stood at the top of the castle tower looking out over the lands they ran together.

"I played here as a child," reflected Aileen.

"Happy memories?" he asked her fondly, and squeezed her hand.

"And sad ones, too."

"And for that you blame me, I suppose." It was pointless to pretend otherwise: loving him hadn't completely tamed her, but he didn't mind that.

"Yes," she replied, still candid. "I cannot ever forget those things, but fighting is the way of the world and I no longer harbour any hostility towards you."

She ran her fingers through his hair, which was just beginning to turn grey at the temples. "It is fitting that the lands of my fathers will also belong to my sons. I've learned to accept."

"And to love?" He still needed her to tell him so sometimes. She understood that.

"Oh yes. You have brought me a great deal, Robert FitzAlan. Wealth and lands, respect and a title, but the greatest thing you have ever given me, the thing which I hold more dear to me than life itself – is the love we bear each other."

He took her in his arms and kissed her.

"Then I haven't done too badly – for a landless Welshman," and taking her hand he walked with her back into the castle.